HUNGER MOON

A Victoria Storm Novel

Loki's Wolves

by

Melissa Snark

HUNGER MOON
Subtitle/Series: A Victoria Storm Novel / Loki's Wolves

ISBN-10: 1492107581
ISBN-13: 978-1492107583

Cover Art: *Farah Evers*
Editing: *Michelle Devon & Lynn Hunter*

Contact Information:

Melissa Snark
P.O. Box 1347
Pleasanton, CA 94566

Published in the United States of America.

The author respects trademarks and copyrighted material mentioned in this book by introducing such registered items in italics or with proper capitalization.

This book is a work of fiction. Names, persons, places and incidents are all used factiously and are the imagination of the author. Any resemblance to persons, living or dead, events or locales is coincidental and non-intentional, unless otherwise specifically noted.

DEDICATION

I'd like to dedicate this story to my whacky family. Without you guys, life would be boring...

ACKNOWLEDGEMENTS

Over the course of three years, several beta readers helped me fine tune HUNGER MOON. In particular, I'd like to acknowledge the efforts of the following ladies: Elanor Finster, Lisa Ryans, LA Freed, Lucinda Gunnin and Rissa Watkins.

My thanks to Farah Evers for designing such a lovely cover.

My editor, Michelle Devon, made an enormous contribution to bringing HUNGER MOON to completion. Michy, thank you so much for all of your hard work and feedback.

Praise for Melissa Snark

"A CAT'S TALE *actually tells a story with all that luscious loving. For that reason, I feel A Cat's Tale, by Melissa Snark, deserves five stars.*"

~**Michelle Devon,** *Texas Straight-Talk Reviews*

LEARNING TO FLY

"*Ms. Snark did a very good job when she wrote her characters, Cassie and Kyle. The relationship between these two was very sweet and a joy to read. But who doesn't love a man with a sexy Irish brogue? Through the entire book I enjoyed watching the relationship between these two play out, while at the same time, waiting to see what was going to happen with Simon Lynch. I was not disappointed in how Ms. Snark had this story play out. This is definitely one of those times where you cannot judge a book by its cover. The content is totally worth it and I look forward to reading more by Ms. Snark.*"

~**Guilty Pleasures Book Reviews**

CHAPTER ONE

Rage—

"Goddess, rage in our hearts and our enemies', it consumes us and we suffer. Are we to live like this forever?"

"Victoria, it is your choice. What life do you wish to lead?"

"You killed my brother, bitch."

"Worry about your own life, Sawyer. Daniel is dead."

Victoria held the blade of her dagger even with his jawline, against the strong column of his throat. Cold steel kissed flesh, but she lacked the will to make the final thrust to sever his carotid artery.

"Because of you." His brown eyes blazed with hatred, more intense and consuming than the inferno raging around them.

Every part of the warehouse was on fire, and there was no way to know how much longer the structure would stand. Cinder and smoke swirled everywhere.

Red-hot embers dusted the bare skin of her face and arms faster than her enhanced healing could repair the damage, but she didn't feel the burn. Fury consumed her heart and protected her from the wrath of flames, but the pain of her loss, the weight of her guilt, crippled her.

"Yes, because of me," she said. She blinked back tears. She should kill him. There was no other choice, because the survival of her pack depended upon stopping the hunters who pursued them, the hunters he led. Doubt stilled her hand. The man's life hung in fragile balance between her desire for revenge and uncertainty.

"Do it," Sawyer said with a sneer, as if he sensed her hesitation. She straddled his chest, keeping one of his arms pinned against his side with her knee. His free hand groped for the shotgun on the ground, just out of reach.

"Has your death wish gotten so strong you're committed to joining him?" She sniffed, attempting to scent his fear, but inhaled a lungful of thick smoke that scalded her throat. Tears filled her eyes and a cough racked her chest.

"I'm going to rip you to shreds." Teeth bared, Sawyer's upper body heaved while he attempted to unseat her. The hunter had plenty of fight in him. Her wolf's strength far exceeded that of any human, even a skilled hunter such as a Barrett man. He gave up obtaining the shotgun and grabbed for her throat with his free hand.

Victoria placed her palm flat on his breastbone and shoved him back.

"Yeah, yeah, I've heard it all before, and yet I'm still here. I'm starting to think you're incompetent, Sawyer."

"Give me a knife. I'll show you incompetent!"

"Now, why would I do something stupid like that?" Despite her taunting tone, doubt twisted her gut into knots. Her hand remained rock steady. The dagger never wavered; the fine edge of the blade bit into his flesh and drew a thin line of blood across the side of his throat.

He's Daniel's brother.

He was also the man who had helped murder her parents and most of her packmates.

The pain of the cut caused Sawyer to grunt; his throat worked while he swallowed, a convulsive clench that betrayed his fear, though his features remained set in a stoic mask.

A hand brushed her wrist, confident and intimate, cool to the touch. Victoria glanced up to stare into a face she knew by heart, every plane and angle committed to memory, although he was far more handsome than her imperfect recollection.

She stiffened.

Impossible! It can't be.

She gazed into the man's familiar face, and the entire world beyond his warm brown eyes ceased to exist: the fire, her pack, the man at the business end of her knife—all of it simply stopped.

She blinked, and her surprise faded. Her mind made the logical leap: it was possible.

He's a ghost.

A strangled snarl emerged from Sawyer's throat, but Victoria did not look at him. The hunter shouldn't have been able to see his brother's ghost. He lacked her gift of spirit sight. She kept a steady grip on the hilt, discouraging him from moving lest he slit his own throat on the blade.

"Daniel?" she whispered. The roar of the inferno engulfed her voice.

A faint smile fluttered across his lips but the expression remained deadly serious. His hand locked tightly about her wrist. Daniel leaned forward. His lips feathered a soft kiss upon the shell of her ear. His honeyed voice murmured as sweet as her memories, causing her excruciating pain, soul deep. She missed him so damned much.

"Not my brother, lover. You can't kill Sawyer."

Victoria's fingers relaxed. The knife fell from her hand. "I won't, for you."

Daniel turned his head and looked his brother in the eye. "There's been enough killing."

Sawyer's features contorted in agony and his hand rose, reaching for his brother. "Danny, I—"

Before Sawyer's hand touched his brother's face, Daniel's body lost substance. Energy crackled in the air, and his form shimmered about the edges. His firm grip grew weaker with each passing second until his hand opened, and he released her wrist.

Her eyes filled with tears. "Please, don't go."

Daniel looked at her; a sad smile touched his lips. "I've got to go, baby."

She closed her eyes, and tears slid down her cheeks. The hot air of the burning warehouse sucked moisture from her skin. Her aching heart pounded, full and heavy, ready to burst. She opened her eyes and forced a brave smile. She extended her arm and brushed his fingertips. "I miss you."

His hand closed on her fingers, and he squeezed. A smiled played on his lips.

"I miss you, too," he said. Then he was gone.

Victoria stood and staggered. She bent and scooped up her knife, and then she shoved it into the sheath on her belt. She glanced at Sawyer, still lying on his back.

He looked as stunned as she felt. He rolled to his side, coughing harshly, but no longer clawed for the shotgun.

Shaken, she looked about her, noticing the fire had worsened. Pillars of flame clawed upward along the walls, licking at the wooden beams that traversed the ceiling.

She scanned the interior of the warehouse and spotted two downed men who had accompanied Sawyer. The hunters had set the building on fire and ambushed the werewolves who had taken refuge within it. A few yards away, her packmate, Rand Scott, lay slumped on the ground. She cast another glance at Sawyer, but he appeared occupied with finding a way out of the building.

Victoria fought past falling timbers toward Rand. Her left shoulder oozed blood from a gunshot. The silver shot lodged in the wound interfered with her natural regenerative ability and weakened her. It had to come out.

With a grimace, she probed the wound with her finger and thumb. Stabbing agony radiated throughout Victoria's shoulder, and she ground her teeth. Her fingers were slippery with blood, but she located the silver slug and ripped it free from her body. She quickly cast it aside before the silver burned the flesh on her fingers.

A wave of nausea washed over her. Victoria hunched over, fighting tears, riding out the pain. Freed of the silver, her body started to regenerate, and her suffering subsided some.

"Goddess, I hate getting shot."

A shower of scalding hot embers dusted her arms and face and burned fabric, skin, and hair, bringing her focus back to her surroundings. Her bright blue eyes stung and watered, leaving her almost blind. She inhaled and coughed hard to expel the toxic fumes and lurched toward her fallen friend.

"Rand?"

The warrior did not respond when she spoke or react when she touched him. She grabbed his shoulders and shoved him backward to inspect his injuries. At seven-feet tall and three-hundred-plus pounds, Rand dwarfed her. His fiery red hair, including his full mustache and beard, appeared gray from soot. A motorcycle accident years before had left him with a prosthetic attachment below his knee.

Dark red blood soaked his white cotton shirt, obscuring the rock band logo on the front. Her heart leapt to her throat. He had taken a direct shot to the torso from a shotgun loaded with silver ammo.

"Rand!" Victoria shook him, but he did not regain consciousness. Shifting her grip to his arms, she hauled him from the ground. Despite her diminutive size, Victoria lifted his considerable weight with ease.

A great crash caused her to turn toward the western side of the warehouse. The wall shattered inward and the enormous form of a creature, half-man and half-wolf, appeared amid a shower of plaster and broken boards. The werewolf stood so tall, he hunched forward, shoulders scraping the ceiling. He lumbered forward. With a turn of his heavy head, he assessed the area, eyes narrowed against thick smoke. The remnants of his torn clothing clung to his body and thick grey-peppered black fur provided protection against the flames. Like a wolf, his ears came to high points, and he sprouted a long, bushy tail from the base of his spine. Much of him remained a man, including his ability to stand upright.

"Paul!" Victoria shouted.

Paul Thornton's entrance set off a chain reaction. One of the timber beams split and brought that entire section of the ceiling crashing down in a shower of debris. A huge crack rent the air, and the roof above Sawyer caved. Victoria's head jerked, and she looked in time to see a boulder of burning debris smash down upon the hunter. A fallen concrete pylon pinned him.

Paul turned toward the destruction and moved in the wrong direction, away from her and Rand.

"Paul!" Victoria's hands hooked beneath Rand's arms. She continued to carry the fallen giant toward their packmate.

Paul turned and lumbered toward them, negotiating the debris. A mouthful of protruding fangs made him difficult to understand. "Are you hurt?"

Victoria thrust Rand toward him. "I'm fine. Can you get him to safety?"

Glowing eyes stared at her through the smoke. "What about you?"

Victoria glanced toward where Sawyer Barrett lay trapped beneath burning debris. Indecision paralyzed her. Her mind warred with her heart. She should leave the man to his fate. She didn't know why she hesitated.

At Daniel's request, she had already spared his life. She had no further obligation. The Barrett family was responsible for the wholesale slaughter of most of her pack, including her parents. Hunters murdered without mercy, using silver, fire—any means within their grasp—in brutal attempts to exterminate her kind. If he died in the fire he had set, it would be poetic justice.

When she contemplated abandoning him, her mind conjured a memory of soulful brown eyes and a mischievous grin, endless nights beneath starry skies, a passion that burned hotter than the desert sun. Her conscience shunned her rage, refusing to sanction her bloodthirsty desire for vengeance. She swallowed hard and sheathed her dagger.

"I'm bringing the hunter. Don't wait. Go."

Paul settled Rand across his shoulders in a firefighter's carry. Always the loyal soldier, he did not question or criticize his leader's decisions. "Don't be long. The roof is going to give."

She nodded, and Paul departed with their injured friend. Victoria watched them go, and then she cast a glance at the fallen hunter. Holding a protective arm before her face, she made her way to Sawyer. She ducked beneath a tumbled column to kneel beside him.

Rubble pinned his lower body and legs, so only his booted feet were visible. He retained consciousness and stared at her with bright eyes. Soot blackened his exposed skin. He stank of aggression and testosterone. Stubborn. Proud. Defiant. Typical Barrett man: like his big brother, *exactly* like his father.

Victoria grabbed a board and cast it aside. She removed cinder blocks and tossed them as though they weighed nothing. Working as fast as she could, she cleared away most of the small stuff and bent to examine the fallen column.

"Why are you helping me?" Sawyer asked.

"I'm a sucker for a pretty face. Hold on. I'm going to lift this off you," she said. She wrapped her arms around the pillar and dug in with all her strength. Victoria pulled upward on the column.

Sawyer cried out in pain.

The fire breathed in and out like angry bellows. Cinder and smoke filled the air until it was all she could smell, taste, or see. Sawyer used his arms to shelter his face from burning embers and took refuge beneath his heavy leather trench coat.

Embers fell on Victoria's exposed face and hands and seared her flesh. The column would not budge.

She released her hold. "Damn, this is heavy."

The entire building quaked, groaned, and threatened to come down. Sawyer stared up at her with an expression full of despair and resignation.

"You can't do it," he said.

His doubt fueled her determination. "I have to shift."

Victoria placed her hands on either side of the column to brace herself and initiated the physical transformation from woman to wolf. Her hands turned to claws, and her ears grew points. Bones cracked and changed, including the elongation of her jaw to accommodate canine teeth. She braced against the pain and endured the terrible crunch of bone and cartilage. Skin distended over her protruding bones while her body pushed and pulled into the shape of a wolf. Ropes of sinew stood out upon her arms and legs while she acquired height and weight, splitting the seams of her soft cotton shirt and denim jeans. Victoria halted the change midway, enabling her to retain use of her human hands but gain wolf strength. Partial transformations required enormous discipline.

Her claws chipped chunks of concrete from the pillar when she tightened her grip. Taut muscles beneath snowy white fur bunched and gathered. She heaved the concrete column from atop the hunter and rolled it to the side. The shifting heap of rubble brought down more ceiling, burying them in a shower of burning debris. She crouched over Sawyer, protecting him from the worst of it, fully expecting a silver knife in the gut for her foolishness.

Rising, Victoria seized his arms and hauled him to his feet. He staggered, leaned on her, and stood with support.

"This way." A mouthful of sharp canine teeth slurred her enunciation.

She tugged on his arm, and the hunter flinched. His survival instincts trumped his innate revulsion, and he cooperated with her efforts to move them toward the hole Paul had created. She could have carried him, but the Barrett men were stubborn and independent. She doubted

Sawyer would have allowed it without a fight.

Above them, the ceiling cracked.

"Watch out!" Victoria dropped her shoulder and tackled Sawyer from behind, propelling him forward. Flames descended on their heels and sent a wave of searing heat across their flank. A sharp spear struck her shoulder, and she howled in agony. The acrid smell of burnt fur and flesh filled her nostrils. She wrapped her arm about his waist and made a blind charge toward freedom through the billowing smoke.

Like a fire giant, the warehouse inhaled, sucking in a deep draught of air, and exhaled, causing the entire structure to split. It exploded outward in a fiery burst.

Outside the burning building, the force of the blast propelled them forward until Victoria landed face down in the hard-packed dirt, Sawyer pinned beneath her. She surged to her feet, grabbed his arm, and dragged him behind her, fearing part of the warehouse might topple onto them at any moment.

Racking coughs doubled the hunter over, but he staggered forward without resistance.

A pair of strong hands seized hold of her arms, providing support, and one of her pack took Sawyer. Victoria peered through stinging eyes and found Sylvie at her side.

"Hold still, sweetie. You've got a chunk of wood sticking out of your back." Sylvie moved to stand behind Victoria.

Victoria gritted her teeth and nodded. "Do it."

She removed it with a fast tug, causing Victoria to cry out.

"Thank you."

"Victory, you scared us to death. I thought you were a goner for sure," Sylvie said, scolding to cover her worry. She lowered Victoria to the ground.

Well into her sixties, Sylvie Thornton possessed the build of a warrior woman: tall and muscular, straight spine and long limbs. She had high cheekbones, a narrow face, and a sharp chin. Her silvered hair, once midnight black, hung straight and contrasted with her golden-brown skin and hazel eyes. Her heritage was a mix of Native American and Norse blood.

"I'm okay, Sylvie," Victoria said, though she gasped for fresh air. While she crouched in the dirt, Victoria spat a vile gob of mucus and soot to clear her throat of ash. She coughed to expel more contaminants.

The sun shone at the midday arc, hidden behind dark clouds in the stormy Montana sky. Victoria breathed in deep and drank in the crisp winter air, wonderful on her skin after the heat of the fire. She initiated the transformation from her in-between form to human. Bones broke and knit and her ears and muzzle retracted; her fur vanished. The majority of her burns and cuts healed. When it was over, she knelt naked on the ground. A bitter-cold northeasterly wind scalded her skin. Victoria straightened and winced when it produced pain from her collection of bruises and burns.

"Did everyone get out okay?" she asked.

"All heads accounted for," Sylvie said. "Take my coat, sweetie."

"Thanks." Victoria pulled on the jacket and fastened the front. "Any sign of other hunters?"

"Not yet."

Victoria craned her head to survey her surroundings and take her own headcount. Sawyer remained on the ground beside the fire hydrant. The human continued to cough up tar but otherwise seemed unharmed. Sylvie's mate, Paul, stood guard over the hunter. He stared at the man with barely-veiled hostility. A short distance away, Rand rested supine in a pool of his own blood, his head in Morena's lap. The whip-thin teenaged girl sat cross legged, her dark head bent so her hair fell over Rand's face. Her cheeks were streaked with tears.

Soft fur brushed Victoria's skin when Sophia, the pack's only non-shifter member, pressed against her leg.

Victoria stooped to pet the pregnant gray wolf and inspect her for injuries. To her immense relief, she found nothing out of the ordinary. Sophia still carried her pups high under the ribcage.

"She's not due for another two weeks yet," Sylvie said.

Victoria nodded. Even though she held a nursing degree, she deferred to Sylvie's expertise on the wolf. The older woman was pack midwife and nanny, with decades of experience.

"Victory, Rand needs you." Sylvie frowned and wrung her hands. "I'm not sure he's going to make it. He's hurt bad."

"Keep watch," Victoria said, indicating Sawyer. The hunter might have been disabled, but Victoria didn't harbor any delusions. Given the chance, he would murder them all.

"Like a hawk," Sylvie responded. She moved to stand beside her mate. Her gaze held no kindness for the hunter.

Victoria coughed. "Don't kill him unless you have to, Sylvie. I went through a lot to save his hide."

"I won't kill him as long as he doesn't cause any trouble."

"Good enough." Victoria hurried to Rand's side and dropped to her knees. She struggled to attain a clinical detachment and regard him as a nurse would a patient, but her professional training failed. She saw only her friend.

"He's weak. He's lost so much blood, and they used silver shot so he's not healing." Morena turned a tear-streaked face to Victoria. The teenager stroked the singed remnant of Rand's bangs from his face.

His eyes opened, but he stared blank into the distance.

"Let me see." Victoria's fingers sought and found his weak pulse. Rand struggled for every breath, gasping for air. He coughed blood and it trickled from the corner of his mouth.

Rand reached for her, but his hands failed to complete the gesture. His lips formed words.

Victoria bent her head close to his mouth.

"The pack?" he asked.

She mustered a smile and took his hand. "Safe, thanks to you."

Understanding lit his face, and he tried to nod. His expression contorted into a grimace. She freed her hands, seized his shirt, and ripped the fabric to reveal his chest, riddled with holes, the scatter pattern of a shotgun blast. Her eyes filled with tears. With her healing magic, she sensed the extent of the damage to Rand's body and knew it was too severe to repair. Still, she had to try.

"Freya, help me." Tears trekked down her cheeks. She marshaled all her strength. "I'm going to try and heal you."

"No! You'll weaken the pack," Rand said. "This is the glorious death I desire."

Red fluid oozed from his mouth. A red spit-bubble formed on his lips and swelled until it burst when he exhaled his dying breath. His hands fell limp to his sides. The light in his eyes extinguished.

Grief closed her throat and caused her to choke. Defeat tasted bitter, but honor bound her to obey his final request. She felt the last of Rand's life slip away. When his soul rose from his body, she caught hold of his ghost. The other members of her pack could no longer see Rand, but spirits were solid to her.

A mournful wail rose from the pack, a plaintive and yearning cry. The collective howl of the wolves lacked the body and volume it had once possessed. Since the war with the hunters had begun months before, their losses had been staggering.

"Stay with me, Rand." Victoria clung to him, tethering his spirit to her so he would not depart. Her duty dictated she attend to his fate. As expected, his spirit appeared confused. The first moments following physical death were disorienting.

"Where else am I to go?" Rand had a bewildered expression on his face. He reached for the injuries that had killed him and examined his chest. "Hell, I'm shot full o' holes. I still hurt like a son-of-a-bitch."

"Your spiritual body will heal. Your pain will cease in Valhalla."

"Valhalla?" Rand's gaze lit with interest. Even as a whelp at his dame's teat, the stories of Odin's hall had enraptured him.

"Valhalla, the Norse warrior's paradise," she said. "You have died a glorious death in battle, brave and selfless, in service to your pack. As Valkyrie, I choose you to join the Einherjar, to dwell in Odin's hall where you will train for the final battle at Vígríðr. You shall dine upon the finest boar and stag, drink the richest ale, and the best mead."

Rand shot Victoria a sly grin. "What of the serving wenches? Are they comely? Will they keep me warm through long nights?"

Victoria smacked his arm. "Aye, the serving wenches are lovely. It shall be my honor to bring your meal, Rand. But know this: You'll be keeping your own damned bed warm!"

The pack listened to her side of the exchange and took comfort knowing Rand's soul resided safely. Her final remark drew laughter from the others. Sylvie snickered. "Tell Rand to mind his manners and not to embarrass us all."

"Nonsense!" Paul said with a hearty chuckle. "Tell Rand to have a helluva good time and to keep a place open for me at his table!"

"Can't Rand hear us?" Morena's timid question brought about a round of laughter.

Rand snorted and then roared. "Tell them I hear them just fine. I'll remain until you can escort me to Valhalla, Victory. Now see to the safety of the pack."

Promise given, he stepped back, fading a bit. Victoria turned to her pack.

"Rand hears you," she said. "I'll take him to Valhalla, but first, we must get the pack out of here."

"What're we going to do with him?" Paul asked. The

old warrior jabbed at Sawyer, still on the ground, the hunter among the wolves he hunted. Barrett sat tense and erect, head held strong and proud, defiant.

Every pair of eyes turned to Victoria, watchful and wary, including the hunter's. Sawyer regarded her, struggling and failing to keep emotion from his face. His hatred burned in his eyes, but his handsome features held surprise and confusion. The scent of his fear betrayed him. She moved toward him, grappling with the dilemma he presented. Alive, he represented a danger to them all, but there was no way she could kill him after Daniel's request to spare his life.

Victoria forced herself to look at the faces around her. Their weary expressions reflected exhaustion that bordered on defeat. Every member of the pack had experienced the loss of someone loved and cherished—Sylvie, a sister; Paul, a brother and nephew; Morena, her parents and an older brother; Sophia's mate had died in Phoenix alongside Victoria's mother and father. Of course, they were pack, family, and drew strength from each other.

The pack formed the foundation of werewolf society with the most powerful wolves holding the highest ranks. A complex set of factors influenced status: age, sex, birthright, physical prowess, cunning, and natural dominance. The dynamics were more complicated when mate bonds formed and children were born, bringing humans and non-shifting wolves into the fold.

The hunters had decimated her pack and left the survivors to scramble to stay alive. Out of the chaos, Victoria had emerged as Alpha, the acknowledged leader. While Rand or Paul might have challenged her, they had not, out of loyalty to her parents and trust in her abilities. The bonds of affection carried more weight than ambition.

"Why does he get to live? It isn't fair." Morena stood with her arms folded across her chest. Her expression conveyed anger and fear.

Sylvie put an arm around the girl's shoulders and

hugged her. "We don't murder prisoners, Morie."

Morena turned her face into Sylvie's shoulder and shed tears. "Mercy doesn't make sense. As long as he's alive, he'll never stop hunting us. He'll bring his father and the others next time. We should kill him now."

Sylvie stroked Morena's short dark hair. "Shush, sweetie. Mercy is what separates us from them."

Victoria crouched before Sawyer to look him in the face. He tilted his head, tossing his dirty blond shoulder-length hair back, and returned her stare. His hatred remained but no longer appeared so blatant. His eyes were wary, and he looked more than a little confused.

Barrett men shared a powerful family resemblance: long limbs, muscular frames, and classical features in the Greco-Roman tradition. They were handsome, but not pretty, truly masculine. Although in his mid-twenties, Sawyer's lashes were long and thick, lending him the false innocence of childhood. She found the resemblance to his older brother uncanny and painful.

She faced one hell of a dilemma. Allowing him to live when the pack needed to cover their tracks might constitute a huge error in judgment. With his knowledge, the others could pinpoint their exact numbers and last known location with accuracy. Like wolves, hunters were most effective when working in groups.

A sigh escaped her lips. "Thirty years of peace between our people wiped out overnight."

"Your people, as you call them, started this. Mine will finish it." His stoic mask dropped, and he bristled with hatred, a heart full of unreasoning rage. He understood that she had spared his life and saved it; still, it made no difference.

She cocked her head and leaned in closer to monitor his scent. Deceit caused physical fluctuations in the body, changes in pheromone levels her sensitive nose could detect. She could literally smell a lie.

"Where's your father, Sawyer? Why isn't he with you?"

Sawyer's jaw hardened. "He's close."

Victoria's nostrils flared, inhaling his scent. He stank of deceit. "You're lying. I think you're alone, except for those two locals who were with you. Your attack was sloppy. You didn't bring backup. Did you come after us without your father's approval?"

He made no response, but his head jerked and betrayed him. Victoria smelled the truth of the matter. His reckless pursuit of revenge had led to his current predicament. No one was close enough to save him if she decided to kill him.

A thin sigh escaped her. "You can relax. I'm not going to hurt you."

That proud head bowed forward, and his tense body relaxed a little. Thinking their conversation over, Victoria started to stand, but he seized her arm.

His voice emerged as a croak, so rough it hurt to hear him speak. "There's something I want to ask you... I need to know..."

"What?" she asked. The confusion and hurt in his voice got to her.

"What the hell happened back there?" He jerked his head toward the building. "Was that Daniel's —"

"Spirit?" she asked. "Yes, it was."

He stared at her. His features hardened with suspicion. "How do I know that wasn't a trick?"

A harsh laugh escaped her, but she cut it short. She wrenched free of his grasp. "Why bother?"

Sawyer gazed at her with agony in his eyes. Beneath that savage hatred, he suffered the same as she: a hurting heart, a wounded soul.

"Why did you murder my brother?"

Victoria stared at him with pity. "You're a fool, Sawyer Barrett. I never hurt Daniel. You're only alive because your brother wanted it. Daniel was my lover. My best friend."

Sawyer was rendered speechless.

Victoria punched him hard enough to knock him out,

and he slumped to the ground, unconscious.

Victoria turned to her wolves. "Paul, give me a hand with Rand's body. We'll have to add him to the fire since we don't have time for a proper sendoff."

"What about him?" Sylvie asked with a gesture toward Sawyer.

"Tie him up," Victoria said. Gathering her power, she rallied the others to action. "Let's go. Jake Barrett can't be far."

CHAPTER TWO

Happenstance–
> *"Goddess?"*
> *"Yes, Victoria?"*
> *"An overlooked length of indestructible ribbon? Really?"*
> *"Shhh..."*

Bifröst, shimmering path of the Aesir, the burning bridge alight with all the colors of the rainbow, ended on a road that led to the towering city gates. The God Heimdallr, guardian of the bridge, dwelt within a gatehouse. Beyond it stretched the eternal city of Asgard, home of the Norse gods. Within the formidable walls, Odin's shining Valhalla stood at the center of the city, rising toward the heavens.

Victoria stepped from the bridge onto the main road leading to the gates of Asgard. The midday sun shone fat and orange at the zenith of its arc in the sky. As Rand followed her, the shotgun injuries riddling his chest healed. His severed leg regenerated, growing outward from the stump, allowing him to shed the prosthetic limb that had burdened him throughout most of his adulthood.

"Look at that! I'm as good as new!" With a gleeful bellow, Rand chucked the prosthesis over the side of the bridge and into eternity.

"Here you will always heal, but take care because the physical injuries you may incur can cause great suffering," Victoria said.

"Stop worrying, mother hen." Rand laughed at her scowl.

His cavalier attitude worried her. It would lead him to trouble. "You should listen to me," she said.

Rand framed her face in his huge hands. "I am listening, Victory! Now stop being such a stick in the mud, and tell me..."

"Tell you what?"

"Does everything still work the same as it used to?" His furry eyebrows waggled in a suggestive fashion.

Victoria slapped his hands away. "Probably better, considering that your health is now perfect, old man."

He bridled in mock outrage. "Who're you calling an old man?"

"You!" She laughed at his expression and softened her tone. "And yes, this is paradise. The pleasures of the flesh are to be had here, the same as the pain. You will find the banquet in Odin's hall to be sumptuous and delicious."

"I had other appetites in mind," Rand said.

Victoria ignored his teasing and marched toward the city gates. A motley assortment gathered outside the fortified walls and formed a disorderly line while they awaited permission to enter the golden city. A squadron of soldiers controlled and guarded the open gates. To her experienced eye, the travelers appeared unremarkable, but Rand gazed upon them with childlike wonder.

"Diverse group." Rand's thick red brow rose at the sight of a Celtic warrior brandishing a copper-tipped spear. The Celt stood beside a soldier armed with an automatic rifle. The pair kept watch duty outside the gates. An entire regiment assumed posts within the interior courtyard. The number of warriors with old-fashioned weapons far outnumbered those with modern ones. As the centuries had passed, Odin's followers had declined precipitously in number. It was the same with all the old gods.

"Members of the Einherjar come from all ages and cultures," she replied. Impatient with the assembled crowd, she plowed her way through the throng.

"Not many women in their ranks, I take it." Rand shot her a provocative look.

She showed her teeth in a wolf smile. "As you have surmised, most of their number is male. Not many women meet glorious deaths in battle."

"Only half the warriors slain in combat are chosen to come to Valhalla. The others go to Freya's hall." A shrewd look accompanied Rand's observation. "So why've you brought me here?"

"A large number of our kin are here," she said.

A look of understanding crossed Rand's ruddy face. "Ah, I see..."

"Do you?"

He nodded. "I think so."

Victoria bit her lower lip, reluctant to voice her concerns to her friend. Thankfully, the interruption of the guards saved her from further explanation. An Einherjar soldier signaled to them.

"You there! Got a reason you're too good to wait in the line?"

Victoria produced the iron signet ring that identified her as a Valkyrie. The ring bore a Valknut symbol, three interlocking triangles known as *Heart of the Slain* that had many meanings. The guard squinted, devoted three seconds of intense scrutiny to the identification, and then gave them leave to pass. They were past the gates and walking the windy streets of Asgard, beneath billowing smoke stacks, amongst the diverse population. Victoria had her reasons for being eager to reach Valhalla, but nothing a few minutes would change.

They stood in the heart of the marketplace. Beside

her, Rand gawked at the sights and smells of the bustling city. "I hadn't imagined so many people living here. Is everyone here dead?"

Victoria snorted. "Goddess, no. Many half-breed children of the Aesir and their descendants live here. The city has a population numbering in the hundred-thousands."

Victoria took his elbow, urging Rand along. "This way."

Rand shook her hand away. "Stop that. I'm not three!"

"Oh, really? 'Cause you could've fooled me," she said with a teasing tone.

She relented and ceased her attempts to hurry him even though Rand slowed their progression through the city. He examined every stall, flirted with every whore, and sampled the local ale.

When they drew closer, Valhalla's roofs of golden shields, supported upon spear-shaft rafters, shone bright in the sunlight. The immense trunks of primeval trees made up the hall's support columns and rose to the sky to satisfy the preference of gods accustomed to wide-open spaces. The structure was miles long and miles across, five hundred and forty exterior entrances capable of accommodating eight hundred men standing shoulder to shoulder, countless hallways and chambers housing the residences of many gods, including Thor's Bilskirnir. Lastly, they passed through the ancient gate Valgrind.

"Now that's ominous," Rand said when they approached the western side of the fortress. He craned his thick neck to peer upward. A wolf, skinned and flayed, hung from its rear legs, suspended off a rampart. A giant eagle hovered in the air above it.

Victoria frowned and bit her lower lip. "We children of Fenrir have an uneasy relationship with the All Father," she said.

Rand grew somber. His good-natured chatter ceased. They passed through doorways, down long corridors, and finally came to the immense dining hall where the Einherjar gathered. At the heart, one-eyed Odin presided upon his throne. Frigg, Queen of Asgard, essence of the earth mother, sat beside her husband. A din suffused the air: jovial voices, hearty laughter, shouted arguments, and the music of minstrels. The occasional chair soared overhead. Mugs smashed into walls and plates shattered upon tables. Serving wenches wound their way between occupied tables, bearing heavy platters laden with food and drink, evading the grabbing hands of enthusiastic Vikings.

Rand inhaled when they entered, drinking in the hearty scent of roasted boar and frothy ale. He glanced about with his mouth hanging open. "Odin's great hairy balls! I've never seen the likes of this place."

"Speak not of The Father's testicles. I have no wish to attract undo attention." Victoria cast a stern frown toward Odin, several football fields distant. The God King's posture denoted brooding while he rested upon his spear and conversed with Thor.

Rand followed her gaze and nodded sharply. Together, they made their way to one of the many rectangular tables that filled the hall. He sat on the end of a bench seat.

"This looks to be a fine place to rest," he said.

"Become acquainted with your neighbors," she said. "I'll fetch you a plate of food."

"Don't forget the ale, wench." Rand raised his hand in a teasing wave.

"Yeah, yeah, I'll wench you." Victoria shot a glare over her shoulder. Her lips curved into an indulgent smile while she wound her way to the roasting fire. She acquired a clean platter and made a run of the banquet tables, piling the boar and pheasant high, and then she snagged a tankard of ale.

When she returned to Rand's table, she found him busy regaling those around him with tales of the modern world. His beefy hands slapped the table in front of him, causing every platter and mug to jump and clatter. "No, I'm not making up stories!"

"You must be, because that's the craziest thing I've ever heard—a man on the moon!" Great guffaws drowned out Rand's sputtering reply. The redhead seemed in his element, having a fine old time of it.

Victoria snorted and approached the table. She intended only to set down what she carried, but a huge male hand upon her elbow prevented the action.

"That for me, wench?"

"Remove your hand, or I'll take it off at the wrist."

Victoria dropped the platter on the table. She slammed down the tankard so hard the brew sloshed over the rim. With a snarl, she whirled upon her assailant, arm raised to strike him. A hand closed on her fist, halting her punch. Staring up into a familiar handsome face, Victoria gasped and almost fell over.

"Daddy!" Victoria flew into her father's embrace.

"It's good to see you again, Victory." Adair Storm dwarfed his diminutive daughter, with him towering more than a foot taller than she was. He had a solid torso and thick limbs. He enveloped her in a hug, and his chest shook with laughter.

Victoria's mother, Katherine, appeared beside her father and joined the family hug. Her smile glowed with welcome. "Oh, Victoria, it's wonderful to see you! We've been waiting for you to visit."

Tears filled Victoria's eyes. For the first time in a long time, she felt warm and safe. Her mother smelled like home, which brought about recollections of a simpler time for Victoria, when life had been carefree.

Mother and daughter shared similar stature: the powerful build of a ballerina, and both failed to reach the five-feet mark. Twenty years senior, streaks of gray marred Katherine's blonde hair, and fine lines delineated the skin about her mouth. Their bright blue eyes were the same.

"Mom, I've missed you so much."

"I've missed you too, sweetheart."

They all spoke at once, a cacophony of voices tumbling together—joyful, concerned, and sorrowful in turn. Victoria could not process every question asked or answer given. She enjoyed a brief state of euphoria, basking in her parent's company. Gradually, they calmed and settled about a table together to speak.

"How long has it been, Victoria?" Adair asked. "You know, time doesn't always pass the same here."

"Two months. Oh, Goddess... Mom, Dad, how have you been? I panicked when I couldn't find you at Freya's hall, but the goddess assured me you were here. I'm sorry I wasn't able to come sooner."

"Surely you didn't doubt we were to be found here?" Katherine gazed at her daughter with dismay. "Our deaths were honorable: in combat, to the death, in defense of our pack."

"Of course, I knew better. It's just—I heard there was an explosion." Victoria stumbled over the implied insult to her parents. She hadn't meant to suggest they had died without honor.

Katherine's expression showed understanding.

"There was an explosion," she said. "Just before the talks began. We were hurt, but so were many of the hunters. Jake Barrett's people must have messed up and set it off prematurely."

Adair's voice and expression communicated his reservations. "I still can't see Jake Barrett being responsible for it. He is an honorable man."

Katherine frowned at her husband. "We've been through this a hundred times, my love. There's no one else who could have set it."

"Daddy, you wouldn't hesitate to believe such a

thing if you knew what that man has done to us..." She choked on her anger.

"Adair? Katherine! Stone the crows! If it ain't good to see you both!" Rand lumbered toward them with outspread arms. He swept both of her parents into a bear hug and another verbal storm of questions and explanations followed.

She crossed her arms and used the precious moments of distraction to regain mastery over her emotions. Eventually, Rand sensed their need for privacy and off he went, calling after a serving wench to bring him another tankard of ale.

Laughing, her parents watched Rand depart.

"He'll do well here," Adair said.

"I expect so," Katherine said, crossing her arms. "Come, let's sit and catch up."

They returned to their table. Adair sat beside Katherine, Victoria across from them. Her father took her mother's hand. "Victoria, it's obvious you're troubled. Tell us what's happened."

Victoria drew a deep breath and pressed her fingers to her temples. In the presence of her pack, she did not dare display doubt or weakness, but with her parents, she was safe to express her feelings.

"Mom, Dad, I've made such a mess of things. The hunters have pursued us from Arizona to Montana, hounded us at every turn. Our resources have run out and the pack is exhausted. Sophia is about to give birth and now Rand is dead."

Anger hardened her features.

"I've made terrible choices and people have suffered. We lost Jasper in Albuquerque, because I made a mistake."

Her parents expressed their dismay in unison.

"Oh, no," Katherine said, and her eyes filled with tears. "Not Jasper, too. He was only a child."

Victoria studied her parents' faces. Her mouth flattened into a grim line. "He's not in Valhalla or Fólkvangr. He didn't die a warrior's death. He was murdered."

Adair and Katherine exchanged a glance that spoke volumes. Her parents knew Jasper's soul had been condemned to Niflheim, the Norse land of the dead, because he had not died a glorious death in combat.

"We will honor his memory," Adair said.

"Honey, what happened isn't your fault." Katherine laid a consoling hand on her daughter's arm. "You must not blame yourself."

"How can I not?" Victoria's lips twisted in a bitter grimace. Her heart ached for Jasper. She had failed to protect the boy, and so she suffered guilt for his death. "It's my fault the pack's dead, my fault you're here!"

"Don't say such things, Victory. We died protecting our pack. We're here in Valhalla together," Adair said.

"There can be no better death and afterlife." Katherine took her daughter's hand. "You were only following your heart. You had no way of knowing what would happen."

"I knew better than to date a hunter," Victoria said. "Daniel could be trusted, but I knew who his family was right from the start. Now we're at war, and I couldn't bring myself to kill one of the Barretts even when I had the chance."

Katherine squeezed her fingers. "Who?"

"Daniel's brother, Sawyer," she said. She revealed in her expression and posture the anguish in her heart. "During the same battle that killed Rand. I should have killed him, but I didn't. I let him live."

She left out the visitation by Daniel's spirit. It was too new, too painful, and she did not yet understand what it meant.

"Victoria, do not feel guilty for having compassion," Katherine said. "You are a priestess and a healer. You are not a cold-blooded killer."

"I've killed."

"Killing in battle isn't the same as murdering a prisoner," Adair said.

Victoria's lips compressed. *It isn't the same as rescuing an enemy either,* she thought, but she kept her mouth shut.

"Honey, you need to stop blaming yourself," Katherine said. "You did nothing wrong."

"I loved the wrong man."

"That's not fair. Think about what might have gone right if things had been different," Katherine said.

Victoria shut her eyes. She sat rigid, jaw and fists clenched. "Mom, please..."

Adair cleared his throat. "Victoria, is your young man here? Perhaps you could seek him out?"

Victoria opened her eyes and shook her head. "He died in battle, but Daniel isn't in Valhalla."

"His faith took him elsewhere," Katherine said.

Adair chuckled. "Spoken like a true priestess."

Victoria and Katherine laughed but the sound carried a brittle note, covering their underlying despair. She knew it frustrated her parents to hear bad news from home and be unable to do anything to help. Adair read their mood with uncanny precision. He covered their joined hands with his own. "Do you know why I nicknamed you Victory as a child?"

She giggled and managed a genuine smile. "Because I never gave up?"

"Not only did you never give up, but you demolished any obstacle in your path with unrelenting determination. In all my years, I've never seen the like."

Victoria felt her cheeks heat, and that embarrassed her even more. "Dad..."

"My point is: I know things are bad, sweetie. I would give anything to be able to fix everything for you, but it is no longer within my ability. You're strong, and you're smart. I have faith you'll lead the pack to safety."

"You're an excellent leader, Victoria," Katherine said. "Be strong and you'll find your way."

Victoria swallowed past the lump in her throat. "Any advice?"

Katherine smiled. "Yes, as a matter of fact. It's time for you to find a mate and bear us a grandchild."

"Mom!" Victoria glared at her mother.

Embarrassed, her father found an interesting spot on the ceiling to study. He cleared his throat. "Good grief, Kat. Is this an appropriate time?"

Katherine snorted. "Will there be another? Victoria has ignored the needs of her wolf for too long."

"I'm right here!" Victoria shifted in her seat, and quelled the desire to jump to her feet. As an 'old maid' of twenty-four, she was all too familiar with her mother's pleas for her to take a mate and settle down.

Adair sighed. "I hate to say it, Victory, but your mother may have a point."

She groaned. "Dad, not you too..."

"Sorry." He shrugged. "But truth is, I'd feel better knowing you had a worthy mate to help you manage the burdens of leadership. I'm not saying a female can't go it alone, but it'd be easier if you had a husband."

"Our entire bloodline will end if you do not have a child," Katherine said. "Our pack has endured for forty generations, but those who survive will surely perish without the protection of an Alpha male. I am sorry, Victory, but it is the way of the world."

"An Alpha male would strengthen the pack," Adair said. "I agree with your mother. You must do this for the good of the pack."

For the good of the pack. Victoria closed her eyes and slowly exhaled. The pack's welfare was imperative, so she made a heroic effort to remove pride from the equation.

Calmer, she opened her eyes. "Okay, what do you suggest?"

Katherine pursed her lips. "Our Lady Freya has granted me a premonition. There is a powerful dominant male wolf without a mate. He would be a valiant protector and provider for the pack."

"Does he have a name?"

"The goddess was not so specific," Katherine said with a wry glint in her blue eyes.

Adair chuckled. "No, of course not."

"She never is," Victoria said.

Katherine ignored them. "Freya has said this is your opportunity to meet your lifemate. A man every bit as strong-willed, stubborn, and contrary as you."

"Sounds like a peach."

Katherine smiled. "It is only a suggestion. Of course, the decision is yours, Victoria."

She sighed, knowing she would regret it, and asked anyway. "All right, so where do I find this Prince Charming?"

"Sierra Pines, California," Katherine said.

To Victoria's immense relief, the subject dropped. They talked, laughed, and the hour grew late. The crowd in the hall thinned out, and Victoria grew restless. Every moment she spent apart from the pack carried a certain intrinsic danger.

"I hate to say it, but I can't stay. I've been gone too long already," she said.

They all stood.

"We understand," Adair said and hugged his daughter.

Victoria moved to her mother's arms next. "Take care, Victoria," Katherine said. "But first, I have a gift for you, daughter."

Katherine extended her right hand and drew the mystical weapon that always hung above her right shoulder — invisible when sheathed, visible when drawn. The dagger was a powerful rune blade, a gift from Freya. Kat offered the dagger to her daughter on her open palms.

Victoria's eyes grew wide. "Mom, I can't..."

Katherine placed the weapon in her daughter's hands. "You can, and you must. I have always meant for you to have it. This dagger came to me from my mother, and you must pass it to your child someday. She is *Vanadium*, and she has served me well. Only one who knows her name may wield her, so guard it."

Victoria nodded her understanding. The weapon felt amazing in her hands, good and right. Fascinated, she wrapped her fingers about the hilt and gave an experimental thrust. The blade sang, slicing lightning-swift through the air, and light shimmered on the surface, moonlight on water. *Vanadium* measured three feet in length—twelve inches of hilt with two feet of blade as thin as a silken ribbon. Victoria almost expected it to flutter when brandished, but it remained true and straight.

"The blade is crafted from the same unbreakable binding that holds the great wolf Fenrir," Adair said.

Katherine's eyes shone with enthusiasm. "The gods commissioned the dwarves to fashion the ribbon *Gleipnir* from six impossible things: the sound of a cat's footfall, a woman's beard, the root of a mountain, the sinew of a bear, a fish's breath, and the spittle of a bird."

Victoria's brow rose. "There are bearded women and fish that breathe." *And maybe even a noisy cat...*

Her father chuckled and reached over to tug the end of his wife's braid. "She has a point, Kat."

Her mother frowned in rebuke to both of them. "This is magic, Victoria. Don't be contrary."

"Sorry." She put on her angel face.

Katherine licked her lips. "As it happened, there was a spare length of ribbon that was overlooked."

Adair chuckled. "Which Our Lady Freya *happened* to acquire. Know this, that blade will cut through anything."

Victoria smiled at her father. "I'd love to test that. How do I sheath her?"

"Thrust the blade toward the sky and let go," Katherine said.

Victoria did as instructed and the dagger vanished.

"Now reach for her," Adair said.

Dubious, Victoria brought up her right hand, and found the hilt of the weapon hanging above her right shoulder. Victoria released *Vanadium*, knowing the dagger would be with her always, patient within her sheath.

"I thank you, mother," she said with a great deal of formality. "I am honored."

"Tell the pack of our love and how we miss them," Adair said.

"I love you, honey," Katherine said.

"As do I," Adair said.

"I love and miss you both so much," Victoria said, and they exchanged hugs and tears.

Katherine bowed her head. "Do you return straight home, Victoria?"

"No, I wish to stop at the temple and pray to Freya for guidance."

Katherine smiled her understanding. "Take whatever Our Lady tells you with a grain of salt."

"Oh, I will. Rest assured."

"Godspeed, Daughter," said Adair.

CHAPTER THREE

Fate—

"Goddess, is this free will or fate?"
"Victoria, must you always ask the questions I don't have the answers to?"
"I'm sorry. I guess contrary is in my nature."

Sierra Pines, California, located within the heart of the Sierra Nevada Mountains, had a small-town, big-money feel. The exclusive alpine community clung to the western shore of Echo Lake, and boasted country clubs, million-dollar homes, and a ski resort. Miles of pristine alpine forest full of deer and elk and other small prey extended in every direction, including the remote and rugged Desolation Wilderness. Fallen Leaf Lake and Lake Tahoe lay to the north.

The picturesque downtown ran along a two-lane Main Street lined with shops, small businesses, restaurants, the library, and a cluster of government buildings, including city hall. Victoria stood before the embossed plate glass door of some first floor legal offices and fidgeted. She checked the crumpled business card in her hand against the name on the door: *Arik Koenig, Attorney at Law.*

The last four weeks had been difficult—hard on her,

harder on the pack. They were exhausted and half starved. Sophia had given birth to her cubs in the back of the pack's SUV, and Victoria had failed to keep her promise to find a safe den for the mother wolf.

To top it all off, Freya's promised Prince Charming had turned out to be...

"A lawyer..." Victoria's mouth contorted in an involuntary sneer.

She envisioned a smarmy bottom feeder with zero scruples and unlimited greed. She wondered what Freya had been thinking, sending her to such a man. She suspected the goddess of a cruel prank.

Victoria turned from the office door and glanced up and down the busy street. The sidewalks were full of pedestrians, and the mid-morning sun shone overhead. On a telephone wire, a pair of ravens sat together like gossiping old women, looking down upon her. The birds emitted raucous *craas*, as if laughing at a private joke. Victoria cast a narrowed-eyed glare of frustration toward them. One of the ravens cocked its head and stared at her with a beady eye.

"Come closer, birdy." Victoria flashed her teeth.

The sleek raven opened its sharp beak. "Craa!"

Victoria's nostrils flared, and she exhaled a long, thin breath. She was running out of excuses to avoid going inside. She had no desire to meet Arik Koenig. Beyond a shadow of a doubt, she did not want a lifemate. A man would only complicate things, restrict her freedom, issue orders, seize leadership of the pack. She gathered her resolve and drew in a deep breath. Her wants and needs were secondary to those of the pack. Everyone sacrificed for the greater good.

As soon as Victoria entered, a secretary behind a teak desk looked up. The receptionist's brow furrowed over her slate-gray eyes. "Good morning. Can I help you?"

"I have an appointment with Mr. Koenig at ten,"

Victoria said. She offered the woman a polite smile.

The nameplate on the secretary's desk read: *Margaret Duane*. Victoria quashed the impulse to fidget while the woman checked the appointment calendar on the computer. The secretary appeared to be in her mid-forties with short black hair and Mediterranean-toned skin. Her trimmed nails and utilitarian style of dress implied brisk efficiency.

"Here you are, Ms. Storm," she said. "Please have a seat, and I'll inform Mr. Koenig you're here. It should be a couple more minutes."

With effort, Victoria reined in the nervous energy that made her want to pace. She took in her surroundings: browns and golds dominated the interior's modern décor, which was elegant but impersonal.

For the meeting, she had worn a crisp white blouse with a V-neckline, mother-of-pearl buttons and cuffed sleeves. Pressed black slacks, a black clutch, and patent leather Mary Jane shoes completed the ensemble. A Chinese hair stick pinned her coiled hair into a ballerina hair bun, a familiar style from her childhood years as a dancer.

"Ms. Storm, Mr. Koenig will see you now. It's the first door on your right." Although Margaret endeavored to maintain a professional demeanor, the woman failed to conceal the combination of speculation and disdain in her gaze.

"Thank you." Victoria rose and moved in the direction indicated. The office door stood ajar. Her tension increased with each step, because the next few moments were crucial. Many wolves attacked, no questions asked, upon discovering an unexpected intruder in their territory.

Victoria felt him before she saw him. His power washed over her with the force of an incoming tide, as dark, mysterious and unstoppable as the ocean. Her wolf rose to answer his in instinctive response, defiant and determined. She challenged his power and altered the irresistible flow so it passed around rather than over her. Before she reached the office entrance, the male werewolf responded to her presence and surged to his feet. He rounded the desk, demonstrating extraordinary grace and strength, and she braced for a physical confrontation. He dwarfed her in both height and weight.

As soon as their gazes met, they locked in a dominance contest. His narrowed eyes pierced hers; the light-pigmented brown irises were the color of honey and eclipsed the whites and round black pupils. *Wolf eyes.*

Victoria did not approach with her head low or avert her gaze. Instead, she challenged him outright, radiating defiance, posture stiff and erect. While they faced off, she regretted the tactical error, but it was too late to rescind. Her stubborn pride permitted no retreat, and it went against her nature to submit.

"Let's take this outside where there are no humans to bear witness," he said in a deep, resonant voice she found appealing.

Aroused, her wolf took an immediate interest in him as a fine, fit male animal. For the first time, Victoria noticed his physical appearance, and her wolf found him more than acceptable. She estimated his age as being in his late thirties. He in no way suffered for the smattering of silver hairs that peppered his dark head. He was a perfect specimen of a man.

Distracted, Victoria broke eye contact, but not to submit. She ran her gaze over his body with blatant approval, lingering on his broad shoulders and chest, muscular arms and legs. He wore a tailored navy suit with a light shirt and dark blue tie. From the way his clothing fit, there was not an ounce of spare fat anywhere on him.

His features possessed splendid symmetry, though a silver scar on his right cheek marred his perfection. The shape of his brow, nose, and lower face hinted at a distant Roman heritage. High cheekbones alluded to his Nordic blood. He cleared his throat, and Victoria scented both his arousal and amusement.

"Did you come to challenge me, or do you have something else in mind?"

His devilish smile hinted at a sense of humor, and Victoria seized on the opening. A ballsy gamble carried inherent risk, but her initial inept blundering had left her with no other graceful out. Her eyes rose to meet his once again.

"I am Victoria, daughter of Adair and Katherine, High Priestess of Freya, Lady Valkyrie, shaman, and healer," she said, making her boast. "I am also the Alpha of my pack, and I am seeking a mate. I have come to assess whether you would make an acceptable suitor."

"You're kidding." He registered surprise and disbelief.

Victoria arched her brow. "I am not."

She pressed her advantage and advanced a step. Lust and suspicion warred on his countenance. His gaze appraised her once again with a blatant sexual interest.

Victoria endured his inspection with pride, well aware she pleased the male eye. She had a high forehead, a narrow nose, and pronounced cheekbones set in an oval face. Her lithe grace suited her petite frame, an ideal ballerina's body, although her passion for combat far exceeded her interest in dance.

Understanding lit those honey-brown eyes. "You're in heat."

"Yes, I'm in heat."

Victoria closed the distance between them and adopted an appeasing posture, sly female approaching a ready male. She extended a bold hand and rested her palm upon his chest, stroking the crisp material of his dress shirt. "You're a handsome and powerful dominant male. Your offspring would be strong and viable."

"I'm flattered." He stared hard, expression unfathomable, and for a second, she feared her ruse had failed. If he insisted upon a physical confrontation, she would be unable to refuse. Submission went against her nature. In a fight, odds were good he would win.

"That was a brilliant recovery." His husky laughter signaled a cessation of hostility. Relief suffused Victoria and her shoulders slumped. She did not bother hiding her reaction from him. His hand rose and his fingers brushed the back of her hand. At his touch, Victoria heated but made no protest when he backed away. She was not ready for any level of physical intimacy with him.

"Thank you. My father was the diplomat." Victoria laughed with him. "Mom and I were always more impulsive: act first, ask questions later."

"Was?" Arik had a good ear.

"My parents are gone." Victoria could not keep the grief from her face. She missed her parents so much. In a way, their short visit had made her longing worse.

Arik's gaze softened with sympathy. "I'm sorry."

"Thank you."

"Please, have a seat. I assume you know my name already, but I'll give it to you anyway. Arik Koenig." He returned to his chair, allowing his head to sink below hers, a testament to his security.

"It's a pleasure to meet you, Mr. Koenig," Victoria said and assumed one of the two leather chairs opposite his desk.

"And you also, Ms. Storm. Now, please, tell me why you're really here."

Her brow furrowed. Having recovered from the social fumble, she wanted nothing more than to get down to business. "What makes you think I'm not serious?"

He regarded her with skepticism. "Well, your practicality is impressive, if nothing else."

She sighed. "My lineage and accomplishments are also impressive if you wish to hear them. Look, I'm not manipulative or political by nature. The fact is that my pack is in a bad way."

Arik hesitated. "I felt your arrival a few days ago."

"If you felt our intrusion into your territory, why didn't you come looking for us?"

"Your pack wasn't being disruptive and stayed close to the highway. At first I thought you were just moving through," he said. "Then, yesterday, I spotted the older couple in town and I realized you were looking for me. I thought it was wiser to wait for you to come to me than risk provoking a confrontation."

Victoria studied him, surmising his motivations. "Thank you. I appreciate the care you've taken with my people."

The corner of his mouth turned up. "Are you really looking for a mate? As flattering as it may be, I'm much older than you are. I'm sure there are plenty of younger males..."

She sighed and waved a dismissive hand. She met his gaze to drive home the force of her conviction. "Yes, there are plenty of impulsive, hot-headed males willing to kill for a chance to mate with me. I don't need that kind of liability right now."

"So it's all about your pack."

"I'm their Alpha. We've been moving for months without proper food or shelter. It's my job to ensure their continued survival, and that's tenuous until I can find us a new home. So yes, it's all about my pack."

He blinked.

Victoria knew her blatant honesty was too much. She and her pack sounded like a disaster and her desperation was unappealing. In his position, she would not have jumped at a chance to mate with her either.

"I can pay bride's price," Victoria said in a flat tone. She reached into her clutch purse and removed the folded square of white silk she carried. She unfolded it and set the talisman down midway upon his desk.

Arik regarded the object with suspicion. A blue silk ribbon formed a neat bow about a lock of hair the color of ripe rye grasses. Shrugging, Arik finally picked it up for inspection. He started and sat up straighter once he felt the potent magic inherent within the object. His eyes widened with awe.

"What is this?"

"The hair of a goddess."

Arik stared at her. "Really?"

She nodded. "Really."

He considered for a long moment and then moved to return the lock of hair to her. "I can't accept this."

Victoria held up a resigned hand, staying his gesture. "Please, accept it as a gift from my pack. If it pleases you, then grant us permission to remain within your territory for a month. One of my pack whelped puppies two weeks ago. We've been on the run even though she should still be holed up in a den, and it's weakening the mother and cubs. We need to remain in one place until they are strong enough to travel."

Arik frowned. "Hardly a fair exchange. This is worth far more than my hospitality for a moon cycle."

Victoria waved a tired hand. "Freya sheds like a cat. It is criminal to dispose of any holy relic in a casual manner, and yet I could knit sweaters of the stuff. Please, accept the gift. I have nothing else of value to offer."

Arik eyed her long and hard. "I wouldn't say that..."

The blatant sexual regard in his gaze excited her. Victoria sat up, squirming with discomfort, suppressing a moan. As much as she despised the admission, she *needed* a male such as that one to serve as companion and confidant.

"I'm not so medieval as to require a bride price, but I am old fashioned," Arik said with a twinkle in his eyes. To her immense pleasure, he tucked the talisman into the pocket of his suit. "What do you say we begin again?"

Her mouth went dry. "What do you suggest?"

"Let's get to know one another while you and your pack are my guests in Sierra Pines. If you will come to my home tonight, I'll prepare dinner for the two of us."

Victoria's spirit rebounded, casting off its cloak of resignation. "All right. I'd like that."

CHAPTER FOUR

Inconvenience—
    "Goddess, Arik has a son."
    "Is this a problem?"
    "Yes, it is."

Hot fat drizzled from the side of beef, fed the hungry fire, and caused the flames to dance higher. Victoria's nostrils flared, drinking in the scent, and she licked her lips. Her stomach snarled, and her sides ached, roiling from a long winter's hunger. The perceptible sound embarrassed her for what it revealed. Her face and throat flushed dark red.

With a chuckle, Arik Koenig cranked the handle of the spit and picked up the basting brush and sauce bowl. When he smiled, his cheeks dimpled and his eyes twinkled.

"Don't be embarrassed," he said. "I admire a woman with a healthy appetite."

The double entendre played well, and Victoria's pale complexion colored more. She smiled and leaned forward so a curtain of pale strands fell forward to cover her face. Her hair hung long and loose about her shoulders, her sole concession to vanity. Sylvie had urged her to wear makeup but Victoria disliked the feel of it on her skin. She wore a black baby doll tee shirt layered under a long-sleeve wool shirt, black jeans and black shoes.

"Thank you for inviting me to dinner, Mr. Koenig." She disliked acting in a deferential manner to any male, but Arik Koenig was a more dominant wolf and senior to her. Her consideration of his courtship did not lessen his ability to intimidate her.

"Please, call me Arik, and you're welcome. It is a pleasure to have you here." He moved closer to her and the sexual tension rose tenfold. His intimate gaze ran along her body.

Victoria smiled and tested his name. "Arik."

"Would you like a beer, Victoria?"

"Yes, thank you." She accepted a Guinness from him and twisted off the metal cap. He opened his own beer. The casualness of drinking from the bottle helped put her at ease.

At least he's not a wine and cheese snob.

Still, she felt underdressed compared to him. His attire was not as formal as the suit he had worn when they met. He wore a long-sleeved linen shirt, tight-fitting jeans, and leather boots. A white apron over his clothing added a touch of whimsy. The logo read: *Natural Born Griller.*

"Arik, do you have a pack?" Wolves seldom chose to live alone. It was in their nature to crave the companionship of their own kind.

He shook his head. "Not anymore."

"But once?" She took care to keep her tone neutral despite her intense curiosity about him. She needed his goodwill. She sensed unimaginable power within him. Wild magic. The true depths remained obscure to her. He could destroy both her and hers in a heartbeat, or save them.

"Once, but that was long ago. Nowadays, it's only my son and me." Arik eased closer so their hot puffs of exhaled breath mingled. The stench of power pervaded him, thick as musk, exacerbating her arousal. Her wolf ached to claim him.

"Your son?" Curious, Victoria tilted her head back. She muzzled her wolf and reined in her wanton impulses before she got herself into serious trouble.

Arik tensed and a shadow darkened his gaze. "Logan."

An alarm went off in her head. She drew back. "Just to be clear, do you have a mate?"

He shook his head. Palpable grief darkened his gaze. "My wife passed away two years ago."

"I'm so sorry." Victoria regarded him with heart-felt sympathy. "As I told you, I lost my parents, so I do understand."

"They were killed by hunters?" It was the logical inference based on what she had already told him.

Victoria hardened her heart. She could not afford the luxury of indulging her grief. Any sign of weakness on her part granted him an advantage. "Every able-bodied adult in my pack was slain, wolf and human alike."

"How did you survive?"

Her pride tasted bitter, as did the knowledge that she should be dead also. "When the hunters came, I was sent to shepherd the disabled, the vulnerable, and the young."

"To get them to safety," Arik said, and his correct assumption acted as a balm to her injured vanity.

"I'm still doing my best to fulfill the responsibility my parents placed on me. We've been running from the hunters ever since."

She saw the question in his eyes before he voiced it. "We lost the hunters in Montana. Traveling as wolves, we laid a trail to the Canadian border and mixed with the local population there. Then we doubled back and came south. The hunters should believe we're long gone."

Arik gave a thoughtful nod, and Victoria exhaled in

relief. Eager to change the topic, she said, "So you're alone then?"

He dwelled on the question, giving it more thought than a simple question required. When the answer came, he spoke with studied precision, reminding her of his chosen profession. "My wife, Lori, was descended from a noble Norse lineage, but she wasn't a shifter. Logan and I are the only wolves in Sierra Pines."

Arik took a swig of his beer, and she matched the gesture, ingesting a small amount. Wolves were not as susceptible to intoxication, but her empty stomach would speed the absorption of alcohol. It was imperative she keep her wits about her.

Perhaps sensing the need to satisfy her curiosity, Arik resumed speaking without further prompting. "Sierra Pines is a quiet little town. I have my own practice, and Lori and I made a home and raised our child here. I'm well regarded by the humans who live here."

She pursed her lips, debating the tact of broaching a sensitive topic. She had concerns beyond casual curiosity about him. His acceptability as a potential mate hinged on several key factors. Shifters tended to have low fertility so his proven virility counted as a plus. However, his son remained a big unknown.

"Ask me," he said. "We both know why we're here."

She gave him a sharp glance. He read her with unsettling accuracy.

"I appreciate your bluntness," she said. "It's well suited to me."

"I learned that on our first meeting." He chuckled and showed teeth. The sultry sound stirred her arousal and heightened her awareness of his intense masculinity.

Given the invitation, she did not intend to mince her words. "Why are you and Logan alone out here in the middle of nowhere? Two males of our breed, even father and son, seldom reside in isolation without females or a pack to provide balance. This area is perfect for our kind, which makes it even odder."

Arik's smile disappeared. The pall of paternal disappointment fell over him, defying his attempt to conceal it. "My son is still young. He went through The Change two years ago."

"Ah, I see." She did not. She shifted with marked unease. She did not smell an explicit lie, but sensed deliberate evasion.

He flashed a predatory smile. "You don't."

"How old is Logan?"

"Twenty." He watched for her reaction.

Victoria failed to conceal her surprise. "Twenty! You're saying he experienced his first Change at eighteen?"

Children born as human manifested their shapechanging abilities between ten and thirteen. In those born as wolves, it happened sooner. If any of Sophia's pups inherited their father's shifter capability, the first Change would occur between the ages of one and three. For a human child, the oldest instance Victoria had ever heard of was fourteen. Eighteen did not begin to scratch the definition of late bloomer.

"Logan should be home soon. You'll have a chance to meet him." Arik spoke with a finality that ended the current topic.

Victoria nodded and watched while he brushed the side of beef with sauce and returned the brush and bowl to the granite counter. She maintained a mask but her inner speculation ran rampant: *What has Arik's son done to engender such bitter disappointment in a loving father?*

The ring of a mobile phone interrupted the strained silence. With a glance at Victoria, Arik removed the device from his pocket and checked the display. "Excuse me a moment."

"Of course," she said.

Arik moved toward the house, and she exhaled as

his departure lessened the tension in the air. Restless, she strolled along the perimeter of the swimming pool in order to admire the lake in the distance. Spotlights along the periphery of the pool defined its clean bright lines, a startling contrast to the five-foot wall of snow at the edge of the shoveled patio. Steam rose from the surface of the heated water, mixing with the chilly mountain air. The impenetrable darkness of Echo Lake lay a hundred yards from the edge of the yard. On all sides, the snow-covered peaks of the Sierra Nevada Mountains towered toward the black starry sky. The crescent moon formed a silvery sliver.

A pair of ravens roosted in a pine tree not too far away, watching her.

Odin's sleek, shiny-eyed creatures... Victoria pinned the birds with her gaze. Unease churned her gut.

"Who are you?" she asked.

The ravens kept their secrets.

Turning from them, Victoria slipped her phone from her pocket and checked the display. No missed calls; no text messages from the pack. What an unbelievable relief to go one day without crisis or drama. She returned the phone to her pocket.

Movement in the trees caught her attention, and she tilted her head to get a better look. Beside the lakeshore, the figure of a woman limped toward the house. Victoria made out brown hair and a splash of red on a flowing white gown.

Victoria took several steps forward and stopped when she reached the wall of snow at the edge of the patio. Her brow pinched, and she opened her mouth to call out.

She caught the scent of a male wolf behind her. Her hackles rose when his whiskey voice mocked her. "Fie, foh, and fum, I smell the blood of a tiny woman."

Victoria spun to face the offending male wolf intruder. Her upper lip peeled back to reveal her canines and a rumbling snarl issued from her throat. He towered over her, standing at least a foot and a half taller, and had at least a hundred pounds of lean muscle on her. He wore a short-sleeve tan shirt featuring a Chinese dragon, faded blue jeans, and black Doc Martens.

She assumed a defensive stance, extending her right hand to reach for her dagger, when he caught her gaze. She found no threat in his amber eyes, only naked lust and wicked humor. His generous mouth twisted into a smirk. In her assessment, he did not present an immediate physical threat.

"Well, halloo, Blondie. Has daddy found himself a new playmate?"

She modified her snarl into a cold smile. They might be wolves, but they were also human. She was a guest in his home. Relaxing her guard, she assessed him with an appreciative glance.

"You must be Logan."

"I must be." He regarded her with a lascivious leer.

Victoria rolled her eyes. She had no doubt. The physical resemblance to Arik became apparent upon consideration. Father and son shared the same high forehead, strong thin-profiled nose, cheekbones and jaw. The boy wore his light-brown hair in a spiky style and lacked his father's sturdy build. Broad shoulders, long limbs, and a narrow waist kept with his youth. In time, he would fill out. She could tell he'd be huge once he reached maturity.

A quick glance over her shoulder revealed that the woman among the trees had vanished. With a shrug, Victoria dismissed the incident.

"You have me at a disadvantage. What's your name?" Logan stepped forward, invading her personal space even more. He tilted his head back, mocking the surrender of his throat.

She refused to give ground, so they were almost touching. "Victoria Storm."

"Victoria—sounds like an old lady," Logan said. "Can I call you Vicky?"

"Do so and die." Victoria glared. She expected he got away with murder, thanks to an uncanny beauty that even a distinct lack of charm failed to eradicate.

Logan threw back his head and laughed, further exposing his throat. He oozed arrogance from every pore. "Are you always so defensive, Vic?"

Her fists clenched, and she reined in the impulse to pummel him. "Does that facile charm work with the little high school girls? Do they call you Wolverine and swoon when you walk by?"

"Ouch." He smirked. "You know, they do. Swoon. But I'm long out of high school and good ol' dad is to blame for my namesake. Is it my fault he's a secret comic book fan boy?"

"Our parents' literary tastes are never our fault." She felt his heat on her skin and longed to wrap her mouth around the thick column of his throat. He smelled delicious.

"The real question is whether it's your fault that you're a bitter disappointment to your father?" She delivered the final cut with a cruel smile.

A facial tick in his jaw showed she had scored a direct hit. His glib tongue formed a quick reply. "It's always easier to slip under my father's bar than to try to go over it."

"A self-professed failure. I'm not surprised. After all, you're still living at home, and let me guess, no job?"

Murderous anger drove the amusement from Logan's eyes. He performed a pantomime of hurt, his hand pressed to his heart. "Wow, they really teach trailer trash how to be mean."

A year ago, his insult would have meant nothing. Thanks to the hunters, she could no longer afford a trailer park as a home for her pack. Rage turned her hands to claws. She killed him with her glare.

"I can recite my lineage all of the way back to Fenrir. My mother's line has produced a werewolf every generation going back a millennium."

"Why'd your mama breed with a coyote then, little girl?"

She must not kill him.

Victoria bit back a slur against Logan's lineage, only because to deride him also meant insulting Arik. Sides heaving, she fumed and forced her hands to revert.

He dismissed any threat she posed with a smirk and a shrug. Balancing on his heels, Logan extracted a small container from his pocket and popped the lid. He threw back his head, tossed candy into his mouth, and crunched it between his teeth. The tantalizing scent of sweet citrus filled the air.

Her stomach snarled. Hunger clawed at her ribs.

Logan's brow shot up and he cast a deliberate glance at her abdomen. He smirked. "Hungry?"

"What are those?"

"Breath mints." Logan held up the container. "Want some?"

Victoria sharply nodded. He tossed her the box, and she caught it out of the air. Without hesitation, she downed the entire contents of the container within seconds. It did nothing to abate her hunger, but it deprived him of his candy.

She hurled the empty plastic box back at Logan, aiming for his face. His left hand flashed, and he caught it out of the air. "You ate all of my candy."

"Sue me," she said with a saccharine smile.

"I would but you don't look like you're good for the nickel."

Her eyes narrowed. Knowing she was just shy of losing her temper and killing him, Victoria turned her back on him.

Asshole! She couldn't help but ask herself if she could handle this boy as a stepson.

With a grunt, Victoria glanced toward the outdoor kitchen. A warm glow emanated from the barbeque pit where the side of beef hanged on a spit over the hot coals. She wished for Arik to return and end her torment.

She decided she should make at least one valid attempt to make peace with Logan.

Victoria returned her gaze to him. "Tell me about Sierra Pines."

He rolled his eyes and made a production of yawning, covering his mouth with his hand before he answered. "Not much to tell. Sierra Pines has a population of fifteen thousand mortals, two wolves, one vampire, and a ghoul."

"Your father tolerates a vampire in his territory?" she asked, tone skeptical. She stared at him but was unable to detect a lie.

"Menja is an exceptional exception." From his smug expression, she could tell Logan would say no more.

She refused to be baited, so the topic dropped.

So much for making nice, she thought.

Her physical attraction to Logan disturbed her. Four years separated them in actual age, but he lacked the maturity and character she found attractive in a male. She might as well return to trading insults with him. At least she felt comfortable with the verbal sparring.

"You're what, fourteen?"

Logan leered, showing teeth and tongue. He dropped a hand to cup his crotch. "Twenty, and in my prime, Vic. The old man is way past his."

"You're disgusting." Victoria allowed her power to rise. She locked gazes with Logan, refusing to allow an unproven male to intimidate her. He might be bigger and stronger, but she had led her pack through hell and high water, and she was more powerful.

Logan looked away first. He rolled his eyes and grinned, refusing to accept the challenge she offered. It was a grave insult. The shock of dismissal set Victoria's teeth on edge. Her jaw clenched and her wolf roiled beneath her iron control, spoiling for a fight. If Logan refused to accede to her higher rank, bloodshed remained her only option for establishing dominance.

Arik's cool power blew over them, dampening her anger. "I see you've met my son."

Victoria smashed a startle reflex and turned to offer Arik a welcoming smile. "I have."

"The food's ready." Arik transferred his gaze to his son.

Logan held Arik's stare for ten seconds and then looked down, conceding dominance to his father. The boy understood how the social ritual worked. However, he had refused to accord her any respect at all by failing to acknowledge her challenge.

Fuming, Victoria marched past Arik and returned to the patio. She reminded herself every step of the way that she was a guest in another Alpha's territory. An attack against Arik's son would not go over well, no matter how much Logan had it coming.

As Victoria took the lead, Arik fell into step behind her. The sullen Logan brought up the rear.

"That was delicious, Arik. I don't think I can move another step." Victoria flopped into a recliner and indulged in a luxurious stretch. She reached far and long with her fingertips and toes, working out every residual crimp.

Her long winter's hunger had abated. She had eaten more than her fill, gorging on the sumptuous meal. He hadn't prepared anything to exceed the culinary skills of the average bachelor, but everything had been tasty.

She experienced more than a twinge of guilt over eating while the others remained hungry, but suppressed the useless sentiment. Guilt served no useful purpose. The betterment of their circumstances rested at the heart of her negotiations with Arik. If she selected a strong mate capable of providing and protecting, the entire pack would benefit.

"It was a pleasure to watch you eat." Arik's throaty chuckle stirred a different hunger within her. His gaze lingered on her, caressing her curves, and she returned his regard with piqued interest. However, Logan's inconvenient presence prevented her from acting on her primal impulses. Arik possessed all of the attractive traits of a dominant male, but his recalcitrant son served to dampen her enthusiasm.

Arik assumed the seat to Victoria's right. Logan stood at the edge of a room, a silent, hostile presence. It surprised her when he stayed. She expected him to leave. In fact, she preferred his absence, but supposed him unwilling to risk his father's wrath.

She moistened her lips with her tongue and studied father and son with marked speculation. Arik commanded attention, compelling obedience through a combination of charisma and authority, regal and solitary in the manner of kings and mountains. In contrast, Logan's aura wildcatted through the room, powerful, unpredictable, and destructive as a storm.

A fundamental wrongness existed at the foundation of their relationship. In a healthy dynamic, a rebellious male Logan's age would have challenged Arik's authority or set out on his own. The boy's sullen obedience combined with his father's obvious shame pointed to major dysfunction.

Victoria realized her stare had fallen on Logan, and she ripped it away. She turned her gaze to Arik, sliding her eyes over his muscular form. Her need intensified, creating a rush of wet heat between her thighs, and she ached to touch him, to taste him, to take him.

Her pensive meditation riled her wolf, who wished

to move on with the business of selecting a mate. She needed to get laid. Her hormones were wreaking havoc with her ability to think. She writhed on the armchair, aware of how both male wolves stirred, responding to the scent of her arousal.

Bold, brash Logan said it aloud. "You're in heat!"

Victoria shot Logan a derisive glare that said, *"Well, duh."* Her condition should be obvious to any wolf with a nose.

Arik shot a scowl at his son. "Don't be rude, Logan."

Victoria's frustration hit a new high, fueling her dislike of the boy and general bad mood. She wanted Logan gone. She lost her temper. "Are you only realizing this now?"

"Dad, she's using pheromones to manipulate—"

Arik's formidable patience frayed enough, so he snapped. "Shut up, Logan. I understand what's happening. This is how the game is played."

"What game is that?"

"Maybe I should go." Victoria sat forward. As much as she enjoyed having the two males snarling at one another over her, she was not interested in petty rivalries. Logan wasn't even a contender as her potential mate.

Arik's eyes arrested her movement. "Please stay."

Logan ignored them and repeated, "What game is that, Dad?"

Arik's anger made him even scarier. He glared at his son.

"Courtship always begins with a food offering from the male. If the female accepts, she is willing to consider him as a mate."

"Ugh." Victoria performed a face smack, her palm to her forehead. The game was up that they were 'getting to know each other' over a nice meal. Arik's declaration made it official and irreversible.

Arik's mouth twisted into a grimace. He understood what he'd done. "Sorry."

"Yeah." She squeezed her eyes shut and offered Freya a fervent prayer. *Please, Goddess, wipe Logan from the face of the earth, and I'll do anything you ask...*

"So what are you saying?" Logan asked. "You two are dating?"

"Logan, you're exhausting my patience."

"And mine," Victoria said.

Logan continued as if he had not heard. His demeanor dripped disdain, and he turned an insulting leer on her. "Are you going to allow this bitch to take mom's place? What the hell does she have to offer that you can't get cheaper from a whore?"

"I can provide the strong son he lacks!" Victoria shot to her feet, adopting a ready stance, and a snarl issued past her bared teeth. Her eyes glowed golden, and her muscles rippled beneath her skin while she initiated the transformation into a wolf.

With a roar, Logan launched across the room at her. Mid-air he underwent the change into his fighting form, the point between human and wolf that offered all of the advantages of hands and feet, teeth and claws, as well as enhanced strength. His body flowed from one shape into the other as if made of water, and the air stank of powerful magic.

She had never seen the like of it.

The swiftness of his change caused her to falter, so her own transformation ceased. She froze, terrified for a split second, just long enough to lose her rage.

"Enough! I will not have you two fighting like animals in my house!" Arik stepped between them. With a sweep of his arm, he intercepted Logan and sent his son flying across the room.

Logan slammed into the wall, creating concentric circles of cracked plaster, and slid to the floor in a stunned heap. Arik remained human the entire time, radiating pure power, a testament to his sublime self-control. His power moved through the room, cool and deep, dampening hotter emotions.

Grappling for self-control, Victoria bent forward and willed her body to revert to human. Her teeth and claws receded; her eyes ceased to glow. Her wolf calmed, and she breathed easier. She sent a silent prayer to Freya that her clothing remained intact.

Logan's body flowed from beast to man, altering with bizarre viscosity. She watched the second manifestation of his magic with marked unease. Once the change was complete, his shirt and jeans hung in torn shreds upon his long frame.

Arik stood over his son. "Logan, go clear your head."

Logan picked himself up off the floor. He shot Victoria a final look of pure venom and then turned to leave without saying another word.

With his departure, the tension dissipated. Victoria exhaled hard and faced Arik in silent embarrassment. Her bad behavior was twofold: she'd allowed Logan to provoke her, and she'd indulged pride without consideration for the pack's welfare.

Damn the boy! Damn me!

Long moments ticked past. When Arik spoke, he retained the air of civility. "I apologize for my son. Logan's behavior is inexcusable, but in his defense, he has no idea what it means to live in a pack. If he is unfamiliar with proper etiquette, then it is on me for being remiss in his education."

Victoria hung her head, aware that her own behavior had been shameful. "You're too generous. I'm the one who should be apologizing. I'm sorry for my behavior this evening. If you want me to leave town, I'll take my pack and go."

He took a long time to respond, long enough that Victoria wanted to kick herself for having cost her pack the opportunity for a home. Her impulsive nature and short temper led her into endless trouble.

At last, Arik shook his head. "I'd like you to stay. It's obvious Logan won't make this easy, but if he's ever going to have a semblance of a normal life, learning to live within a pack will be good for him."

Why would he phrase it so: a *semblance of a normal life*? Unease stirred in her stomach. As much as she disliked his choice of wording, she breathed a sigh of relief. If nothing else, her pack retained his hospitality for the moon cycle.

"Victoria, do you want to stay?" He rested his hand upon her shoulder. His power washed over her and soothed her frayed nerves.

"I want to stay." She would never submit to any male, but Arik Koenig might be the partner she needed. Her wolf found his strength and steadiness reassuring. He possessed an even temperament she believed she could learn to trust.

Decision made, the residual tension from the confrontation with Logan left her body. Arik filled her with a sense of security. Her wolf desired nothing more than to feel his muscular body against hers. From his patience and sensitivity, he promised to be a wonderful partner in bed.

His nostrils flared, and he leaned in closer, drinking in her scent. Arik rubbed his palms across her shoulders, thumbs digging into the tense muscles of her neck. The air hummed with his power. His wolf pressed against hers, testing her defenses, but Victoria held her ground. According to his rank and power, she should have yielded but her indomitable nature refused to allow surrender.

Arik chuckled. "You're a magnificent woman, Victoria. Have you always been so stubborn?"

She laughed, understanding his amusement. Few females dared to stand toe-to-toe with the boys. "Always."

His jaw worked, and his pupils dilated. His strong

hands continued to knead the knotted muscles of her back. His aura deepened to dark red and took on a silky texture. The intrusion of his wolf grew seductive, making the penetration part of the courtship.

Quicksilver, Victoria's awareness shifted to the press of that powerful male body against her own. The linen of his shirt clung tight to bulging muscles. He filled out his jeans, leaving little to the imagination. Her nostrils flared, drinking in the musk of his arousal and the heat of his breath.

Reaching out, she caught the front of Arik's shirt with her hands, gripping the fabric hard enough to tear it, and hauled him to her. She might have been small, but her strength was considerable.

His lips parted, and Victoria captured his mouth, devouring him with starved aggression. He tasted male and meaty, delicious. Her tongue thrust past his parted lips, and they dueled for control of the kiss with playful rivalry.

Her hands shifted to claws, but she didn't even feel the white-hot pain that blended with the pleasure. Her nails created rents in the front of his shirt, baring that muscular wall to her touch. His hands slid across her back, caressing her skin through the fabric of her shirt.

The shrill ring of her mobile phone served as a rude interruption. With a frustrated snarl, Victoria ripped her mouth from his, and he echoed her growl. She forced her hands to return to normal. She dug out her phone and flipped it open.

"What?"

"V-V-Victoria?" Morena stammered in her distress. "I'm so sorry. I didn't want to interrupt, but I didn't know what else to do. Sylvie said to call you."

"Morena, calm down and tell me what's happening." Victoria used her voice to assert her dominance. A sick feeling of dread filled her gut. Through the pack magic, she sensed that something awful had happened. Once the conduit opened, the distress and sorrow of every member of her pack poured into her.

"It's—" Whatever the explanation, Morena's next words faded to static, and then the call dropped.

"Damn it!" Victoria glared at her phone and gripped it hard. She reined in the impulse to smash the device against the wall. Dropped calls and poor reception were constant issues with the disposable cellphones the pack used to stay in touch.

She looked up and found Arik watching her. His eyes held frustration and resignation. They shared an intense look of longing across the span between them.

"I'm sorry," she said. "I have to go."

He nodded. "They're your pack. Go. Will I see you again?"

"Yes." She hesitated and then darted toward him to steal another hard kiss. "I'll call you."

CHAPTER FIVE

Grief —
  "Goddess, why?"
  "I'm sorry, my priestess. It is the way of things."

Just after midnight, Victoria pulled her white VW Golf into the parking lot behind The Fireside Inn, located south of Sierra Pines and North of Highway 50. She took the parking space to the right of the pack's Tahoe. Paul and Sylvie's pickup was to the left of the SUV.

The hotel sign had the letters "F R S E I N" in large block letters across the top. Beneath that, a wooden cabin was interposed over a bright red flame, a combination that screamed *firetrap* in Victoria's mind. A garish red glow came from the lit vacancy sign attached to the bottom of the main billboard.

Three weeks before, Morena had purchased the Golf from a salvage yard outside of Boise, Idaho. On a typical morning, the little car took three minutes of constant key turning to start, not to mention a prodigious amount of praying and swearing. The suspension rode worse than a mule with a bad back; the seats were little more than metal frames. Every time she shut the engine off, Victoria prayed it would be the last. She despised the vehicle with a fiery passion. However, as Sylvie said, "Beggars can't be choosers, Victory, and it's better than walking."

The hotel consisted of a main lodge and two rows of dilapidated cabins tucked in the woods. A fresh dusting of snow covered the parking lot, and small flurries continued to fall, drifting at a horizontal angle on the wind before touching the ground. Thanks to the snowpack on the roofs, the shoddy structures possessed a charming, whimsical air. Icicles hung from the eaves and several feet of snow pressed against the windward sides of the cabins. Her entire pack occupied Cabin #7.

Earlier that same day, Sylvie had negotiated terms with the hotel's manager, a skinny man named Phil who had bad teeth and a nervous tic on the right side of his face. In exchange for rent, the pack would clean cabins. The deal had gotten them out of their vehicles and into a dwelling with a real roof and electricity for the first time in weeks.

With dread weighing on her, Victoria stepped into the cabin's main room and closed the door behind her. She found the pack waiting for her with sorrowful expressions. Her gaze sought and found each of their faces in turn. Paul and Sylvie huddled together; the mated pair clung to each other. Gaunt Morena crouched on the floor with her shoulders hunched forward. Sophia lay atop a beaten braided run before the fire, her furry form curled about her pups.

With every passing second, Victory's sense of wrongness multiplied. Her jaw clenched so hard she thought her teeth might break. "What's happened?"

When no answer came, she turned to Sylvie for answers. "Sylvie?"

"I'm sorry, Victory." Sylvie stepped forward, holding out her hands to offer a small bundle wrapped in a blanket. Grief filled her hazel eyes.

Her stomach turned, and bile rose in her throat. A harsh moan of denial tore from her. Victoria staggered forward, and Sylvie deposited the bundle into her Alpha's arms. "No. Oh no, no, no..."

"There was nothing to be done for it," Sylvie said. The Beta wolf knew the right words, the empty words, but her voice lacked conviction. Tears ran down her cheeks. Grief made her look older than her years. Victoria folded the top of the blanket back and stared down in stricken horror at the lifeless body of a wolf cub. It was Minnie, the runt of the liter.

"This is my fault." A harsh sob brought Victoria to her knees. She clutched the tiny body of Sophia's dead cub to her chest and cried. Her tears soaked into the towel and the pup's soft fur.

"No, sweetie, it's not your fault. Hush, don't say such things. You're doing the best you can with the hand you've been dealt." Sylvie embraced her, offering unqualified support. Sharp keening rose from her throat, and Victoria tilted back her head. The pack took the cue from their leader, and rushed forward to join in mourning the death of their smallest and weakest member. They locked together in a huddle, sharing a physical and empathic connection.

At the center of the pack, she experienced every nuance of their loss, sadness, and regret. Aside from herself, no one blamed her. The pack did not condemn; the pack did not criticize. They loved her without condition or restraint, and she them.

The persistent press of Sophia's furry body against her ankles drew Victoria back to reality. Urgent whines of hunger came from the three living pups that were too young to understand anything but their own need.

Scrubbing away her tears, Victoria handed the precious bundle back to Sylvie. With a smooth motion, she removed her shirt and then kicked off her socks and shoes. She undid her belt and shimmied out of her jeans. Naked, she dropped to her hands and knees and undertook the painful transformation into a wolf.

On all fours, she crossed the family room to where Sophia's cubs huddled together on the rug before the fireplace. The three pups retained fuzzy baby fur and blue eyes. It was too soon to know if they would inherit their father's shapechanging abilities, but they were the future of the pack.

The others moved aside, making way for her, although she held their undivided attention. The pups recognized her by both sight and smell. They greeted her with eager whimpers. Mick, the largest of the pups, shoved his nose into her mouth, licking and whining. His brother and sister, Roman and Gypsy, did the same.

Their begging produced the instinctive gag reflex of an adult wolf. Victoria regurgitated the contents of her stomach, depositing digested meat on the floor of the cabin. The three puppies swarmed the food and gulped it down with avarice.

Victoria backed away and settled on her haunches in order to watch the puppies consume the first solid meal they had eaten in over a week. All three were thin and fragile; healthy cubs would have been plump and robust. Likewise, Sophia's ribs showed against her sides.

Sophia did her best to produce enough milk for her offspring, but she could not keep up with their voracious appetites. The responsibility for the pack's cubs fell to all the adult members. When food was scarce, the cubs ate first.

After they'd eaten every scrap, the pups continued to sniff and lick the floor searching for more. Roman grew tired first, and yawning, returned to his mother. He curled against Sophia's side and buried his face in his mother's fur. Gypsy followed next, and bold Mick was the last to snuggle into a tight ball with his nose tucked into his tail.

When they awakened, they would be hungry again.

Victoria heaved a heavy sigh. The long day had left her weary, longing for sleep. Her energy reserves had bottomed out an hour ago. She fought it, but a huge yawn peeled apart her jaws.

"Tell me about it." Sylvie settled a hand atop her head, burying her fingers in Victoria's pure white fur. Victoria was larger than the average coyote, but smaller than most wolves, and the top of her head only reached to Sylvie's hip. Shortness plagued the females of her mother's bloodline.

With a grunt, Victoria got to her feet and headed toward the kitchen. She shifted to human and donned her clothing. The pack watched her every movement with anxiety. Sylvie, Paul and Morena followed her, but Sophia stayed with her pups.

"What happened this evening?" Paul settled against the cracked Formica countertop. The old warrior stooped forward, favoring his bad back. His limbs twisted like the branches of an ancient oak tree. He squinted at her through his right eye; his eyelid drooped closed over his left.

"Yes, what happened, Victoria? Please, tell us?" Morena clung to Sylvie's hand. The teenager's brown hair stuck out at every possible angle from an assortment of bright-colored clips and bands.

Victoria hesitated, considering what to disclose. She always guarded her words around her pack, weighing potential interpretations and impacts. She kept a close eye on their morale.

Sylvie's hazel eyes lit with hope. "Did it go well?"

"It went better than I expected. There is food and shelter." Her lips twisted into a bitter smile. "More than I've been able to provide."

"Don't be so hard on yourself, sweetie," Sylvie said. "February has always been a cruel month for our kind, Victory. The Cree call this the month of the hunger moon."

Victoria summoned a wan smile for her friend. "Do you have any sage Native American advice for filling our bellies?"

The old woman patted Victoria's back. "No, I'm

afraid not. We just have to keep doing what we're doing, and we'll make it through. Things will get better. You'll see."

Morena danced with impatience. "Tell us about him!"

Victoria arched her brow. "Him?"

"What of the dominant male?" Sylvie asked, interceding on the teenager's behalf.

Victoria bit her lower lip. "There were two dominant males."

Sylvie got a knowing look in her eyes. Her fine brow lifted. "What did you think of Arik Koenig?"

Victoria deliberated before answering. "He is strong, strong enough to protect the pack, but he is also cool and distant. I sense there is more to him than he lets on. He is hiding something, and it makes me cautious."

Sylvie chuckled. "You sound suspicious."

She felt sick to admit the depth of the distrust she harbored for Arik and his hostile son. "I am."

"What are you going to do about it?" Paul asked.

Victoria stared at the linoleum floor of the cabin. Her face molded into a determined mask, and she looked up. "Whatever I have to."

Unease rippled through the pack, but Victoria countered it, projecting unshakeable confidence. "We need to build a funeral pyre for Minnie," she said, directing their attention toward what had to be accomplished so they could bury their dead puppy.

"I'll gather wood," Paul said.

Sylvie wrapped an arm around Morena's shoulders. "We'll all help."

Around nine-thirty the next morning, Victoria arrived before the Sierra Pines public library opened and perched atop a low planter wall rather than wait inside the detestable Golf. Her wolf metabolism ran hot, so the cold didn't affect her as much as it did regular people.

The library was a small A-frame building made of redwood logs with square windows. Snow capped the roof and icicles decorated the eaves. The breeze created interesting harmonics as it played upon the ice, the illusion of indistinct words whispered upon the wind.

Victoria closed her eyes and tilted her face toward the winter sun, soaking up the meager warmth it offered. She listened, trying to bring the voice into focus in order to make out the meaning of the message. Try as she might, it remained indiscernible, but the sound soothed her wolf and lulled her into a sleepy state. She drifted for a time, dreaming of hunting in the wild forest. Her paws flew across pristine snow and the scent of prey swelled her nostrils, the throbbing of a frantic heart echoed in her ears. The irresistible allure of fear, adrenaline, and fresh meat drew her deeper.

The raucous *craa* of a raven rudely woke her. Victoria opened her eyes and found the black-eyed creature perched above her on the library's rooftop. It cocked its head and returned her stare with smug amusement.

"A strange place to nap."

Her head snapped forward, she checked a snarl, and glared at the intruder. Victoria smelled nothing extraordinary about the woman, and yet she had managed to approach undetected, a feat that should have been impossible.

A quick glance toward the parking lot revealed a white Toyota 4-Runner in the space beside the Golf. Victoria returned her gaze to the woman clad from head-to-toe in snow gear. The human was short with stunted limbs and a body like an apple. She had a mean gleam in her coal-black eyes and a hairline of steel gray visible beneath the raised hood of her jacket.

Victoria managed a frosty smile. "Good morning."

"Library's not open yet."

"I'm aware of that." Victoria showed her teeth in a smile. "I'm waiting until it opens. Are you the librarian?"

"I'm Delores Sanders, the *head* librarian."

"Ah, quite the distinction." Victoria maintained a bland expression and weathered the woman's fierce stare. Aware of the librarian's disapproval, she leaned back against the retaining wall, legs extended like a slutty model. Her tight red sweater with its plunging V-neckline and skin-tight jeans contributed to the overall impression.

Disgust flashed in the older woman's eyes. "I'm surprised you're not freezing."

"Oh, I'm a hot-blooded breed." Tongue-in-cheek, Victoria managed to keep her smirk hidden until the woman turned her back.

With a huff and a stomp, the librarian ascended three steps to the locked entrance of the building. She removed a heavy keychain from her pocket and opened the glass doors.

Victoria trailed the librarian into the building. She waited while the woman turned on the lights to reveal a cozy lobby. The wooden reception desk matched the oak floors. A children's section was to the immediate right.

"You're new in town." It was not a question.

"I'm visiting for a couple days. My name is Victoria." She kept her tone polite and endured the woman's obvious dislike only because she needed access to whatever limited resources the small library had to offer.

A grunt acknowledged her introduction. Delores stepped into an alcove adjacent to the entrance, a small room with linoleum floors, cubbies, and coat hooks. She set about removing her snow gear, starting with her gloves. A gold wedding band covered in scratches fitted over her gnarled ring finger. Both her hands bore numerous age spots. Beneath the bulky jacket, she had on an oversized knotted black sweater, black leggings, and flats.

Victoria had rehearsed her story in advance. "I'm a grad student at the University of Nevada, and I'm working on my thesis on the local history of the area. I'm wondering if you have an archive of past editions of the local newspaper."

Delores swung back to stare at her through narrowed eyes. "Are you looking for anything in particular?"

She smiled. "I'll know when I see it."

The librarian snorted but it seemed her sense of duty outweighed her dislike of Victoria. She emerged from the alcove and turned right, heading deeper into the library. "Of course, we keep everything on microfiche. I'm sure we have everything you need. Both the *Sierra Pines Gazette* and the *Echo Lake Daily* are available."

"Microfiche?"

"We keep the machine in the basement due to a lack of space on the main floor." Delores either failed to notice Victoria's incredulity or simply did not care.

She followed the librarian down a flight of wide concrete steps. Midway, the staircase reversed direction. They entered a dark space much cooler than the floor above. The scent of years of accumulated dust clung to every surface.

Victoria's nocturnal vision adjusted to the darkness before Delores switched on the lights. Boxes stacked to the ceiling cluttered every inch of spare space. Exposed pipes ran along the ceiling and north wall, and a groaning furnace occupied the entire southwestern corner of the building. The librarian made an unerring path straight to the wall switch and flipped it. Flickering fluorescent lights came on overhead.

"The microfiche viewer is through here." She showed Victoria to a small secondary room off the main area about the size of a walk-in closet.

Delores hit another light switch to illuminate the area. "The microfiche is stored in these cabinets. Do you have a specific timeframe you wish to view newspapers from?"

Victoria licked her lips. "About two years ago."

The older woman shot her a critical glance and pursed her lips, but made no comment. Instead, she showed Victoria to the appropriate cabinet, and demonstrated how to recover and view stored newspaper images.

"I'll be upstairs if you need anything," Delores said.

"Okay, thank you for your help." Victoria concealed a grimace. The older woman made her uneasy. Being political went against her direct nature but Victoria also tended to be pragmatic. There were times when honey could get her where she needed to go.

The librarian left. Breathing a sigh of relief, Victoria got down to the task. She had nothing but questions, and the future of her entire pack depended upon the choices she made. She couldn't trust their fate to Arik Koenig without doing her due diligence.

An hour later, she found what she sought, a newspaper article in the *Echo Lake Daily* dated two years prior.

Two Slain in Brutal Attack

Friday night, police discovered the bodies of a man and woman slain outside of a Sierra Pines residence. Emergency operators received the 911 call at 1:35 A.M. from local attorney, Arik Koenig. Officers from the El Dorado County Sheriff's Department were first on the scene.

Authorities have not yet released an official statement regarding cause of death. Officials at the coroner's office confirmed the identity of Lori Koenig as the female victim. The identity of the second male victim remains unknown at this time.

Details obtained from a source close to the investigation indicate an animal attack might be the cause of death.

Grim-faced, Victoria printed out a copy of the article, which went on to talk about the prestigious status of the Koenig family. She folded the printout and tucked it into her back pocket.

She spent another hour scouring newspaper stories, searching for another mention of the murders until her eyes grew tired from squinting at the small, smudged print. At last, her gaze fell upon another noteworthy title in an article dated four days after the original. Her brow knit and she leaned forward to study the brief paragraph.

Slain Local Man Identified
Last week, the Echo Lake Daily reported the deaths of local Sierra Pines' resident, Lori Koenig, and a then unidentified man. Sierra Pines Chief Coroner Audrey Pascal has released the name of the previously unidentified victim as Gregory Sanders, a local businessman. Cause of death has been attributed to a rogue bear attack.

"That's it?" Victoria frowned because she had expected more information. After all, how many sensational double deaths could a community the size of Sierra Pines possibly have? The press should have been all over it.

"What's that you said?" The head librarian's severe voice came from the entryway to the small room.

Victoria swiveled in her chair toward the librarian. Her eyes narrowed, and her thoughtful gaze settled on the woman.

Delores Sanders — she has the same last name as the slain man.

It seemed an unlikely coincidence. Whether it was her wolf-like instinct for danger or simply human premonition, Victoria suspected the librarian of something. There was no proof other than a vaguely uneasy feeling in her gut, but that had rarely failed her.

"Maybe I can be of assistance?" Delores asked.

Victoria surged to her feet. "Thanks, but I think I've found what I need," she said.

Delores's lips formed a frosty smile that never touched her eyes. "Of course, I just wanted to check and see how you were doing. After all, you've been down here for hours."

"Actually, I'm finished," Victoria said, squaring her shoulders. Her stomach roiled, but she didn't know the source of her unease. One thing she knew for certain, Delores Sanders set her teeth on edge.

"Well then, make sure you clean up after yourself," Delores said and departed the small room.

Victoria stared after the woman, frozen in place until she felt her wolf finally subside. Abruptly, the basement felt terribly claustrophobic, and she wanted nothing more than to escape its narrow confines. In a hurry, she turned off the microfiche machine and returned the film to its original location within the cabinets.

Upstairs, the library appeared unoccupied. Victoria passed the librarian at the reception desk and gave a final suspicious glance.

"Thank you for visiting," Delores called after Victoria while she exited the library.

Outside, the sun had reached its zenith in the sky. Breathing hard, she dug her disposable cellphone out of her pocket. She read the phone number written across the back of Arik's business card and waited in tense anticipation while it rang.

Arik answered. "Hello?"

Victoria gripped the phone harder and struggled to make her voice sound as normal as possible. "Hi, it's Victoria. Would you like to meet for lunch?"

"Is this good for y'all?"

The waitress indicated a corner booth with high sides that came as close to facilitating Arik's request for privacy as anything else The Broken Bend Café had to offer.

He looked to Victoria and arched his brow; she nodded her acceptance. The corner table of the busy diner allowed a degree of anonymity. They wouldn't draw attention as long as they kept their voices low.

"This is fine, thank you." Arik remained standing until Victoria slipped into one side of the booth. He sat opposite her, causing the vinyl seat to creak when he settled his bulk.

"Blue plate special today is the chicken fried steak with sweet potato fries and mixed veggies."

The server passed each of them a menu. Her name-tag read: *Dolly.*

"Would y'all like something to drink?" Dolly asked. She spoke with a brisk Dixie accent. She was a little taller than Victoria but had a much stockier build. In her early sixties, the waitress sported a tawny beehive of hair and wore her red lipstick like a second skin.

"Coke, please," Arik said.

"Is Pepsi all right?"

"Pepsi is fine."

Dolly's gaze transferred to Victoria.

"Soda, also. Thank you."

Dolly pursed her lips. The waitress turned toward Arik and excluded Victoria with her body language. "Have you had enough time to decide?"

"I'll have the chicken fried steak, sweet potato fries, and mixed vegetables." Arik surrendered his menu to the server.

"Good choice, Suga'."

Dolly regarded Victoria with none of the deference she had shown Arik.

"I'll have the same. Thank you."

Dolly scribbled on her notepad and then seized the second menu. She left without another word.

"She doesn't like you," Arik said, his tone even.

Victoria heaved a sigh. "It does get old."

"I take it that happens a lot."

She shrugged to indicate ambivalence. "She's reacting to my pheromones, perceiving me as a threat or competition even though she doesn't know why. The female members of my pack seem to be unaffected."

"Are they?"

Victoria laughed. My, but the man turned an interesting phrase. "Okay, not entirely. Every time I go into heat, Sylvie busts out the knitting needles. Somewhere, she must have an enormous stockpile of baby booties and blankets."

His smoky chuckle resonated through her entire body. He said nothing to indicate the talk of children disturbed him. In fact, his expression remained agreeable, and she marked another point in his favor.

He noticed her watching him. His jaw worked while his gaze slid over her again. She smelled the scent of his arousal; her own body quickened in response.

He chose to pursue the verbal conversation while their nonverbal exchange continued, an evocative mix of caution and arousal. "You can't be surprised to provoke such reactions. Most humans can sense what we are on an instinctive level."

"No, I'm not surprised." Victoria stared at him, attempting to read those honey-brown eyes. He guarded his thoughts and emotions well. "She didn't react to you as a threat. So far, no one has."

"I've gotten good at hiding my true nature." He flashed even white teeth and settled back against the red vinyl booth. He sat with his limbs splayed in an aggressive and masculine manner. He had just a hint of sexy stubble on his jaw.

Beneath the table, his foot touched her calf. He

made no move to withdraw, and she welcomed the teasing touch. Their interest in one another was not a secret. The courtship dance promised to be fun and challenging.

Victoria took a sip of her drink. The diner's old jukebox pumped out the opening beats of *Sympathy for the Devil*. Arik's foot tapped to the rhythm against the white porcelain floor.

"So you like The Stones?"

His eyes lit with sincere enthusiasm. "Yes."

"You're wondering why I picked this as a meeting place?"

Wariness crossed his face. "Yes, I wondered. From the aroma coming out of the kitchen, it appears to have been a good choice."

Victoria grinned. "My dad always said not to judge a restaurant by its appearance but by the line of people waiting to get in."

"Sounds like a smart man."

Unexpected sadness robbed her smile. "He was."

Arik paused for a moment, watching her. "At first your request to meet me in a roadside diner confused me, but then I thought about it from your perspective. It's a clever choice."

Victoria glanced about the shoddy interior of the little restaurant. The pockmarked parking lot and the garish billboard out front did not create a great first impression until one noticed how the lot remained full morning, noon, and night. The ripped and faded vinyl booths, the chipped floors, the flickering overhead lighting all served as turnoffs, but a variety of hearty smells wafted from the kitchen.

"You understand why we're here?" She did her best to conceal her surprise but failed to keep it from her voice.

"Of course." He settled his hands atop the table. Those long, strong fingers drew her attention. She wanted to feel his caress on her naked flesh, pushing apart her thighs. She desired his throat against her lips, his blood on her tongue.

"You've seen my home, met my son, and ascertained my ability to provide. Now you wish to observe how I interact with humans, because an inept mate can be a greater liability than no mate at all."

"I guess you have me figured out." Victoria tipped her head, acknowledging the accuracy of his assessment.

His perception astonished her, almost as much as his honesty. The depth of his cunning made her feel like a small fish swimming with large predators. As much as she hated to admit it even to herself, he intimidated her.

So far, Arik did not appear offended with her machinations, but she wondered if all that would change once he became aware of the other reason she had wanted to meet with him in public.

"Actually, there's at least one thing I don't understand." Arik leaned forward and locked gazes with her.

Victoria sat taller and stared straight into his eyes. She could not look away without acceding dominance to him; the timing of his challenge took her unprepared.

"Shoot," she said.

"I've done some checking. Your bloodline is ancient and distinguished. You're the daughter of Alphas, Priestess to Freya, and a healer. If you're everything you say you are—"

The implied insult caused her to stiffen. "I haven't misrepresented myself."

His hand covered hers; his voice smoothed and soothed. "I didn't imply you have. Allow me to finish."

She nodded and allowed her fingers to curl around his hand. "By pedigree and accomplishment, you're royalty among our kind. You're twenty-four, so how is it that you're just now seeking a mate?"

Victoria licked her lips. She deliberated on her words. "In the past, I've rejected plenty of eligible males."

Dolly arrived with their food, and they waited in tense silence while the waitress set down the plates. Victoria's stomach growled the moment the tantalizing aroma hit her nostrils.

"Is there anything else I can get for y'all?"

Arik shook his head and withdrew his hand. "Nothing else. Thank you."

Dolly left. Victoria dug into her food. She maintained good table manners but she exercised no hesitation about eating in front of her date. She had more urgent priorities than giving her suitor the impression she never ate.

"Are you the only adult bringing back food for those cubs you mentioned?" Arik asked with undisguised concern.

He startled her during the act of swallowing. Victoria choked on the food and managed to force it down. She grabbed for her drink and finished the rest of the soda.

She set aside the glass. "Yes. The others are busy most of the day with work. Sophia, the mother, is lactating, so she's providing milk, but it means she eats more."

"You mentioned a litter. I take it, Sophia is a wolf?"

Victoria inclined her head. "Her mate was killed in Arizona. She's not a shifter."

"How long until the cubs are weaned?"

His scrutiny made her uncomfortable.

"Another month or so." She hesitated and then broached a sensitive topic. She wanted to be clear that her pack had not abused his hospitality. "I've forbidden hunting in your territory."

He pressed his lips together. His brown eyes flashed with something she could not name. Victoria dismissed the impulse to make excuses for her own lack of employment or usefulness. She carried her guilt within. She refused to show weakness or doubt before this man.

"Go on with what you were saying before. I'm sorry to have interrupted," Arik said.

She shrugged, unsure of how to tell it without sounding arrogant. "Before hunters destroyed us, my pack was large and prosperous. I had the luxury of time, and so I pursued my education. I hold a nursing degree from Arizona State University and two years of experience as an RN. I've never been in a hurry to take a mate."

Arik considered her, and it took discipline not to squirm under his regard. She had the distinct impression he had an agenda, known to him, unfathomable to her. Upon their first meeting, they had discussed her motivations for taking a mate and her preference for a mature male.

"How did you wind up in Sierra Pines? It couldn't have been an accident," Arik point-blank asked.

Victoria breathed a sigh of relief; no more dancing about the fire. It was time to brave the flames.

"Freya sent me to you."

His sublime control slipped for a second, and she perceived his astonishment before his mask slid back into place. "Freya, you say?"

"The goddess commended your prowess," Victoria said, in a transparent bid to appeal to his ego. She favored him with a sly smile.

He grinned and chuckled. "Consider my vanity satisfied. Now, what aren't you telling me?"

She licked her lips, debating what information held relevance. She doubted it mattered that the prophecy had arrived via her mother, and she did not trust him with her deepest doubts.

"The goddess seldom sends me anywhere for simple reasons," Victoria said. "I can't help but wonder if there's more."

He stared at her with scary intensity. "What more could there be?"

She allowed her shoulders to lift and fall in a careless shrug. "Only the goddess knows."

"That's an evasion. You can't ask?"

"I can, and I have asked. She has chosen not to answer."

Arik leaned back and regarded her with cool intensity. His food sat untouched. Victoria pushed away her empty plate. She understood his suspicion and his frustration with her lack of answers.

She sighed. "Look, my goddess is under no obligation to give me explanations. She dictates her desires, and I do my best to fulfill them. I can conjecture that she has a hidden agenda for sending me here, but it's nothing but speculation."

"But you do have a theory?"

Her reluctance increased tenfold. "Yes, I do."

"Let's hear it." He waited and watched. The stubborn set of his jaw communicated his intractability.

Victoria snapped her teeth in annoyance. "Fine. I'm wondering if I'm here because I'm supposed to help you."

She had the satisfaction of seeing his jaw drop. "How would you help me?"

She threw up her hands. "I have no idea!"

Arik slowly shook his head. "Faced with uncertainty, are you content to be paired with a stranger because your goddess dictates the suitability of the match?"

She could see the man had the makings of a trial attorney. Anger filled her eyes. Her lips parted in a silent snarl. "I am not a coveted broodmare; you are not a stallion."

"But you are a bitch in heat."

The gloves were off. Victoria refused to allow him to objectify her or coerce her into subservience. While she could ill afford the luxury of pride, pride and honor were all she had left of any real value.

She rose from the seat and placed her hands on the table. She leaned upon her hands so they were nose to nose. "Damned straight, I am."

Arik laughed and those honey-brown eyes lit with affection. "Your honesty is admirable. I've never met another woman quite like you, Victoria."

She rocked back. His sudden change of demeanor threw her. "Was that some sort of test?"

"I just wanted to be sure to get a sincere response."

"So you provoked me."

His head dipped forward in a graceful nod. She sat back and exhaled through her nose, watching him for a full minute. She might not have appreciated his tactics, but in his place, she likely would have done the same thing. It wasn't worth holding a grudge over.

"Fair enough," she said. "But it's my turn to ask you a question."

"Ask."

"Tell me about your wife."

CHAPTER SIX

Wait —

"*My Lady, was that you?*"
"*No, it was not.*"

"My wife?" Arik spat the words with venom. His eyes glimmered with golden sparks, and his hands formed fists. His wolf reared in a vulgar display of power, and the mortals about them shivered in fear. Conversations died, and the diner filled with thunderous silence.

Victoria nodded. "Your wife."

A great darkness passed over Arik. Grief and rage filled his eyes threatening to overpower the impressive control he maintained. Eventually, he opened his hands and relaxed his fingers.

Victoria breathed and then realized she had stopped for a time. The human customers in the diner stirred and shivered. They forgot because the mortal mind preferred not to confront things outside its comfort zone. They resumed their activities as if nothing had happened.

"Very well, what would you like to know?"

"How did she die?"

He stared at her with murderous anger. "Not how she lived?"

"I care about that too, but it seems a less urgent matter."

"You've been doing your homework." His game face slid into place, the composed mask he wore when his emotions were closest to the surface. They had not known each other long, but Victoria had learned much about him in that short time.

"Yes, I have. I don't like sneaking around, but I have to protect my pack." She did not so much as bat an eyelash, all too aware of the tension between them. Everything rode on the answers he provided. If Arik had killed his mate, the humans around them would provide her only safety. He would not reveal his true nature, destroy the public identity he valued, and possibly provoke a mob.

"You could have just asked me."

She tilted her chin in acknowledgement. "I could have, but I didn't. The newspaper said it was an animal attack. I need to know what really happened."

Dolly chose that inopportune moment to intrude. The waitress sidled alongside the table and reached for their empty glasses. "I'll get y'all refills. Is everything all right?"

Victoria summoned a pleasant smile. "We're fine. Thank you."

"Can we have the check please?" Arik asked.

Dolly left again. Victoria turned a questioning glance toward Arik. If he refused to explain his wife's death, then he left her no choice other than to assume the worst.

He met her gaze with a level look. "Let's wait until she comes back. She's been watching us. Asking for the check takes away another excuse to interrupt."

"Ah."

Satisfied with the explanation, she settled in to wait. Dolly returned with the refills and the bill. The waitress surveyed them with bubbling curiosity and then left them alone.

"Logan killed his mother."

Victoria gaped and then closed her jaw with an audible snap. "Logan! Your son? How is he still alive?"

Arik exhaled through his nose. "The night my wife died, I was in Reno on business. Logan underwent his first transformation into a wolf without a dominant wolf present."

"Goddess." Horrified, Victoria covered her mouth with her hand. Of all the scenarios envisioned, it was worse than she could have imagined. She shuddered to think of the emotional toll such a thing must exact on a family.

His shoulders hunched forward, and his voice altered whenever he spoke his son's name, conveying his immense shame and sorrow. At last, she understood the reason for it.

"As I mentioned before, Logan failed to experience his first transformation in adolescence, so his mother and I assumed he would be human."

She nodded but did not interrupt. It was a reasonable conclusion. The majority of shifter children with a wolf or human parent inherited no shapechanging abilities. Only when both mother and father were shifters was it certain that the child would become one also.

"Lori spoiled Logan," Arik said. Bitterness tinged his voice, but also remorse. He suffered from awful regret. "She indulged him, and he wasn't taught the ways of our kind. It was my fault for allowing it. I was disappointed in him, my only son, and I allowed it to cloud my judgment."

She offered no condemnation. He had plenty of his own. "Why would Logan kill her? I don't understand that. He must have been provoked somehow."

Arik's beast roiled under his stringent control. His upper lip pushed out due to the elongation of his fangs, and Victoria knew she'd made a terrible mistake confronting him in public. She hesitated, but reached out and took his hands, accepting his rage. Lava poured into her, scalding hot, challenging her ability to contain her wolf.

A tentative connection formed between them, as tender and delicate as a new blossom. It was weaker than pack magic, less enduring than a mate bond, but still, it was something.

Arik calmed and gave her hand a slight squeeze in thanks. "Lori was having an affair."

"The second person killed. The article mentioned a man."

He nodded. "After his first change, Logan's beast would have been in control. He must have reacted to what he perceived as an invading male. Lori and her lover were out back by the pool when Logan found them. He killed her lover beside the pool and then chased her down to the lakeshore."

"Goddess, he's a berserker." She felt sickened, torn between sympathy and revulsion. Arik had lost his mate and his son to the same horrific event.

"Yes, I believe he must be a berserker. His first transformation came at the age of eighteen and without warning. To this day, he possesses the ability to shapechange with unusual swiftness."

"So I saw," Victoria said and shuddered while she recalled Logan's uncanny talent.

"The night it happened, I knew something was wrong. I left immediately to drive home, but an unexpected blizzard blew in, and the roads snowed under. It took me hours to get through. When I got here, I found Logan asleep next to his mother's body, covered in her blood."

"You didn't kill him?" She could not hide her amazement. No one would have blamed him, and he would have been within his rights. The slaying of kin carried the severest penalties under their laws. As Alpha, it was his duty to execute Logan.

"He's my son. I love him." Arik's voice broke and she caught a glimpse of the most awful torment in his eyes. His lips shook, betraying his affection. He had a great heart, capable of powerful emotions, beneath his cold exterior.

Her teeth sank into her lower lip. "Does he know what he did?"

"When he awoke, he had no memory of what he'd done, but he knows. There was no way to protect him from it."

"Do you have his wolf under your control?" The thought of the damage Logan could cause to her pack filled her with dread. Berserker werewolves were the stuff of legend, capable of horrible atrocities. They were as rare as they were dangerous. Without a more dominant wolf to command his beast, Logan would lose all control, all humanity.

"His wolf submitted to my control as soon as he realized what he'd done, and guilt has kept him submissive these last two years. There are occasional juvenile outbursts, but he doesn't want to hurt anyone else."

Victoria lacked Arik's faith in his son's integrity but she kept her mouth shut. Her one encounter with Logan had not gone well, to say the least. Her opinion of the boy was biased.

"What did the police investigation find?" It made sense that Arik had taken steps to shield his son and alter the crime scene. The fierce protective streak he possessed for his son reassured her that love and loyalty lay beneath that cold mask.

"The police investigation concluded cause of death to be an animal attack, a bear, as a matter of fact."

Victoria stared down at the table for a long time before she looked up again. "What happens if you ever lose control of his wolf?"

Arik's expression grew grim. "Our laws are clear. If I

can't control him, then I have to kill him. If it comes to that, then I'll do what I must. Until then, I intend to protect my son to the best of my abilities."

"And you control him only with his consent?" She wet her lips. The knowledge cast her first meeting with Arik's son into a new light. Logan scared her more than ever.

Arik's brow furrowed. "Yes. He's too strong-willed for me to coerce into submission. I'd have to break him, and I know my son. Logan would die first."

"I'm having second thoughts about whether staying here is the best thing for me and my pack."

He nodded and looked at her in a way that unsettled her further. She never felt comfortable with how much Arik seemed to perceive. "I understand, and I can't say I blame you. We share a powerful attraction, and I believe we'd be compatible as mates."

The vinyl booth creaked as he shifted his weight, restless within the tight confines. She understood his desire to move given the serious nature of the conversation.

"Logan and I didn't exactly hit it off." Victoria made a face, scrunching her nose. "Right off the bat, he called me short and slutty. I lost my temper, and it went downhill from there."

Laughter glinted in his eyes, and his lips formed a smile. "Logan can be... difficult."

"Difficult is one way of putting it." Victoria huffed in annoyance. While she appreciated the fact she and Arik shared a pragmatic approach to the business of selecting a mate, she disliked being a source of amusement.

He regarded her with a keen intellect, considering and calculating. Her wolf felt drawn to him. He commanded attention and inspired a desire to obey. He had all the makings of an excellent Alpha, and the incongruity of his lone wolf status struck her as disturbing. There was still more going on than she knew, more secrets yet awaiting revelation.

"Are you going to leave?" His question betrayed his impatience.

Victoria cocked her head. "Freya sent me to you. I must trust in the wisdom of my goddess. While I see many advantages to staying, I perceive the inherent danger as well. Tell me something, doesn't it concern you that I almost got into a fight with your son?"

He hesitated for too long, and she ground her teeth. "The despair of life without purpose or companionship is overwhelming Logan. I'm worried he may take his own life," he said.

Dread stabbed her gut and twisted. She swallowed bile. Suicide would doom Logan to an existence of eternal misery in Niflheim, the frozen realm of the dishonored dead.

"Goddess..."

"You implied your goddess might have sent you to me for an unstated reason. If you and your pack could help me, it would be to provide Logan with some semblance of a normal life."

"I understand," she said. As a healer, she ached for Arik and his son and wanted nothing more than to help them. However, as a pack leader with numerous burdens and obligations, she harbored deep reservations regarding his appropriateness as a mate. Her life was already too complicated.

"Will you stay?" He inclined his head, indicating it remained her decision.

Victoria sank her teeth into her lower lip. She stared into his eyes and strived to find the strength to trust. She weighed whether she should remain and risk her pack or go and incur the dangers of the open road, whether she should run again or throw her dice and see where they landed. Suspicion encrusted her heart, making it impossible for her to put blind faith in Arik. In doubt, she turned to her goddess. Freya sent her to him. In Freya, she placed her trust.

After a lengthy delay, Victoria made her decision. "I would be honored if you would meet my pack."

His aura lit up with pleasure, the same as his smile. "I would be honored to make their acquaintance, Victoria."

In a subdued mood, Victoria returned to cabin #7 after three-thirty in the afternoon. The entrance led to a main room and the utilitarian kitchen, connected via an open floor plan. The building had two small bedrooms and a single bathroom. A huge stone fireplace took up the entire wall of the family room.

When she entered, Sylvie looked up from her seat on the brown couch. A fire crackled and popped within the hearth, throwing a welcoming wall of heat. Her knitting needles paused for a moment and then flew into motion again. A tiny blue hat dangled from the end of the needles.

"Hello there," she said.

Victoria stopped and stared. She frowned. She injected plenty of vinegar into her voice. "What are you going to do if I have a girl?"

With a blithe smile, Sylvie reached over and removed an identical hat done in pink from her wicker basket. "Be prepared."

Victoria resisted the urge to smack her own forehead with her palm and instead grumbled under her breath. She walked to where Sophia curled before the fire on a braided rug. "Where is everyone?"

"Morena's taken a shift cleaning cabins, and Paul's at the gas station." Sylvie rose from the couch and made her way into the cabin's small kitchen. "You should see this."

Victoria almost fell over. She released an audible gasp, floored at the amount of food within the fridge. "Where'd that come from?"

"A delivery man brought it around while you were out." Sylvie closed the fridge and picked up an envelope off the counter. She offered it to Victoria. "This came with it."

She accepted the envelope, which had her name written on the outside, and flipped it over to find it unsealed. She extracted a single piece of paper, folded into neat halves, and opened the note. Bold, masculine handwriting jumped off the page.

> Victoria,
> Please accept my gift.
> Arik

"You read this?" Victoria finished reading and looked up.

"Wasn't much to read, but yes, I read it. I needed to know where such a gift was coming from before I accepted it."

"It's a generous gesture." She struggled to keep her tone neutral, even though ambivalence seized her emotions. On the one hand, she wanted to offer Arik profuse thanks. On the other, she wanted to give the food back. It put her in debt to him, not a position she wished to be in.

"Now that's the sort of man I can give my wholehearted approval to," Sylvie said. "Be sure to express our gratitude."

"Yes, of course, I'll thank him." Victoria walked back to Sophia and stooped to give the mother wolf a reassuring pat on top of her head. "Hey, girl, how're you doing?"

In response, Sophia whimpered and lifted her head. Her tongue lolled from her mouth and her tail thumped the floor. She licked Victoria's hand in welcome.

Sophia had dark gray fur with tawny dappling and cream-colored legs and belly. She was average-sized for a gray wolf, measuring five-five from nose-to-tail, weighing around a hundred pounds. She carried several generations of werewolf genes but possessed no shapechanging abilities of her own.

Any one of the cubs might grow up to become a shifter but it was too soon to tell. Gypsy and Roman resembled their mother in coloring while Mick, the eldest, had reddish-brown fur like his deceased father. All three still had baby blue eyes.

Sylvie returned to the couch and resumed knitting. "Did you find out anything more about Arik Koenig or his boy yet?"

Victoria buried her fingers in Sophia's thick fur. She scowled, staring into the fire. "The son isn't a boy."

Sylvie's needles clicked together, and a contemplative expression crossed the older woman's face. "Is he enough of a man that you'd consider him as a prospective mate?"

Victoria rejected the idea out of hand. "No!"

Sylvie's hearty laughter rocked the room. "Well then, that makes matters of courtship less complicated than they could be, doesn't it?"

Victoria knew better than to rise to the bait. She changed the subject. "If we're going to stay in Sierra Pines, I could work again. The city has a small medical center."

"Nurses are always in demand. It would be good for you."

"I'd like that."

"You're not the type to stay at home with children. It's a good thing you have me to be a nanny to your young ones." Sylvie stared into the distance with a dreamy gleam in her eyes, a breathy sigh in her voice.

Victoria shook with silent laughter and shook her

head. "Speaking of... Where are the cubs?"

On cue, the three puppies swarmed into the main room. The pups bounced and wobbled on uncertain legs, falling over one another. Yapping up a joyful storm, the wrestling cubs stampeded across the linoleum floor.

Sylvie laughed. "They're full of the Dickens today. See the good that a real meal does for them?"

A rush of shame caused Victoria to hang her head.

"I've failed the pack," she said. "I can't even provide enough food to keep the pack fed. We're forced to accept charity just to get by."

Sylvie's mouth opened with dismay. "Victoria, you must not blame yourself like this. We all understand why we can't hunt here. If word should spread of wolves in an area where they're known to be extinct, it would bring a swarm of hunters."

Victoria scowled. "It's my job to provide for the pack, Sylvie. I'm a failure..."

Using the pack magic that connected them, the older woman projected her staunch support. "Oh, hush! The sacrifices you make for us are more than enough. Just keep doing what you're doing. Think of what it will mean for the pack to have a strong Alpha male again."

The prospect of subjugation to a male as powerful as Arik caused Victoria to suck in a deep breath. Despite her attraction to him, she still did not trust him. For selfish reasons, she loathed sacrificing personal freedom, but her duty demanded it of her.

"For the good of the pack," she said without thinking.

Sylvie blanched. "Victoria, are you courting Arik for our sake?"

Victoria winced. *Damn it!*

She'd allowed her inner doubts to show. She adopted a soothing tone and tried to cover. "Of course not. He is strong. Strong enough to protect and provide for—"

"The pack," Sylvie said. She stared at Victoria with a bleak expression, eyes full of heartbreak.

Ashamed, Victoria looked away. She welcomed the sudden skirmish that broke out in the kitchen between the pups. A kitchen chair tipped over, falling to the floor with a clatter, and Roman barreled across the floor, straight into Sylvie's ankles.

"Oh, you scoundrel! Come here!" Chuckling, Sylvie bent and picked up the squirming cub. She held Roman with one hand under his belly; he licked the fingers of her other hand with his pink tongue.

In search of her brother, Gypsy disappeared around the corner of the couch, exploring with quivering excitement. The eldest and boldest of the pups, Mick, barreled past Victoria. He headed straight for the entryway.

"Mick!" Victoria called after the straying puppy.

She felt the intruder before she saw him.

Every hair on her body stood on end, and a chill ran the length of her spine. A snarl erupted from her throat, and she whirled to face the intruder threatening the pups. She lunged to her feet and then froze upon coming face-to-face with Logan.

He stood in the kitchen with the yelping Mick at his feet. She had no clue how he could have gotten into the cabin undetected. It should not have been possible. On the couch, Sylvie realized the danger and had succumbed to horrified paralysis.

Logan smiled, and a chunk of ice formed in her gut. His amber eyes glimmered with reflected fire from the only source of light in the room. She feared the puppy was as good as dead.

"Hey there, boy, aren't you precious. Who's the cute one?" Logan sank to a crouch. His huge hands wrapped around the cub, and he lifted the puppy from the ground. He held Mick against his chest and stroked his finger across the top of the cub's head.

Innocent to the danger, Mick yipped and licked Logan's jaw. Her heart broke just to look at them. She could not stand to lose another cub. She did not have it in her to withstand another senseless death or another heartbreaking funeral.

Sensing the danger to her pup, Sophia lunged to her feet. She stood with her head low and her tail bristling. A growl rumbled from her throat.

Victoria's head jerked toward the mother wolf. "Sophia, stay!"

"Goddess, help us." Praying aloud, Sylvie snatched up Gypsy from the floor. She retreated toward the bedroom, carrying the other two cubs.

Victoria would beg if it would save Mick's life. "Logan, let him go. He's innocent. He's done nothing to harm you."

Logan stared at her hard. For a second, he seemed uncertain, but then a cold mask rendered his expression unfathom-able. "You think I want to hurt him?"

She edged forward a step. "I think you want to hurt me, and he's convenient, but you don't have to use him to get to me. I'm right here."

Logan's fingers flexed, stroking Mick's head. He had an odd look on his face that confused and frightened her worse than any threat. "What would you sacrifice for him?"

"My throat. My life. Anything. You have my word I'll surrender to you. Please, please, let him go." Tears filled her eyes, and she begged without a semblance of pride.

Logan ruffled the puppy's fur and glanced down, then up. His mouth twisted into a grimace, then into a smile. "You know, I came here intending to confront you. I wasn't sure what I was gonna do, but it was clear to me that you were nothing more than a calculating, selfish bitch after my dad's money."

He extended his hands and offered her the cub. Victoria rushed forward and snatched Mick from his grasp. She fell back to a safe distance, clutching the pup to her chest. Her heart slammed against her ribs, and the heaving of each breath filled her ears.

She stared at Logan in disbelief, her expression an open question. Her lips formed a silent word. "Why?"

His brow quirked; he shook his head. "I was wrong. I can see that you're just doing what you have to in order to keep your pack safe."

Moving with unexpected celerity, he retreated through the front door, gone before she processed the meaning of his words. The brittle tension in the room exploded into broken shards of confusion and relief.

Victoria stared after him. She passed Mick to Sophia. Without hesitation, she ran after Logan, following him out the front door and into the snowy winter day.

She caught up with Logan in the parking lot. He had his back to her, walking toward a parked vehicle. Victoria didn't hesitate; she charged him at top speed. She knew how fast he could change shape. She would not make the mistake of underestimating him again.

Logan turned on his heel as she bore down on him. Victoria extended her right arm high and grabbed hold of her dagger's hilt. *Vanadium* appeared in her hand. The ribbon-thin blade glittered with a thousand rays of refracted light, creating a rainbow effect.

"Fuck!" Logan sounded as impressed as he was astonished. He slipped into a defensive stance but Victoria was already on top of him. She hit his chest with her full weight. Her momentum propelled him into the side of a cabin, and she pinned him, one hand pressed against his chest above his heart. She held the tip of her weapon at his throat.

Wait. A silken whisper filled her mind, startling her into compliance. She did not know the voice, but it felt familiar nonetheless. It repeated: *Wait.*

Logan's hands touched her sides and she felt his razor-sharp claws against her ribcage, the tips positioned to gut her. His threat was implicit: mutually assured destruction.

She did not care. She snarled into his face, showing her teeth. Her eyes glowered; her power encircled them. "You dare come here threatening my pack. *Our young.* I should kill you where you stand."

Wait. Still in her mind, the voice stayed her hand. She felt compelled to obey.

Logan's power rose alongside hers, and his eyes turned to liquid gold, molten depths to drown in. He stared at her, body held tense. His heart thudded beneath her hand, a potent and hypnotic rhythm.

Her core heated with her awareness of his superb physique. In that moment, she wanted to fuck him as much as she wanted to kill him. Victoria's mouth contorted in a grimace, and she damned her undisciplined hormones for her attraction to such an inappropriate male.

Logan's expression changed, and his jaw worked. The aggression did not subside; it altered form. Without warning, he released his hold on her sides and held up hands already returned to human. "No matter what else I might be guilty of, I don't kill pups. I picked him up because he was cute. I had no idea you'd assume I wanted to hurt him. That's all, I swear."

She gnashed teeth. She wanted to rip the heart out of him, but also knew that her unreasoning anger came from fear. If she could not control it, then it would become her master.

Glaring, she backed away from him, dagger still drawn. "You murdered blood kin—your own mother. Killing a cub would mean nothing to you."

Logan blanched and staggered. Her words moved through his heart as effectively as the blade of her dagger. Unbearable hurt and rage showed in his eyes. "You're a fucking bitch, Victoria."

"Yes, I am. Now get the hell away from here. Don't come near my pack again. Next time I *will* kill you."

With a final hateful glare, he left.

CHAPTER SEVEN

Logan—
"Goddess, I don't know what to make of him."
"I'm sorry, Victoria, I don't either."

The white wolf glided across pristine snow. Starlight illuminated the night. The hunger moon had entered a new phase, an emaciated shadow of its former self. The woods along the lakeshore were silent, save for the occasional foraging deer. The prey caused her tail to quiver and her nose to twitch with predatory interest, but she passed them by and ran on.

Victoria had left the Golf parked in a scenic pull off about a mile north of the Koenig residence. Traveling as a wolf permitted her to approach the property over dense, difficult terrain. She moved stealthily, slipping between the trees, decreasing her chances of detection.

She emerged from the forest into a clearing located beyond the boundary of the yard. Thick-trunked pines surrounded the field, and the house was visible through the trees. A stone-lined path led to the boathouse, and a thirty-foot dock stretched out over the opaque plane of dark water.

In the center of the clearing, Victoria underwent a complete transformation to human. Her clothing remained behind in the car, so she walked naked through the winter night. Her bare feet left tracks in the deep snow, and she shivered despite her natural resistance to the cold.

Victoria shoved her loose hair back from her face and slipped the band she wore on her left wrist over her hand. She pulled her hair into a neat ponytail.

Stepping with care, she moved through the clearing. "Lori, are you still here?"

The silence stretched with no response. With a sigh, Victoria turned toward the lake and considered her options. Sneaking around behind Arik's back carried considerable risk, and she hated to leave with nothing to show for it.

Victoria cleared her throat and tried again. "Lori Koenig—you showed yourself to me once already. There must have been a reason. Will you come out and tell me what you want?"

She waited. *Nothing.*

With a huff of frustration, Victoria turned to leave.

A frigid blast of air beat down on her. She ducked her head and raised her hands to protect her face from the frozen wind. It stung her eyes and caused them to water. The stench of fresh blood flooded her nostrils.

The wind abated, and Victoria looked up to find an apparition before her. "Lori?"

Silvery light swirled about the spirit's form. Unblinking amber eyes flecked with green and red stared straight through Victoria. Her light brown hair framed an oval face, and she possessed sculpted beauty like a marble statue. Her bare arms and torso bore deep slashes. She wore a white flowing robe, torn and bloody. The lower half of her body blurred and faded so she appeared to float.

"This is where I died?" The spirit's voice conveyed her uncertainty. No self-awareness shone in those disturbing and familiar eyes.

Victoria glanced heavenward and shot off a quick

prayer for patience. "Yes, this is where you died. My name is Victoria. Do you remember revealing yourself to me the other night?"

Recognition finally crossed the spirit's countenance. The scent of blood grew stronger as she manifested, coalescing from a wispy phantasm into a solid figure. "Are you Logan's friend?"

Victoria snorted. "Friend is a bit of a stretch, but yeah, for the sake of argument, if it will help you to tell me what you want from me."

The spirit extended her arm. "Logan is in danger. I fear for him."

Victoria reached out and caught the spirit's hand, seeking to provide a real connection. "Lori, I need for you to focus. You can speak to me because I'm a shaman, able to see and communicate with spirits."

The spirit stared at her in confusion. "Victoria?"

"Yes, Victoria. Now, how can I help you?"

"Logan is in danger."

Victoria sighed and throttled her impatience. She wished, just once, she could meet a coherent ghost. Apparently, it was too much to ask.

"No, Logan hurt you, Lori. Do you remember how you died?"

Tears filled the spirit's eyes. Her hands trembled in Victoria's grasp. "No, Logan is my son. Please..."

"Lori, your spirit is tormented because you were murdered. You're reaching out to me because there's something that has prevented you from moving on." She sought to keep her voice gentle but insistent.

Lori moaned. "No..."

Perhaps if she changed her tactic... "Lori, are you seeking justice? Tell me who killed you."

The spirit wept and shook. While she grew distressed, Lori's body lost form and substance. She started to fade. "No, I— Please help me? I can't—"

"Lori, I want to help you but you need to tell me

what it is you seek. Justice? Revenge?"

The ghost shook her head. "No, neither."

"What is it then?" Victoria grew more desperate with each passing moment. In a second, the spirit would be gone and she would still have nothing concrete to go on.

"Mom?"

"Logan!" Lori whirled toward the house. The wind kicked up again and assaulted Victoria with biting cold.

"Mom!" Logan's shout filled the night. The thunder and crash of his approach destroyed Victoria's communion with the spirit.

"Shit!" Furious, Victoria turned toward the house. A moment later, she performed a double take in surprise. "Lori, how is it that he can see you?"

The tormented spirit offered no answers. Instead, Lori floated toward her son with arms extended. Logan perceived only the welcoming embrace of his mother. Victoria watched with dread, expecting the worst, a spirit hell-bent upon revenge.

"Logan, no! Stay back!" The wind swallowed her voice. She surged forward in an attempt to protect him, but then hesitated out of self-preservation. She considered Logan more unpredictable and dangerous than a wild animal—a wolf capable of slaying blood kin.

Logan crossed the distance between the pool and the clearing, making impressive time through the fresh snow. He struggled and floundered in the occasional deep drift, but moved forward with single-minded determination. When he reached his mother, she tilted her head back and released a horrific moan of such wretched suffering it turned Victoria's blood to ice.

Logan's arrival in the clearing triggered a startling change in their surroundings. A crescent moon appeared overhead in the blood-red sky. A blizzard blanketed the ground in a white death shroud. Lori Koenig vanished from Logan's arms and appeared on the ground. She lay on her back, limbs splayed and clothing torn. Her amber eyes stared sightless and her splayed ribs revealed a decimated chest.

A deep red pool spread outward from her body, polluting the pure fallen snow. The scent of fresh blood became so prevalent, her mouth salivated, and at the same time, her stomach turned in revulsion. Her kind did not consume the flesh of man or wolf. It was taboo.

"Mom, no. Oh, god, I—" Logan sank to his knees beside the body and gathered his mother into his arms. A harsh sob racked his chest, and he strangled on the expulsion of air and tears. He fell upon Lori's body and pressed his face to her throat.

"I'm sorry. I'm so sorry." He wept in abject grief, repeating the apology until it grew indecipherable. Victoria viewed him in pity and disgust—a part of her longed to comfort him, another to kill him.

Lori's arms rose from the snow, open hands reached for Logan's head. She threaded her fingers through her son's hair and held him to her breast. "Shh, baby, don't cry. Logan, listen—"

"Mom." He lifted his head. Tears glistened on his cheeks.

Lori gripped his face and forced her son to look her in the face. "Logan, it wasn't your fault. Do you hear me? You mustn't blame yourself."

As Lori spoke, she faded, taking the crescent moon and the blood-red sky with her. The blizzard wind died to little more than a breeze. Within seconds, the spirit vanished, leaving Logan and Victoria alone in the clearing beneath the new moon.

Nausea threatened to overwhelm Victoria. As always when dealing with spirits, she felt too much. She empathized with Lori's suffering and Logan's anguish. The worst, the harsh realization that Lori Koenig's murder was not at all as it seemed. The truth was not a neat, simple thing.

Desperate, Victoria reached out and seized Logan's arm. She pulled him to a seated position and spoke with urgency. "Logan, pay attention. Do you remember anything from the night your mom died? Anything at all?"

Logan blinked through his confusion and then shook his head. He wiped the tears from his face. He leaned forward, chest against his knees, and ran a hand through his hair.

His voice emerged rough and raspy. "No, I don't remember anything at all."

"It's vital that you try."

His gaze focused on her. "You're naked."

"Oh, stop acting like a horny teenage boy for five seconds!" Victoria punched his bicep. Then she grabbed his arm and hauled him to his feet. She spun him to face the house.

"Look." She pointed to the broken trail he had created leading through the snow to the clearing.

"What am I looking at?"

"Look how hard you struggled with a wolf's strength to travel across a few hundred feet of chest-deep snow. Imagine how long it would have taken your mother. Think about how fast you move compared to a human."

He stared in silence and then made grim reply. "You're saying that both murders should have happened beside the pool."

Victoria nodded and released his arm. He remained seated on the ground. "Your mother wasn't killed by a berserker wolf. She was stalked and then slaughtered."

"You don't think I did this?" His question contained more hope than conviction. His shock ran deep, but his rage churned at the core of his being. He terrified her.

Victoria retreated from him toward the woods. "What I think is irrelevant."

Logan surged to his feet and pursued her. "Wait. Please. I need your help."

"I can't help you."

He stopped in his tracks. "What the hell are you doing here then?"

"I needed more information to form a complete picture. It's too bad that your mother's spirit isn't more coherent, because I would like to help her."

"What now?" Despair filled his beautiful eyes.

"Now?" she said. *What now? What comes next?*

"Yes, now."

"Now... what I need is to take my pack and get the hell out of here before we wind up under the control of a psychotic Alpha who murdered his mate, or saddled with a damaged boy who murdered his mother. Either would be our end."

He blanched. "Vic..."

Victoria shook her head. "Sorry, Logan, but I've done you all the favors I'm gonna do."

"You call this a favor?" Logan's outrage carried him into her face, arms spread in an angry gesture. He grabbed hold of her arms and dragged her off her feet.

She scrambled to escape. "Let go!"

"No, why should I? You've screwed me, Vic. Why don't you just pull that damn knife and stick it in?" His desperation made him careless. He left himself wide open.

Victoria kicked him in the gut hard enough to wind him and knock him to the ground. "You know what, Logan? You're an idiot. All I've done is ask your mother to name her killer. It's not my fault that she couldn't."

He knelt on his knees in the snow and stared up at her with eyes bright with unshed tears. His despair twisted her insides into a horrible mess. "What you've done is give me hope. That's way worse than slitting my throat."

She denied him with a shake of her head. "You should be grateful."

He gaped at her and his expression grew ruthless.

"Grateful? For what? Am I supposed to be grateful that my dad might've murdered my mom?"

"Call it whatever the hell you want!" She turned her back and ran from him, fleeing from more responsibility. Her conscience nagged her every step of the way. She owed Logan and Arik more than a cold shoulder, but her obligations to her pack were already more than she could bear.

She made it three strides before he caught her. He seized her elbow and spun her to face him again. He loomed large and angry. "You know what, Vic? You're a bitch. Worse than that, you're a coward."

The insult to her honor struck home. "I am not!"

"Denying it doesn't make it any less true!"

Red blurred her vision, and she roared her rage. With a yank, she ripped her arm from his grasp and punched him in the face. Her fist connected with his chin. Logan staggered backward and collided with a pine tree. Branches snapped and cracked, and the impact brought down an avalanche of snow.

Logan howled in anger and shook off the snow. He rebounded and charged straight into her. He tackled her and wrapped his arms around her waist. Together, they plowed through a stand of young pines and left the ground littered with debris.

Victoria landed flat on her back in a snowdrift. The intense cold upon bare flesh caused her to yelp. His powerful body provided a startling contrast, scalding hot to the touch. It awakened unexpected urges that she preferred not to think about in relation to Logan. Her mouth watered, and she licked her lips, resisting the desire to taste his throat.

His hips settled between her thighs, and he rocked against her. His primal musk filled her nostrils; he awakened her need. Growling low in her throat, she dug her fingernails into his back, gouging scratches in his shirt and flesh.

"Fuck, you smell good." Logan buried his face against her throat and inhaled her scent. His touch, violent just moments before, grew gentle. One hand stroked her hair; the other followed the curve of her body. Through the denim of his jeans, his arousal pressed against the juncture of her thighs. He had her pinned.

"Get off me," Victoria snarled through bared teeth. She forced her eyes open, resisting her body's enjoyment of his touch. She bucked her hips in an attempt to dislodge him.

"You want me." He fought to remain atop her.

"I hate you!" Victoria struggled harder, shoving him away. "Get. Off."

Logan lifted his head and looked her straight in the eye. "So you can hit me again? Is violence your answer to being wrong?"

"Don't you dare! Your little brain dictates your every action." Summoning her wolf, Victoria used her anger to fuel her transformation. Her power spilled forth, and her wolf ascended to dominance.

When she changed, her eyes glowed golden, her face and fangs elongated, and her ears grew to points. Her hands and feet turned to claws. Her limbs grew longer, the same as her trunk, and fur covered her entire body. She stopped midway in the bipedal wolf-man form werewolves used for combat.

With the increased strength her transformation provided, she lifted Logan into the air. She expected him to transform also, but he remained human even though his power rose to meet hers. Hefting him, Victoria threw him toward the dark lake.

Cat fast, Logan landed on his feet and settled into a defensive stance. Victoria advanced, adopting an aggressive posture, spine stiff and head high. She expected Logan to come at her any moment, and she braced for his terrible transformation. They were close in power, but his superior size and strength allowed him a distinct advantage.

Victoria did not understand the delay; his attack should have come with the swiftness she knew he possessed. His continued failure to transform infuriated her. "Change!"

"No."

"Change, damn you! Fight me!" She lunged at him and lashed out with her claw. She struck his right bicep and left a set of deep parallel gouges. Blood ran from the wound and fell onto the white snow.

Logan growled but controlled his beast. He smirked, taking a perverse pleasure in her towering frustration. With deft grace, he dodged her next blow. "I don't think so."

Her frustration peaked and she gnashed her teeth together. "Why? Why won't you fight me?"

"Because it gives you an easy out if we kill each other. You don't like who I am, so you resort to violence. You don't want to hear what I have to say, so your solution is violence."

He stopped moving and absorbed another slash to the chest. She left another set of bloody wounds over his left pectoral. "This doesn't lessen your cowardice, Vic. It proves it."

"Change. Now." Victoria towered with fury. She backhanded Logan and drove him toward the edge of the lake. A shallow bluff hung over the water.

"Go on. Run away. Screw with people, and then tuck your tail and run. Run away so you don't ever have to solve a problem or trust someone. Run away. It's what you do best, coward."

Pure hatred burned in his amber eyes.

The insult struck home more deadly than silver, flaying her ego to the bone. He took distinct pleasure in driving his point home and twisting the blade. *Cowardice.* It was too damned close to the truth. For months, she had run from everything—hunters and responsibility—

to her great shame.

Howling, Victoria grabbed hold of Logan and hefted him above her head. She took three huge strides toward the edge of the bluff and heaved the wretched male high and far. If he'd never come down, it wouldn't have been long enough for her.

Logan flew through the air and then hit the dark water below. An enormous splash served as the final punctuation on their confrontation. She watched long enough to be sure he surfaced and then she left. If Logan had been angry before, getting drenched might push him into a frenzy.

Without any regard for stealth, she ran back to her car on two legs even though travel on four would have been more efficient. She did not want to stop and take the time to transform to a wolf, only to change back a few minutes later. Shapechanging consumed an enormous amount of energy and left her ravenous afterward.

She had left the Golf unlocked with the keys in the ignition and her clothing folded on the front seat. Inside the car, Victoria writhed into her jeans and pulled her shirt over her head. Fully dressed, she flopped back against the seat and rested for a few luxurious seconds. Her rapid breathing and racing heartbeat made her feel like she'd just fled the scene of a crime.

Victoria opened her eyes and scooted into the driver's seat. She fastened her seatbelt and reached for the keys dangling in the ignition. The engine produced an awful whirring sound and failed to start. Swearing, she let go of the key.

Logan's angry howl filled the moonless night, informing her he was coming after her. He wasn't far away.

"Shit." She'd forgotten about the persnickety nature of her getaway vehicle. If she'd been thinking, she might not have dunked Logan into an ice-cold lake. She cranked the ignition again, and the transmission yowled in agony.

Metal screamed, and the roof of the Golf caved inward under the impact of a heavy object. A spider web of cracks spread across the front windshield, and Victoria ducked her head to avoid having it smashed.

"Logan!" Victoria grabbed for the door but the mangled mass of metal refused to budge. The little vehicle rocked and groaned under repeated impacts; she suspected he was bouncing on top of the car. The roof collapsed further and broken glass flew everywhere.

Victoria twisted within the small enclosure, trying to get into a position to rip through the side of the vehicle with her claws. She secured a solid grip on the frame when the entire Golf shifted, turning sideways and then upward with alarming speed.

His shout filled the night. "Time to get wet, Vic!"

"Damn it! Logan, I'm going to kill you!"

His laughter answered her threats. Victoria braced when Logan heaved the Golf into the air. It soared and then fell, and hit the lake with a tremendous splash. Water poured in through the broken windows and flooded the car.

Hyperventilating, Victoria sucked down several gulps of air and then held her breath as the icy water of Echo Lake swallowed the car. It was dark—so dark she couldn't see her hand in front of her face. Navigating by touch, she used her claws to rip her way out of the crushed cube of metal that formed her prison.

Victoria kicked free from the car and it continued to sink, disappearing into the watery depths. For a timeless eternity, she floated in the darkness without any sense of up or down. It may have been seconds or a minute before she achieved enough orientation to determine which way was up. She sent up a quick prayer and then swam for all she was worth.

By the time her head broke the surface, the burning in her lungs filled her entire chest. She gasped for breath and floated until she located the closest shore. The short swim took less than a minute, and she emerged drenched and unhappy onto the snowy beach.

Logan waited for her on the shore. Naked and human, he stood with one arm propped against a pine tree. His slick hair lay flat against his skull and water dripped from his limbs. The deep lacerations she had left on his arm and chest had already begun to heal.

Victoria trudged out of the lake and marched past him. He trailed along behind her. "I need your help."

She whirled on him. "Say that again. I dare you!"

He peered at her with a hopeful smile. "Please?"

She stabbed at him with a finger. "You're crazy! It occurs to you to ask nicely *now*?"

Logan grinned. "I asked nicely before, but you weren't listening."

Victoria glared. She considered drawing her dagger and taking his head. He had destroyed her car. She also agreed with every accusation he had made, which was why the insults had angered her so much. She considered cowardice a vile thing, and to be guilty of it brought dishonor upon her.

"Vic..."

"Fine!" Victoria threw up her hands. "I'll help, but you're paying for my car."

Logan arched his brow. "If we stop at an ATM, I can take out a twenty."

"Ha ha, very funny. I'm serious."

His face lit with a triumphant smile. "All right, I doubt it'll break the bank. Until you get another one, you can borrow my car for the duration."

"Done." She grumbled and glanced down at herself. "And I need to borrow your clothes dryer."

He smirked. "I'll loan you the dollar."

"Pizza will be here in forty minutes." Logan replaced the landline on its base. He walked to the fireplace and picked up an iron poker he'd used to stir the fire. He had on a dark red shirt and jeans. His feet were bare and his short hair was a tousled mess, the result of hasty finger combing.

"I hope you ordered more than one. I'm starving." Victoria finished towel drying her hair and sank into a black leather recliner with an exhausted sigh. She wore an enormous white cotton bathrobe while her clothing tumbled in the dryer. The neckline plunged to reveal her cleavage. Her nose told her the robe belonged to Arik; the scent enveloped her.

"Yup, four large combos." Logan flopped onto the couch opposite her. A glass-topped coffee table stood at the center of the room.

"What are you going to eat?"

"Wow, was that a joke?" Logan stared at her, mocking astonishment. "I thought you didn't have a sense of humor, Vic."

"I don't. I'm starving. Stop calling me Vic."

He flashed an unrepentant grin edged with a leer. "Hey, I'm buying you pizza. Does this mean we're a-courtin'?"

Victoria glared and threw a throw pillow at him, which he ducked. "You can deduct what I owe you from what you owe me."

"Yeah, yeah, talk to my lawyer," Logan said.

"And while we're talking tallies, you owe me a new cellphone." She dug into the robe pocket and tossed her disposable phone onto the table. "Mine is dead, and it's your fault."

Logan gave her phone a dismissive glance and then dropped an expensive smart phone onto the table.

She stared at it and then released an exhausted sigh. "Fine," she said. "We're even."

He snorted. "We're far from even. That thing was a

piece of crap. My phone is worth your car."

Too tired to fight with him, she sank further into the recliner. "It was the only phone I had."

Logan's expression softened. "I'll get you a new phone."

She nodded. "Where's Arik?"

"He works late."

Victoria exhaled in relief. If Logan's father arrived home, there would be all manner of awkward explaining to do.

"Hell, dad works all the time. I wouldn't worry about him coming home and interrupting." He added a suggestive brow wiggle.

"Fine, let's get down to business, and spare me anymore of your mindless banter. You're not witty or cute."

"I love emotionally unavailable women." Intent, Logan leaned forward and gave her his undivided attention. "Go on."

She stared at him and attempted to penetrate the flippant exterior he showed the world. Her lips began to form words, but they failed her.

His eyebrow rose. "What?"

"There's nothing vicious about you."

She got to him. His face revealed embarrassment before he recovered that cocky grin. "Ah, but I am vain and horny."

She ignored him. "Logan, your mother's spirit is tormented. The fact she remains tethered to the place she died and has not passed into the afterlife means she cannot move on until there's resolution."

He stopped breathing, then resumed. "What does that mean?"

"Most likely, she seeks justice, to have her killer revealed or punished."

Another interruption occurred in his breathing and his heart skipped a beat. Raw hope, painful to look upon, crossed his face. His lips formed words without sound: *her killer.*

"Can't you ask her?" Agitated, Logan rose from his chair and moved closer to the fireplace. He took to restless pacing before the hearth, hands moving with agitation.

"Will you stop that?"

He swung on her. "How the hell am I supposed to turn my emotions off? I'm not a machine!"

"Fine! I tried to talk to Lori, but she became agitated. She couldn't name her killer. She expressed concern for you, said that you were in danger."

Logan stopped in front of the fire with his profile to her and stared into the flames. He ran an agitated hand through his hair. "I can't believe my father killed my mother."

Victoria stared at him. He spoke with real conviction, not the sentimental wistfulness of a fool. She found his loyalty to his father to be strange and endearing, given the tension she had witnessed between the two men.

"You prefer to believe it was you?" Victoria asked. She had no qualms about playing Devil's Advocate. The more she learned, the closer she came to the truth.

Logan shot her a blistering look, brimming with scorn. "What I prefer to believe is that neither of us killed my mother. Who do you think did it?"

"What I think doesn't matter." She shrugged. "But they say that the husband is always the prime suspect."

"No!" Logan's fist struck his palm. "You don't understand! You weren't there! My father mourned for my mother. He believed I murdered her, and he controlled the instinct to kill me even though I wouldn't have tried to stop him. I begged him to kill me."

The firelight reflected off wetness on his cheek. Logan loved his father without condition or reservation, in spite of the emotional baggage between them. Nausea churned her gut. It would destroy what was left of Logan's world if Arik proved to be the murderer. She smashed the sympathy with ruthless determination. She couldn't afford to lose her objectivity or to let her guard down.

"The only way to turn this into a win-win is to prove someone other than you or Arik murdered your mom," Victoria said. "That should be our objective."

Logan swallowed and nodded. "Where do we start?"

Victoria chewed her lower lip. She wasn't a cop or a private investigator. She had no more idea than Logan did on where to start, although, she trusted her impartiality more than his.

"Let's start with the murder. Was there anything you recall that seemed out of place? A foreign scent or tracks in the snow?"

Logan's lips compressed, forming a flat line. He shook his head. "No, nothing. I was covered in her blood, and..."

"Logan." She straightened in her seat and started to stand. Logan shuddered and swallowed a sob. He held out his hand, palm toward her, in a gesture designed to stop her. His aura swelled to engulf the room, leaving her awash in his grief and rage.

She trembled under the onslaught. "It's okay, Logan. Let it go. We'll investigate this and uncover the truth."

"How?"

She thought about it but felt like she was grasping at straws. Finally, she went with the foremost thought in her head. "We need to get our hands on the original police file and find out what their investigation revealed."

Logan looked up. Light shone in his eyes. "I think I know someone who can help us get the file. Let me make a call."

"Okay."

The doorbell rang, signaling the arrival of their food order. Her stomach rumbled with hunger. She could have smelled the pizza two miles off.

Logan snickered. "Hungry?"

"Shut up."

He laughed and reached for his wallet on the mantle. His car keys were beside it.

"Give me your keys," Victoria said.

Logan shot her a nasty glance. He hesitated and then tossed her the keys. Victoria caught them with her left hand.

"Try not to drive it into the lake." He headed to answer the front door.

Victoria flashed her teeth at his back. "You hope."

He stopped in his tracks, and it was her turn to laugh. With real pleasure, she threaded her middle finger through the ring and held the keys against her palm.

A smug smile played on her lips.

What a sweet thought.

CHAPTER EIGHT

Thrice marked? —

"Goddess, he bears the marks of two of Loki's three children: wolf and serpent."

"It is so."

"Will Hel mark him also?"

"I do not know."

Logan turned his red SUV onto a small side road. Walls of plowed snow lined both sides of the street. He parked and turned off the engine and then climbed from the vehicle.

Victoria shoved open the passenger side door and stepped out. She followed him around the car. So far, he hadn't disclosed their destination or the identity of the friend who could help them. Her curiosity was piqued.

"This is it."

Victoria stopped in her tracks. "This is a cemetery."

Logan snapped his fingers. "Damn, you're observant. Can't put one past you, Vic."

She bored holes in his back as he approached the tall wrought iron fence. The eclectic collection of headstones and mausoleums visible through the bars made the cemetery appear historical.

"Why are we here?"

Logan glanced over his shoulder and smirked. "I figured you'd think I was getting fresh if I took you to the dump."

"Gross, now I need to scrub my brain. TMI: I don't need to know where you go to masturbate."

Logan scoffed. "Oh, yeah, right. Like I'd take you to my happy place."

She counted to ten and then tried again. "Why are we here?"

"I told you, we're meeting my contact about obtaining the police file on my mom's murder."

Victoria frowned. "You're being deliberately dense."

"Am I?" Logan bent his knees and performed a standing jump, twelve feet up and over the fence. He came down on the shoveled walkway.

"Yes, you are." Tilting her head, she gauged the distance, and then leapt. She cleared the fence and landed on the path beside Logan.

The night was darker than most due to the new moon, so both wolves relied on their nocturnal vision to navigate. Logan led her through a maze of gravestones and trees, heading toward the center of the cemetery.

"Why are we meeting your contact in a graveyard? And who even has contacts outside of television?"

"Evan isn't a friend," Logan said. "Contact fits. I'm not sure what else to call him."

"Do you even have any friends?"

Anger flashed in his eyes. He glared but made no reply. His failure to answer made her regret the bitchy question. She and Logan were on a slippery slope with the insults.

Her breath emerged as a puff of hot steam in the frigid night air. At a glance, the cemetery appeared calm enough. She perceived only an occasional spiritual blur dancing above a grave.

"Do you see them?" Logan asked.

The unexpected question caught her off guard. "Yes,

but I'm surprised that you can."

A shrug rolled off his shoulders. "Second sight runs on my mother's side of the family. I've always been able to see ghosts, as far back as I can remember."

They passed a crypt and an eerie sensation passed through Victoria, causing her skin to crawl. She stopped in her tracks, staring at the small Gothic structure. "What's in there?"

"Old Torment." Logan circled back to take her elbow.

She arched her brow at him. She sensed a story there. "What does that mean?"

Logan urged her along. "Long story. Keep moving. He'll leave us alone so long as we leave him alone."

Victoria craned her neck to stare at the crypt as they passed, a hundred questions in her mind, but she shoved her curiosity aside. A part of her did want to know; another part knew she was better off not asking. Finally, they reached a storm drain.

"Wait here." Logan ducked inside. She heard him call out in a soft voice. "Evan? Are you here?"

Logan's footsteps faded as he moved further from her. She stood outside the storm drain and listened but heard nothing else. Her impatience grew by leaps and bounds. Finally, she couldn't stand to wait any longer.

She entered the storm drain, and her nose curled at the rank smell of rotting organic matter and frozen pools of standing water. It was warmer inside of the pipe than she'd expected but also pitch black, challenging even her wolf's night vision.

"Logan?" Taking careful steps, Victoria moved forward, relying upon her other acute senses to find her way. Sniffing, she picked up Logan's scent and followed it for over a minute through the muck and debris.

Ahead, she heard the hushed voices of Logan and his friend. She approached using stealth, both curious and cautious. As she drew closer, the stink of death flooded her nostrils, and she recognized the source as coming from the *thing* talking to Logan.

Victoria snarled, displaying her teeth, and her eyes glowed, providing illumination within the dark sewer. Her angry growl ended the conversation. She charged forward, claws ready, intending to eviscerate the undead creature.

"Whoa!" Logan whirled and his long arms flashed out. He caught Victoria about the waist and swung her around.

The dead thing emitted a scream of terror and retreated further down the tunnel. Rumbling with a continuous growl, Victoria struggled to be free from Logan's hold.

"Take it easy there, Lassie. Good girl."

"Let go! It's getting away!" Her claws slashed at empty air, seeking to rend and tear the dead thing limb from limb. Logan's superior strength held her back.

"Vic, that's Evan you're trying to kill." Logan dropped his voice to a hiss. "Remember Evan? Evan, I need his help to get the police file on my mom's murder. Evan, we're meeting him here. Does any of this ring a bell?"

"Hi, my name is Evan. It's a pleasure to meet you." The thing held up a timid hand in greeting. Its voice registered in the falsetto range, giving it a breathy, child-like sound.

"You're protecting that thing?" Victoria punched Logan on the chest with her clenched claw and then hit him again, directing her frustration against him until he released her. He let go, but he kept his body between her and Evan.

"Evan's a ghoul, not a thing. Granted, he's among the living-impaired, but he keeps to himself. He doesn't hurt anyone. Snacks on the occasional stale corpse, but hell, everyone likes junk food every now and then, right?"

Victoria huffed and hit Logan's chest again with both fists. "That's disgusting."

"I'm sorry you don't like my choice of food, but it's really my business," Evan said.

Victoria turned her entire attention to Logan, trying to comprehend his reasoning. Maybe he didn't understand.

She tried to explain. "Logan, it's undead, an abomination. That rotting corpse has a soul trapped within. It must be destroyed so the spirit can move on."

"Excuse me, but I'm not rotting," Evan said in weak protest. It sniffed. "Maybe a bit rancid."

She started forward and Logan shoved her back with a frustrated snarl. "What part of no is unclear to you? The *n* or the *o*?"

Her hands created a wringing motion; she envisioned his throat between them. "*How* can you protect it?"

Logan leaned forward so she could see the glow of his eyes, and the gleaming threat of bared teeth. "I am not going to let you hurt him, Vic."

"Stop calling me Vic!" She wanted to scream with frustration. Why did Logan always have to be so damned contrary? It made no sense to her.

An expulsion of air escaped his lungs. "Look, my dad sanctions Evan within his territory. This ghoul is under his protection, so you shouldn't destroy him without checking first."

"Your dad doesn't even know we're here! Don't play games with me!" She considered the ghoul, huddled about fifty feet down the tunnel behind Logan.

Finally, she grunted. "Why don't you or Arik kill it?"

Logan issued an exasperated sigh. "You shouldn't kill something just because you don't understand it."

Victoria regarded him with patent disbelief. "Are you even a wolf?"

Logan gestured with open arms. "Oh, come on! This

is California. We're tolerant of differences, remember?"

"I'm from Arizona."

"All is made clear."

Victoria huffed, but acceded and put up her hands to show she would not attack. "Fine, let's get this over with."

"Evan, you said you could get us into the evidence area." Logan stood with his arms spread, hands looking to commit violence. His irritation with his pet ghoul caused Victoria to snicker.

A dim maintenance lamp illuminated the dark tunnel. Evan cowered at a safe distance. He was short and wore rags, but aside from those details, Victoria still had not gotten a good look at him. Shadows seemed to enshroud the ghoul.

"I said I knew how to get *to* the evidence area. I never said I could get the door open," Evan said. "This is an old maintenance entrance that leads into the police station's basement."

"It's locked."

"Of course it's locked. It's a police station," Evan said. "You're a werewolf. Can't you rip the door off the hinges?"

"Yeah, as a matter of fact there are all kinds of things I could rip to shreds," Logan said with a threatening glare.

"I don't believe you'd hurt me. We're friends," Evan said, but his voice was uncertain, and he trembled in fear.

Victoria shook with silent laughter so hard it became difficult to breathe. She had tears in her eyes, listening to the two of them. She pressed her hands to her sides to relieve the pain.

Evan stuck out his hand, palm up, and waited.

Logan swore up and down the spectrum of shocking words. He shot her the evil eye, causing her to laugh harder. Maybe he'd learn. She could not have conjured a more appropriate twist than the current development. Finally, Logan yanked out his wallet and tossed a roll of twenties at Evan.

The violent gesture caused the ghoul to flinch. Then, he scrambled to snatch up the bills from the soggy ground.

"Two hundred, as we agreed?" Evan asked.

Logan's teeth gnashed together. "One hundred. Our agreement was that you'd get us into the evidence area. You didn't deliver. Now get lost before I let Arizona here off her leash."

Victoria growled low in her throat and took a menacing step toward the ghoul. Evan squeaked and departed with alacrity, heading down the tunnel. In the blink of an eye, he vanished from sight.

"Next time, get it in writing." Victoria checked the ground but the ghoul had managed to gather all of the money before he left.

Logan grumbled and regarded her with a sour expression. He did not seem to share her amusement at their predicament. He turned the knob and found it dead-bolted. "Do you know how to pick locks?"

She snorted. "I'm many things: spirit speaker, healer, nurse. Regardless of what you think of me, I grew up in a nice neighborhood with a nice family. We did nice, boring things together. I can't pick locks or disarm security systems.

"You're ruining my fantasy."

"What about you, Silver Spoon?"

"My spoon was gold, baby, solid gold." Logan regarded the sturdy metal door and then gave it a rattle, checking its strength. He looked to Victoria and arched his brow. He had a gleam in his eyes that she did not like at all.

"Logan, what are you thinking?"

"That Evan had the right of it. Ready to have some fun?" Logan gave her no opportunity to formulate a reply. He stripped off his shirt and kicked off his boots. His jeans came last, sliding over lean hips, muscular thighs and trim calves. He folded his clothes and handed them to her for safekeeping.

"Are you sure this is a good idea?" Victoria remained skeptical, but she had no alternative plan.

"You got a better idea?"

"Nope."

He turned his back to her and for the first time she noticed the tattoo on his back just above his ass. It was an Ouroboros Serpent, a dragon eating its own tail.

Victoria let out an admiring wolf whistle, using her teeth to create the sound. Her gaze lingered on his tight buttocks as much as the intricate artwork.

He shot her a cocky smirk. "Enjoying the view?"

"It would figure that you'd have a tramp stamp."

"Ouch." He pantomimed hurt, hand to heart.

She smiled and shook her head. "Nice ink."

"Thanks." Logan's quick glance and expression revealed his surprise at the compliment.

"Does your father know you have a tattoo of the world serpent?"

"It's a dragon and yeah, he knows. It's my back, not his." Logan turned back to the door. "I got it on spring break in Cabo when I was seventeen. Woke up hung over and there it was."

Victoria snorted. "No idea how you got it?"

"Not a one."

"You're such a cliché."

"I'm not. I never know where to put the accent mark."

Logan braced, assuming a wide stance, and initiated the transformation to a wolf. He halted the change midway, augmenting his natural strength while retaining the use of his hands. As before, he shifted with terrifying speed, far faster than normal.

"Ready?" He aligned his claws along the edges of the door, creating deep indentations in the metal.

"Ready." Victoria flexed her hands, echoing his action. Her adrenaline surged with the rush of excitement. Granted, most human police probably did not load their guns with silver bullets, but breaking into a police station carried inherent risks.

The metal doorframe groaned while he applied his considerable strength. The edges warped and the door separated from its hinges with a final broken groan. Taking two steps backward, Logan set it down and propped it against the tunnel wall.

"I'd hate to have to explain that to the insurance company." Victoria stepped into the opening and scanned the area, searching for signs of torn wires or other security devices. She found nothing.

Head cocked, she listened but heard no alarms or sounds of approach. She turned toward Logan. "Shouldn't there be a security system?"

"Sierra Pines is a small town. Who would want to break into the police station?" Logan bent to pass through the doorway. He underwent a quick transformation, reverting to human, and Victoria handed him his clothing.

She studied the area while Logan dressed. Auxiliary lighting provided illumination, revealing tall steel shelves full of cardboard boxes and bins. The entire criminal history of the town, contained within one room. The aisles were narrow and the floor bare concrete.

"How are we supposed to find anything in here?"

"Dunno. There must be a computer or a filing system." Logan looked as perplexed as she felt. Law-abiding werewolves had no business breaking and entering.

"I'll go look. You stay here and try to figure out the

system for how things are arranged on the shelves."

"Yes, ma'am, I'll get right on that." Logan performed a sloppy salute. His tone dripped sarcasm.

Victoria grinned and left him in the aisle, inspecting the assorted boxes. She made her way through the basement, exercising a great deal of caution. At the far end, she located a stairwell, filing cabinets, an old office desk, and an older computer.

Victoria took a seat on the creaky rolling chair and turned on the desk lamp. She touched the mouse to bring up the logon screen. The 'Administrator' account required a password for access. The password was not 'password' or '12345'.

"Well, that exhausts my hacking skills." She leaned back in the creaky chair to contemplate her next movement. She opened and closed the desk drawers, rifling the contents, and turned over the mouse pad. She flipped through the day calendar.

Nothing.

Victoria spun in the chair in order to examine a set of shelves holding dozens of navy binders. Each bore the label "Evidence Log", arranged in chronological order. She located the correct binder for the date of Lori Koenig's murder and removed it from the shelf. She flipped through the pages until she found an entry for 'Lori Koenig'.

Logan emerged from among the shelves, carrying a couple of cardboard boxes stacked atop one another. He had an open manila file folder in his hand.

"Found it," he said.

"That was easy, maybe too easy." She sounded suspicious even to her own ears. She closed the binder and returned it to its original spot on the shelf. She performed a final inspection to be sure everything was as she had found it. Then she stood and rounded the desk.

Logan shrugged. "Sierra Pines doesn't have many violent deaths."

"Did you find out anything useful?" She indicated the open folder.

"I don't know. There's a lot here." He snapped it closed and offered it to her. "Apparently, Sheriff Trash performed a thorough investigation."

"Sheriff Trash?" She accepted the file folder. She stared at Logan, expecting another juvenile joke. Instead of humor, she found guilt.

"Uncle Mike is our local sheriff extraordinaire and also my mom's brother." Logan wore a harsh mask. His eyes in particular betrayed his misery even though his tone remained flippant.

"Does your Uncle Mike know about shifters?" She opened the folder and scanned the contents.

"Yeah, he's family."

"His initial notes indicate he believed it was murder," she said. "I don't understand how he could have concluded it was a bear attack. Unless..."

She looked up. The air around Logan vibrated, bottled rage without release, guilt without exoneration. "Could he have been involved in the cover up?"

Logan brooded in percolating silence, tension building in his muscular frame until she feared an eruption would demolish his control.

"Logan? What aren't you telling me?"

Bitterness edged his chuckle. He stood with his shoulders hunched forward, fists clenched. "Hell, yeah, Uncle Mike collaborated with dad. They did what was necessary to protect me and hide the truth."

It seemed too typical, a rich white kid who had a lawyer father and a police chief uncle getting away with murder. She bit her tongue to curb the sarcastic remark. She was not there to judge, but rather to investigate. Her invitation came directly from the spirit of one of the two victims.

"Why didn't you just ask your uncle for the file instead of breaking into the police station?" she asked.

"Uncle Mike hasn't said two words to me or dad since mom's funeral."

"Why'd he help cover it up then?"

Logan shook his head. "I don't know."

"Didn't you ask?"

"No." He made the flat reply and glared at her. She paid particular attention to what Logan said about the murder. If he were telling the truth, then his story would not change. The deeper she dug, the less sense things made.

"There's something hinky about this whole thing."

"My dad didn't kill my mom," Logan said but to Victoria he lacked the absolute conviction he'd demonstrated a few hours before. Doubt was an insidious thing.

"What about your uncle?"

Logan glanced at her, eyes widening in surprise. "No way. Uncle Mike and mom were tight. He's a good guy."

She made an audible exhalation, expressing her frustration. "Well, someone killed your mother, Logan, and it sure as hell wasn't a bear."

She held up the file folder and folded back the page to show a photo taken from the scene of the murder. "Those are wolf prints in the snow."

Those amber eyes focused on the photo and stared. Victoria watched him for any sign of reaction, but all she saw reflected was weary acknowledgement.

He cleared his throat. "These boxes are going to take more than a few hours to go through. Let's take them with us."

"Okay." Rifling the file, she found a snapshot of a man and studied it with a scowl, the man who had died along with Lori Koenig, her alleged lover. She didn't show Logan but tucked it into her back pocket. She returned the folder to the evidence box and turned off the desk lamp.

A thought occurred to her. "That cemetery we passed through on the way in? Is your mom buried there?"

"Yeah, we have a family plot."

"How about the man with her the night she was killed? Is Gregory Sanders buried there too?"

He thought for a second. "I think so. I remember 'cause there was a funeral conflict. We had to reschedule to Sunday."

"I want to stop in the cemetery on our way back," Victoria said. "And see if the ghost of Mr. Sanders has anything to say about his murder."

Logan stared at her in real surprise. "You can do that?"

"Yep." With any luck, the man's ghost would prove more helpful than Lori Koenig had. She figured he couldn't be any worse.

The silence of the moonless night penetrated to the bone. Victoria shivered and edged closer to Logan, seeking his companionship rather than his heat. No stranger to spiritual happenings, the dance of whorls moving at cyclonic speed through the graveyard exceeded her experience. The dead were out in droves. In startling contrast, a peaceful sleepiness hung over the snowy mundane world of men.

"Have you ever seen this before?" she asked, and touched his elbow, a gentle nudge to get him moving. He carried both of the stolen evidence boxes.

"Nope, gives new meaning to restless dead." He glanced down at where her hand clung to his elbow. His brow lifted.

Victoria tightened her grip. The wind blistered her face; a woman's frosty whisper filled her ears: *Don't trust him. Don't turn your back on him.*

Choking suspicion gripped her. Victoria released Logan's arm and scrambled backward, almost falling over a gravestone. Her sudden movement caused him to swing toward her. She brought up her arm and grabbed for her dagger. *Vanadium* appeared in her hand.

A startled snarl erupted from Logan. He dropped the boxes and lowered his head. His golden eyes glowed and highlighted his flashing fangs. He shifted into a defensive stance, not quite crouching, and his power crawled across his skin, creating bulges and ripples, muscles liquid with the start of transformation.

"Vic, what the fuck are you doing?" Logan roared a challenge. He stepped sideways, removing himself from easy striking range.

Kill him, the wind whispered. *Kill him before he kills you.*

It wrapped her in a lover's embrace, a cold fury, a blood frenzy. She succumbed without a whimper. She followed his retreat, intending to take his head, but a misstep led her to stumble.

Reckless Logan rushed forward and caught her before she fell. His arms held her steady. The near fall jarred her and knocked the sense back into her.

"What am I doing?" Victoria stared at him in distant horror and became aware of the feathery weight of her dagger in her hand. Horrified, she thrust the weapon upward, returning *Vanadium* to its sheath above her right shoulder.

Strength deserted her, bringing a wave of weakness, and her head hurt. She pushed Logan away and staggered toward the wrought-iron fence. She clung to the bars, sweating and panting, close to heaving the contents of her stomach. Tears streaked her cheeks.

Logan left her alone, standing some distance away in restless uncertainty. "Vic?"

"Do you hear it?" Even while she asked, the hypnotic whisper expired, leaving behind an eerie whistle as the gale moved through branches.

"Hear what?" Logan's brow furrowed.

She shoved the moment of insanity aside, too over-whelmed to deal with it. She turned from him, watching the spirits busy at their whirlwind waltz, bursts of mist and myth.

"They know something is going on," she said.

"Yeah, well. Who you gonna call?" The corner of Logan's mouth pulled down, indicating his displeasure.

"Do you ever stop cracking stupid jokes?"

He stared at her. "Beautiful and humorless. You must be the woman of my dreams."

"Shut up." Despite his best efforts, she perceived the tenuous nature of his self-control, so fragile, so like her own. He shared her mood—frayed nerves and ragged temper. How long would it be before they tried to kill each other again?

She turned away from him and spotted a directory near the entrance of the cemetery. Without a word, she strode to it and scanned the list of names until she located the correct grave plot. Logan trailed her at a safe distance to Gregory Sanders's final resting spot. A gray granite headstone marked the site.

Victoria stood on the plot. "No sign of our Mr. Sanders in residence. He's not in the grave."

"Huh." Logan's skepticism permeated the simple sound. "If his dominoes aren't here, then where do you reckon they are?"

"Dominoes?"

"Y'know, his bones."

"Oh." Victoria glared. "I wasn't referring to his phys-ical remains. I meant that his spirit isn't in residence within the grave."

Curiosity lit his expression. "How can you tell?"

"I have a sense for it. Here, come stand on the grave." Her shoulders rose and fell in a shrug. She stepped aside to make way.

Logan placed one foot, then the other, where she indicated. His expression humored her until the bland smile fell off his face. "It feels... empty."

"Exactly. Even when a person's soul has moved on, the body contains memories, a shadow of who the person used to be, called a shade. I'm going to summon the shade now and speak with it. You need to leave. Take the boxes back to your car and wait for me." She shooed Logan toward the fence and his vehicle, taking no care for diplomacy or hurt feelings. She needed him gone so she could concentrate.

"See, that's where you're wrong." The stubborn set of his jaw and squared shoulders made it clear he had no intention of leaving. "I have to stay."

Victoria marched toward him. Her hands hit his shoulders, shoving him, even though she failed to move him. "You haven't been cleared of murder, remember? Every summoning carries the risk of also calling the spirit back. The last thing I need is to summon a vengeful spirit that awakens to confront his killer."

Logan's eyes flinched. He fell back a stride. Cruelty proved an effective weapon, serving her purpose, because she did not have the time or the inclination to cater to his fragile ego. Later, she might apologize, maybe.

"Fine, whatever," he said. "I'll be at the car. Maybe I'll wait for you."

She issued a sigh of relief, and he stormed away.

"Stay there," she said, calling after him. "I'll come when I'm done."

Victoria stood at the foot of the plot and considered the snow-covered ground. A proper summoning ritual involved both song and dance, and she preferred to have an accompanying drummer. Without Paul to play for her, she would have to make do.

Victoria stripped her clothing and folded it into a neat pile beside the headstone. She loosened her hair from her ponytail and shook out the blonde tresses. Naked amid the trees and gravestones, beneath the moonless starry sky, she lifted her arms in a graceful salute to the night.

Her dance started with controlled motions, tight and precise, the discovery of tempo and position. She created a rhythm in her throat, swayed to that beat, gyrating raised hands and arms, undulating hips, feet pounding out the steps. Her heartbeat drove the pace, faster and faster, building to an energetic crescendo. The dance became the all of things, obliterating her sense of time and self, defining her entire existence. She danced, oh how she danced upon the dead man's grave.

Victoria threw back her head and allowed her voice to ascend, emitting a howl to fill the night with her wolf's song. The music swelled from her soul. Many restless spirits swirled about her in frenzy, attracted by the summoning ritual. She ignored them and sang on, her pain and her loss, the death of her parents and pack. The faces of everyone she'd loved and lost filled her mind, imbuing the magic with tragedy.

Alone, I am so very alone, she sang. The memory of Sophia's pup, the lifeless furry body wrapped within the blanket, broke her heart. Her entire body trembled with the depth of her hurt. Tears streaked her cheeks and her heart ached.

The spirits sensed her weakness and swarmed her, grasping at her hair and arms with wispy hands. They were wretch-ed creatures, stranded on earth without substance or form, desperate to steal her life force, her power, in order to feel alive if only for a second. They formed a cacophony of howls and moans, individual voices drowned out beneath the needful din.

Out of nowhere, a second voice joined hers, deep and masculine, his howl speaking of his own loss and suffering. Shocked, Victoria stumbled and lost the rhythm of her dance, creating a hiccup in the music.

More spirits rushed at her.

Logan picked up the verse, and he carried the song. His magic commanded the crazed spirits, strong and authoritative, dominating them into submission. The ghosts cowed and shrank from her, withdrawing their insubstantial hands.

Ever more distant, a chorus began, and the voices of her pack gave their support across the miles. Steadfast Sylvie spoke of hope and love; Paul, of courage and honor; Morena and Sophia added their strength and blended their voices to reinforce the message of the Beta wolves. She lived for them, her beloved pack.

Victoria recovered the steps to the dance. Her howl soared, challenging Logan for the dominant role, and their voices vied in a discordant contest for control. Sparring, they moved up and down the vocal range, confusing the pack's chorus while they strived to follow. It was a mad pell-mell tumble, creating chaos within her magic.

Stop! I will kill you! Victoria roared her anger into the music. Furious, she turned in Logan's direction and found him a hundred yards away on the far side of the fence. He took one look at her expression, dissolved into laughter, and his voice fell out of the chorus. Satisfied, Victoria resumed control of the song.

My Lady of the Vanir, grant your power unto me, Victoria entreated, weaving her plea into the music. In another land, her distant hall, Freya heard the appeal of her Valkyrie and answered. Victoria experienced divinity while the essence of the goddess moved through her. Power shimmered upon her skin, focused in her hands, glowed brilliant and bright.

Gregory Sanders, come to me! I command you! Her howl ascended to the top of her range and dominated the night. Victoria fell to her knees atop the grave and plunged her arms up to the elbows into the snow. She dug deeper, groping the frozen soil, encountering rocks, dirt, and decaying bits of dead things. Finally, she found the shade she sought.

With a shout and a lunge, Victoria ripped her arms free and dragged the summoned shade of Gregory Sanders from his grave. The skeleton formed and then flesh coalesced on the bones. His face came last, round and heavyset with flabby jowls and beady eyes. He hung in the air like a black and white still image, flesh lacking color and muscles slack without expression. A few wisps of hair capped his otherwise bald skull. His rounded gut indicated a sedentary life with too many beers. His legs turned to mist below the knee.

"I have summoned you and I command you." The contest of willpower would come once the shade realized his predicament.

"Command me? How?" His mouth opened and fat worms poured forth. The ravenous larva swarmed the ground about her bare feet, wriggling cold and slimy against her toes.

Her gorge rose, and she fought to keep the contents of her stomach down. She tasted digested pizza and bile. Turning her head to the side, she spat to empty her mouth and clear her throat to get chunks from her nasal passage, and then she spat again.

The shade laughed, a wicked cackle.

"Name your killer, Gregory Sanders."

"My killer?" He regurgitated more of the larva.

"You will stop that now." Victoria shook with rage. She strived for control. To rend the shade to shreds would defeat her purpose. "No more tricks, Sanders. Name your killer."

Gregory grinned, demented and delighted. "My killer is the Trickster."

"His name!" Victoria applied her power in conjunction with the command. The shade's resistance perplexed her. Her strength should have been that much greater.

"My killer is a shapechanger!" He crackled with defiance. A maniacal giggle caused the thing to shiver and shake. His mouth fell open and a single long worm slithered forth.

She summoned her most potent magic and asserted her will upon the dead thing. The shade vibrated, losing coherency, but was unable to leave because she had not yet released it. "Why are you protecting your killer? Name him! I command you!"

"My killer serves Loki, the son of Faribault and Laufey, the father of Fenrir, Jörmungandr and Hel! *Larð skal rifna ok upphiminn!*"

"Were you Lori Koenig's lover?"

The switch in tactics took it off-guard. The shade replied without thought, "No."

They stared at one another, duelists faced off on the field of combat. The shade broke first. "Why?"

Victoria smirked, showing her teeth. "You're fat, ugly and old, whereas Arik Koenig is a virile, handsome man. It is impossible she would have chosen you over him."

"You bitch!" Rage suffused the shade, bringing ruddy tones to the colorless face. He offered a ferocious resistance, attempting to escape her control, hands reaching for her throat.

Victoria tilted back her head and laughed in his face. Her mockery fed the shade's rage. His human façade failed; a twisted and hideous thing writhed in the air. It defied description, an amorous mass, huge in size and immense in power.

A wraith.

"Your mask is removed! I see you for what you really are! Gregory Sanders was your puppet! Wraith, name your killer!"

"I will be your killer!" Hideous laughter surrounded her. Dark tendrils battered her, striking on all sides. Pain blossomed along her every nerve, and she felt fear.

"In the name of Freya, Lady of the Vanir, be gone!"

The fiendish wraith opened its mouth. Gravity shifted toward that gaping maw, huge and impenetrable, the essence of hunger. The airflow shifted toward the hole, sucking up snowflakes and debris and soon, her.

The darkness rushed straight at her. She did not retreat. She faced the trial head on. She would die as a warrior, and there could be no more glorious death. Logan's distant shout echoed through the night, and then he roared a challenge. She could not see him, but she knew he would not arrive in time.

She saw then that the wraith's mouth did not open to nothingness. It was a portal to hell.

Victoria screamed her defiance. Hands raised, she sent a white-blue starburst into the maw while it engulfed her, closing on all sides. Her pain eclipsed everything, and she fell into blackness.

CHAPTER NINE

Something fishy —
  "Goddess, how many small-town librarians require an at-torney to manage their finances?"
  "Victoria, is this a light bulb question?"

"Damn it, Vic. Don't die on me. Please, God, let her be okay." Big hands ran across her body, lifted her so she dangled, and shook her like a ragdoll. Logan's voice penetrated her slumber, urgent and demanding. In-sistent fingers sought and found her pulse. "Thank you, God, Goddess, whoever. Thank you."

Logan crushed her chest, maybe seeking to finish what the wraith had failed to accomplish. His arms en-circled her, hands against her back. He groped her ass, and she decided he probably didn't intend to kill her af-ter all.

Cold, so fucking cold.

Her awareness set her teeth chattering. She shook from head to toe. Every muscle screamed with pain. It even hurt to breathe. She pried one eye open in order to confirm what touch and smell had already told her.

"I'm still alive."

"I don't know how." From his expression, Logan shared her astonishment. His wandering hands contin-ued to caress her body.

She glared at him. Her shivers persisted, so strong that her bones ached. "Stop that."

Logan chuckled, but his hands stilled. "You're ice cold, Vic."

"Tell me about it. The wraith," she said, turning to the urgent matter. "What happened to it?"

Logan cocked his head; his black pupils eclipsed the amber irises of his eyes. "It ran."

"Because of me or because of you?" Her teeth knocked together, reminding her of an old-style manual typewriter.

Logan shrugged. "Dunno. At the risk of you biting my head off—" He clutched her against his chest. His heat warmed her until her violent trembling subsided. She had no idea how much time passed but the alarmed howls of her pack reached her across the miles. She lacked the energy to answer.

The more time that passed, the worse it got. The pack's fear and despair reached her through their bond, motivating her when nothing else succeeded. She stirred and lifted her head from the pillow of Logan's pectoral.

"Answer them," she said in a raspy voice.

Logan tilted back his head, exposing the strong column of his throat. He released a short howl, telling the others to wait. It wasn't ideal, but the pack ceased their incessant wailing. She heaved a sigh of relief.

Logan started to stand, cradling her in his arms. She stirred again, craning her head to the side. He grunted in annoyance. "Will you stop struggling?"

"I need my clothes."

Logan huffed, but he bent, and through acrobatic maneuvering, he managed to snag her clothing and shoes from the ground. He thrust the bundle against her chest. "Here."

Her arms closed around the stuff. "Thanks."

The corner of his mouth curled into a smirk. "Don't thank me. I like you better without them on."

She resumed struggling. "Put me down. I want to get dressed."

He ignored her and set out at a brisk clip for the car. "Dress in the car."

She hit his chest with her knuckles. "Damn it, Logan."

"You're too weak to walk, Vic. Don't embarrass yourself by insisting."

"I'm going to kill you," she fumed but subsided. *Damn his insufferable smugness. Double damn him for being right.*

"Yeah, promises, promises." He hefted her, altering the carry hold so he took most of her weight over his right shoulder.

Victoria released an indignant squawk.

Logan reached the fence and took a running start. He swarmed the barricade, using one hand to grab the bars, the other to secure his hold on her. In the space of two seconds, they cleared the top. Logan landed square on both feet on the other side. He slung her back to a cradle carry. Victoria glared at him but held her tongue.

Logan placed her in the passenger side seat of his vehicle. "Wait here. I'm going back for the files."

"Right. Don't forget our stolen evidence." She used the opportunity to shimmy into her clothing for the second time that evening. By the time he returned, she was dressed. She settled into the seat, arms folded, and nursed her wounds.

Logan put the files into the back and rounded the SUV. He climbed into the driver's seat and waited until she pulled on her seatbelt before he started the engine. Considering his promise to lend her his car, he sure seemed to be doing a lot of the driving, not that she was in any condition to drive herself anyway.

The trip back to her motel passed in absolute silence. She appreciated his ability to hold his tongue. At the same time, his restraint astonished her because words were his weapons and armor. When they were closer to The Fireside Inn, Logan's tension increased, the scent of unease and anger flooded her nostrils. He set her more on edge with each passing second, and she had no idea why.

The SUV pulled into the parking lot before he finally broke the silence. "I'm going to help you inside."

His combative tone startled her. "Okay..."

They climbed from the vehicle at the same time. As soon as her feet hit the ground, a wave of dizziness swept Victoria. She blinked and looked up to find Logan hovering over her.

What the fuck is his problem? She swayed, trying to organize her exhausted thoughts, when her pack charged into the parking lot.

Logan assumed a fighter's stance—hands prepared, feet spread—and looked her straight in the eyes. His jaw set with stubborn determination. Then he turned to confront the pack.

Morena arrived first, transformed to a wolf, slinking with her head and tail low. A threatening rumble issued from her throat, and she advanced to Victoria's left, flanking Logan.

Paul and Sylvie, both human, followed a moment later. Paul's good hand formed a claw; his mate brandished a dagger. The pair of Beta wolves bracketed Victoria on either side and formed a solid united front against their enemy.

"You were warned to stay away," Paul said.

"I don't listen so well." Logan's power spilled forth and his skin rippled as he initiated the change. The white bled out of his eyes, leaving solid amber irises. Wolf eyes.

"Stop." Victoria slammed the order down and backed it up with all of the power she possessed. As their Alpha, she asserted her willpower as the pack's most dominant wolf through their shared connection.

The drastic action had its intended effect: her pack froze.

Logan remained free of her command, but he yielded and remained human.

She took a steady step toward Logan. She traded a loaded look with him, and then placed her back to him. The deliberate gesture carried implicit meaning. She addressed him and her pack. "This is my fault. I leapt to unfair conclusions; I made accusations grounded in fear. He is not a threat to the pups. I was wrong. I owe Logan an apology."

The wet sound of breath inhaled through clenched teeth betrayed Logan's surprise. Victoria turned to him. "I'm sorry."

He accepted the apology with a sharp nod. "Thank you."

Victoria released her hold upon the pack. Morena made an immediate retreat; Paul stood his ground. Sylvie leapt forward just in time to catch her Alpha as Victoria toppled over, the last of her strength exhausted.

"Wait," Victoria said before Sylvie dragged her inside. With the other woman's help, she turned back to Logan. "You owe me something."

He stared and then smiled. He dug out his car keys and tossed the ring to her. She caught them but only because he used an underhanded throw.

"Vic?"

"What?"

"Can someone give me a ride home?"

Paul grumbled something about crazy people beneath his breath. "I'll take him."

Words impinged upon her consciousness, scolding with passion, but evoking feelings of love and belonging. Victoria lifted her eyelids just enough to see a sliver of light. With a reluctant smile, she edged further toward wakefulness, surrendering the seductive embrace of slumber.

Sylvie's mothering hand stroked her forehead. "Victory, you scared us to death. Thank the Goddess you're safe. I don't know what craziness you've gotten yourself wrapped up in with that fine young fox, but mark my words, no good will come of it..."

Familiar bodies pressed about her on all sides, keeping her warm and safe. She knew the scent of each member of her pack, her family, as well as her own. She listened and the even rhythm of hearts and breaths told her that everyone slept except Sylvie.

Victoria occupied a crowded double bed. Beneath the covers, she wore nothing and Sylvie's thigh served as her pillow. The rest of the pack lay in a dog pile atop the comforter. Paul slept on his stomach with one arm dangling off the edge of the mattress. Morena curled in a tight ball, her nose buried beneath her gray and white tail. Sophia slept across her legs, and the three cubs pressed against their mother's side. Still sleepy, she stifled a yawn and her restless movement attracted Sylvie's attention.

Sylvie's hand stilled and then slid from Victoria's forehead. She scooted to the side of the bed and stood. "How are you feeling, sweetie?"

"Better. Starving." Victoria squirmed out from under the covers, doing her best not to disturb the others, but Sophia stirred and lifted her head. Victoria sent a pulse of reassurance through the pack's connection, and the gray wolf lowered her head and went back to sleep.

She took a shaky step and discovered the summoning spell had left her weaker than she had hoped. Her body bore no outward sign of injury, but her muscles ached from head to toe. Her limbs felt leaden and the constant gnawing of her stomach testified to the amount of energy she'd expended.

Victoria pulled on her clothing and then she and

Sylvie slipped from the room. In wordless agreement, they made their way to the kitchen and sat at the small round table in the dining nook. The chairs were scratched and rickety. Victoria's creaked when she shifted her weight.

"The pack is exhausted," Victoria said, settling with a slight groan at the cramps in her back and legs.

"Hardly a wonder. That song last night was intense. One of the most draining I've ever experienced. What were you trying to do, raise the dead?" Sylvie asked.

"It sure felt that way." Victoria summoned an edgy smile that never reached her eyes. "Thank you. For the help last night. Without the pack, I'd have been lost."

"Aw, sweetie, without you, we'd be lost." Sylvie leaned over and gathered her into a fast hug.

Blinking back tears, Victoria wrapped her arms around her Beta wolf and counted her blessings. Her time spent with Logan had shown her what an abysmal existence life could be, and she would not soon forget. No matter how bad things got, the members of her pack always had each other. When they awakened, she intended to make sure each knew of her gratitude and the value of their contribution.

"Now that's enough of that. Stop crying." Sylvie waved a scolding finger and sat back. "We're like old women, all of this yammering and sobbing."

Victoria laughed and used the side of her hand to clear the tears from her cheeks. "Bite your tongue."

"Consider it bit."

Still chuckling, Victoria glanced around in a vain attempt to find a clock. The sunlight filtering in through the front window told her it was mid-morning. "What time is it? My cellphone is dead."

"Just after ten." Sylvie studied Victoria with an insinuating gleam in her hazel eyes. "What happened to your phone, Victory? For that matter, what happened to the Golf?"

"They got wet." She frowned, hoping to discourage further inquiry even though she knew it to be a foolish endeavor.

"That sounds like one heck of a story."

"Nope, no stories. The Golf has gone to a watery grave at the bottom of Echo Lake and that's all I have to say about it."

"Humph." Sylvie flashed a knowing smile. "How did your lunch with Arik go?"

"Well," Victoria said, "we've agreed he should meet the pack."

Sylvie stared at her. "Victory, why are you frowning? Doesn't he please you?"

"Oh, he pleases me well enough. He's fit and handsome."

"What's wrong then?"

Victoria linked her hands, resisting the desire to wring them. She waged a brief but fierce internal debate. She hesitated to share her doubts, incendiary in nature and lacking proof. Ultimately, Sylvie functioned as her confidant and advisor, and leaving her in the dark would be unwise.

Victoria exhaled and ran her hands through her hair. "Goddess, Sylvie, what's not wrong? I've gotten involved in a hopeless mess, and I don't know how to get out."

Talking fast, Victoria confessed everything to her second, the murder of Arik's wife and his twisted relationship with his son. She talked about Lori Koenig's ghost and the debt she'd incurred to reveal the dead woman's killer. She ran on for a time about Logan's aggravating stupidity. Sylvie listened in silence, offered the encouraging nod and the requisite "hmm", but otherwise allowed Victoria's explanation to run its course before she spoke.

Sylvie regarded her with open shock. "What will Arik say when he finds out you're investigating the murder of his mate without his knowledge or consent?"

Victoria sighed. "It's not that simple. I have to be one-hundred percent certain Arik didn't murder his mate and frame his son, and then use the guilt to subjugate Logan for two years."

Sylvie's jaw dropped. A tremor passed through the Beta wolf. She leaned against the counter for support. "Such a thing would not even have occurred to me."

"I know. I hate the fact that it occurs to me, but I have a duty to the pack. If Arik becomes my mate and our Alpha, we're committed to an ironclad rule. He's too powerful for it to be any other way."

"It doesn't have to be that way. Your father was very dominant, but he was always fair and kind."

"The difference being Dad wasn't a stranger," Victoria said. "We loved and trusted him. I know nothing about Arik other than what he's told me, and that hasn't been much."

Sylvie nodded and returned to cooking. She poured Victoria a glass of milk, but she didn't speak again until she set two plates on the table. She took the chair across from her Alpha.

"What of Logan?"

Victoria grabbed her fork and dug in. "What of him?"

"You don't think he's capable of having murdered his mother," Sylvie said with a sage nod.

Victoria stopped mid-bite, the fork frozen on its way to her mouth. "I don't?"

Sylvie bestowed a long stare. "You apologized to that boy in front of the entire pack and declared him a non-threat to the pups. If that's not a declaration of trust, I don't know what is."

Victoria flushed. "That doesn't mean I think he's innocent. It means I don't believe he's dangerous..."

"Mmmhmm. I see the subtle distinction."

Damn, Sylvie knows just how to employ the sharp edge of

sarcasm. Victoria bit her lower lip and said nothing. She resumed eating.

"Do you believe that Arik Koenig murdered his mate?" Sylvie continued her inquisition.

"Why does everyone keep asking me that? It doesn't matter what I believe. The truth is in the evidence."

Sylvie's expression rebuked her. "Others might buy that BS from you, but don't you lie to me, Victoria Svana Storm."

Victoria cringed and held up a defensive hand. "Don't use my middle name! Anything but that!"

With her trademark stubbornness, Sylvie refused to succumb to distraction. "What does your heart tell you?"

Victoria glanced heavenward. "Fine, I don't believe Arik murdered his mate and framed his son. Not in my head or my heart, but something still doesn't add up. There are too many inconsistencies."

Sylvie reached to clear the empty plates. "Good, then you must do whatever's necessary to satisfy your conscience, as long as it's the right thing for the right reasons."

Victoria nodded, grateful for her Beta's approval. She had other concerns but hesitated to ask. Some things were too dangerous to voice aloud.

Sylvie arched her brow. "Go on, spit it out."

Expression grim, Victoria plunged ahead. "Sylvie, you're trained in the bard tradition. If I repeated something from one of the old languages, could you translate it for me?"

Sylvie put her hands on her hips. "No promises, but I can try. There's a lot more I don't know than what I do, but I can do my best. What do you need?"

Victoria licked her lips and then did her best to repeat the phrase Gregory Sanders's wraith had screamed. *"Larð skal rifna ok upphiminn.* Do you know what it means?"

Sylvie blinked and cocked her head. She remained

silent, lost in thought for a time. Victoria left her to think. She used the opportunity to wash and rinse the dirty dishes. She stacked the clean ones beside the sink for drying.

"It's from the *Sonatorrek*," Sylvie said. "A rough translation is: *The Earth shall be rent and the heavens above.* The reference is *Ragnarök*, the end of the world. Why do you ask?"

Victoria's face remained clear of expression. She managed a neutral smile. "No reason."

"Mmmhmm." Sylvie regarded her with that knowing look again, but Victoria had run out of explanations.

"I'm going to grab a shower and go into town. This has the makings of a big day."

"Yes," Sylvia agreed. "Especially if we're to meet Arik Koenig."

"Yes, that's correct. We'll see you Thursday. Good-bye." Margaret Duane hung up the phone and turned back to her computer. The dark-haired secretary returned to work, oblivious to her watcher.

Standing outside the polished glass door to Arik's office, Victoria flexed her fingers but didn't reach for the handle. One, she didn't have an appointment. Two, it was his place of business. Three, she was underdressed, wearing only a tee shirt and blue jeans. Four, she needed to see him.

A nimble figure stepped in front of her, blocking her view of the secretary. Astonished, she tilted her head back and stared up into Arik Koenig's forceful eyes. He held his head high, a regal beast wearing a man's skin, a king in every sense of the word.

His mouth formed a silent "hi".

Victoria raised one hand and mouthed the greeting in return. The sight of him forced accusations and confessions from her mind and left her mouth watering for the taste of him.

He tilted his head to the side and used his brow to invite her inside. A grin curved her lips, and she pushed the door open. Hesitation was not part of her character. Neither was cowardice or silliness.

She reached for his hands and pulled him to her. The feather soft caress of his lips against hers created a shiver of delight in her loins. She licked his lower lip and nipped at the tasty tidbit. The scent of his arousal teased her even as he withdrew and released her hands.

"I wasn't expecting you," he said. "I thought we were getting together tonight."

"I'm sorry. I know I don't have an appointment."

"Don't apologize. It's always a pleasure to see you. Come inside."

Victoria nodded her agreement. At her back, she felt Margaret glaring poison-tipped daggers. The secretary didn't bother to hide her jealousy or her hostility until Arik turned to her. Then, she flushed and scrambled to recover.

"Margaret, hold my calls."

"Yes, Mr. Koenig."

Victoria laid a hand on Arik's elbow to halt him. He stopped and glanced at her with curiosity. With deliberation, Victoria turned her head and captured Margaret's gaze. She touched her voice with power. "He is mine."

Margaret turned a boiled lobster shade of red and cowed in her seat. The secretary dropped her eyes, acceding dominance. Satisfied, Victoria dipped her chin.

Arik chuckled and shut the office door behind them, preventing his secretary from eavesdropping. "I apologize. Margaret is very protective of me."

"Of course." She mustered a neutral smile. Without a doubt, Margaret coveted Arik for herself. Any healthy heterosexual female would want him. The man oozed primal charisma.

Arik remained standing so Victoria did also. She put her back against the door, adopting a defensive posture. She regretted the choice, but done was done. Altering her stance would have given too much away.

Victoria exhaled a stream of breath. "We need to talk."

He waited, but she did not speak. Seconds ticked past. Arik noticed her tension. He grew alert and ready. "Victoria?"

His prompt jarred her into action. "I assume you heard the howling last night?"

Arik scowled. "Everyone heard the howling last night. You were too close to populated areas. There's an article in the paper this morning, speculating that wolves have spread to the area. We'll be lucky if we're not inundated with hunters before the week is out."

Victoria blanched and her heart stopped beating in her chest. Her hands opened, fingers spread wide and flexed outward. "Oh, Goddess! I'm so sorry, I didn't think of that!"

After a moment, the harshness left his expression. He stepped toward her and laid a reassuring hand on her arm. His power held authority; his confidence filled her. "If the hunters come, then we'll deal with them. Desolation Wilderness is a protected wilderness area. If the hunters aren't careful, the place will be crawling with conservationists."

"That would be something to see." Victoria mustered a tentative smile. His rock-solid confidence reassured her. She craved him and the protection he offered. It would have been so easy to yield to his magnetism and accept his words with complete faith, but she did not feel it.

Succumbing to temptation, Victoria leaned against Arik and wrapped her arms about his waist. The attraction sizzled between them, and her wolf desired him with painful intensity. She turned her face into the side of his throat and nipped at the spot just below his ear, not breaking skin but hard enough to leave a mark.

His power moved across his skin and surged into her. His wolf's aura penetrated deep in an act of erotic foreplay. A rumble emerged from his chest, lower and lustier than a growl, intensified within his throat. She bit his earlobe and suckled; his lips found her throat and his teeth nibbled at her skin.

Victoria opened her mouth and released Arik's ear. She rocked back on her heels; her hands clutched his arms for support. Her diminutive size left her at a disadvantage when dealing with such a large male, but she knew how to improvise. She seized the length of his tie and used it to draw him down to her. He came without a fuss, his hands sliding across her back.

His lips were smooth and firm, his teeth slick and hard, his tongue wet and supple. He tasted like a feast within the center of famine. Shapechanger body temperatures ran hotter than human, so together they generated a ton of heat.

Victoria broke the kiss to gulp air. "I really should say what I came here to say."

"So say it." Arik kissed her again.

Victoria slid her arms around his neck and threaded her fingers with his hair, enjoying the silken thickness.

"You're like a mink," she said when they came up for air again.

Arik grunted to convey his offense. He straightened, and her feet left the ground, so that she clung to him for support. He nuzzled her neck. "I must disagree. I'm much more agreeable in temperament than a mink."

Victoria laughed and threw back her head, allowing him unimpeded access to her throat. "I meant your hair, lover."

Arik drew back. He looked her in the eyes in a way that had nothing to do with dominance, everything with seduction. "I'm not. Not yet. But I will be."

The implicit promise, threat, enormity of his words left her with no option other than to hold firm to her convictions. She released her grip on his neck and slid down his body. She landed on her feet. "I came here to talk."

"Then talk."

"I have no idea how to say this," she said in a rush. "Even in my head, it sounds crazy. So I'm going to go ahead and blurt it out. Something in Sierra Pines is dreadfully wrong..."

Arik's dark brow jumped. "What do you mean?"

Her hands clenched to fists, so hard her nails bit into her palms. "That's the trouble... I don't know exactly. It's just a feeling, but I sense something, *someone*, watching me. Everywhere I go there are these ravens, and I hear a voice—*a woman's voice*—whispering on the wind."

"You're right; that's awfully vague," Arik said.

She felt his skepticism, a palpable force that erected barriers between them. In frustration, Victoria snarled low in her throat, unable to put her deepest instincts into words without sounding crazy. If Arik had been a member of her pack, he would have heeded her warning without hesitation, but the foundation of trust between them was so fragile.

"Victoria, I don't want to insult you but you have to realize how this sounds," Arik said.

The phone on Arik's desk buzzed, indicating an interoffice call, and interrupted them. His expression conveyed annoyance. He hesitated when the phone rang again. "It must be important or Margaret wouldn't interrupt, not after I instructed her to hold my calls."

Like hell she wouldn't...

Victoria mustered a smile. "Go ahead. I can wait."

Arik pushed the intercom button. "Yes?"

"Mr. Koenig, I know you said no interruptions, but Delores Sanders is here to see you. I've explained you're in a meeting, but she insists it's an urgent matter."

Arik's silence communicated his displeasure. The intercom crackled. Although his expression remained impassive, Victoria sensed his inner debate. She sighed when she realized her opportunity to confess had slipped away. She'd let herself get sidetracked into an unrelated tangent about paranoid suspicions and missed the opportunity to tell him about her escapades with Logan.

"Mr. Koenig?" Margaret said.

Arik exhaled so his nostrils flared. He cleared his throat. "Yes, please send her right in, Margaret."

"Yes, sir."

Arik hit the button to turn off the intercom. With an apologetic expression, he rounded his desk. "I'm sorry. I feel obligated to speak with her. Can we talk later?"

Victoria's stomach dropped. *The librarian.*

"Delores Sanders... You do know who she is, don't you?" Victoria asked, a scowl on her face.

"She's the widow of the man who was murdered alongside my wife. Ironically enough, I handle her financial matters," Arik said, stone-faced and severe in tone.

"Oh," was all she said. However, her suspicions were aroused, and Victoria's brow furrowed.

Why would he continue a professional or personal relationship with that woman after what had happened?

"What is it?" Arik asked.

A perfunctory knock on the office door interrupted them. Arik opened it to admit his visitor. "Mrs. Sanders, what brings you by?"

Arik stepped aside to admit a flinty-eyed, steel-haired woman in her fifties wearing a charcoal suit with a pencil skirt. The wearer lacked the legs necessary to boost it into an attractive ensemble.

Victoria squared her shoulders and stared the older woman straight in the eyes. She refused to flinch or drop her gaze before a human, and the inexplicable desire to slink past the librarian was not acceptable.

"I have urgent business to discuss with you, Mr. Koenig," Delores Sanders said in her diamond-hard voice.

Her gaze settled on Victoria; cruel amusement glinted in those black eyes.

"Why, Victoria Storm." She flashed a shark's smile. "Imagine running into you again so soon, and at my attorney's office, of all places. Are you conducting more... research?"

"Extensive. Research." Victoria showed her teeth, an *I-eat-sharks-for-lunch* sneer. The viciousness of her reply drew a sharp glance from Arik.

"Mr. Koenig, thank you so much for your time." Victoria reached out and grabbed Arik's lapel. With a sharp tug, she pulled him down to her level and claimed his mouth in a hard kiss.

"I'll see you later?" Arik asked when the kiss broke. At a glance, the unflappable attorney appeared serene, but his hot and bothered gaze lingered on her.

"Tonight." Victoria nodded.

They had plans for dinner.

Victoria strode past Delores and encountered Margaret in the lobby. From her vantage, the secretary would have witnessed all that happened within. Margaret's expression bordered on shock and contained a lethal dose of disapproval and disgust.

Victoria ignored the secretary and walked on. She did not stop until she reached the parking lot, and a suspicious thing occurred to her.

That's it!

Her clear blue gaze lit with realization and she snapped her fingers. "I never told that witch my last name."

CHAPTER TEN

POW—

"Miss Morie took him down."
"Indeed she did, My Lady."

The meet and greet of her pack with Arik took place at his home. They gathered on the back patio, and he once again rolled back the pool cover. She could not fault his hospitality. The man knew how to put together a lavish spread. Victoria had not seen the likes of it since her parents' twentieth wedding anniversary.

"Victory, you should try the meatballs. They're delicious. They're venison." Morena held up a plate of appetizers for her inspection. The Omega wolf's overeager offering resulted from nervousness. It disturbed Morie to be eating when her leader was not.

There were times when wolf and human social dynamics clashed in ways that left Victoria with a world-class headache. "Morena, thank you, but—"

"*Victory?* Is that your nickname?" Smirking, Logan appeared beside Morena, speaking with a tongue-in-cheek smugness that made her palms itch. "If you don't want those, I'll take them."

Logan reached for the plate of meatballs. Victoria knocked aside his hand. "Those are mine."

"The caterers brought enough for everyone!" More-

na scrambled to get out of the way while the two dominant wolves squared off. She sidled to the right and
retreated toward the pool.

"Yeah, well I don't see your name on 'em." Logan
stalked forward, his stance assertive and aggressive. He
didn't spare the meatballs as much as a glance.

At last! Victoria leapt with excitement at the conflict.
Logan had denied her a dominance showdown long
enough to make her reckless in her enthusiasm to put
him in his place for the last time.

"You don't call me Victory, not unless you plan to
die." Her gaze locked with Logan's, steel-eyed and determined. Stiff-legged, she advanced on him, eager for a
fight.

"Guys, please, they're only meatballs! I can get
more!" Morena dropped the contested plate on a bistro
table and shot off in the direction of the banquet.

"Why can't I call you Victory... Victory?" Logan did
not press forward or retreat. He stood his ground, back
to the pool, faced off against her. His wolf rose, a seductive shadow, darkness challenging her brightness.

Ten feet away, activity came to an abrupt halt. Arik,
Paul and Sylvie ceased their discussion of music to
watch the unfolding drama. Sophia, her pups at her feet,
made an uncertain but curious exploration of the snow.
It was the cubs' first outing.

"What's going on?" Paul turned an interested stare
toward Logan and Victoria.

"Haven't those two established rank yet?" Sylvie
sounded astonished and amused.

"Not yet," Arik said. "It's still under negotiation."

Victoria ignored them. Her unblinking stare cen-
tered on Logan alone. "People who matter may call me
Victory. You do not."

"Oh, that stings." Logan blew on his pinky finger
and waved it under her nose. Victoria snarled and
reached for his throat.

"Make way, coming through! Meatball express!" Carrying three plates stacked atop one another, Morena sprinted toward the two dominant wolves. A second too late, the Omega wolf applied the brakes and went into a skid. Out of control, she yelped her surprise.

Victoria registered Morena's entrance right before the Omega wolf careened straight into Logan and knocked him off balance. His face bore a look of blank surprise, and he stumbled toward the pool's edge.

"No!" Victoria grabbed for Morena but it was too late. Eye contact was broken; dominance remained unresolved. Morena, Logan, and three plates of venison meatballs crashed into the deep end of the pool.

"Argh!" Victoria wrung her hands around an imaginary throat and then heaved a sigh when Morena's dark head surfaced. Reaching out, Victoria caught hold of her Omega's hand and dragged her dripping companion out of the pool.

Logan also broke the surface, coming up in the center of the deep end. The meatballs sank toward the bottom. He spit out a mouthful of water and flashed a grin. "This is starting to feel familiar."

A growl rumbled her throat. "I'm going to kill you."

On cue, Morena wailed and burst into theatrical tears. "Victory, I'm so, so sorry! Please, please don't kill me! I'll clean the mess up!"

The Omega wolf dropped to her knees and wrapped her arms around Victoria's legs, shackling her leader. The groveling grew more dramatic. "Please don't kill me! Give me another chance! I can do better!"

Helpless, Victoria glowered at Logan as he swam to the edge and pulled himself out of the water. About that time, Sylvie swooped in and pried Morena free from her legs.

"Hush now, silly." Sylvie wrapped her arm around Morena's shoulders. "Victoria doesn't mean you. Now come inside, and I'll help you get dried off."

Sylvie's voice faded while they strolled away, but Victoria heard the older woman murmur words of praise. "Miss Morie, you did real good..."

In the blink of an eye, Morena dropped the theatrics and peered over her shoulder. She watched to be certain Logan and Victoria were not at one another again. The Omega's expression was intent and intelligent.

Scowling, Victoria caught Morena's gaze and held it. The Omega wolf grinned and dropped her eyes, leaving her leader with no other recourse. She could not take measures against a submissive wolf.

"She's only doing her job," Paul said.

Victoria exhaled and waved her hand. "I know, I know."

"Logan, fetch some towels and the pool net," Arik said. "Then go get cleaned up."

"Aye aye, Cap-e-tain." Logan shot his father a mocking salute, then obeyed but without alacrity. Dripping, he disappeared around the side of the house and returned with a net.

"I'll go give Logan a hand." Chuckling to himself, Paul joined Arik's son beside the pool.

"Are you okay?" Arik came up beside Victoria and spoke in a voice pitched for her ears alone. His fingertips caressed her shoulders with the precision of a pianist to a keyboard, drawing forth a note ringing with tension. His touch soothed her wolf.

"Not really, but I'll endure. I've survived far worse." Victoria offered him a lopsided smile. All things given, the formal introductions had gone rather well, regardless of the mischief and mayhem, and meatballs in the pool. "I'm glad you sent the caterers away."

Arik chuckled, a dark velvety laugh that caused her every nerve ending to prickle. "I figured something was bound to happen but not that. Logan has never had the benefit of a pack. He doesn't understand the social dynamics."

Victoria exhaled and studied the man beside her. She longed to nip at his neck or run her hands along those muscular arms. "My pack is so small. It's so difficult to explain this is all that remains of what was once a great pack."

"I do understand." His tone resonated with an odd quality, and Victoria cast him a quick glance.

"You know, I believe you do." Her intuition told her that he had experienced a similar loss at some point in his tragic past, something in addition to his wife's death.

"Better than you might think," he said in a tone that filled her with foreboding.

"Thank you."

Surprise flittered across his face. "For what?"

"For granting us sanctuary, for the gift... for everything. You've been more than generous." Her gesture encompassed a vague area around her, indicating all and nothing.

"You're welcome." Arik slid his arm around her shoulders and tucked her close to his body with a familiarity so very right. Gazes locked, blue and brown, communication couched in empathy, devoid of dominance.

"Do you want to tell me about it?" she asked.

He hesitated and then nodded. "I grew up in Ironwood, a suburb of Reno. My parents were Alphas. We were a small pack but prosperous. Lori and I forged our mate bond in high school, and Logan was born our senior year. I attended grad school, and Lori stayed home with our son. Eventually, I assumed leadership of our pack when my parents chose to retire. It was during my final year in grad school when tragedy struck."

"Was it hunters?" Victoria held tight to his arms.

"No, although, hunters would have been preferable."

"How so?"

"My family on my father's side has an old legend

going back several generations. The long and short of the story tells of a *seiðr*—a witch—who once enslaved our bloodline to do her bidding. My grandfather found a way to break her control and escaped decades before I was born."

Victoria's skin crawled with fear and dread. She experienced the premonition of something awful about to happen, an immediate sense of danger. Uncanny certainty manifested within her gut. "The witch came after your pack."

"Using magic I've never understood, she influenced our beasts. She created dissension and strife and even possessed our weakest members. She turned the pack against itself, wolf against wolf. I managed to get Lori and Logan to safety but my decision to save my mate and child cost me everything. My parents, my pack: no one else survived."

Arik showed no visible sign of weakness, maintaining a controlled demeanor, but through their touch, Victoria sensed the awful torment he carried in his heart. Like her, his burden of guilt was worth more than one lifetime.

"What happened to the witch?"

"I killed her." Arik's noble head lifted and his dark eyes shone with fierce passion. His bloodthirsty nature was worthy a Viking king.

"Good, I'm glad." Victoria took satisfaction in his triumph. She shared his lust and enthusiasm for vengeance. Someday, perhaps, she would have her own, if she ever had the guts to kill her dead lover's brother.

Her stomach lurched, and she shoved the unbidden thought aside. "Is that why you left Ironwood?"

"Yes. We couldn't stay. There were too many bad memories."

She blinked away tears. "I think I'd feel the same way about Phoenix."

Arik's arms tightened about her. "Lori had relatives

here so we relocated to Sierra Pines. After what had happened, I never looked back, but I've never forgotten."

He looked her straight in the eyes. "That is the reason why I've never taken leadership of another pack."

"Oh." Understanding punched her in the gut, creating a wave of nausea to think about how much anguish Arik must have endured. In her desperation to protect her pack, she had thought of no one's feelings but her own.

"I come with a pack. It's not negotiable."

Arik regarded her with warm amusement. "I'm well aware, Victoria. You're a woman well worth the resumption of responsibility."

Flushed with pleasure, Victoria leaned into him. She rubbed her face against his neck and nipped at his throat. Arik chuckled and held her close.

Following an indeterminate silence, Arik asked, "When are you going to tell me what's going on with you and Logan?"

Victoria did not show surprise because she'd been expecting the subject to come up. No Alpha male worth his weight could have failed to notice the disruption she and Logan had created the night before. Either Arik's patience was that of a saint or he'd already received an explanation from Logan.

"We should speak in private," she said.

"Let's go into my study." Arik indicated the back door to the house.

"Okay." She followed him into the house.

"This is a lot different from your office at work."

Victoria took the time to look around when she entered the room. The furniture and accessories included a lot of leather and glass to create a look of sparse elegance. The walls were tan and the large fireplace was the focal point of the room.

Arik made a sound of agreement. "I hired an interior designer to do my workplace."

She stopped to study a computer that looked like it had fallen out of another decade. The machine sat atop an exquisite handcrafted desk, tucked into the corner of the room. Victoria circled to take a better look at the relic. "Is that a floppy drive? Does it still work?"

Arik shot her a sour look but then smiled with good-natured humor. "It doesn't boot any longer. I just haven't gotten around to throwing it away."

"Wow." Chuckling, she exchanged a long look with him, and they shared a good laugh. When the mirth died away, a comfortable intimacy remained.

He touched her hand and gazed at her with serious eyes. "What was it you needed to tell me earlier at the office?"

Victoria bit her lower lip and licked it, then took the plunge. "Logan asked me to help him prove he didn't murder your wife."

Genuine confusion clouded Arik's eyes. If the man were a liar, she felt he should hold office. If an actor, he belonged on the stage. He did not utter an immediate denial or declare the impossibility of the matter but considered it for a while.

"How?" he asked.

Victoria looked him right in the eye. "We broke into the police station and stole the files on the investigation into your wife's death."

He appeared stunned and then furious. A vein throbbed in his temple, his jaw set, his hand clenched. He spoke with fierce intensity but not volume. "You what?"

Victoria took a deep breath. "We—"

"I heard you the first time!"

Victoria glared and her temper flared. "Don't be rude!"

He rocked back on his heels, unaccustomed to defiance. Victoria stared at him, held his gaze, refused to yield. She was not any happier with her own indulgence in illegal activities than Arik, which made it worse. Duplicity compounded her guilt.

Arik's nostrils flared. "My apologies. You were saying?"

"Logan believed he might find proof about his mother's true killer in the files. Perhaps some piece of evidence overlooked or misinterpreted by human cops. He asked for my help."

She left out her initial refusal, because she believed it served no productive purpose to go into the dirty little details. Besides, Arik already knew she and Logan harbored an intense dislike of one another. She figured there was no sense in rehashing the obvious.

"He asked, so you saw fit to help him?" Arik's tone carried skepticism.

"I didn't have another vehicle or cellphone to spare."

"Excuse me?"

"Nothing, sorry." She waved her hand, dismissing the off-colored remark. "Yes, I agreed to help him, for my peace of mind as well as his. I apologize for not coming to you sooner. I tried to tell you in your office before we were interrupted."

Arik stared at her, expression implacable. "Well, this explains why Logan refused to submit to me today."

Her stomach lurched. "He did?"

Arik nodded. "It's the first and only time I've asked that he's said no, but it's a huge thing, Victoria. Logan is a berserker, so I must maintain control of his beast. If his resistance goes on much longer, I'll lose my hold on his wolf."

She licked her lips. "What if he's not? Not a berserker? Not guilty?"

Arik's expression turned intractable. "As much as I would love for Logan to be innocent, I was there the night Lori died. When I found Logan, he was asleep, drenched in his mother's blood. It was in his hair, on his hands, his mouth..."

She shuddered at the implication. "I'm so sorry for what you've been through."

Arik shrugged off her sympathy. "What makes you think he might be innocent? For that matter, what's happened to convince him of it?"

"There's been other evidence."

"What evidence?"

"You're aware I speak with spirits?"

"You've mentioned as much."

"Your wife's spirit revealed itself to me in the clearing down by the lake."

Arik's eyes grew empty, then filled with heartbreak and despair. "It's where she died."

"Lori asked me for help. She didn't state what sort of help — not in so many words — but she showed me how she died. Logan saw her too, which surprised me."

"Second sight runs on Lori's side of the family. Logan has never shown any signs of having the gift."

"He saw her. He spoke to her, and she told him it wasn't his fault."

"Did she say he didn't murder her?"

She bit her lips, thinking long and hard. "No, she didn't say that."

Arik exhaled. "Fine, say I believe you about Lori's ghost. Of course, she's going to say it wasn't his fault. It was the first time he'd experienced The Change. He was in the grip of blood lust; he had no control over his actions. Lori loved Logan more than life itself. She would forgive him."

Victoria gave him a moment. "There's more evidence. You're not going to like it, but you must hear it."

"Fine." From the look in his eyes, she had almost exhausted his patience.

"Did your wife love you?"

Fury flashed in his eyes. She had stabbed his pride with a venomous stinger. "I thought she did before I found out she was cheating on me."

Among her people, adultery constituted a huge loss of honor. Many shapechangers would have considered Arik well within his rights to kill his cheating spouse. Victoria dug the crumpled photo of Gregory Sanders from her pocket and handed it to Arik.

"What's this?" He took the picture and spared it a glance. No recognition lit his eyes.

"Do you recognize him?"

Arik shook his head. "No."

"That's Gregory Sanders, the man your wife was supposed to be cheating on you with." Victoria scrutinized his reaction, searching for any hint of deception but found none.

"I don't know him." His fist crushed the photo.

"You don't recognize him at all? You must have seen his body."

Arik scowled. "The body was... eaten. What was left wasn't recognizable, even if I had been paying attention. My focus was on protecting Logan."

"Take a good look at him. I want you to really see him."

At her insistence, Arik looked at the portrait again, and then thrust it back at her. His growl of anger served as a sharp warning.

Her next words were so very soft. "He is fat, old, and unattractive. Even if your wife were inclined to be unfaithful, why in a million years would she sink so low?"

Her inescapable logic tripped him up. Arik considered the matter before answering. "She wouldn't. Lori liked nice things. Expensive clothes and shoes. Pricy jewelry. Attractive men."

"As a woman, take my word on the matter. *That* is not an attractive man."

Arik remained so still his aura acquired a scary quality. She sensed single-minded determination beneath that stoic exterior. He wasn't someone she ever wanted to cross.

Finally, he said, "It's a valid argument. It was her brother, Mike, who suggested she was having an affair. I had my hands full with Logan and had no reason to think he would lie."

"Mike as in Sheriff Mike Trash?" Victoria asked.

Arik nodded. "Is there any actual physical evidence? Proof that Logan is innocent?"

Victoria's mouth formed a grim line. "No."

"Nothing at all? Was there anything in the file?"

"I don't know. Logan took the file." Her distress redoubled with each passing moment. "Arik, please, *listen*. Last night, I summoned Gregory Sanders's shade. He admitted he wasn't your wife's lover. The wraith I brought back was not the ghost of a mortal man. It was... monstrous."

"Did he name his killer?"

"No, I tried, but it was able to evade direct questions it didn't want to answer. I have no explanation, because such a thing shouldn't be possible. When I summon a shade, it is mine to command."

"So we're back to circumstantial evidence and your gut feeling." With a grimace, Arik sized her up. "What are you thinking, Victoria? Maybe I murdered my wife, framed my son, and then spent two years playing puppet master over Logan?"

She flinched because she had held those exact suspicions. There was no point in lying when she wore the truth on her face. "It had occurred to me, but no, I don't believe you're capable of something so wretched."

"I suppose that's something." Arik's anger achieved new heights. His power thrummed, vibrating with controlled rage, and extended well beyond the confines of the room.

"Arik, if you'd just listen to me—"

"Victoria, I don't understand why you're involved in this, and it needs to stop. You're making things worse for Logan, indulging this wishful thinking. It might seem like you're helping him, but hope is going to kill him."

"I don't believe Logan killed your wife." Victoria opted for blunt honesty over a more diplomatic tactic. She possessed a measure of cunning but preferred a brutal confrontation to manipulation. "Logan and I have been at each other's throats since the moment we met, and he hasn't lost control yet. I don't like him, but he's not a berserker. And he's not a murderer."

"That's the first time you've shown your cards," Logan said from the doorway. He had managed to approach undetected, slipping in under Arik's flagrant display of power.

Startled, Victoria looked his way.

Logan met her eyes. "Thanks for that, but you're wrong."

"What?" she asked.

Logan entered the room and walked toward his father. He moved as if he carried the world on his shoulders, full of despair, on the verge of defeat, and she feared for him.

"Logan?" Arik awaited his son's explanation.

Logan drew down a shaky breath and stopped before Arik. "I've been going through the police files all day. There's nothing, no tracks in the snow aside from mine and mom's. So unless we're looking for a killer who leaves no trace, it had to be me."

"What about scent?" Victoria asked. "Scent wouldn't show in the file."

"I wasn't paying attention," Logan said, grasping at the thin hope. "Everything from that day is a blur."

Arik rumbled deep in his chest, then shook his head. "There were no foreign scents; nothing that didn't belong. I'm sorry, Logan."

"Yeah, it's okay." Logan's breathing acquired a deep and labored rasp. His shoulders slumped in defeat, disturbing to witness in a dominant wolf of his strength. "I—I've been staring at the photos for hours. I'm starting to remember. I did it."

Victoria bit off a growl. Her hands formed fists. Her energy ran quicksilver across her skin. "You idiot, of course you're projecting guilt after hours of staring at photos of your dead mother!"

"Victoria, that's enough!" Arik's eyes radiated solid gold light. His anger emanated from deep within, causing the skin of his forearms to ripple and bulge, a precursor to transformation. The display shut Victoria up when words would have failed.

Arik turned to his son and placed a hand on Logan's arm. His voice underwent a remarkable transformation from fury to tender. "Logan, son, it wasn't your fault. We've been through this countless times; nothing has changed. I understand your desire to make it otherwise."

Logan ran his hands over his face, rubbing away tears, and then he pushed back his hair. He hung his head and hunched forward. The tears fell harder, faster, broken sobs threatening to tear his chest apart. "I was desperate to believe some unknown monster had killed mom. It was me; it was me."

"Logan, let me command your wolf," Arik said. "You have to submit. I don't want to force you."

"You can't force me, Dad, not without my cooperation, and we both know it."

Arik's mouth formed a grim line. His power rose and encroached upon his son's aura. "Logan, our laws are clear. A berserker must remain under the control of an Alpha at all times or be destroyed."

"Being destroyed is preferable to a life without freedom." A silent struggle broke out between father and son when Logan's wolf refused to submit.

"You can't mean that." Arik laid a hand on his son's arm.

Logan shoved his father away. "I do mean it. I can't

do this any longer. I'm through being subject to your control, Dad. I'd rather be dead."

Arik's face twisted in pain. He stared at his son, expressionless. "Logan, I can't lose you, too. You're all I have left."

Father and son shared so much grief and anguish it hurt to watch. Unable to witness more, Victoria turned away and stared out the sliding glass door of the study. There were icicles on the eaves, the glitter of dancing light, mystery and romance, a seductive whisper, a lover's kiss.

Spellbound, Victoria leaned forward and focused her attention to the spectacle outside, the drama unfolding in front of her. Reflected within the ice, she caught a glimpse of a beautiful woman, bold and blonde, laughter like crystal bells. She had blue eyes with black irises in the shape of ravens. Her pale hair wore a coat of frost.

"I see you, ravens." Victoria spoke without meaning to, so the sound of her own voice startled her. Shivers ran along her spine and gooseflesh rose on her arms. With a shake of her head, she woke herself up.

"Stop, this is wrong—all wrong! Can't you feel it?" With a burst of energy, she charged across the room toward the males. Logan and Arik both stared at her; the surprised looks on their faces indicated she'd been forgotten.

"Victoria," Arik said her name as a distinct warning.

She ignored him. "No, listen to me. The evidence points to Logan's innocence."

"What evidence? There is no evidence. I've listened to everything you've said, and I've been more than fair. Now it's time for you to listen to me." Arik's voice rose along with his power, energy burning with anger. He stalked toward her, towering over her, but she held her ground.

His hands closed on her biceps, and he leaned in close. "I've welcomed you and your pack into my territory as guests and tolerated conspicuous disruptions that have endangered us all. As of this moment, it's over. I forbid any further behavior on your part that endangers my son. Do you understand?"

Victoria stared him straight in the eye. "No."

"No?" Arik's control over his form slipped; he started the transformation.

"No. I am not yours to command."

"Let me put it this way then..." Arik spoke with the full authority of his position as Alpha male. He possessed the strength to back it up. "I've enjoyed your games, indulged your manipulation, and been more than patient. It's time for us to seal the mate bond. Then you will be mine to command."

Victoria's heart stopped in her chest, and she strangled a scream of frustration.

"No," she said. "No. No. No."

CHAPTER ELEVEN

Dishonor—

"Victoria, this is unacceptable."

"Yes, Goddess, I know."

"Priestess, heed me, this will not end well."

"What would you have me do, Goddess?"

"Better than this."

"No."

Arik's brow rose. Claws tipped his hands and gouged her arms. "No? You don't seem to understand, Victoria. This isn't a request. I'm going to seal the mate bond if I have to command your wolf without your consent."

"No has one meaning. And you'll have to do more than command my wolf. You'll have to kill me." With a powerful surge, Victoria drove his hands from her arms. She failed to move Arik backward, but she'd made her point. She claimed her ground and left no doubt she would fight him.

A soft growl erupted from Logan. "She said no. Dad, you're so wrong right now it's not even funny. You can't protect me from life."

Arik turned his angry glare on his son. "Logan, I'm warning you. Stay out of this. This is between Victoria and me."

"Really? Because I heard myself say no." Her fine features formed a harsh mask, blue eyes burning bright, mouth set in a hard line. "Do not discuss me as if I am a possession."

"You accepted my courtship. I am within my rights as Alpha." Arik's power swelled as he let his wolf off the leash. Victoria braced because she knew what to expect. Their gazes locked and the dominance stare down commenced. His energy engaged hers.

His power created a crushing weight that felt as if it would suffocate her. Sweat formed on her brow and her breathing grew strained. Victoria froze in place, trembling and then shaking as every limb strained to keep her upright. He was powerful, ungodly powerful, stronger than she'd thought. He'd kept much of it hidden.

"Dad, this is wrong!" Logan seized his father's shoulder.

In a desperate bid to be free, her will rose and bucked him. She tried and failed more than once to dislodge the aura attempting to subdue hers. If she surrendered and submitted, the pain would cease. He would take her over, assume command of her beast, and she'd be his wolf in every sense of the word.

Should I surrender? she wondered. *Not happening.*

"Dad, you've got to stop!" Logan's shouts roared past them.

Victoria's energy was almost tapped out while Arik's seemed inexhaustible. Her aura shrank, retreated, and started to collapse. Seconds passed and she knew she could not win or hold out much longer. She was Thor holding up the World Serpent. Soon her strength would give and Arik would win.

"I demand you prove your worth in combat." Victoria threw down the challenge. Her voice was cold and steady, edged with fear and hatred.

Arik blinked. His attempt to subdue her wolf

ceased. "If this is a joke, it's a poor one."

Surprised, Logan stopped interfering and fell back a pace.

"No joke." She chose her words with precision, so he would *know*. "It is my right as the contested female. When two competing males have both initiated a courtship, the female has the right to demand they fight."

"Who's the other suitor?" Arik asked.

"If you refuse, you lose face and your claim on me is forfeit."

"Victoria..." Arik showed teeth when he spoke; his wolf stared out of his honey-brown eyes. If he'd tried to kill her then, Victoria wouldn't have been surprised.

"Logan." She spat the name. "Logan has made a formal gift of food, and I accepted."

"The hell you say?" Logan arched his brow, but did not sound surprised.

Arik's head jerked toward his son. The men locked gazes, not for dominance, but rivalry and speculation. The stench of testosterone in the room busted balls.

Logan turned a challenging grin toward Victoria. "Come on now, sugar. We agreed to go Dutch on the pizza."

"Logan would have to offer you food, which you accepted, for this scheme of yours to work. It would have to be a gift," Arik said. The attorney in him was not above splitting hairs.

Victoria made eye contact with Logan. She smiled, nice and sweet, and said just two words, her gauntlet: "Breath mints."

Realization dawned in those amber eyes, a light going on, and his grin widened. She caught a glimpse of chagrin and a flare of primal aggression for a brief moment, then he hid it fast. And he hid it well. With a mock bow in her direction, Logan bent and took up the imaginary gauntlet with a flourish.

"The lady commands us to the field of combat."

Arik took one look at his son's face and groaned. "Logan, you didn't..."

"Sorry, Dad, but I did." Logan smirked. He shook his head and paced clockwise from his father toward Victoria. The severity of the situation seemed to escape him.

Or maybe, Victoria thought, *he understands all too well.*

"So I guess we're gonna have it out, huh? What're the rules? Rapiers? Pistols at twenty paces?" Logan asked.

"Logan, this is no joke. These combats end in death." Arik directed a look of pure contempt toward Victoria. In that moment, he must have hated her for involving his son in their dispute.

Despite an awful burden of shame, Victoria held her head high. She had used trickery to entangle Logan in her scheme and pitted father against son in the worst sort of manipulation. When the situation reached its resolution, no matter what the ending, her honor was in tatters.

She met Arik's gaze with cold eyes and a colder heart. He would not coerce her into a mate bond and enslave her against her will. She would not allow it. "You backed me into this corner. I have no other choice."

"I might say the same." Arik's determination remained hard and fast, shoulders squared, set on following the course he'd chosen to the bitter end.

Between them, there could be no reasoning. No compromises.

Victoria turned to Logan. "You have the right to refuse to fight."

"That true?" Logan looked to his father for confirmation in a tacit slight to her integrity, but she could not blame him.

Arik tilted his chin in acknowledgement. "Either of us can refuse combat, and it nullifies both courtships.

However, it is impossible to refuse without losing face."

Victoria turned pleading eyes on Logan. If there were any hope of one of the two dominant males choosing reason over status, it rested with Logan. He had no standing within the werewolf community to damage.

"Say no. No one's going to think any worse of you for it," she said.

Bitterness flashed in Logan's remarkable eyes. "Right, cause I've got no one."

Arik's jaw clenched, and Victoria paled.

"Logan, this is a farce. Please, say no. I don't want anyone to get hurt because of me. As soon as this is settled, I'll take my pack and leave town. I swear: You'll never hear from us again."

"She's right, Logan, you can back down without losing face," Arik said. The Alpha glared at Victoria. "I will not relinquish my claim. You have made this about proving my worth as a man and a leader. It is about honor. I am Alpha; I will not submit."

"My honor is no less important." Victoria's nostrils flared, and she returned Arik's stare. He had tried to force her against her will. In her mind, her own transgressions paled to insignificance in comparison. This challenge represented her only path to freedom.

Neither would back down.

Victoria looked to Logan, hoping he would be the voice of reason. "Logan, it's up to you."

Logan wore an indecipherable expression. He returned their expectant gazes, those amber eyes glittering with specks of gold and green, and the seconds ticked past.

Outside, the wind whispered through the pines, and a raven's *craa* filled the night.

Logan shook his head. "Sorry, Dad. I won't lie down. Not this time."

Victoria stifled a snarl of frustration. *Stupid, stubborn males!*

Her teeth snapped together with an audible click. "Fine. My pack must be present to witness the fight. The winner shall be my mate and our Alpha male."

They gathered deep in the wilderness, miles from the closest human habitation or road. Arik and Logan attended, as did Victoria and her entire pack. A sliver of moon hung in the starry sky, and a fierce wind blew down off the mountains. A natural clearing in the alpine forest served as the designated battleground. The terrain sloped west, and snow covered the rocky ground.

"I don't understand how this happened," Sylvie said.

"I had no other choice," Victoria said. If she said it often enough, she might start to believe it, but she seemed no closer to convincing her Beta wolf than herself.

Sylvie turned a disapproving stare on her leader. "That boy wasn't even a consideration. You told me so yourself."

"I know what I said."

"Then what the hell happened? Because I'd sure like to know."

Her shoulders hunched forward with shame before she squared them. "I tricked Logan. I accepted food from him, and then I pretended it didn't mean anything until it suited me to do so."

"This is wrong, forcing a father to fight his son."

Victoria's fingernails dug into her palms. "I'm not forcing anyone to do anything. Both of them have the right to back out of the fight."

Sylvie's hazel eyes called her a liar. "And wind up branded a coward? No man worth his salt would do such a thing."

"Sylvie, please..."

"Oh, Victoria, I sure do hope you know what you're doing."

"Arik left me with no other choice."

Sylvie gave her a hard look. "Did he? Or did he hurt your pride?"

Her cheeks stung from the heat of embarrassment, the chilling bite of the tempest. She had no answer, so she stomped the snow beneath her feet and stared up at the sky.

The pack and participants moved through the clearing, beating down the snowpack. Strength and skill would determine the outcome of the combat, not the vagrancies of luck over an unpredictable playing field. An aura of gloom-and-doom hung over everyone except the pups, who frolicked and wrestled under their mother's watchful gaze.

Sylvie grasped Victoria's arm and spoke with urgency. "Victoria, there's something I must tell you. I did some more research of the line from the *Sonatorrek* you cited — *Larð skal rifna ok upphiminn*. It is more than a prediction of *Ragnarök*. It's a father's lament for the death of his sons. I have a terrible bad feeling about this, Victory. You must find some way to stop this fight. If this is prophecy, then the wicked forces at work here will win."

"The only wicked forces at work here are male pride and vanity."

"More than male pride and vanity are at play here," Sylvie said with a disapproving frown.

Limping, Paul approached the female wolves. "Sylvie, my mate, the challenge has been made and accepted. It is about honor and glory. The outcome is no longer in Victoria's hands."

Sylvie regarded her mate with exasperation, lips compressed in a tight line. "Honor and glory, glory and honor. It is always the same with you men."

Sylvie's reprimand earned her an impudent grin from her mate. "I happen to recall a sultry beauty who once issued such a challenge. I fought not one but two other opponents to prove my worth and win her as my own."

Sylvie's dusky complexion threw heat, and she turned her face away to hide a pleased smile. "Stop it, you old rogue. I'm sure I have no idea what you're talking about."

Victoria mustered a faint smile that didn't reach her eyes. "Excuse me. I'm going to leave you lovebirds alone."

Arik and Logan had assumed positions on opposite sides of the clearing in preparation for the coming fight. She hesitated, glanced from one to the other, and then walked toward Logan. She tilted her head back in order to gaze up at him. "Why are you doing this?"

Logan regarded her with wariness. "Aren't you going to wish me a glorious death? Maybe slip me some tongue to repay me for my noble sacrifice?"

Recognizing the attempt at misdirection, she refused to allow his leer to distract her. "Logan, you don't have to fight. Backing out isn't the same as submitting. It's as simple as declaring you no longer want me."

His callous smile stopped her cold. "That's funny, Vic, because I never said I wanted you in the first place. You used trickery to get me out here, and now you want me to tell collaborating lies to get out of it. Sorry, but I'm not playing your game."

Her scowl forced her face into a rigid, painful grimace. Her temples pinched and she felt a migraine forming behind her eyes. "It's not a game. You know why I'm doing this. Logan, *please*. I've given you sufficient reason for you to withdraw without losing face. The deception was shameful; pitting you against your own father is dishonorable."

Logan shoved his face into hers, almost knocking her off her feet. "Look, there's something you don't seem to get, so let me spell it out. *This has nothing to do with you.*"

His vehemence shocked her. She rocked back on her heels and stared at him with a hanging mouth. Her jaw snapped shut. "What does it have to do with?"

"Nothing involving you, so go back to your precious pack and leave me alone! I'm through indulging your monumental ego—everything is not about you!" Logan swung his arm toward her in a gesture designed to drive her away. He wore his flippant demeanor as armor, but she saw past his mask. His eyes held despair and desperation, devoid of hope.

Realization came to her then, and it tasted of ash. Dread filled her, and she stared at him and backed away. "Oh, Goddess," she said. "You intend to die. Suicide by ritual combat."

Logan's face betrayed the truth of the matter, but he didn't offer verbal acknowledgement. "Don't worry about your freedom. After this, my dad won't want you anymore. He'll release you without sealing the mate bond."

Logan hesitated and then said, "Tell him it wasn't his fault, okay?"

"Tell him yourself!" Victoria glared daggers at him. She wanted nothing more than to rush him and pummel him senseless.

Shaking, she took a step backward. "It won't work. Arik will know if you're not fighting for real. He'll be able to win without killing you."

Logan smirked; his cocky brow rose. "I think you underestimate my powers of annoyance, little one. Rest assured, I'll be fighting with everything I've got. Any pain would be worth the look on your face if I won. Imagine, *me* as your mate."

"I'll kill you first." Thanks to Logan's talent for getting under her skin, she bristled with anger and stung pride. She had no idea whether her hostility stemmed from ego or fear, but she suspected a good measure of each played a part in it.

"Will you wait until after the honeymoon? I'm such a romantic fool. I can't wait to get into your pants." Logan thrummed a hand over his heart.

"If your father doesn't kill you, then I will!" Fuming, Victoria stalked away. She would waste no more time, expend no more energy on the obnoxious jerk. He deserved to die.

"You already have, Vic. You already have." Logan's laughter followed Victoria across the snowy clearing, taunting her while she returned to stand with her assembled pack.

Favoring his prosthetic leg, Paul walked out to meet her. They shared a solemn nod. He continued to the center of the clearing where he would serve as the mediator. Victoria joined Sylvie and Morena at the edge of the clearing. Sophia and the pups maintained a safe distance near a thick copse of redwoods. She turned to face the battlefield. Arik stood to her far right, Logan to her left.

Arik finished undressing and placed a neat pile of folded clothing into the backpack he had brought for the occasion. The Alpha stood tall and proud, radiating unshakable confidence. Every gaze rested upon him. The sheer magnitude of his presence had a lot to do with his superb physique, and even more to do with his compelling charisma.

"Mmmm, that's one fine specimen of a man," Sylvie said. "Look at that sculpted definition."

"Sylvie!" Teenage Morena giggled and blushed, scandalized.

Sylvie smiled. "I'm old, but I'm not dead yet, Morie."

"He's gorgeous," Morena said, but her gaze remained riveted upon Logan.

Logan had also shed his clothing and dropped them in a careless tangle on the ground. He was taller than his father and carried less muscle on his lean frame. His big hands and feet alluded to his potential in a few years when he finished filling out.

Sylvie snorted and cast a quick glance at Logan. "Too pretty for my taste."

"Oh no, he's perfect." Morena clasped her hands, her gaze far off and dreamy.

"Shush, show respect." Victoria shot a scolding glance at her packmates but her reprimand lacked heat. Who could blame them?

"We are. Believe me, we are," Sylvie said. Her jolly tone set the teenager to a fresh round of giggling.

Alpha wolf and Beta wolf traded a long look. Sylvie's eyes were serious. Her antics served the sole purpose of lightening the mood for Morena.

"Thank you," Victoria said, mouthing the words.

Sylvie inclined her head in acknowledgement.

Craa! Craa! Grating birdcalls echoed across the snowy clearing. Victoria searched and located a pair of enormous ravens perched in the branches of a pine tree. The wind whispered something wicked through the trees, and her stomach cramped. Cruel laughter rang out, bell clear, and chills swept her spine.

"Odin watches," Sylvie said. "This must be an omen."

"It is an omen," Victoria said. "Good or bad is the question."

Paul cleared his throat. "Listen up, everyone. When it comes to a courtship challenge, the pack's enforcer performs the duties of mediator. Seeing as how we're shorthanded, I guess this falls to me. I'll call for the start and the end of the fight. I'll also declare the victor.

"The rules are simple. A fight to the death unless one of the contenders surrenders. There may be no outside interference; acceptance of surrender is mandatory.

"As with love and war, all else is fair. Is this understood and agreed upon?" Paul asked.

"Aye." Arik inclined his head to indicate his assent.

"Five by five." Logan saluted, fingertips to his temple in cavalier acknowledgement.

"Begin." Paul signaled for the challenge to start and moved off the field. Both Logan and Arik waited until he was clear. Paul stood beside his mate.

Victoria expected Logan to rush Arik, utilizing his frightening speed, but the men made a measured approach. They walked toward each other and stopped three paces apart. Facing each other, they exchanged bows and then assumed sparring stances.

"Mmm, looks like they've done this before." Sylvie wrung her hands in subconscious anxiety.

"That's some form of martial arts." Victoria did not recognize the discipline, but it explained their cool familiarity with one another.

Paul grunted. "*Savate*. I used to practice it 'fore I lost my leg."

Squared off, Arik and Logan traded a series of punches and kicks, movement flowing smooth and supple. The start of the fight lacked the customary bravado, the exchange of insults that accompanied the physical violence. The men said nothing to each other.

Paul's jaw worked. "Not a very blood-thirsty pair, are they? I've never seen a warm-up workout in a courtship challenge 'fore."

"Looks to me like neither of 'em wants to be out there," Sylvie said.

"Goddess, nothing about this makes any sense." Victoria pressed fingers to her temples and tried to block out the raucous *craas* of the ravens and the wind's cruel laughter. Fine fingers of fog surrounded the clearing; magic rode thick on the mist.

Her thoughts were disjointed: *A woman's voice... Magic... connected to Arik and Logan. We're being influenced... Who's in control?*

Abruptly, her thoughts clouded, and her heart filled with a cruel combination of rage and guilt. Striving to maintain her focus, Victoria felt as if she had found and then lost an important thought. Her hand rose to her mouth. "If I could just..."

Logan launched an open-handed strike, the same as a dozen others he had already thrown. However, in the split second before the punch connected, his hands underwent a swift transformation into claws. He left deep gouges along the length of Arik's forearm. A mighty growl tore from the Alpha's throat, and he started to shift to a wolf. His hands turned to claws, his teeth elongated to canines. Fur appeared upon his skin.

Paul sucked his teeth, hissing hard. "First blood! Yeah, that's gotta hurt."

Bloodlust launched Victoria forward, and she started toward the combatants. She underwent a partial transformation of her own and grew teeth and claws. Sylvie and Paul surged after her but stopped when she reined in her wolf. Panting, she slid to a halt.

Head bowed, she struggled for self-control. She chanted the mantra: "*None may interfere.*"

"How was that, Dad? You always say to use my natural speed to my advantage." Logan launched another assault against his father.

"Approval-seeking behavior will stop you from becoming a full dominant, Logan." Arik's eyes shone burnished gold. Blood flowed from his injured arm and fell on the snow, staining it red. He favored his right side while the injury healed, and turned away from his opponent.

Arik put out his left hand and grabbed Logan midcharge. He redirected the younger male's momentum and swung him toward the edge of the clearing. The throw propelled him into the trunk of a tree. Logan's collision cracked branches and bones. He let out a pained yelp when he went down.

"This is wrong. This is wrong." Victoria shifted from foot to foot. Wild energy coursed through her body, wreaking havoc with her heart rate and breathing.

Cramps caused her sides to ache so she stumbled and almost fell. Sylvie and Morena reached for her and kept her upright.

Arik seized the advantage while Logan was down. He delivered a kick to his son's shoulder and then another to his ribcage. Logan coughed up blood and rolled away from the blows, lessening the severity of each impact. He attempted to regain his feet, but Arik did not allow the recovery. He blocked the first and the next. Finally, Logan managed to stand.

Lightning fast, Logan rose from the ground and roared his defiance. Bloody saliva dripped from his glistening fangs and matted the black fur of his muzzle. Rushing forward, Logan wrapped his long arms around his father and raked the older male with his claws, opening long gouges across Arik's abdomen and ribs.

"This is wrong. Can't you feel it? There's something... something in the air, something... I have to stop this!" Victoria yelled. She struggled; Sylvie and Morena tightened their grip. Her desperation grew with each passing second. She twisted and almost broke free, but Paul wrapped his arms around her waist and added his weight.

"Calm down, Victory," he said.

"Let me go!"

"No, Victory, you must not interfere." Sylvie grunted from the exertion of restraining her Alpha. In fear and confusion, Morena whimpered, and Victoria screamed her frustration.

Arik seized Logan's arms, preventing those wicked talons from doing further damage to his belly. Father and son grappled, pitting strength versus strength. Still more human than wolf, Arik underwent a fast and forced transformation, attempting to keep pace with Logan. His body contorted, undergoing excruciating alterations. The entire time, he had to keep moving. He sprouted a thick dense coat of black fur.

Father and son were terrible to behold. They clashed, lightning and thunder, as vigorous and glorious as two gods in their conflict. With a swipe of his claws, Arik opened lateral incisions across Logan's chest and delivered a vicious bite to his son's shoulder. Logan growled in pain; Arik's jaws locked onto him.

"You know something, Dad? This is good; this is right. It's been a long time coming." Logan released his hold on his father's torso to grab the jaws locked on his shoulder. He seized his father's upper jaw in one hand and lower jaw in the other, and wrenched them apart with all of his strength.

A sickening crack accompanied the broken jaw. A wretched howl rose from Arik, and Logan dropkicked his father to the ground.

The younger male leaned over the older. Logan smirked down at his father. "Mom blamed you for the death of your pack. You know that, don't you? She might've claimed otherwise, but deep down, you knew. You always knew. The booze, the valium... She drugged herself senseless trying to escape *you*."

Victoria redoubled her efforts to be free. She bucked her three packmates again, and then Sophia's mouth closed on her calf. "Let me go! He's leaving himself open on purpose!"

Logan's voice rose to a shout. "Do you hear me, Dad? It was your fault! The pack died because of you! I didn't kill mom. You did!"

With an awful roar, Arik surged to his feet and caught Logan's undefended abdomen with his claws. The slashes began beneath the ribcage, angled inward and down. He cut sharp and deep and opened his son's gut. Logan's intestines spilled from the injury.

Clutching his stomach, Logan whimpered and sank to his knees.

Arik threw back his head and howled in victory. His wolf crested the pinnacle of power, the forest and the mountains resonated with the strength of his voice. Icicles shattered and shards of ice rained to the ground; snow tumbled from the sides of the mountains in avalanches. It was primal, a howl heard through time, from the very beginning to the bitter end.

The mist evaporated; the wind stopped laughing.

"My fault." Great painful sobs racked Victoria. She went limp, dangling in her pack's grip, and they released her.

Paul stepped forward. "The winner is known. I declare it to be Arik Koenig."

Victoria staggered into the clearing and halted opposite Arik. Shocked, they stared at one another across a vast divide. The horrified expression in his eyes mirrored hers.

My mate.

The Alpha's broken jaw hung open in an obscene display; bloody gouges covered his body. Arik broke eye contact and his heartbroken gaze dropped to his son who lay limp on the ground. Victoria had never witnessed such utter destruction of a soul.

"Logan." His busted jaw resulted in his voice sounding as a harsh croak. He fell to his knees beside his son. Arik grasped Logan's hand and lay on the ground. He pressed his face to Logan's throat and a devastated howl tore from the Alpha, then terrible sobs.

Victoria looked away and took a blind step. A cold hand grasped her ankle; she looked straight down into Logan's amber eyes. She flinched, but curbed the impulse to jerk away.

"Hey, Vic," Logan said. He reverted to human but the extensive injuries did not regenerate. His spilled guts covered the ground.

She sank to her knees and touched a hand to Logan's shoulder. Her fingers came away wet with blood. "I can't heal this. I've healed cuts, broken bones, minor burns. Never anything like this."

"Wow, real tears. For me?" Logan's chuckle turned into a wet cough and blood ran out the side of his mouth.

Victoria touched her cheeks and felt wetness, but she wasn't sure if it were her tears or his blood or both. Sick with guilt, she took his hand between hers. "I'm sorry. I'm so sorry. There's no justification for this. No excuses. I didn't want to see you die no matter how often I threatened it."

Arik's head reared back, revealing his jaw had already begun to heal. He completed a rough transformation into a man and knelt naked in the snow beside his fallen son. "Logan, this is my fault. I'm sorry."

Logan tried to sit up and failed. Gasping in pain, he fell onto his back. He grasped for his father's hand. "I made my own decisions, Dad. It's not your fault. I wanted this. I knew exactly what buttons to push. I always did."

"Logan, hang on. We can get help." Tears streaked Arik's face.

"Too late." Logan succumbed to another bout of coughing. His heartbeat weakened and stuttered.

"Vic, wanna know a secret?" She could barely hear him. His hand would have slid from hers if she had not held fast.

Turning her head to the side, Victoria moved her ear closer to his mouth. "What? Logan, what?"

He smiled at her. "*I understood all along.*"

He exhaled his last breath, and his heart stopped. Logan died with his eyes open.

CHAPTER TWELVE

Sacrifices —

"Victoria, you must understand, this is not without cost to me also."

"I understand, Goddess. I do. Only too well."

Dead eyes mocked her.

A harsh wind blew through the clearing, loud and moaning, scalding flesh and sucking tears. A vampire wind, a mocking wind, a tormenting wind. It fed on their pain and suffering. Cruel laughter boomed through the night, riding the cyclone, circling like a predator stalked prey.

"Two years ago, I lost my wife; tonight, I have slain my only son." Arik's hollow voice lacked heart or hope. He spoke empty words that came from a dead place inside. "I will not live to the dawn."

Victoria blinked, and her careless eyelids released fresh tears that tracked down her cheeks. The tempest stole the proof of her grief, the same as the others. She stifled a moan and struggled to reconcile her truths.

Am I to add Arik to the list of deaths I've caused?

She stared into dead eyes and discovered bright flecks, green and red, within the richest amber. Without the light of his soul, they were like beautiful pieces of glass.

Logan's spirit did not rise from his body.

"Freya, help me," Victoria said, whispering the prayer. She already suffered anguish, grief, and suffocating guilt because of the deaths she had caused: Daniel, her parents, Jasper, and others.

With the whimsy of a cat, Freya answered some prayers and ignored others. Her goddess was never predictable, but it shocked Victoria when Freya's golden voice caressed her consciousness and said, *Victoria, you must see clearly.*

A stream of visions flooded her mind: ravens, dark magic, a woman's cruel voice commanding the basest emotions to create discord among wolves.

Arik's seiðr. The witch.

Arik passed a tender hand over his son's face, closing his eyes for eternity. His son's death had destroyed Arik's will to live. Defeat enshrouded the Alpha.

"In Freya's name, if you die tonight, I shall exact revenge for both you and your son upon our enemy." Victoria looked up to Arik so he would know she swore the oath with complete commitment. Her watching goddess bore silent witness.

Arik stiffened. "What do you mean?"

"This is the work of the *seiðr*, your witch. I could feel her, but I didn't understand until it was too late. She has used magic to manipulate us, turn us against one another. She inspires fear, anger, pride... Hatred."

Arik growled and flashed savage teeth. His eyes reflected blood lust. "I killed the *seiðr!*"

"She will win if you die, Arik."

Angry, he gripped her with strong hands, lifted her from the ground and slammed her to it again. The impact jarred her bones. "I ripped the heart from the witch and ate it!"

Victoria stared at him. Fear seized her, not of death, but of him. "Then she lives on within you. She is here, now, with us. The laughter on the wind... Can't you hear her? She is the woman within the ice. I have seen her and heard her since I came here, but I did not understand. I think I do now."

He regarded her as if she were crazy, his heart full of disbelief and distrust, and made no reply.

She had no means to reach him. She wasn't his priestess. After all, she had forced him to fight his son. She exhaled. "Arik, I will try to explain everything to you as many times as you need, but ultimately, it is going to come down to faith. I have no solid evidence. I need for you to believe me."

"I can't," Arik said. "Not without some sort of proof."

The stubborn male turned from her. He tilted back his head and released a chilling howl, colder than the frozen night, penetrating both earth and sky so the world mourned with the wolf. His power ebbed and flowed across the landscape, drowning them all in inconsolable sorrow. The rest of the pack joined in, sharing his pain, grieving with him. It was the way of wolves.

Victoria, alone, remained silent and stared at Logan's corpse. Arik's rejection stung, but it was what she had expected and deserved.

Still, Logan's spirit had not risen.

A wise wolf marked the end of life with sadness and regret, celebrated the greatness of the person who had passed, and then moved on. An individual passed into memory, spirits into the afterlife, and the pack remained. A wise wolf lived within the pack and for the pack, and the pack meant never being alone.

Logan had not been in her pack.

Victoria had never been a wise wolf.

While the others howled to mourn Logan's passing, Victoria stripped away her clothing. Her fingers curled under her shirt and tugged it over her head. Her jeans caught over her shoes, and the struggle to kick free knocked her to the ground. Her actions created such a ruckus that the grieving pack noticed and turned their attention her way. By the time she shed the last shred of clothing, the howling had ceased. Even Arik fell silent. Perplexed, they watched her every move.

Victoria staggered to stand over Logan's body, and Sylvie made the logical leap. Aghast, she grabbed for her Alpha's arm. "Victory! What are you thinking?"

"His soul has not left his body. I can bring him back."

Paul supported his mate. "The boy is not even a member of our pack. You cannot risk so much for a near stranger."

Morena whined in sharp disagreement, but the Omega wolf lacked the courage to speak. Instead, she scurried on the heels of the Beta wolves, wide-eyed and worried.

Sylvie shook her. "Listen to us. Victoria! What you are considering violates our every tradition! The boy is dead! It is forbidden!"

"Sylvie, let go! I have to do this. I have to try." Victoria yanked her arm in an attempt to free it, but did not use her full strength. Her reluctance to hurt Sylvie hampered her movements.

Sylvie released her and staggered, moaning a warning. "The gods would curse you should you succeed. Pray, Victory, listen to reason."

"Tell me what's going on." Arik delivered a command, no room for disagreement or dispute. Victoria ignored him and circled around Logan's body, trying to find a way to approach him without walking through his spilled guts. The rest of them, however, reacted strongly to his command. Sylvie's entire posture altered, head lowering, to demonstrate submission. Paul and Morena followed suit. Sophia slinked away to rejoin her pups.

All of them feared him.

Arik gentled his tone. "Sylvie?"

"She is going to attempt a resurrection," Sylvie said with a defiant glance at Victoria. "You must stop her."

Victoria regarded Arik with open defiance, standing strong and proud. "I'm going to do this. You'll have to kill me to stop me."

Arik's gaze burned her. A thin ray of hope shined through his darkness. "Can you really do this?"

Her mouth flattened to a grim line. "My mother accomplished it once, a long time ago."

"I was there," Sylvie said. "The gods exacted a terrible price."

"But my father lived."

Sylvie turned to Arik, beseeching him. "She was with child, and she lost the baby."

Arik's face froze. "Victoria?"

Victoria's jaw clenched; she shrugged. "I'm not pregnant."

Arik deliberated a second longer, and then nodded. "Do it. Bring him back. If the gods come, then I shall stand in their path."

"Spoken like a true Viking," Victoria said without humor. It was an old and tired joke, but it was appropriate.

Arik caught her hand in his, holding fast. "Victoria, if you can save him—"

He cut the sentence short, but she filled in the blanks: no price too high, no barrier insurmountable. If she failed to bring back Logan, Arik would have no reason to continue to live.

No pressure.

"I'll do everything in my power." She gripped Arik's hand and stared into his eyes. Understanding passed between them, a common goal, a shared purpose. They each had a part in Logan's death and would do anything to make matters right.

"What can I do?" Arik hovered close and yet his vast reservoir of power might as well have been light years distant.

"Nothing. There's nothing you can do because we're not packmates." She squeezed his fingers and let go to make her point. "Your magic is strong, but if you touch me while I'm healing him, it will seal the pack bond and make you one of us."

Moving with deliberation, Victoria straddled Logan's body, one foot to either side of his chest. She looked to those she loved best. "Will you help me?"

Grim faced, Sylvie nodded and stepped forward. "We're with you, Victory."

"Godzbedamned." Paul threw back his head and laughed, though there was little joy or mirth in the sound.

She extended her hand toward her assembled pack. "I need you."

The pack came in response to her summons, surging forward to make physical contact. Joined hands linked them together. They touched her to complete the circuit. Even the cubs, bustling with excitement, gathered to press cold noses to Victoria's ankles. Together, they formed a living, breathing battery.

The pack's power poured into her, and Victoria knelt over the prone body, ignoring the squishy mess beneath her bare feet. The scent of fresh meat and perforated bowel slammed her nostrils, appealing and revolting all at once. His abdomen gaped open like an anatomy doll, ropey lengths of reddish intestines strewn everywhere.

Touching him turned her stomach, but it was necessary. She had to touch the corpse in order to repair it, and time was of the essence. Beneath her hands, his skin was still warm, and his soul lingered within the shell, but it would not remain for long.

She started with the nasty bite wound on his shoulder. A missing chunk of flesh marked the place where skin and muscles had separated from bone. It was a serious injury but less daunting than his midsection. Bracing, Victoria placed her hands over the shoulder injury, and energy sparked between her hands and his bare skin. The resultant hum made her teeth ache. The smallest cuts and abrasions responded first to her healing aura. Her entire being resonated with the pack's power.

Groping blind, she sought and found a beat, not a rhythm, but one note repeating. Healing did not come naturally to her. She had learned the craft under her mother's tutelage. She took the beat and focused the pack's power, weaving raw energy into a spell. She channeled the magic, giving it focus and direction, substance and form.

The healing energy moved into the bite wound while she mastered the flow, and then it moved deep down to repair his insides, and then moved outward toward the surface of the body. His skin grew last. By then, all of the secondary wounds were gone—along with the pack's energy.

Victoria exhaled and stared down at the gaping abdominal injury and the mess of perforated bowels on the ground. She swallowed a frustrated sob. It was more than she had ever attempted, and she had no idea where to start. With the pack's energy tapped out, starting with the least serious injuries began to look like a mistake.

Logan's soul emerged from his body, filling her with panic. His ghost settled across from her. His crouch mirrored her position, and he wore a sad little smile. Amber eyes mocked her.

Arik and the pack could not see him.

Logan glanced down to inspect his remains. "Oh, snap. What a mess I am."

"Don't leave." Victoria made the impulsive decision to do something. Shuddering, she plunged her hands into the mass of spilled guts and began shoving intestines back into his abdominal cavity. Mirroring her actions, the pack followed suit. They gathered up bits and pieces of Logan and returned the tissue to his body.

"Just like Humpty-Dumpty. All the King's wolves..." Logan laughed at her desperation.

"Shut up!" Victoria snarled so that her incisors elongated and her eyes turned gold. "Shut up, and get back into your body!"

Logan stopped laughing and sighed. "Vic, let it go."

The ghost vanished, his destination unknown to her. She couldn't keep track of everything going on around her. He might have departed or returned to his body as she commanded—impossible to tell. She prayed he'd done the right thing.

"Victory, the pack is exhausted," Sylvie said. The gentle warning made Victoria aware of heavy hands and trembling bodies. Sides heaving, the adult wolves clung to her with the last of their strength; the pups had already fallen away.

"Hang on a couple more minutes, please." With heroic effort, she summoned all of the power at her command, tapping the last of her reserves. She gathered the energy into a white bright burst and sank the entire star into Logan's abdomen. His entire body convulsed as impulses traversed nerve pathways. His lungs drew a single breath. His heart pounded out a single beat and then subsided.

"I will not give up." Tears trekked Victoria's cheeks and she began the impossible task of mending the butchered intestines.

Hopeless.

There was too much damage and not enough energy or skill at her command. She needed a miracle. She knew she would fail, but she would try anyway because surrender was not an option.

"Some things are meant to be." Arik's strong hands pressed against her back, fingers curling over her shoulders. His power came as a tsunami. Victoria gasped and shuddered, her eyes and mouth opening in reaction as an unstoppable tide flowed into her. She caught a glimpse, then, of the source of his power. He tapped into the land, and so his strength was as the vast sky, the lake, and the earth. His energy lifted her on a wild and wonderful ride, and she drifted on it, too tired to fight the current.

Arik tilted back his head and released a long howl to mark his admission into the pack. His power flowed through Victoria and then spread outward into the others, binding them all together. He energized the exhausted members. New connections were born, and the structure of the pack reorganized with Arik at the center, providing stability and support.

Connection defined the pack, tying each wolf to the others, bonds born of empathy and kinship. Arik was the first new member into the pack since Victoria's assumption of leadership. His admission plunged her into cold water. He represented a clear and present threat to her leadership and role as the dominant wolf.

The male Alpha's fierce howl died away, and an interval ensued as the members of the pack adapted to the new dynamic. Victoria threw back her head and allowed her howl to ascend into the night. In turn, each of the others howled, affirming their rank within the pack: Sylvie and Paul in unison, Sophia, and finally Morena. The pups were too young to be concerned with status.

Her implicit regulation to second rankled. She twisted around to snarl a warning at Arik, teeth bared, bristling with challenge. She growled to voice her dominance, still straddling Logan's damaged body. Arik's proximity brought their chests and thighs together, and Victoria's she-wolf quickened with arousal. Conflicted desires drove her aggression: She resented him and she wanted him.

He had fought for and won the right to mate with her. She would claim him and make him hers, united in all things, rank and power, one voice. Her clawed hands reached for him, intending to take him in the snow with the pack to witness their union.

Arik caught her gaze and captured her wrists. His grunt of exertion emphasized the strain he was under; the power he placed at her disposal was not without cost. He commanded, "Victoria, help Logan."

She returned to her senses with a thud. Her instinctive reaction shamed her, making her feel like nothing more than an animal, ruled by primal urges, a slave to her hormones.

She turned from Arik and reached for Logan. She stroked her hands across his upper thighs and followed the narrow curve of his hips, framing the bloody incisions with splayed fingers. The power at her disposal thrummed deep and sensuous throughout her body, and she reveled in it. Now, she not only had the beat but the rhythm.

With a flicker, she directed the magic. Healing the gory injury wasn't a finesse job. She used brute force to knit severed tissues and conjured flesh from pure power when she ran into gaps. Beads of sweat formed on her brow, but her meticulous attention never wavered from the task. She rebuilt a complete and intact digestive tract from the tattered remains.

"Logan?" She spoke to his soul, waited and listened, but received no reply.

The last of his intestines healed and flesh grew over the organs. As the healing neared completion, it picked up speed as if his body knew to cooperate.

New skin stretched taut across his stomach, recreating six-pack abs. His gooey parts were all back inside him where they belonged. She stroked a hand across that beautiful body, testing the integrity of her work, and found it satisfactory.

"Logan?" Victoria tilted her head to the side and listened again.

No answer.

Raising her arm over her head, Victoria slammed her fist down onto Logan's breastbone and sent a fresh surge of power through his body, the act designed to energize his heart. She waited but his heart did not beat.

Victoria redoubled her efforts and struck him with repeated blows, fist to sternum. She kept at him until his bones threatened to break. She grew tired, and her blows weakened. His heart refused to restart.

Her pack fell away, retreating from their frenzied leader, and huddled together. From the looks on their faces, they feared for her sanity, but she didn't have time to offer reassurances.

Arik seized her arm and stayed the next blow. "Victoria, he's gone."

Sides heaving, Victoria stared at him. Her chin trembled and tears clouded her vision. He could not be gone, could *not*, not after what she and the others had done to bring him back.

"No!" She wrenched her wrist from Arik's grip and gathered all the power left between them. Praying, she threw her hands into the air and summoned her goddess to her aid. "Freya! My Lady of the Vanir! Grant your power unto me!"

"Victoria!" Arik's shout rose to compete with her voice, but she ignored him.

"Freya, please, bring him back!" She seized Logan's body and hauled him from the ground. Arms raised, she lifted the corpse above her head toward the stars. The bright white halo of her goddess enveloped her. Her frustration peaked, because she did not hear the voice of the goddess answering her pleas.

"Freya! I beg of you! I invoke your name! Do this for me, and I will pay your price!" Lunging, Victoria slammed the corpse to the ground. He landed on his back; limbs flopped to his sides. Her arm rose overhead, hands turned to claws, as she prepared to rip open his chest in a fit of fury, undoing everything she had accomplished.

"Freya!" Her final shout reached the heavens. Victoria struck Logan's chest with her right hand and her claws gouged deep wounds in his flesh.

"Priestess, I am here." The unearthly voice of the goddess surrounded her. Bright light enveloped her, radiating from beneath her skin. The goddess passed through Victoria and into Logan. The stench of burnt flesh filled the air where Victoria's open hand touched Logan's chest. With a shriek of pain, Victoria yanked her hand away.

Freya's golden aura appeared overhead, and Logan's body lifted from the ground. The holy light cocooned him, obscuring him from sight. "Victory, I hear your pleas, and I answer. What do you ask of me?"

Bright, so very bright, and yet it felt like a dream. The sweet resonance of Freya's voice made her weep. Exhausted, Victoria fell to the frozen ground and knelt in the bloody snow. Arik and her pack watched with reverence as the goddess became visible within shining brightness at the center of the clearing.

The Norse deity was taller than any mortal, the epitome of warrior and woman. Her long tresses were golden as ripe rye and her eyes were blue as northern glaciers. She wore a dress made of flowing water; the color changed with her mercurial mood.

"Freya, give him life."

"Victoria, if I do this, the price will be dear," Freya said. "When the time comes, you will owe me a life. Do you understand?"

Victoria nodded her head. "Aye, I understand. When the time comes, I owe you a life."

"I grant him a kiss." Golden grace, the goddess bent and pressed a single kiss to Logan's lips. All watched in awe.

The goddess withdrew and the cocoon of light dissipated. Logan's body lowered to the ground. When the last of the brightness faded, she saw his chest rise and fall with shallow breaths, and his heart beat with the even rhythm of sleep. A bright red burn, the imprint of her hand, marred his chest above his heart. He was a beautiful, empty shell.

Victoria froze. "He has no soul."

Freya's light began to fade. "I'm sorry, my priestess. I have given him life, but I cannot do more. His soul has gone to Odin's hall, Valhalla."

Victoria grabbed her goddess's hand, holding her there for a few precious seconds. "Wait! Please. How long can his body live without his soul?"

"Three days. You have three days to recover his soul, or his body will die. I am sorry, but it is all that is within my power."

Victoria bowed her head and released Freya's hand. "Thank you, Goddess. We are grateful."

Arik sank to one knee and bowed. "I thank you for my son's life, and you have my eternal gratitude. I will not forget the debt I owe you."

Freya's smile glimmered, and her appreciative gaze lingered on his noble profile. Her husky laugh sang with serenity. "I will not forget such a fine offer, but for now... Protect my priestess, wolf."

Arik bowed his head in assent. Freya vanished.

"I will go to Valhalla," Victoria said.

She rose and staggered a pace, seeking a reflective surface so she could follow her goddess on the spirit roads. Her heavy feet tripped, and her vision blurred. When she stumbled and pitched forward, Arik caught her in his arms.

With a murmur, she succumbed to exhausted sleep.

CHAPTER THIRTEEN

Mr. Cash—
> *"Do you have a favorite song, Victoria?"*
> "Hurt, *by Johnny Cash."*
> *"Was that not a cover?"*
> *"Yes, but he owned it."*

Terrible cramps twisted her gut, knives at work, carving her abdomen into jagged slivers. The stench of malevolent magic awakened Victoria, jarring her from a sound sleep to a state of readiness. She opened her eyes to discover she lay naked in a strange bed beneath soft flannel sheets. The comforter and pillows smelled of goose down, but the bed lacked the distinctive scent of a regular occupant.

Guest room.

She rolled over and squirmed out from under the covers to stand and survey her surroundings. Blackout curtains covered the windows and cast the room into darkness. The red glowing eyes of another wolf gazed at her from across the room. The intruder crouched close to the ground, tail held straight and stiff. It had a longer body and more solid mass than she possessed.

Victoria narrowed her eyes and issued a challenging growl. She sniffed in confusion, because common sense contradicted what her nose was telling her. The other wolf was female and familiar.

"Morena?" Her voice contained a high note of disbelief.

Morena snarled, teeth bared and ears laid flat. Her muscles bunched and she sprang at her leader, closing the short distance between them in a single leap. Victoria managed to bring up her arms in a defensive gesture, protecting her face and throat. The Omega wolf's weight knocked her off balance, and she fell over backward.

Glistening teeth snapped at her face, spraying spittle and ribbons of saliva. The wolf's breath huffed hot on her face. Morena lunged for her throat, and she blocked those snapping jaws with her arm. The wolf latched on, sinking her teeth into Victoria's forearm. Pain lanced through her arm and shoulder.

"Morena! What the fuck are you doing?" Victoria checked her own instinctive impulse to shift to her canine form. If she allowed her beast to rise, she risked losing control of the already vicious situation. Instead, she summoned her power and attempted to calm her packmate.

Morena locked her jaws and shook her head from side to side. She ripped a chunk of flesh from Victoria's forearm. Blood sprayed the goose-down comforter and Victoria had to use her injured arm to stop those wicked teeth from ripping open her throat.

The soft feather mattress provided no purchase, so Morena gained the advantage. She crouched atop Victoria's chest and pinned her down. The Omega wolf's claws dug into her torso, leaving long parallel scratches.

The fresh pain propelled Victoria toward anger and overrode her reluctance to harm her pack member. With a burst of adrenaline, she surged off the bed and used all of her strength to hurl Morena across the room. The wolf landed in the corner, but charged the bed again as soon as she had recovered her feet.

Victoria leapt and met Morena midair. She tackled

the other woman and wrapped her arms around the Omega wolf's body. They landed on the ground in a heap.

Victoria beat the other wolf to her feet. "I don't want to hurt you, Morie. Please stop fighting me."

Morena snarled and foamed at the mouth. No recognition lit her eyes, only feral rage. She was not in control of her faculties. Howling, she lunged at her Alpha again.

Victoria met the younger wolf's charge. She caught Morena about the throat and then pitched her toward the bedroom window. The Omega wolf yelped when she struck the heavy material of the blackout curtain and the windowpane behind it. The curtain tore from its rod; the window shattered with a great crash. Then the whole thing collapsed on top of Morena.

Victoria dashed forward and snatched the corner of the curtains. She pulled the heavy material over Morena's head, covering the Omega wolf with the thick black fabric. With a grunt of exertion, Victoria wrapped her good arm around Morena's throat in a stranglehold and bore down, applying her full weight.

Morena struggled to escape, but she reacted from rage and not reason. Her claws ripped through the blackout curtain but the improvised restraint held long enough to serve its purpose, restricting vision and air.

In a furious contest of strength, Alpha struggled with Omega. Grunts, groans, and the occasional gasp filled the room. The exertion left Victoria soaked in sweat, as if she'd endured a terrible fever. Curls of wet hair clung to her skin, and blood from the injuries to her arm and torso streaked her body.

With stubborn determination, Victoria kept her arm locked tight about Morena's throat and rode out the bronco ride. Morena bucked and twisted, but her resistance weakened. Making a final bid for freedom, the Omega wolf jerked and then went limp except for her angry snarl. Finally, she subsided altogether.

Victoria released her chokehold. Hands shaking, Victoria pulled the curtain off the unconscious werewolf and bent to check Morena's throat for a pulse. The wolf had steady breathing and heart rate. She twitched and whimpered in her sleep.

"I'm sorry, Morie. I never wanted to hurt you." Victoria wrapped her arms around her unconscious packmate and hugged her hard. She buried her face in the Omega's fur and inhaled her scent. Tears coursed down her cheeks.

Sunlight streamed through the broken window and the glass shards cut into her knees, but Victoria could not release her desperate hold on her packmate. She was terrified. It was midday, and she had awoken to a nightmare where her pack had turned on one another. Logan was among the living dead.; Arik may very well have taken his own life.

"Victoria?" Arik's concerned voice came from the doorway.

"You're alive!" Startled, Victoria's head jerked toward him. She released a strangled cry of joy and relief, and released her hold on Morena. She sprang across the room and caught him about the waist. She latched on with all of her strength, squeezing so hard she forced the air from his lungs.

Arik hugged her in return, encircling her slender form in his arms, providing her with a fortress of strength. Her tears soaked into his cotton tee shirt. He felt solid and wonderful. Her world was a little bit better.

"Where are the others? Are they safe?"

"Yes, everyone is okay. Paul and Sylvie are outside with Sophia and the cubs, getting some fresh air. Everyone was going stir crazy waiting for you to wake up." Arik cradled the back of her head with his hands and pressed a kiss to her forehead.

"What the hell happened to Morena?" Victoria twisted around to watch her packmate with renewed wariness.

"She volunteered to sit with you. The last time I saw her, she was fine."

"She's not fine now." Fear bordering on panic threatened to seize her. She tightened her grip on Arik and clung to him for support. "Morena attacked me."

"I saw. I didn't want to interfere," Arik said.

"Thank you." He scored points for having the sense to let her resolve the conflict on her own. If he had interfered, Victoria might have attacked him to defend her Omega. Instinct was a powerful thing.

The Alpha murmured something indecipherable — an assurance or platitude — then his tongue stumbled into the awkward silence of a man unaccustomed to voicing his emotions.

Victoria did not suffer from his verbal affliction. "I'm going to rip that fucking witch limb from limb."

"I'm right with you."

She jerked away and stepped out of his arms. Her blue eyes burned bright. She drew back her arm and clobbered Arik on the chest with her fist. The force of the blow would have sent a human flying into the wall. The Alpha absorbed it and stood his ground.

A look of chagrin crossed his countenance. "What was that for?"

"For not listening to me when you should have!" Victoria scrubbed at the tears on her cheeks with the back of her hand. She wanted to hit him harder but curbed the impulse.

"I guess I had it coming then," Arik said. His dark eyes and tense posture communicated tiredness and tension. "Are you okay?"

"My arm and chest hurt, and I'm starving." Victoria's gaze strayed to Morena, twisting with sorrow and anger.

Arik scowled. "The *seiðr* is growing bolder, more powerful. She's gone from manipulating our emotions to taking outright control of the weakest member of the pack."

Victoria stared at him, mouth open. She closed it, afraid of what she might say. Could it be so easy? She had expected to pull teeth in order to convince him of the witch's existence. Once again, the sense of a Twilight Zone awakening struck her.

When she didn't respond, Arik reached for her injured arm. "You're bleeding."

"I'll heal once I eat something. Help me move her." Victoria indicated Morena.

He nodded and went to the unconscious wolf and hefted her in his arms. He set her down on the bed.

"I'll fetch some restraints." He directed a look in Victoria's direction. "Watch her?"

"Hurry, before she wakes." Victoria sat on the bed beside Morena and stroked the wolf's fur. Arik left and then returned a couple of minutes later carrying silver shackles and chains. The restraints included a silver collar designed to fit a wolf.

"Where did you get those?" Victoria shuddered and stared at the fetters but did not protest when he put them on Morena. Still, she failed to hide her disgust. Human hunters used similar restraints when they took prisoners for interrogation. The silver prevented shapechangers from shifting forms.

"I had them made for Logan," Arik said. "It was right after Lori died, and I worried about having trouble controlling him. We never used them. Silver had no effect on Logan."

Victoria stared at Arik. Her brow rose. "Logan is immune to silver?"

"Yes." Arik locked the last shackle into place.

"That's... amazing." *Epic*, as in the heroes of legend.

Arik flashed a sardonic smile. "Nothing else was

common about Logan. Why should that be?"

The Alpha's expression underwent rapid change, an awful moment of realization. "Shit. I don't know whether to refer to him in past or present tense anymore."

Victoria trembled. Due to exhaustion and injury, she couldn't control her outward expression. "Where is he?"

"I put him on his bed in his room. He's still... asleep."

Victoria grabbed his hand and reached for him through the pack bond, offering her comfort and support. The day before, she would not have taken such a familiarity.

"When did you decide to stop being stupid and believe me?"

Arik's lips twisted in an ironic little smile. "This is a lot like being married again."

At the reminder of their unresolved relationship, Victoria's mouth twisted at the corner, not smiling or frowning. Their engagement would last until they had sex and sealed the mate bond, then they would be married for life. Wolves did not divorce.

"You'd know better than I," she said.

He arched his brow. "Do you want to discuss this now?"

She shook her head. "No, we've got too many other problems to face. Let's take care of the high priority stuff first."

From the look on Arik's face, her pragmatism continued to surprise him. "I agree."

She glanced around and for the first time wondered about clothing. "How long have I been unconscious?"

Arik's hungry gaze traveled the curves of her body. He licked his lips. "Almost twelve hours. It's almost noon. C'mon, let's get you food and clothing, then get our pack to safety so we can deal with my witch and help Logan."

"Say 'we' again." Victoria grabbed his hand. Her

eyes were bright with tears. It hurt to breathe. She'd been alone—bearing the burdens of leadership alone—for so very long.

He stared at her and smiled, a real smile that reached his eyes. "We."

"We." Her smile grew in response to his until she wore a silly grin. She tightened her grip on his hand, stroked the hair on the back of his wrist. "Our pack, our witch."

Victoria hauled Arik toward her. Her stomach growled for food; her wolf clamored for sex. Too many conflicting needs. She pressed a hard kiss to Arik's mouth, using her lips and teeth and tongue, and suppressed the desire to nip him and taste his blood.

They separated, breathing hard. "You'd better feed me, or I'm going to bite you."

Arik laughed. "I'll head to the kitchen and make you something to eat. Your clothes are on the dresser. The bathroom's across the hall."

"Okay, thanks," she said. As Arik departed, she called after him. "I want raw meat!"

She located a neat pile of folded clothing on the dresser. They were different from the ones she'd been wearing earlier. Sylvie must have provided them. She carried her stuff into the bathroom and turned on the water in the shower to let the water warm. A quick examination of her reflection in the mirror revealed half-healed injuries caked with dried blood. Her hair looked like a bristle brush.

She showered and without dressing returned to the guest bedroom to check on Morena. The Omega wolf remained unconscious, but an examination of her neck, wrists, and ankles revealed raw burns from the silver. Victoria's stomach churned, but she acknowledged the necessity of keeping Morena chained, at least until they figured out how to overcome the witch's control.

In the kitchen, Arik presented Victoria with a

butchered strip of raw beef. The second the scent of fresh meat hit her nostrils, she shifted to her wolf form. She fell on the steak and devoured it with voracious hunger, tearing and gulping chunks of meat. Arik watched her eat and maintained a respectful distance.

She shifted and dressed while Arik cleaned. She took a seat in a kitchen chair to lace up her shoes. "What convinced you?"

Arik's brow rose. "Convinced me of what?"

"That I'm right about the witch. Face it, last night, when I tried to convince you, you wouldn't listen to me."

Arik looked her straight in the eye. "Victoria, last night I saw you resurrect my son from the dead and call down a goddess from the heavens. You possess such grace that Freya granted your prayers in person, and you possess such honor you were willing to give your life to see my son live. Who am I to question your integrity?"

Her foot hit the floor with a thud, and she stood. "Thank you. You have no idea how much that means to me."

"I made a mistake trying to force you."

"I don't know how to submit." The difficult admission cost her.

Arik nodded. "I won't try again."

She licked her lips. "It was wrong of me to put you in the position of fighting your son or losing your honor."

Their apologies blended, voices crossing over, speaking over one another. But she stopped talking when Arik said, "I admit: I can be stubborn, even obstinate..."

She flashed teeth. "Thick-headed."

Arik shot her a warning glance, and she laughed. "C'mon, you left yourself wide open."

He chuckled and pulled her into a hug. His breath ruffled her hair. "I'm sorry."

Victoria kissed the underside of his jaw. "I'm sorry too. Are we good?"

"We're good."

They fit well together despite the difference in their sizes. She tilted her head back to look him in the eyes, and they shared a long look. Their exchange had nothing to do with dominance but rather communication. Finally, she had a consort and companion; the burden of leadership no longer fell on her alone.

She broke the silence. "Can I see Logan?"

Arik took a step back. "This way."

He led her to a bedroom off the main house and opened the door. He stepped aside to allow Victoria to pass. She entered the dim room and glanced about out of curiosity. Overall, Logan was surprisingly, *shockingly*, neat. She had expected more of a hurricane-hit, lived-in look.

Built in bookcases, crammed with thousands of books, took up an entire wall. Rock band posters decorated the space over the bed, including a black and white poster of Johnny Cash giving the world the bird.

It made her smile. "I wouldn't have expected *that*."

Arik snorted. "Logan and I share a passion for old rock music."

"Yeah, I saw the collection of vinyl albums in the family room."

Arik waited a beat. "Logan calls it old folks' music."

"Well, he's an ass."

They shared a broken laugh. She summoned her courage and faced the bed. Logan lay on his back beneath a dark blue sheet, turned down at his waist. His chest rose and fell with shallow breaths. He lived but suffered from a conspicuous lack of the animation that defined him. It disturbed her to witness his degradation.

"Is it true you named him after the comic book hero?" Victoria asked, breaking the uncomfortable silence. Guilt sickened her. For the sake of personal vanity, she had pitted father against son. Her arrogance had gotten Logan killed and had destroyed Arik's will to live. She felt she had no honor left.

Arik snorted. "Logan's named after his grandfather."

"It figures." She swallowed past a lump. "This is my fault."

Arik shook his head. "No, it's mine."

She stared at Logan's closed eyes, remembering the way he'd stared at her in death. She didn't want to argue fault with Arik; more than enough blame to go around.

"Has he stirred at all?" she asked.

Arik's tangible despair reached her through their pack bond. "No. He appears to be in a deep coma."

Victoria checked Logan's pulse and found it to be slow and steady. "If you can obtain the equipment, I can put him on an IV-drip and a catheter."

"No." Arik's tone vetoed the idea. "If we can't recover his soul, then his body must be allowed to die."

"I agree. His soul has gone on to Valhalla. I'll go after him just as soon as we get the pack moved to safety."

"Is that the right thing to do? I can't help but wonder. Logan's soul is in paradise. His suffering has ended."

Arik's anguish made her chest hurt. She feared for him. If he chose to end his own life, Valhalla would not be waiting for him. There would be the frozen eternity of Niflheim, the Norse land of the dead where the Goddess Hel ruled. There would be no joyous reunion with his deceased family and friends.

Victoria grabbed his hand. "It is always better to be alive! In life, there is suffering but there is also hope, creation and the potential for joy. Death—even in paradise—is static. It is eternal monotony."

He held her hand as if it were his lifeline. However, she sensed his remoteness. Arik possessed an impenetrable emotional detachment. So many years alone had left him isolated in an inner fortress. He would allow her to get only so close; there were limits to how much of his turmoil he would share.

"We need to move the pack," Arik said. "Get them somewhere safe. If this goes down like it did before, then the seiðr's powers are strongest after nightfall."

Victoria jumped to action. "I'll fetch Sylvie and the others. The explanation should come from me. They'll be frightened and confused once they find out what's happened to Morena."

Arik acknowledged the wisdom of sending her. "I'll pack provisions and get Morena into my vehicle. Don't waste any time, Victoria."

She nodded and headed for the door but hesitated before plunging into the snowy yard. Her thoughts were full of hunters and witches, a world thick on threats.

"Arik?"

Arik looked at her, a question in his honey-brown eyes. "What?"

"Where is safe?"

"Desolation Wilderness. Now go."

Victoria nodded and went. She cursed the loss of her cellphone. She exited the house via the backdoor and crossed the back patio where she picked up her pack's fresh tracks in the snow. She smelled Sylvie, Paul, Sophia and the pups. At least they were all together.

Victoria set out at a brisk clip, following their trail. A half mile from the house, she came to an abrupt stop. A mild breeze blew west off the lake; it was bright and sunny. Alert, she scanned her surroundings, searching for the source of her unease.

The sound of a round being chambered split the silence, revealing the location of her stalker. Victoria spun and stared down the barrel of the shotgun. She met the eyes of the man who believed she had murdered his brother.

"Hello, Sawyer."

CHAPTER FOURTEEN

Sacrifice—
  "Goddess, is this the right thing?"
  "Victoria, it is the thing that you are going to do, right or wrong."

"Hello, Victoria." Sawyer Barrett held the shotgun trained on her. He had rock-steady aim. The hunter stood forty feet away within the eaves of a redwood. The lowest branches were so laden with snow, no green was visible.

Victoria lowered her head and her muscles bunched into knots as she gathered her strength. She calculated the distance to him, estimating the five seconds separating her fangs and his throat: less time than it took to pull a trigger, far less than it took a bullet to travel the same distance.

Long seconds dragged past. Sawyer's brown eyes were hard. Sweat beaded his upper lip, and his breath emerged as heavy puffs of vapor. His heart pounded, beating out a steady *thud thud* rhythm. He smelled of tension and hesitation, a terrible combination in a hunter.

Victoria grew impatient with the silence. "How did you find me?"

"Trade secret."

She rolled her eyes. "It was all the howling."

He dipped his head forward. "Dead giveaway, every time."

He answered too fast. She would have the vehicles searched for tracking devices if she survived the encounter. Victoria sighed. "Look, are you going to shoot or were you hoping to get my number?"

Sawyer's jaw worked. "I want to know about my brother."

Victoria closed her eyes and exhaled. Then she looked him straight in the eye. "Sawyer, I don't have time for this right now. I'm dealing with a witch who's trying to take control of my pack, and I need to get the soul of an annoying guy back from the dead. Why don't we set up a meeting for next week? You have my word that I'll show. As long as I'm still alive, that is."

He gestured with the shotgun. "You're going to have to make time, Victoria."

She stared at him and then glanced around the empty forest, testing the air for the scent of other hunters. "You're here alone, aren't you, Sawyer? That's foolhardy and risky. Hunters are dangerous to us because of your numbers."

She narrowed her eyes. "One man alone against a pack of wolves..."

He ignored the implicit threat. "Stop delaying."

"You don't trust me enough to lower the shotgun, but you want me to tell you about Daniel? Why would you believe me?"

"Leave the reasons up to me."

"Don't give me orders and think I'll obey."

His lips twitched in what might have been a smile. "I found some photos of you on my brother's phone. Let's say they were real friendly looking."

Her lips formed a thin smile. "Fine, I can prove I knew your brother. When you were six, you almost drowned while your brother was babysitting. Your mother ran to the market, but he was playing video games. He blamed himself."

Sawyer's complexion paled beneath his tan.

She continued. "Daniel squeezed the toothpaste from the middle of the tube and never put the cap back on, so it formed this disgusting crust. His favorite music was heavy metal: Metallica, ACDC, Iron Maiden. His favorite color was blue."

The color of my eyes, she thought, was what he would say when she was in his arms.

"His favorite food was bacon, and he lost his virginity to Christy Cortez in the eighth grade behind the bleachers during a school dance."

She could tell by the look on his face she had him listening, at least, if not convinced. "Daniel liked to do this thing when we had sex—"

"Whoa, okay, I've heard enough!" Sawyer held up a staying hand, so rattled the barrel of the gun dipped. "Very convincing, although, the bacon was sorta a gimme."

Victoria exhaled. "Look, Sawyer, don't take this the wrong way, but I'm up to my eyeballs in trouble. I don't have time for any shit, so if you're not going to listen to me—"

"I want to hear what you have to say. I'm not leaving without answers." He kept the shotgun's muzzle pointed downward, no longer aimed straight at her. It was a minor concession, but she was willing to take what she could get.

Victoria stared at him for a long moment, debating the wisdom of making a break for it. By the time he could aim and get off a shot, she stood a good chance of reaching the nearest stand of trees and cover. Running did her no good when Jake Barrett and his people would pursue them to the ends of the earth. Sawyer presented an opportunity for resolution without more bloodshed.

The torment and despair in those soulful brown

eyes convinced her. Victoria exhaled so her breath formed a cloud of vapor on the cool air. "Fine. You're getting the abridged version."

"Okay, fine."

"After we started dating, Daniel used to take me hunting with him. Or rather, I should say, Daniel's definition of a hot date was a hunt and then takeout back at his place. Or sometimes we'd just drive out into the desert and hang out in the back of the Chevelle with the top down." She laughed, an empty sound, because the memories hurt. Nostalgia just wasn't her thing.

"You're telling me Daniel's idea of a date was a hunt?"

Victoria challenged him with an arched brow. "You're telling me otherwise?"

His throat rumbled with a hoarse chuckle. "Point taken. What did you hunt? I can't see *you* — "

Victoria bared her teeth. "Can't you? Try using your imagination then, because there aren't many things wolves love more than a good vampire hunt."

"Okay, I guess it's not that much of a stretch. How come he never told me any of this?"

She shrugged. "You were away at college. He said you didn't need hunting in your life anymore. I think he wanted to protect you."

"He was my older brother. He was always trying to protect me, even when I didn't need it. I can't believe he didn't tell me," Sawyer said with terrible anguish.

"He didn't tell anyone from your family," Victoria said. Bitterness gave the words bite.

Sawyer's mouth twisted. "How the hell did the two of you start?"

"Hunting together? It's a long story. I don't really have time." She glanced at the sky, thinking about time ticking past. How long before Arik came looking for her or the pack stumbled across them on their way back to the house?

Sawyer shook his head. "Never mind, tell me how he died."

"We were hunting vampires. It was my fault." Her expression betrayed her guilt. It was not the smartest thing to say to her dead lover's brother, but it was the truth.

Sawyer's grip tightened on the gun and the barrel shifted toward her. "Is that a confession?"

Victoria blinked and tears fell. "I didn't sense the vampire until it was too late. The wound that killed Daniel was too severe for me to heal. I tried to save him, but I failed."

Sawyer swore. "How long did this go on—your thing with my brother?"

"A year, give or take. In the beginning, it was on-again, off-again. But near the end, we were together whenever our schedules allowed."

Sawyer clenched his teeth. "I thought wolves mated for life," he said, trying to poke holes in her story.

Victoria stared at him. "We do, but I'm a modern woman living in a modern world. We used birth control, and besides, Daniel never asked. I think maybe he wanted to, but he wasn't ready to go against your father."

"Wait, you blame my father for this?"

"Who else would I blame?"

Sawyer swore again. "All those people died for nothing. Why the hell didn't you or one of your people come forward and tell us the truth?"

She sneered. "As if anyone can tell Jake Barrett anything! My father tried. He arranged that meeting with your dad and he went unarmed. He walked right into an ambush. I'll tell you this, Sawyer Barrett, your brother's killer is still out there but it sure as hell wasn't me."

"What the fuck is that supposed to mean?"

Victoria started to answer but then a distant sound through the trees caught her attention. She tilted her head back to listen. A wolf howl pierced the thin veil of daylight filtering through the snow-laden trees. It was Sylvie, leading the charge.

Sawyer leveled the barrel of the gun straight at her. "Tell them to back off."

Paul's deep-pitched call filled the air, and then Sophia's and the yips of the pups. The pack had the scent; they were coming. Sawyer knew he was in trouble.

"Fuck." He rubbed his jaw and backed up.

"Sawyer, please, put the gun down. Trust me. I can protect you." Risking a gunshot, she moved forward and got within ten feet of him before the sound of breaking branches announced the arrival of the first wolf.

Sawyer spun toward the newcomer. A black wolf the size of a pony crashed through the trees. Reminiscent of the Norse legends of Fenrir, he had immense jaws and huge paws, and the glowing eyes filled with fury. He let loose a fearsome howl.

"Arik, no!" Victoria launched herself into the air. The leap of her arc carried her into the path of the shotgun. She felt the impact and then the blast deafened her. The shot caught her in the side, entering her back, hard and shocking, as if a bomb had gone off inside her chest.

"Arik, don't kill him, please. We were talking." She staggered forward, remaining between the men. Behind her, Sawyer cursed a blue streak. No more shots rang out.

Arik performed a forced partial shift, enough so that he had hands to catch her before she fell. His honey-brown eyes held shock and amazement. "You took a bullet for me."

"Consider it a wedding present." She mustered a smile but her joke fell flat, and she would have also but for Arik's arms holding her up. A crushing pressure against her lungs caused her breath to come in short gasps. She looked down and saw nothing but blood.

Arik looked past her and growled at the hunter. Victoria tightened her weakening grasp on his arms.

"Please."

Arik lowered her to the ground, and she lost all sense of the passage of time. Events seemed to unfold with surreal slowness and yet too fast for her mind to process. The others reached them, and the air was full of howls, men's angry shouts, and her pack's frightened whimpers.

Sylvie fell to her knees with a moan. "Oh, Goddess, not you, too. Victory, we can't lose you, too."

Paul squared off opposite Sawyer. "Arik?"

"Hold off," Arik said. "Victoria doesn't want him dead."

"None of this would have happened if we'd killed him the first time," Sylvie said with shocking bitterness from such a sweet person.

"The bullet wasn't silver."

Every head turned to stare at Sawyer. Expressions ranged from relief to disbelief. Through a white-hot haze of pain, Victoria gathered all of her remaining strength. She experienced the physical regeneration occurring as her injuries closed. Her body would force the shrapnel out, so long as it was made of lead.

Victoria lifted her head from Sylvie's lap. "I believe he's telling the truth."

"If the bullet had been silver, she'd already be dead." Sawyer maintained a white-knuckled grip on the shotgun. Victoria suspected the hunter had reloaded with silver. He'd had plenty of time.

"Arik, let him go," she said. "No more bloodshed. Please."

Arik leveled a stare at Sawyer. "Do you want to live?"

Sawyer's swallowed so his Adam's apple jerked. "Yeah."

"Leave and do not return. If you come near my mate or my pack again, I will kill you."

Sawyer cast Victoria one final glance. The word *mate*

left him shocked. His expression conveyed confusion, and finally, understanding as he completed the mental calculation and realized the dynamic had changed. Then he moved from his vantage beneath the redwood and headed for the road.

"Sawyer, wait." Victoria struggled to sit up.

Sawyer stopped in his tracks and glanced back. "Yeah?"

"Is your brother's phone still active?"

He stirred. "Yeah, I think so."

"Good. I'll give you a call when I'm ready to talk, once this current crisis is over. I'll answer all of your questions about your brother. Until then, stay the hell out of my way, do you hear me?"

"Yeah, I hear you." Sawyer departed, disappearing into the trees toward the road.

Arik bent and gathered Victoria into his arms. Excruciating pain caused her to see white, and she lost her tenuous focus for a second. "Goddess, that hurts."

"I'm not surprised." Arik turned to the pack. "We're leaving."

Sylvie and Sophia spread out to round up the pups. Arik placed his mouth beside Victoria's ear and pitched his voice for her alone. "Your involvement with the hunters is more intimate than you led me to believe."

"Yes." Tears filled her eyes. "I loved the wrong man. A whole lot of people are dead because of me."

Arik pressed his lips to her forehead. "You don't love me, and yet you took a bullet for me."

Victoria blinked and looked away. Funny how her heart hurt when she'd been shot in the side. "Love doesn't matter. You're my mate."

"Excuse the interruption." Paul appeared to Arik's right. "We've got the pups rounded up. Need to get a move on before the critters scatter again. Where're we headin'?"

"Up to the house," Arik said. "Morena's already in

the back of my vehicle. Let's move out."

Arik took the lead with Victoria cradled in his arms. Sophia and Sylvia rode herd on the pups, and Paul brought up the rear. Swift and silent, the wolves melted into the forest.

Victoria awoke, cradled in Arik's arms, to the crunch of feet upon unbroken snow and wolves huffing for breath. His steady pace created a rhythmic rocking she found soothing. The fresh scent of pristine wilderness filled her nostrils. The stench and noise of civilization was gone.

Victoria opened her eyes to catch a glimpse of a dizzying blue sky overhead, bright like eternity. She made a huffing sound, and Arik broke stride and came to a halt. The other members of the pack, traveling in a single line formation, followed suit.

"Did I fall asleep?" she asked.

Arik lowered his head and nuzzled her face. "You passed out and missed the car ride. The blood loss was extensive, but I believe the bleeding has stopped."

"I'll have to shift to finish healing." There were limits to what her body could accomplish without the reformative process of shapechanging.

"We'll stop in a moment to do that."

Her lips touched her mate's cheek; the tip of her tongue licked salt from his skin. She attempted to lift her head, but weakness overwhelmed her. She settled for tilting her head back in order to gaze at their surroundings. It was a valley with a river running through, mountains high on either side.

"Is this Desolation Wilderness? It's breathtaking."

Arik nodded. "This is Desolation Wilderness."

Sylvie's hand touched Victoria's forehead. "Sweetie, you've taken years off my life today."

"I'm sorry, Sylvie. I'll try not to get shot in the future."

"Hrmph." Sylvie snorted and moved away.

Victoria struggled to see around her again. "Where's Morena? Is everyone here?"

"Don't worry none. I've got Miss Morie." Paul appeared at the periphery of Victoria's vision. He carried the Omega wolf—still bound in silver chains and wrapped in a heavy blanket—in his arms. The old werewolf moved with great difficulty under the combined burden of his prosthetic limbs and Morena's weight. With a grunt of relief, he lowered Morena to the ground and rested.

Sophia and her pups swarmed into sight. The cubs bounded through the snow with energetic zeal, perceiving the pack's desperate flight into the wilderness as nothing more than a great adventure. Sylvie moved to cut off their rambunctious advance, herding them away.

"Put me down. We need to attend to Morena," Victoria said.

"We need to heal you first." Arik lowered Victoria to the ground. He helped her out of her tattered and bloody clothing.

"Damn, there goes another outfit," Victoria said. She yipped when her bare buttocks and legs encountered the frozen ground. She attempted to change shapes on her own and failed because she lacked the energy necessary to fuel the transformation.

With a frustrated sigh, she turned to Arik and found him waiting. "I can't shift right now. I don't have enough strength."

"There's no shame in asking for help, Victoria."

Her chin set into a stubborn jut, provoking chuckles from Sylvie and Paul.

"Victoria doesn't ask for help," Sylvie said. "Not even when she was a little girl. Had to do everything her own way."

"Girl used to give her mother fits."

Arik snorted, but at least he didn't laugh at her. With a shake of his head, the Alpha stood and stripped away his clothing. He shed his shirt, soaked with her blood, and allowed it to fall with a wet glop onto the fresh snow. His shoes and pants followed, preserved for future wear.

He reached for Victoria and the rest of the pack crowded forward. At their approach, Arik stiffened and a discordant note rang through the pack's aura. Victoria bared her teeth in a snarl and the others froze. Every wolf from Sylvie on down to the youngest pup quivered in reaction to the perceived rejection.

"You've lived outside of a pack for too long, Arik," Victoria said. With a gesture, she called the others to her. They came, bubbling over with love and concern, and seized hold of her hands and arms. A cold nose pressed into her side as one of the pups struggled to find his place.

Arik approached last, and the others parted before him and then closed behind, like the stream about the rock. He took her hand, and a collective sigh whispered through the pack.

"You're right," Arik said.

Victoria flashed a cheeky smile. "Of course, I'm right."

His eyes laughed even though he maintained a stoic demeanor. "Ah, is that how it is?"

Arik bent and his power spilled forth, flowing into her and then the pack. Wolves whined, barked, and squirmed as the pack's magic ignited into a brilliant blaze. The wildfire grew and spread along every pathway open to it and created new avenues, strengthening the whole.

When the magic built to a crescendo, she drew it into herself. An enthusiastic shout escaped her as the energy crawled across her skin and the transformation to wolf took hold. Tendons burst and pain blossomed, but it was the pleasurable aching and tearing of rebirth. Fur sprang from beneath her skin and bones snapped, reoriented, and fused together. The change progressed, and her injuries healed as she slid into her second skin.

Healthy and whole, she gained her feet and shook off the lead shot her body had pushed out of the wounds. The others pulled away, and she trotted from the throng as a small white wolf. Aware of her mate's gaze upon her, she pranced for him.

Arik stared. "By Odin's eye, you're glorious."

Victoria preened, basking in his male admiration, right up until a moment later when Arik said, "But I've seen bigger coyotes."

Victoria snarled and her hackles rose. Stiff-legged, she advanced and dared him to repeat the deadly insult.

Call me a coyote, will you! Posturing, she lunged and Arik evaded her snapping jaws.

Sylvie chuckled and caught Victoria in her arms. "Arik, a wise man speaks of his mate's loveliness and keeps such comments to himself."

Paul chuckled. "Our Victory has been known to call out wolves three times her size for such a remark."

"Oh, yes," Sylvie said. "Remember when Victory challenged Rand? He called her itty-bitty, and she smacked him so hard he fell over." Mixed sorrow and amusement hit the pack's aura, a splash of cold water.

"Ah." Arik managed to bend his smirk into a repentant smile. He held up a conciliatory hand to the still snarling Victoria. "Peace and my apologies. Your beauty is unrivaled and startled me so I spoke out of turn."

Crafty lawyer... Victoria held her head high and sniffed. She ran her tongue across the back of his hand. She knew his scent and his taste. *Mate.* Energy coursed between them, touch intensified, and their gazes locked. Arik reached for her ruff, burying his fingers in the thick fur. She tilted her head back and whined, frustrated with the depth of her need. She balanced the demands of her body against her duty to pack, always finding duty more pressing.

Arik produced a rumble deep in his throat. Tension electrified the pack and they stilled, watching with fascinated intensity. Mindful of their audience, Arik grunted and withdrew his hands from her fur. Bereft, Victoria whined again in protest.

"Let's help Morena," Arik said.

Victoria barked in agreement. The limited vocabulary of a wolf vexed her, but she needed to remain one long enough to recover some of her strength. Another change so soon would leave her exhausted.

Arik went to where Morena lay on the ground. He pushed aside the blanket, unveiling the Omega wolf, still bound in heavy silver chains. Although she kept her eyes closed, her sides rose and fell as the result of rapid panting. Blood had crusted and dried on the silver chains where they burnt into her flesh.

When Arik touched her head, Morena's eyes snapped open. Her lips peeled back from her teeth and a fierce snarl rocked the wolf. Froth foamed from her lips, and her blood-shot eyes glowed with crimson fire. Her ferocious struggle to be free produced fresh blood from the injuries caused by the restraints.

"Goddess," Sylvie said. Her horror spread through the pack. Sophia and the pups recoiled, tucking their tails, and retreated from the spectacle.

Victoria moved closer to show Morena she wasn't afraid. She pressed her side against Arik's leg and placed a paw on Morena's back. The Omega wolf flew into a renewed display of fury, growing and thrashing, but Victoria remained clear of her teeth and claws.

"What's wrong with her?" Paul asked.

"A *seiðr*," Arik said. "A witch has taken possession of her. We must free her."

The Beta wolves exchanged a glance. "The entire

pack again?" Sylvie asked.

Victoria barked an immediate denial.

Arik's hand settled on her neck again. "No, this is too dangerous to risk Sophia and the pups. Victoria and I will do this together. Take the others and move back into the trees until we say it's safe."

They watched and waited until the rest of the pack had taken refuge beneath a stand of pines. Victoria turned back to the rabid Morena and surveyed her packmate with grim determination. Yet another member of her family in danger, another fight for survival. She wondered how many more battles she would fight and whether it would ever end.

Arik knelt beside her in the snow, and together, they pressed against Morena. He rested his hands on the back of the Omega wolf's neck, and Victoria pressed paws and nose into the fur above her spine. They completed a circuit and opened to the evil presence that occupied Morena.

A bitter cold wind sprang up, lashing down upon their heads, cutting like a whip. The frozen force penetrated fur and sinew. The wind boomed, creating a deafening thunder, and Victoria folded her ears against the onslaught. She listened and heard it again.

There!

Arik shouted something to her, but his words were lost to the wind. She strained to hear him, but the tempest drowned him out, leaving only laughter. Cruel cackling surrounded Victoria, instilling a sickening horror and fear, so she shook. Great fury rose up in her, and she whirled as if the hounds of hell were snapping at her heels. The taunting laughter retreated, and she followed with snapping jaws and glistening fangs.

Victoria plunged into the snow, seeking to destroy her tormentor, and ran into the trunk of a redwood. The enormous old tree had branches burdened with ice and snow and a hundred delicate icicles ringing with the witch's voice. She reared onto her hind legs to reach the lowest branch and bit through the bases of an entire row of icicles. She shook the tree and brought down an avalanche of snow that landed on top of her and buried her deep.

Arik's hands found Victoria beneath the snow and hauled her to the surface. Bristling, she snarled and showed her teeth. His hand closed on her mouth, shutting it, and his arm encircled her body. With a grunt, he hauled her off the ground. Victoria emitted a startled yip, and her anger took a new course over the indignity visited upon her.

"Stop letting the witch distract you. Biting icicles isn't helping Morena." Arik dropped Victoria to the ground. She landed beside the Omega wolf.

The sight of Morena bound in silver and helpless knocked some sense back into Victoria. Still growling, she reined in her anger and focused it into a more productive avenue. Arik's large hands found her shoulders. As a magus to magic, he summoned his power, calling it forth. Victoria trembled from nose to tail, quivering with excitement at the first delicate stroke of his energy. She cleaved to him, her potency to his, faithful and fervent to her mate's cause.

Before, when they had joined in an effort to save Logan, the tsunami of power had overwhelmed. This time, she expected and welcomed the flood of energy. She responded to the coupling with eagerness, and opened to him, allowing his primal essence to flow into her.

"Observe and learn," Arik said, speaking not only to Victoria but also to the watchful pack. "For this is mine alone to teach. Our kind has lived too long in the cities of men, surrounded by machines and human artifice, losing our connection to the primordial beast."

The Alpha commanded all then. His power originated from within and without, surrounding them, just as the lake and the mountains and the sky above. His will created an act of becoming. Victoria watched him, determined to learn his secrets.

The cold fire of the aura borealis burned in his hands; he held his palms down and bathed Morena in the light. The Omega wolf's body jerked and writhed with convulsions. The witch's cruel cackling turned to a shriek of outrage, and the lashing wind kicked up and blew that much harder.

"In pure places, in wild places, my wolf is your master, *seiðr!*" Arik shouted over the witch-wind. "I am this great wilderness! I am the immovable mountains, the vast lake, the infinite sky. I am everything, and you are nothing!"

His power rose and soared. The endless wellspring spilled over into Victoria. She used it to fuel her transformation to human shape and to replenish her depleted reserves. Her exhaustion receded, and she felt refreshed. Once again, it gladdened her heart to have Arik at her side. She could not have asked for a stronger, fiercer mate.

Then, to her amazement, the energy moved to the rest of the pack without the benefit of physical contact. It filled Sylvie and Paul, Sophia and the pups to overflowing. When one wolf could contain it no more, the living, breathing *thing* moved on in search of a new home. It reached Morena last.

The violent convulsions ceased, leaving the Omega wolf limp on the ground. The witch wind died away, becoming a gust, then a breeze. Finally, not a current stirred the air. With it went the *seiðr's* wicked laughter, leaving behind the broken beauty of the winter day.

Morena gurgled, choking on blood. Red froth bubbled from her mouth, forming a cascade of foam to the stained snow. The Omega blinked and turned her head to the side. Her brown eyes held pain and confusion. She struggled and then whimpered under the burden of the silver chains.

"Help me unchain her." Victoria grabbed for Morena and cursed when the restraints burned her fingers. She secured a firm hold on the Omega wolf's furry ruff. "Morie, shhh. Don't struggle. Stay still and we'll get you free."

Arik removed the chains and discarded them. "The burns are deep. This is more than she can heal alone."

"I'll help her." Victoria gathered the passive Morena into her arms. She summoned her healing magic. Out of habit, the rest of the pack started forward, prepared to provide the energy necessary to fuel Victoria's magic.

"Wait. I want to try something." Victoria held up a staying hand and the others stopped.

She tapped into her personal power, and then reached for the gateway to Arik's wild magic. The initial impulse struck her as being as reckless as drilling into the side of an immense dam, but she needed to test the boundaries of what she'd learned. The magic responded to her bidding, a trickle rather than a torrent, supple and pliable to her command.

When Victoria removed her hands, Morena's injuries had healed. The Omega wolf's fur remained matted with dried blood, but she rested on her side in the snow, breathing easy.

"You learn fast," Arik said. His gaze held admiration.

"Thanks." Victoria hid a smile of pleasure and adopted a modest posture, although she wanted to do nothing more than dance across the clearing.

"Allow her to remain a wolf," Arik said.

Victoria nodded. "Agreed. No sense in her changing, and then having to change back." She petted Morena's head and murmured a few words of reassurance to be sure the Omega wolf understood.

Arik addressed the pack. "As you've witnessed, there's a witch attempting to destroy the pack. This witch is my enemy from long ago, and I had thought her destroyed."

"The witch uses magic to take control of our beasts. It's how she turned Morena against me," Victoria said. She and Arik exchanged a look. What came next would be difficult.

"Victoria and I have discussed this," Arik said. "We've agreed the witch is a foe we must confront alone. If we remain together, she will divide us and turn us against one another."

The dire predication caused a shiver of unease to traverse the pack bond. None of them felt safe.

"Sylvie, Paul, you're to take the others deep into the wilderness preserve," Victoria said. "Live as wolves. Hunt to survive. Avoid humans at all costs."

The Beta wolves traded glances.

"For how long?" Sylvie asked.

"Until you are called." Victoria allowed her gaze to travel from one member of her pack to the next. She used her influence to soothe their agitation.

"And if you don't come?" Paul asked.

"Then this is an excellent place to live and hunt," Victoria said. Her stern tone brooked no argument. Her pack knew her well enough to know when it was okay to argue and when her mind was made up.

Victoria took a deep breath. "I'm going with Arik, but I won't be coming back."

The pack stirred; Arik shot her a sharp glance.

"Logan's soul must be retrieved from Valhalla before three days have passed," she said. "As a Valkyrie, it is my right to choose members of the Einherjar from the souls of those slain in combat. There is precedence for a soul being taken from Odin's hall, but there is also a catch."

Sylvie, schooled in the traditions, grew pale. "A warrior must be left in place of the one departing. Victory, you plan to remain!"

Paul sputtered in outrage and whines of distress rose up from Sophia and the pups. Morena alone remained silent. Victoria exerted her power and managed to cool hot tempers until her mate turned against her.

Arik snarled. "No! I will not allow this!"

His opposition caught her unprepared. She turned astonished eyes toward him. "I thought we were in agreement! Logan must live. Only then will honor be satisfied."

"I'll stay in his place," Arik said.

Victoria shook her head. "No, you must destroy the witch."

Sylvie caught hold of Victoria's arm. "Honor be damned! That boy wasn't even of this pack!"

Every head turned to Sylvie, eyes wide with amazement.

"Sylvie, please, listen to me," Victoria said.

"No, you listen, Victoria Svana Storm! Your duty is to this pack! Your duty is to mate with the Alpha male our goddess has provided and to produce a healthy and viable heir! Your duty is to your bloodline! Your family's heritage and honor depends upon you! Now I have mourned with you and supported you and done all I'm able to ease your guilt. But enough is enough!"

Fury transformed Arik. He started to shift, slipping into wolf form. "Beta, you speak out of turn!"

Victoria moved between Arik and her Beta even though the older woman's harsh words smarted. "Sylvie speaks her mind. She always has; she always will. Without her wisdom, I'd be lost."

Both Sylvie and Arik turned to Victoria. The Beta wolf looked relieved and the Alpha perplexed.

"You shame me, Sylvie," Victoria said. "But you're right."

A terrible silence reigned. Arik's grief threatened to edge out everything else, it was so overpowering in its bleakness. Victoria wrestled with the concept of resignation, giving up. It felt like submission and ran against the grain of her very character. Her indomitable spirit rebelled. She refused to quit. Her determination turned the tide of her mate's sorrow, and the mood of the pack shifted.

"I refuse to give up on Logan," Arik said. He gave precise voice to Victoria's thoughts; it might as well have been telepathy. Victoria's head lifted, and she grinned.

"We refuse to give up." With the last ounce of strength in her body, she would fight. Spirits lifting, the pack echoed the sentiment: do or die.

"I'll go along and remain in the boy's place."

As a body, every member of the pack turned to gape at Paul. The Beta wolf exhaled so his nostrils flared, and then repeated the unbelievable offer. "It's the sensible sacrifice. I'm old and crippled and a burden to the pack. Prosthetic limbs don't change shapes, so I can't even turn completely into a wolf. Just coming out here was a struggle. I'd be unable to remain here with the pack for any length of time."

"Paul, no! Don't you dare! Don't say such things!" Tears flooded Sylvie's eyes, and she grabbed for her mate's hands.

"Paul, you're never a burden." Victoria envisioned every time the old soldier had come to their aid: rescuing Rand from the burning warehouse, working at the gas station, carrying Morena through the snow in spite of his lame leg, a thousand other ways and times. The pack would long ago have collapsed without him.

Paul stroked his mate's gray hair. "Shush, now, Sylvie. Don't cry. I've lived a good life. What I want now is a good death, an opportunity to earn my place in Valhalla. Woman, you won't deny me that."

Arik cleared his throat; his voice emerged choked. "That you would sacrifice your life for my son who is not even of your pack—"

Victoria winced and Sylvie cringed.

Talk about your words coming back to bite you in the ass.

Doing her best to conceal a grimace, Victoria wrapped her arms around Sylvie's shoulders, offering her friend support.

"The boy is the son of our Alpha. He may not be pack, but that's good enough for me. Besides, I figure it was sorta inevitable that he'd become pack if things hadn't gone south the way they had," Paul said with the unwavering loyalty others had always prized in him.

"I can't go on without you, you old fool," Sylvie said with tears streaming down her cheeks.

"Nonsense, woman, you'll manage fine. You always do. You must stay behind and watch after Morie, Sophia, and these pups. I expect you'll be along when you're ready, my goddess, in glorious fashion. Then we'll be together 'til world's end."

"Don't flatter me; I'll have none of that." Sylvie slipped free of Victoria's grasp to go to her husband's embrace. Her grudging acceptance spread through the pack's aura along with great sorrow.

"Victory, what say you?" Paul asked.

Victoria's mouth turned up at one corner, a forced smile forming on her lips. She counted yet another member of her pack lost, and her heart broke. "I say Rand will be overjoyed to see his old friend, and the rest of us will feel the loss."

"Eh, doubt you'll even notice I'm gone." Paul gathered Sylvie close and took her away from the rest of the pack. "Excuse us. I must speak alone with my mate."

Morena crawled on her belly to Victoria. The Omega pressed her face to her Alpha's knee and whimpered because she could not speak. Likewise distressed, Sophia and the pups crowded close, wet noses and furry bodies all about her. Victoria hugged each in turn. Her throat hurt and her heart ached, so great was her love for them. Tears filled her eyes, spilling down her cheeks.

Victoria adopted a scolding tone. "We must go. Hush now, and be brave. Morena, you must be attentive to these pups. Sylvie is old, and Sophia will need your help. Feed them; teach them to hunt."

The pack shed many more tears in the hours to follow. Words spoken, advice given, final goodbyes said and then repeated. As the acting pack leader, Sylvie shifted to her wolf form last.

The strenuous walk out of the valley took a heavy toll on Paul. He traveled with great difficulty over the rough terrain, limping and at times dragging his prosthetic leg. He accepted help only over the most difficult patches. Arik and Victoria respected the old warrior's dignity, though either could have hefted and carried Paul up the side of the mountain.

Winter's early nightfall overtook them before they completed the journey. At the crest of the trail, they turned back for one final glimpse of the pack. Far below, the figures of the six wolves formed black dots against the snow.

"What if it's the last time I ever see them?" Victoria asked. An awful and paralyzing fear struck her, and she tilted back her head to release a long, thin howl.

Distant, the pack answered, emitting mournful cries that carried for miles on the frozen night.

CHAPTER FIFTEEN

Messengers—
"Goddess, I don't like this man or his message."
"Take care not to succumb to clichés, my priestess."
"I'm not going to slay him... But I'd like to."

Victoria scowled at the vanity mirror and flipped the visor closed. "I look like I haven't slept in a week."

"Have you?" Arik asked.

Victoria hesitated. "I guess I have. I've been knocked out plenty of times."

Arik chuckled as the SUV pulled into the driveway. He pulled into the detached garage and used the garage door opener to close it behind them. "You're radiant, Victoria."

From the backseat, Paul snickered. "Aye, there's a man who doesn't require schooling in the husbandly arts."

"By the Goddess, keep it up!" Victoria shot her wise-cracking mate a narrow-eyed glance. Only his bland expression and the fact that he had not added 'dear' saved him from being smacked.

The men shared a laugh that went on after the SU-V's big engine subsided. Victoria rumbled and bristled for the sake of appearance, but she didn't really resent their humor at her expense. It was good that they had managed to form a bond in such a short time.

Arik seemed to delight in ribbing her about their newly formed status.

Great Zeus!

"Are we going to get married?" The question burst from her.

Arik cast a sly glance her direction. "Would you like to get married?"

Victoria blinked and bit her lip. Her mind raced.

Well?

It had been so long since she'd thought of the future in terms anything more concrete than where shelter or the next meal was coming from.

Would Arik want a prenup? If we manage to save Logan, could I stand the wicked stepmother jokes without killing him again?

Paul chuckled. "It's not a good sign when a woman has to think that long about her answer."

Something glittered in Arik's eyes—she thought it might be disappointment. He turned away to get out of the car, and she grabbed his hand. "Yes, I want to marry you."

His smile lit her up, a joy that confused even as it pleased. "We'll put it on the list?"

She laughed and pressed a quick kiss to his mouth. "Sounds like a plan."

She pushed him from the vehicle and exited on her own side. Paul joined her outside the garage, and they waited while Arik closed the door and secured it with a padlock.

During the night, fresh snowfall had covered the walkways that surrounded Arik's house. "Your front walk and driveway need to be shoveled." Victoria followed behind the two men.

Arik shot her a grim glance, brow furrowed, lips compressed. He appeared years older and drained of energy. "Shoveling the walk is Logan's job."

A leaden weight settled in her stomach. "Oh."

"I'll call a service in the morning," Arik said.

"But we must—" Victoria bit off her automatic protest. She followed Arik's meaningful glance to Paul and then nodded. The old warrior required rest. They had lost a day but two remained. Plenty of time to travel to Valhalla, barter with a god, and return with Logan's soul.

"I'm sorry to slow you down, but I'm gonna need to rest before we undertake another adventure," Paul said, well aware of the subtle communication taking place between the Alphas.

"We'll get a fresh start in the morning," Victoria said. She patted Paul's forearm while Arik fished for his house key. He tested the knob and it turned.

Arik grunted, sounding surprised. "Odd, I must have forgotten to lock up."

"Hardly surprising, all things considered," Victoria said.

"It's not like me," he said.

Arik led the way into the foyer and shut the front door behind them. With a twist of the knob, the deadbolt clanked into place. The three wolves stood for a frozen moment, heads cocked, listening to the quiet house. Nothing seemed amiss.

"I'll show you to a guest room," Arik said to Paul.

"Thank you." Paul followed Arik, hobbling with an awkward limp. The old warrior seemed dispirited and exhausted. Victoria bit her lower lip and smothered her mothering impulses for the sake of male pride. He wouldn't want a fuss.

"I'm going to check on Logan," she said.

Arik's grunt acknowledged her. "Okay."

Their journey through Arik's sprawling ranch house took them down the same hallway. Arik and Paul turned right at the first doorway; Victoria continued down another twenty feet to Logan's room, located on the left.

Victoria paused outside of the room for a moment, bracing for the sight of Logan's soulless body. That was when she caught the first scent of an intruder. Her nostrils flared when she inhaled deeper. Alarmed, she opened the door and stepped inside the room. She froze dead in her tracks.

A man stood over Logan's body, holding a pistol.

A roar bellowed from Victoria's chest, a cry of fear and protectiveness, as a wolf to her cub. Her hand shot into the air, grabbing for her mother's dagger, always over her right shoulder. She found it with unerring accuracy. The weapon came like a faithful lover to her call, whispering encouragement within her mind, and the delicate blade cleaved the air. From a standing start, she charged toward the intruder, releasing a ferocious battle cry.

Startled, the man looked up and turned his head toward her. His body followed the motion, and he swung the gun up and around. Victoria swung *Vanadium* overhead, angling the point toward the man's heart in a downward arc. The dagger sang in her hands, a seductive melody, begging for the taste of blood.

He shouted and she caught a glimpse of round eyes, wide enough to show the whites, before the gun discharged. Bracing, Victoria expected the almost familiar feel of metal ripping through her chest. However, the shot went wide and high. A puff of plaster chips and dust exploded from the ceiling. Victoria never slowed or hesitated. She followed through on her attack, and the man fell backward so the tip of her blade cut him, slicing through his shirt and scratching his flesh.

A red stain appeared on the front of the man's shirt along the cut.

First blood...

The man landed on his backside on the carpet, still clutching the gun. Hefting *Vanadium*, Victoria stood over him and raised it above her head. She gripped the hilt with both hands and angled the blade to strike the intruder's neck in a decapitating blow.

"Stop!" Arik's angry command dominated the room.

Acting from instinct, Victoria froze, obeying her mate. The man did the same. Arik bounded into the room to stand beside her over the intruder. Her mate's hand caught her wrist, staying her blade.

"Easy," he said. "Lower your arm."

With Victoria's cooperation, Arik guided the dagger so the blade no longer hung like a guillotine over the intruder's head. He released a tired sigh. "Victoria, this is my brother-in-law, Mike. Mike, this is Victoria Storm."

Victoria blinked. "Mike Trash, the sheriff?"

"That would be me." From his seated position, Mike continued to clutch his firearm. Hardened suspicion glittered in those brown eyes, and he stank of fear. The man wasn't in uniform, and nothing in his brown sports coat over a light blue shirt suggested his profession.

Victoria's jaw hardened. "I don't care who he is. I found him standing over Logan with his weapon drawn."

Arik eased between her and the sheriff. "Mike, she's right. You'd better have a damn good explanation for what the hell you're doing in my house with that gun."

The sheriff started with a few choice words before he got around to explaining. "Fuck, Arik, I dropped by because I needed to speak with you. I tried to call you three times today but got your voicemail. I called your office, and Margaret said you hadn't come in, so I stopped by to investigate. When I arrived, I found the front door standing wide open. I called out, and no one answered, so I drew my firearm and proceeded inside. I found Logan like this."

The sheriff indicated Arik's son with his head. "What the hell is wrong with him?"

"He's in a coma." Victoria made eye contact with

Arik, urging him without words not to share too much information with this stranger. Family or not, she didn't trust him.

Arik turned his head toward her so the light from the hallway cast his profile into a silhouette. "You haven't spoken to me since Lori's death, Mike. What was so urgent it had to happen today?"

The sheriff's jaw worked. He attempted and failed to conceal a resentment so powerful the air vibrated with tension. "Can I stand?"

"Put the gun away," Arik said.

Mike made a show of holstering his firearm and gestured at Victoria. "What about her?"

"Victoria?" Arik released his grip on her arm.

"Fine," Victoria said, sounding every bit as sullen as she felt. With a twist of her wrist, she thrust *Vanadium* back into her sheath, affixing it to its position over her right shoulder. The display caused the sheriff to gape, and even Arik's lips parted, an admiring gleam in his eyes. Victoria smirked and enjoyed their awe. As much as they'd learned about one another in a short time, they still had their secrets.

While Mike climbed to his feet, Victoria took the opportunity to study him. The sheriff appeared to be in his late-forties to early fifties with a rectangular face, ears that stuck out a bit, and a receding hairline. His piercing, intelligent brown eyes were his best feature. He stood a handful of inches taller than Victoria and appeared fit. She thought him good-looking, not quite handsome, but cute.

From the look on the sheriff's face, he didn't know what to make of her. Victoria cast a quick look down at herself. She was a strange sight, to say the least. She wore Arik's oversized coat as if it were a dress, zipped all of the way to her throat. Her feet were bare. Arik was dressed in a spare change of clothing he had carried in his car.

Arik turned his head toward his son, and interesting shadows obscured his expression. "Let's go to the study."

Victoria cleared her throat. "I need to check on Logan."

"I'll wait in your office, Arik." Mike slipped past the two wolves into the hallway. Arik lingered, waiting for Victoria.

Victoria bent to check Logan's pulse and breathing. "He's in normal range for one of our breed."

"Good."

"Can I go change?" she asked.

"Sure." Arik glanced around Logan's room. He hesitated, frowning, and then opened a dresser drawer and extracted a pair of sweats with a cinch waist and a tee shirt.

Arik offered her the clothing. "Will these be okay? I don't have anything else on hand in anything close to your size."

"They're fine, thank you." Victoria shed her coat and pulled on the clothing. Even clean, the garments carried Logan's scent, a painful reminder of his current condition, but one she'd have to live with.

From what Victoria had seen of the house's layout, the floor plan followed a simple U-shape with living quarters in the wings. The main branch of the house contained the kitchen and dining areas, a large family room, Arik's study, and a utility room. The three-car garage was detached, and patio doors led out onto the deck and the pool. Farther down the hillside, the back of the house faced the lake.

Arik followed Victoria into the study where Mike waited, staring out the sliding patio door that overlooked the pool. The sheriff stood with his arms crossed over his chest, shoulder propped against the doorframe.

HUNGER MOON

Despite his relaxed posture, he reeked of tension.

As she entered the room, Victoria made noise to alert the human to her presence. The sheriff turned toward them, and Victoria took a seat on a shiny blue leather and stainless steel chair that matched the rest of the study's decor. The chair had a matching footstool she didn't use.

"I bet this cost more than my first car." She ran approving fingers across the sleek surface. The suppleness of the leather was unparalleled.

Arik shut the door behind them. "That depends. What was the make and model of your first car?"

"Lori bought that on a trip to Boston," Mike said, his tone sharp and accusatory.

Victoria forced down a rush of anger and came to her feet. Thanks to him, she could no longer enjoy the beautiful chair. She refused to apologize, but at the same time, she felt sorry for the man. Her suspicion of him, however, overrode everything else.

"Would you like something to drink, Mike?" Arik asked.

The sheriff's jaw worked. "No. Thanks. I quit."

Arik nodded. "Let's get down to business. You wanted to talk."

Mike's gaze slid to Victoria. "What about her?"

"Victoria is part of my new pack," Arik said.

Victoria's brow rose. She noted the omission, but decided not to stake claims in front of this stranger. She preferred to trust Arik's judgment.

"I wasn't aware you'd adopted a new pack, but I suppose it makes sense, considering what I do know," Mike said.

Arik leaned against his desk. "And what's that?"

"I knew there were wolves in the vicinity. Now it's none of my business, but you should be aware. Folks have been talking. People heard howling going on near the cemetery and outside of town. There was a broadcast about it on the local radio station this morning and an article in the Echo Lake Daily."

Victoria resisted the urge to plant her hand on her face. She wondered if she would ever learn from her indiscretions. "The howling was my fault. I'm sorry. I'll make sure it doesn't happen near town again."

Mike shrugged. "As I said, it's none of my concern."

Arik's eyes narrowed, and his jaw worked. After a thoughtful pause, he said, "More brought you here than the howling, Mike. So what is it?"

Explosive tension built, and the sheriff's gaze made pointed accusations. "There was a break in two nights ago at the precinct. A solid steel utility door was ripped off its hinges. Nothing was taken but the files for the investigation into Lori's death."

Arik walked around his desk and reached underneath. He pulled out both of the stolen boxes and stacked them atop one another. He pushed them toward Mike. "I found these in Logan's room yesterday."

The sheriff accepted the stolen goods and performed a cursory inspection. "Why the fuck would Logan steal these?"

Arik spared Victoria a glance. "He got the notion into his head that he wasn't responsible for Lori's death. At first I was skeptical, but after reading your notes, I started to wonder. There are a lot more questions than answers."

"What the hell are you implying, Arik?"

"Implying? Nothing, Mike. I'm asking you. You told me that Lori was having an affair with the man selling her drugs, and I *believed* you. I never even questioned..." Arik leaned forward. His hands rested on the edge of the desk, his white knuckles dug into the wood.

The sheriff's jaw clenched, and his eyes lit with anger. He struggled with his answer. "I said it to get back at you, okay? Later, I regretted it, but at the time I was so fucking angry —"

Arik rocked back, incredulous. "Get back at me? For what?"

"For not putting that bastard son of yours down after he murdered his mother! Lori was my sister!" Mike's shout filled the room, and dead silence followed its wake. The man's unbelievable audacity brought a snarl to Victoria's lips. The tears on his cheeks saved him from her fist.

Arik waited a long time to speak before he composed a careful response. "Logan had no control over his actions, and you knew it. I lost my wife. Logan lost his mother and has to live with that knowledge every day. And you were angry because I didn't kill him?"

"Yes! I was pissed! I love that boy like my own son, but Lori was the only family I had left after our parents died. She was all I had; she was all I had."

The man's naked grief hurt to witness. Victoria looked away.

"I loved her, too," Arik said.

And still do.

Victoria felt it, through the pack bond, at the heart of his deepest emotions, the ones he kept hidden behind a stoic façade.

"Damn it, Arik! It was your responsibility to put down a berserker wolf! It was your fucking duty!"

"I know." The weight of his admission crushed Arik. "I have brought dishonor upon myself, but I couldn't. I can't. I'd already lost my entire pack, then Lori. Logan was all I had left."

"I blame you for this," Mike said, shaking his head. "I blame you."

"I know you do, Mike." Silence, then Arik said, "Why did you write the report to cover up the murder if you felt Logan needed to pay? I never asked you to call it an animal attack."

"Logan came to see me after Lori's funeral."

Arik drew back with genuine surprise. "What did he

want?"

"He asked me to kill him," Mike said. "He said you couldn't, and he didn't have the stomach. He brought silver bullets and a .45 revolver over and asked me to 'put him down'. That's how he said it. Put him down like some sort of mad dog."

Mike blinked, and his eyes were bright with tears. "I wanted to. God knows, I tried. I chambered a round, and I put the barrel to his forehead. But when I looked at him, all I saw were Lori's eyes staring back at me... All I could think was, he's the closest thing I've got to a son."

Mike ran an agitated hand across his scalp. "Hell, I taught that boy to fish, and he used to come over on Sundays and watch football with me. Lori would've had my scalp if I'd done anything to hurt her son."

Victoria cleared her throat. Frayed nerves, blurred vision, and exhaustion dragged her down. At the same time, her skin crawled with restless energy, and it took an act of will not to prowl the confines of the study. She had too many questions without answers.

Her impatience broke her silence. "Who was Gregory Sanders? If he wasn't Lori's lover, then how were they involved?"

Arik and Mike traded a look rife with meaning. Arik gave a slight nod. "Sanders was a drug dealer who dealt prescription meds," Mike said. "He worked out of Tahoe and had a rap sheet a mile long."

"Lori was addicted to barbiturates," Arik said. "She mixed tranquilizers and alcohol. I tried several times to get her into rehab, but it never stuck..."

"I knew about Sanders," Mike said. "I suspected he'd been selling to Lori for years, but I never caught him. I didn't want — "

Victoria nodded. "You didn't want to bust your own sister. I understand. Did Logan know about Sanders?"

"I don't know," Mike said. "But during the investigation, the thought occurred to me. Maybe Logan caught

Sanders selling to Lori beside the pool. I figured he flipped out and murdered Sanders first, then Lori when she tried to escape. The evidence supported the scenario."

"I've had similar thoughts," Arik said.

Victoria bit the inside of her lip. The explanations made sense, but if they were correct, it destroyed the last hope that someone other than Logan had murdered Lori.

"Mike, if you were so angry with me, why did you conclude the investigation and call it an animal attack? I never asked for any favors," Arik said.

The sheriff's face emptied of color. "It wasn't for you, Arik. The night after her funeral, Lori's spirit appeared to me, the same evening Logan came to me. After I failed to shoot him, I threw the gun in his face and sent him away. Then I got shitfaced. Lori came to me. She spoke to me; she touched me. It wasn't a dream. It wasn't a hallucination. It was her."

Mike shook with the depth of his need to have someone—anyone—believe him. Victoria reached out and laid a hand on his arm. "It's okay. We believe you. I've seen her too."

Mike did a double take and stared at her open-mouthed. "Who the hell are you?"

Disturbed, Arik interrupted. "Mike, what did Lori say to you? I need to know."

"Which time?" Mike asked.

"You've seen her more than once?" Victoria asked.

Mike nodded and swallowed. "The, uh, first time, she begged me to help Logan. She said it wasn't his fault."

Arik appeared disturbed at the turn the conversation had taken. "How many other times have you seen her since?"

"Just the once, last night."

"What did she say?" Victoria leaned so far forward

she almost fell over.

"She came to me again. It's why I'm here tonight. At first, I thought I was dreaming. But then I realized I wasn't, and it was happening again."

Arik burst with impatience. "Mike, what did Lori say?"

"She begged me to help Logan. I didn't understand until I saw Logan like that..."

Mike's lips formed words. His distant gaze saw more than the people before him. *"Water will end the witch."*

Victoria grabbed hold of the lapel of his sports coat. She shook him. "She said what?"

"She repeated it three times: *Water will end the witch.*"

Victoria opened the front door, and Mike stepped onto the porch. He carried the two file boxes, stacked one atop the other, in his arms. He glanced outward into the clear night before he took a step and then stopped.

Not a hint of snowfall or a wisp of fog obscured the bright light of stars and the crescent moon. Victoria gazed at it and thought of her pack, miles distant beneath the hunger moon, and wondered if they were looking up, too. She missed them with quiet desperation.

Mike's back remained to her.

"I don't really know who you are," he said, speaking over his shoulder.

Victoria's brow arched. "That's okay. I'm still working that out myself."

He turned to face her. His lips twisted, more grimace than grin. "In any case, thanks."

Victoria bobbed her head.

He stood there as though he wanted to say something else, but he remained silent. Her already frayed patience dissolved further. She couldn't just close the door on him. The man qualified as her mate's kinfolk, so she felt a sense of obligation to him.

"Would you like an escort to your car?"

"I may only be human, but I do have a gun. I'm parked across the street. Thanks, but I'll manage."

"As you said." She didn't argue. She wasn't any more eager to tromp into the snow and cold than to debate the human's competence.

"I'll review the entire case again tomorrow to see if anything out of the ordinary leaps out at me." He looked at her with an expression of expectation.

Victoria stared at him. She wondered what the man wanted from her. "Thank you. Arik and I appreciate your help."

The sheriff left.

Victoria watched his taillights recede into the distance and shut the front door. She threw the deadbolt and started toward the bedrooms. When she turned, she came face-to-face with Paul.

"Can't sleep?" she asked.

"I heard the commotion," Paul said. "Is there anything I can do to help?"

Victoria went to him and wrapped her arms around his waist. Paul enveloped her in a bear hug. "Thank you," she said. "But you should get some sleep. Tomorrow is going to be another big day, and I want to get an early start."

Paul pressed a fatherly kiss to the top of her head. "Take some of your own advice, will you?"

She smiled "Good night, Paul."

"Good night, Victory."

Victoria padded barefoot through the house, navigating the dark in the direction of the master bedroom. Halfway there, she stopped dead in her tracks. An awful sound reached her ears, terrible sobbing coming from within Logan's room.

She hesitated outside of the room and debated whether to enter. She felt like an intruder and doubted Arik wanted her invading his privacy, but she couldn't leave him to suffer alone, grieving for a lost pack, lost spouse, and lost child. He was her mate.

My mate.

Her heart ached in her chest. She pushed open Logan's door and slipped inside. Arik stood with his back to her, facing his son's bedside. His shoulders hunched forward and shook with violent emotion. A strangled moan tore from his throat, and the scent of his grief filled her nostrils.

She went to him and wrapped her arms about his waist. She turned her head to the side and rested her face against the corded muscles of his back. Her cheek only came to the small of his back due to the vast difference in their heights. Arik stiffened, rejecting her touch, but Victoria held on. She threaded her fingers and waited until his muscles grew supple. She pressed her fingertips into his abdomen and relished the silk of skin over sinew.

"Mike left," she said.

"Thank you for escorting him out. It was difficult seeing him."

"It hurts you to have Lori's spirit appearing to Mike and Logan—"

"And you. A stranger."

"I am a medium. Spirits often appear to me."

"Victoria, I'm no fool. Lori was lost to me years before her death. She was my lifemate, but she couldn't deal with the pain of living, so she used pills and booze to escape. I turned more and more to my work, and it was Logan who suffered the most. I've made so many mistakes I wish I could take back."

Arik's terrible recrimination knew no release. He directed the full force of it inward. For all his great and enduring strength, Victoria knew he was close to breaking. She kissed his back.

"Arik, no one's perfect, not even parents. *Especially* not parents."

"My failings as a father go way past missing a baseball game or yelling at him for something he didn't do."

"He loved you."

"And I murdered him."

Knowledge filled her with terrible certainty. "You still intend to die if we can't save Logan? This is only a temporary reprieve?"

"Yes."

Victoria shuddered. She felt sick with guilt and fear. Desperation drove her, because she could not bear to have another death weigh on her.

"It's my fault Logan's like this," she said.

Arik turned in her arms. "I killed him—gutted my son with my bare hands."

Victoria squeezed her eyes shut. "You fought over me. It doesn't matter. We could argue forever over the fault of it. We're both to blame." She opened her eyes and looked up. "I swear to you, on my honor—or whatever's left of it—I'll bring his soul back from Valhalla."

"What will you do if Logan won't come?" Arik asked.

Victoria blinked. The question startled her because the possibility hadn't occurred to her. She had worried about the mechanics of it and the timetables. Logan's cooperation hadn't been a variable in her computations.

"If he won't come, I'll make him."

Arik's mouth tugged into an ironic smile. "You did notice that we're discussing Logan?"

Victoria's face set into a mask of determination. "What would you give to get him back?"

Arik's smile vanished. "Anything. Absolutely anything."

Victoria tilted her head back and stared at him, an unanswered question. She waited with brittle expectation. Understanding shone in those dark eyes.

"Ah, I see," he said.

"Do you? You love your son; you don't love me."

Arik nodded. "I see. My answer is: Do whatever is necessary to bring Logan home. I'll ask no questions and make no accusations."

Victoria tipped her chin forward and considered the matter settled. She dismissed it. Instead of pursuing further conversation, she tightened her grip on Arik's waist and stifled a yawn.

"It's been a long day," Arik said, looking down upon Logan's body.

Victoria followed his gaze and almost jumped out of her skin when she discovered Logan's startling amber eyes open and staring straight at her, accusing, no longer mocking.

"We should close his eyes so he can sleep," she said.

Arik stirred. "I closed his eyes."

"They're open now."

He inspected his son and reached a hand down to lower Logan's eyelids. "Must have been a reflex."

Victoria shuddered, eager to be gone from the room.

"Must have been," she said.

Arik escorted her into the hallway and stopped at the entrance to the guest bedroom where Victoria had awoken earlier that same day.

"Do you need anything?" he asked.

Victoria shook her head in disbelief and watched to see if he intended to follow through on the preposterous idea that she belonged in a guest bedroom. Arik dropped a quick peck onto her forehead and headed down the hallway. The door of the master suite shut behind him.

With a sense of the surreal, Victoria turned and flipped the light switch on. The overhead lamp illuminated a room that looked like a hurricane had blown through. The mattress lay at an angle across the box spring. The broken curtain rod lay on top of the dark green drapes on the floor beneath the window. Broken glass covered the carpet. She'd have to remind Arik to call a glass company in the morning, in addition to the sidewalk service.

He could not seriously expect her to stay in a destroyed room.

She glanced into the hallway to see if the man had come to his senses. She counted to thirty, and still Arik did not return. Victoria paced the length of the bedroom with restless energy, allowing the misguided male an opportunity to see the error of his ways.

When he failed to come back, she charged out the door and down the hallway after him. She found the door to the master bedroom closed but not locked. She opened it and entered a room decorated in the same blue hues that dominated Arik's study. A framed print of van Gogh's *Starry Night* hung over the bed.

The sound of running water reached her ears, and she headed for the bathroom, shedding her clothing along the way. Her borrowed shirt landed beside Arik's discarded pants. She lost the sweatpants inside the bathroom door and entered an enormous bathroom.

Her feet were swift and silent while she crossed the cold tile floor. Waiting for her with an expression of studied expectation, Arik stood naked in a glass-walled shower beneath the spray of the shower head. The hot water created a cloud of vapor, steaming up the clear glass.

When she approached, his dark head adopted a forward tilt; his posture indicated readiness for physical confrontation. Without pausing, Victoria yanked the glass door of the shower enclosure open. Her hungry gaze traveled up and down his athletic form. She admired the clean lines of his body. The sight of him—her need to touch and taste every inch of him—set her on fire. She breathed deeply, inhaling his musky male scent.

Her skin tingled when she stepped onto the wet tile, and every muscle in her compact body bunched while she gathered her strength. Her wolf peeked out from beneath her human façade. The hint of fang protruded beneath her lips. The golden glimmer of her eyes created fascinating refractions across steam and glass.

Arik met her regard with a savage grin, and his gaze caressed every inch of her naked body. She endured his inspection proudly, aware that her cool beauty pleased the male eye.

"You're gorgeous, Victoria," he said.

Her eyes narrowed, and she smirked. "You're not hard to look at either."

He chuckled and his eyes danced. "Always the smart mouth."

"I'm a smart woman. Don't worry. I'll keep it simple so you can keep up."

"Yeah, do that." He grinned, then he laughed heartily, and his hand rose in invitation.

She took another step forward. His power rose between them, jutting and formidable as the mountains. She stopped a distance from him—no other parts of their bodies touching—and that male appendage pressed against her stomach. Wolf and woman, she found him pleasing, in no way lacking.

"Has your obligation to duty brought about your decision to submit?" Arik asked, daring to taunt her with Sylvie's sharp reprimand.

Victoria flashed her teeth and a growl rolled from her throat. Her power rose up to meet his, strong, glorious, and defiant. "I have come to claim what is rightfully mine, and I will not be the one submitting."

"Is that so, little wolf?" A sultry chuckle escaped him, causing his chest to reverberate. Eyes dancing with amusement, he bent forward and his mouth captured her lips in a rough kiss. Tongues and teeth clashed in a playful contest for control, and she committed the dis-

tinctive, delicious flavor of him to her memory. It became known to her—a part of her—and belonged to her
as he soon would when they sealed the mate bond. The
scent of his arousal was a potent aphrodisiac.

Victoria surged against him, locking her hands behind his neck, her legs about his hips. His big hands
settled on her back. Long fingers stroked the line of her
spine and then slid to her ass to splay across the curve of
her buttocks. He bent his head and tasted her breasts,
cupping the small, firm mounds within his hands, teasing her nipples to high points with calloused palms.

Hot water rained down upon their skin but their
bodies burned with even more scalding intensity. Holding her, Arik turned and placed her back against the
cold tile of the shower wall. The startling contrast in
temperature caused her to jump, surging against him,
and the kiss broke on her gasp. She laughed against his
throat, fingering wet strands of his sable hair, and then
pressed her mouth to his throat and tasted the skin just
beneath his ear, licking and nibbling.

He pressed the head of his shaft against her, positioned to enter her, but held back so their slick flesh slid
together. No penetration happened. Victoria moaned
and rocked her hips, urging him to sink deep into her
body. Her shiny teeth flashed and delivered a punishing
bite to his shoulder, drawing a taste of blood, a slight
scratch that healed immediately. The copper tang of his
blood on her tongue drove her wild, and she reached for
him, and into him, with all her strength, physical and
spiritual.

A connection flared into existence, a shining silver
thread that stretched between them, shimmering with
potential. It promised eternity. An unbreakable bond.
Nothing severed a true mate bond, only death brought
release from the lifetime commitment, and according to
some legends, not even death.

Victoria knew the legends to be true. Her parents'

mate bond had endured, even in death.

Arik met her gaze. "Are you sure this is what you want?"

She stared deep into his honey-brown eyes and considered his question, giving it the weight it deserved. She admired his intelligence and respected his courage. Arik embodied the traits she desired in a mate: strength, stability, physical prowess, an even temperament, wisdom. He offered everything she wanted and needed in order to provide her pack with a stable home.

They lacked love, but maybe what they had would be better. Safer. Saner. In time, she would learn to love him, and maybe he would love her in return.

"I want this," she said in a steady voice, never wavering in her conviction or her commitment. "I want you."

He thrust deep and hard, sinking into her to his hilt. He cleaved a path through her flesh until he reached her core. She gasped and clung to him with all of her strength. While he moved against her, she channeled all her personal power into forging a lasting bond. Arik's wild magic merged with hers, energizing her wolf with primal energy until she tilted her head back and released a low, wailing yowl.

His primal howl echoed within the confines of the room. He rocked against her, driving into her body with steadily increasing intensity. She met every surge, pulling him to her, holding him fast. Every thrust ratcheted her pleasure higher, and the pressure in her core built until she thought she would explode.

On the verge, Victoria grasped at Arik's broad shoulders and stared into his face. His features were set in tight lines, his discipline stressed to the limit. She turned her face toward his throat and her eyes cast a golden glow upon his skin. She placed a light bite on the underside of his jaw and an answering growl rolled from his throat.

Their souls touched, fused, and the mate bond sealed.

Victoria's eyes lit with the joy of possession.

"Mine," she said, meeting his gaze.

He flashed a wolfish grin. "Yours."

He sank into her one last time. Victoria clenched her inner muscles about his shaft, deliberately destroying his self-control. He lunged against her with unrestrained violence, pummeling her slick channel. Then his entire body grew rigid, and his face contorted as if in the agony of pleasure. His head tilted back, and he howled to raise the roof, a glorious declaration of his power and dominance.

A convulsive shudder began in her center and swept her body. The white and bright burst of energy erupted from her core, consuming her entire being in a rhapsody of light and heat. She closed her eyes and surrendered to the climax, the entire time experiencing Arik's shared ecstasy through their bond.

At long last, she was no longer alone.

My lifemate.

CHAPTER SIXTEEN

Chivalry—
> *"He is right to protect you."*
> *"Et tu, Milady?"*

Victoria took a sip of her piping hot coffee and swept the surrounding trees with a sharp eye, scanning for ravens. She saw none.

In the front yard, a workman busily shoveled snow, clearing the sidewalk.

While she watched, Paul's battered Ford pickup rolled into the Koenig driveway. Victoria shot down the sidewalk, breaking a fresh path through the portion not yet shoveled in her hurry to reach the vehicle.

"Do you have them?" The idle of the engine hadn't faded, and he wasn't all of the way out of the vehicle, but she crowded him in her impatience.

Paul laughed and waved Victoria back. "Yes, yes, I have them. Give an old man space to breathe, youngster."

The snow crunched under approaching footfalls, and Arik appeared in the driveway, moving at a sedate pace. The proximity of her mate caused her skin to heat, and Victoria cast a sly glance over her shoulder, regarding Arik with veiled admiration.

"What are you both so excited about?" Arik asked.

He placed his hand on Victoria's elbow, and energy crackled between them.

The mate bond...

It was new, fascinating, and more than a little scary. It tied them together now, always.

"These daggers are relics, passed down through our pack from one generation to the next since before our ancestors set foot on this continent's eastern shore," Paul said. He reached onto the bench seat beside him and picked up a black rectangular case. He handled it with reverence, tucked against his chest with his prosthetic hand, and contorted in order to slide out from behind the steering wheel.

"Gotta say, I hate all of this damn blasted snow," Paul said while they passed the workman who watched them from the corner of his eye while he pretended to be intent at his task.

"I love it," Victoria said.

"Arizona was dusty an' hotter than hell, but at least there were no snow drifts."

"Can I give you a hand with that?" Arik's tone contained only polite consideration, but his eyes were bright with curiosity.

Victoria chuckled at the comical interest in her mate's honey-brown eyes. "Paul, give Arik the case. He needs to feel useful."

"What a load." Arik grinned at her, showing teeth, but he accepted the case from Paul, tucking it under his left arm. Then he opened the front door and held it.

Victoria waited until the door closed before she spoke. "We're going to need a large open area. Privacy is necessary."

"I have a home gym," Arik said. "It's not huge, but it's big enough."

Victoria nodded. "Can we see it?"

"Sure." Arik led the way to the side of the house opposite the master bedroom where Victoria had not been before. Arik presented a room containing a treadmill, a weight set and an area covered in blue exercise mats.

"Will this work?"

"Yes, this should be fine," Victoria said. "Thank you. May I?" Victoria reached for the black rectangular case.

Despite his curiosity, he had not opened it. She set it upon a contour table and flipped the latches. She lifted the lid to reveal two ritual daggers resting on black silk. The blades were twenty-four inches long and made of pure silver. The hilts were iron, allowing shifters to wield the weapons without being burned, and featured short guards engraved with a pattern of inter-locking knots.

"These have been in my family for centuries," Victoria said. With reverence, she lifted one of the daggers from the case and presented the hilt to Paul. He accepted the weapon.

"What're you gonna do with the body?" Paul cast a cunning glance at Arik while Victoria picked up the other dagger.

Arik rose to the bait. "What body? No one said anything about a body. You're kidding, right?"

"No, we're not kidding," Victoria said. "Only the dead or those in service to the gods may enter Valhalla. I'm permitted to come and go because I serve Freya as a Valkyrie."

Arik turned to stone. His tension caused them both to stop moving. Victoria exchanged a pointed glance with Paul who lifted his brow and shrugged.

"Arik, I'm sorry. I thought you understood," she said.

"How is this supposed to go down?" Arik asked in a way that made it clear he was miles from okay.

"Paul must die in combat," Victoria explained. "Then his sacrifice will be considered worthy. Any other death would render him ineligible to serve in the *Einherjar*. This cannot be faked. The gods would know."

"So you intend to fight Paul to the death?" Arik said.

"Yes."

"Aye," Paul agreed. "My death, that is."

"I cannot allow it," Arik said in a forbidding tone.

Victoria bristled. Her hands formed fists. "You've already agreed that Paul should be permitted to make this sacrifice."

"I am not objecting to Paul's sacrifice."

Victoria challenged Arik, standing on tip-toe to speak face to face, at least the best she was able given their considerable difference in heights. "What are you objecting to then?"

Arik stared her straight in the eye, an immoveable rock. "You cannot be permitted to risk yourself in a fight when you may be carrying our child."

Paul gasped and swung on her. "Victoria!"

"Oh." Her indignity vanished and left her feeling deflated.

"Even the slightest injury to a pregnant mother can result in miscarriage." Arik sounded so much like Sylvie he might have been channeling the absent woman.

Victoria crossed her arms. "That's a gross exaggeration."

Arik glared. His jaw had a classical stubborn jut.

"I'm not pregnant." Victoria threw up her hands in protest. She looked from one male to the other. Arik stared at her, intransigent; Paul stared, too, disapproving and stern.

The silence stretched. Victoria had argued herself in a circle. As much as she resented the stricture, she agreed with it in principle. "Okay, I'm probably not pregnant."

Paul crossed his arms over his chest. "I refuse to risk the life of a child. Your mother would be shocked."

Victoria rolled her eyes. Without a doubt, that final zinger came from his sense of obligation to Sylvie. "The supposed shock my poor, dead mother would suffer far exceeds anything she ever expressed in real life."

Paul harrumphed. "Your father would have your hide."

Victoria nodded. "True enough; that he would."

The three wolves engaged in a bout of determined silence, looks exchanged, battle lines drawn. Finally, Victoria made a face and threw up her hands. "Fine! You win. I'll sit it out."

She flipped the silver dagger and presented Arik with the hilt. He plucked it from her fingers.

"You've made the right decision, Victoria," he said.

"Like I had another?" Victoria bared her teeth at Arik, but it was only for show. Her anger lacked real heat. Disgruntlement made her a sore loser. Paul gave an approving nod and appeared satisfied with the compromise. He faced the coming confrontation with true Viking zeal.

Fighting to hold back tears, she edged closer to Paul. "Are you sure about this?"

Paul smiled with easy confidence. "Of few things have I ever been surer. Courting my glorious Sylvie; pledging my fealty to your father."

"If I were half the leader my father had been such sacrifices would not be called for." Victoria crossed her arms, desiring comfort, wishing to shake the numbness.

Paul leaned over to give her a bear hug. "Nonsense, sacrifices are always called for. It is the mark of a good leader's wisdom that appropriate sacrifices are made."

Victoria clung to the old wolf and did not argue. Once made, second-guessing the choice served no useful purpose. She released Paul and turned to survey the room.

"The space is tight, but in many ways, it's ideal for knife fighting." Victoria paced while the males stripped to their pants and moved onto the mat.

Arik's brow rose high when Paul removed his prosthetic hand and replaced the attachment with a hook.

His lips curved into a smile. "Why do I have the feeling I might be in trouble?"

Paul flashed a wolfish grin. "Don't worry, youngster. I'll go easy on ya."

Victoria ceased her pacing. "Arik, do you know how to fight with daggers?"

The Alpha gave the knife an experimental heft. "I think I can manage."

Both males assumed a guard position and held the dagger right-handed. Arik brought the dagger forward and high, and stood with his left hand back. Paul adopted a wider stance, arms spread, his hook positioned and ready to strike.

Exchanged nods signaled the start of the duel, and they maneuvered about the mat, studying each other's guards.

Gnawing her lower lip, Victoria also braced. It killed her to stand aside and watch while the men fought. She wanted to be right there in the thick of things.

The battle started slowly. Arik and Paul exchanged a series of feints, dancing in and out of one another's guards. Paul moved with an economy of motion, darting in a swift thrust and then stopping short and withdrawing before the dagger hit. Arik responded with a low feint. His silver blade flashed faster than the eye could follow.

"Ha!" Paul's left hook struck out, catching Arik's wrist as he ended his feint. The older man dragged his opponent off-balance and toward him. The Beta wolf thrust his silver dagger toward the Alpha's torso. Arik's left hand locked onto Paul's wrist, and the two males grappled with one another.

The grapple ended when the men separated, shoving each other away. Each fell into a guarded position again, but not for long. Again, Paul acted as the aggressor, advancing upon Arik with a shout. Paul stepped in, shoved Arik's dagger up and away, and went for an undercut.

The swift tip of Paul's blade cut a lateral incision across Arik's abdomen. The Alpha snarled and his eyes lit with his wolf's primal rage. Victoria leapt into the air, shouting at the top of her lungs. She curbed the instinct to rush forward and join in the fray.

"Come on!" Paul returned to a wide guard stance, arms and legs spread. "Stop holding back! Let's finish this!"

Arik answered with a growl, and dropped his guard in favor of a full attack. The Alpha charged at the Beta wolf, bringing both his greater weight and strength to bear. Paul intercepted Arik's attack, and the two males grappled with one another, hands locked on wrists, daggers raised high.

Paul's prosthetic leg slid out from under him as Arik forced him back. The Beta wolf snarled and marshaled his strength, giving a mighty shove, but he failed to recover. Paul wobbled and fell backward, losing his grip on Arik's knife hand.

Freed, Arik's dagger hand surged toward his opponent's body. The silver blade sliced a deep incision across Paul's chest and blood spilled from the injury. Arik reversed the blade and thrust again, this time cutting clean through Paul's jugular in a killing blow.

Arik caught Paul before he fell.

"I'm sorry," Arik said with tears on his cheeks. "I'm so fucking sorry."

Paul gurgled a reply; words unclear, thanks to his slit throat.

Victoria sprang forward, and a spray of blood from Paul's severed jugular struck her. Her hands were on his shoulders before his heart stopped beating. "Paul, stay with me!"

Paul's spirit rose from his body and experienced a moment of disorientation. He blinked several times in quick succession before glancing about. Victoria seized hold of his spirit and secured a tight grip upon his arm.

"Victory?" Paul's eyes focused on her.

"I'm here. I'm with you Paul. There's nothing to fear." She turned her head to address Arik. "I'm going now. I'll be back as soon as I'm able."

Arik nodded. "Godspeed."

"Thank you."

She maintained her grip on Paul's spirit and groped for the weapon he had dropped. All of the blood made the mat slippery and rendered her search both frustrating and futile. Victoria shed angry tears and finally Arik placed the hilt of his knife in her hand.

Taking great care, Victoria wiped the bloody blade clean on her jeans until she could see her polished reflection in the silver. She gazed into the reflective surface until the world turned inside out and upside down.

The Shadowlands mirrored the physical world in many ways. Victoria still stood within Arik's home, inside the gym. However, the edges of the room shimmered with distortion. Walls were solid; locked doors stayed locked. Staring straight at something caused it to go out of focus, but a sly glance stolen from the corner of the eye revealed a clearer image.

Paul stood shoulder-to-shoulder beside Victoria in death, as he had done in life. He adapted fast to his surroundings and glanced about with avid curiosity. Unlike Rand, he demonstrated the good sense to stay close to her without her having to scold him.

He shoved the fingers of his good hand into the gaping hole in his throat. "I thought my wounds were supposed to heal up," he said with bubbling impatience.

Victoria chuckled. "It will, and your leg and hand will regenerate as soon as we set foot in Valhalla."

"That can't happen soon enough," Paul said. "I sure as hell have missed 'em."

Laughing, Victoria hefted the silver dagger and carved a symbol into the air over her head. Using the tip of the blade, she traced the pattern, reciting an ancient Norse incantation. A faint glow appeared before her, growing brighter until it burned with every primary color.

Paul made a sound of awe. "Bifröst, the rainbow bridge."

"Yes." Victoria shooed him ahead of her. "Step swiftly. Valhalla awaits."

The Norse God of Justice did not wear a blindfold or carry scales. His eyes were wide open, and he carried a double-edged sword in his left hand since a giant wolf had bitten off his right centuries before.

Tyr, God of War and Laws, towered over the tallest of mortal men. As gods tended to reach god-sized proportions, so did he, and his hall also covered a sweeping expanse.

When Victoria and Paul entered Tyr's chamber, the god's head turned in their direction, setting his red tresses to swinging. His eyes glowed as bright and fierce as the forge. The top of Victoria's head came to Tyr's waist, and Paul reached his sternum.

Tyr sprang from his throne and drew a great sword, longer than Victoria was tall. "What is your business here, wolf?"

Victoria stopped a fair distance from Tyr, deeming it unwise to get too close to the god. "Peace, Mighty Tyr. I am Victoria, Valkyrie and Priestess of Freya."

Tyr's great nostrils flared. "Who is your companion?"

"My companion is Paul Thornton, also a loyal wolf and valiant warrior of my tribe."

"My Lord." Paul dipped into a deep bow from the waist.

"What is your business in my hall, wolf?"

"Mighty Tyr, I seek your permission to bring a member of the Einherjar with me when I leave Valhalla," Victoria said. "Paul Thornton will remain and take the warrior's place. He is a worthy soldier and has made the sacrifice of his own free will."

Victoria indicated Paul with a small flourish of her hand. Paul bowed his head. "My Lord, it would be an honor to serve the Einherjar."

Tyr frowned and abided time before he spoke. "I have no reason to grant such favors to your kind," the god said with great scorn. "Fenrir is the sire of your breed."

Victoria bristled but reined in her quick temper. "True enough, but I have served Freya and the Aesir my entire life, as did my mother. I would not be held to answer for the doings of Fenrir but rather my own actions."

Tyr sneered beneath his great bushy mustache and peered at her through ferret eyes. The god moved his right arm, which ended at his wrist, and waved the stump with a flourish. "You know then what the wolf Fenrir cost me."

"I know of the deceit of the gods to bind Fenrir with the unbreakable ribbon, *Gleipnir*. I know of your courage in placing your right hand between the wolf's jaws," Victoria said. She met Tyr's stare and did not blink. She did not back down.

"You know the story, Valkyrie Victoria, but what do you think of it?"

Victoria considered her reply and said, "I think if one were to place his left hand within my jaws while attempting to bind me with an unbreakable ribbon that one would soon be missing both his hands."

Expressionless, Tyr stared at Victoria, and a vein throbbed in the god's temple.

Beside her, Paul stopped breathing. Victoria held Tyr's gaze and waited.

Abruptly, the god threw back his head and roared

with laughter, booming through the great chamber like thunder. "Ha, a good one! I can't wait to tell Thor!"

When his laughter subsided, Tyr waved a dismissive stump at the pair. "Take the warrior of your choosing and leave this one in his place."

Victoria dropped a deep bow. "Thank you, Mighty Tyr."

CHAPTER SEVENTEEN

Outrage—
"You sent my mother with cryptic messages and fashion accessories!"
"Would you rather that I'd sent your father?"

"What the hell are you wearing, girl? You don't expect to attract a man lookin' like *that,* do you?" The saucy serving wench stopped to study Victoria's attire. Her disapproving gaze took in the loose, baggy fit of the masculine clothes and then her eyes popped when she noticed the dried blood crusting the leg of the blue jeans.

Victoria mustered a neutral smile, well aware she looked like shit. "I have a man, thanks."

"Well, don't you want to keep him?" The servant flipped her dark hair over her shoulder and swooshed her skirt as she turned away. She disappeared into the crowd.

Rand snickered and slapped his knee. "She got your go—oomph!"

Victoria waited until Rand put up his hands to signal surrender before she removed her elbow from his gut. "You were saying?"

The huge redhead shook with silent laughter, tears bright in his eyes. Finally, he produced a gurgled sound that might have been "nothing."

"Paul, I've got to go." Victoria placed a hand on her friend's shoulder. She offered him a sad smile when he looked up at her. At the table beside him, Rand also ceased his guffawing and gave Victoria his attention.

"Already?" Rand asked. "You only just got here, Victory. You haven't seen your mom and dad yet."

Victoria continued to smile, though her heart hurt. "I'm sorry, but I have to go. I'll catch up with mom and dad next time. Rand, please tell them I love them..."

"I understand." Paul rose and hugged her. "Find the boy and return as fast as you can. The pack needs you. Your new mate needs you."

He turned her over to Rand who attempted to squeeze the life out of her with his tree trunk arms. He dropped a kiss on top of her head. "Take care, Victory."

"You too, Rand."

"Victoria, I can't believe you're leaving without even saying hello."

Victoria whirled and came face-to-face with her mother. Katherine stood with her hands on her hips, a smile on her lips, and a glint of anger in her bright blue eyes.

"Mom!" Victoria rushed forward to give her mother a hug, ignoring the older woman's disapproval. She knew from experience it was for show.

Katherine laughed. She stood back and looked her daughter up and down. "My Goddess, you look like you've been through the ringer. What happened to you, daughter?"

"More than I have time to say," Victoria said. She gazed into her mother's face, and thought about the one thing she knew Katherine would want to hear. She opened her mouth, but nothing came out; an unaccustomed shyness tripped up her tongue.

"Never mind all that," Katherine said, placing her hands on Victoria's shoulders. She steered her daughter through the dining hall. "Freya sent me."

"Freya sent you to what? Mom, why does Freya always talk to you about me instead of telling me things herself? And where is dad?" She spoke loud out of frustration, making herself heard over the din. Raucous congregations of warriors gathered in the dining hall that evening. There were ten thousand soldiers, dining, drinking, and making merry.

"Your father is around." Katherine pulled Victoria behind a small stage often used for musical and theatrical skits. The backstage area had a number of rooms used for props and changing rooms for the performers.

Katherine recovered a small package from some cubbies along the wall. "Freya sent me because she knew you wouldn't listen, darling. She says you're trying to get a man to do what you want and it's important, but you hadn't bothered to clean yourself up."

"Mother!" Victoria's cry of outrage filled the room.

"Don't *mother* me, Victoria." Katherine surveyed her daughter with bleak disapproval and used her belt knife to cut the binding on the package. "Goddess knows, Freya has the right of it when she says you lack common sense."

Victoria threw up her hands. "This from a goddess who has cats pulling her chariot!"

"Ah-ha! Perfect!" With a wide smile and a flourish, Katherine unfolded the contents of the bundle to reveal a black leather corset with a lace up bodice and a pair of black leather trousers. The matching boots boasted five-inches of stiletto heels.

Victoria took one look at the outfit, better suited to an S&M club than Odin's hall, and shook her head. "Mom, seriously, you're embarrassing me."

"It's my job to embarrass you, sweetheart. Now take off those hideous things so I can have them burned."

Victoria scowled and refused to budge for a whole minute. She met her mother's gaze and stared and stared and stared. Katherine never blinked, gazing back at her with a blank expression. Finally, Victoria gave in. "Fine, I'll change. But it'll make no difference. Logan doesn't notice me anymore than I notice him."

"Don't lie to your mother, Victoria." With a satisfied smirk, Katherine settled back to supervise. Under her mother's watchful eyes, Victoria shed her clothing and washed up before donning the new outfit. Katherine helped with the lacing and adjusted the fit of the pushup bodice.

Victoria narrowed her eyes. "If I move wrong, I'm going to pop out."

"Just wear it, Victoria. You'll make a huge impression on the warriors of the hall."

"Correction: My boobs will make a huge impression." She inspected her image in the mirror with an impatient huff. The outfit revealed more skin than it covered. "Fine, I'll wear it. Tell me why."

"Put on the boots, darling. I want to get the whole effect." Katherine took a step back.

Victoria fumed but did as instructed. She laced up the boots, then pranced and struck a pose. "What do you think?"

Her mother rocked back with a husky laugh. "Do you remember how to walk in heels?"

Victoria smirked. "Twelve years of dance lessons. I know how to do more than walk; I know how to dance."

"It broke Madame La Fleur's heart when you gave up dancing for martial arts."

Victoria danced a few steps for her mother. She moved with grace and precision, and used her long legs to sweep the room following a full spin. "Take that, Grace Kelly."

Katherine clasped her hands and beamed with tears in her eyes. "You're beautiful, Victoria."

A hot blush caused her cheeks to flush. At a loss for words, Victoria hugged her mother. Her heart ached for all the times to come when they wouldn't be together.

She wanted *this* with quiet desperation — the fussing, the silly interactions, the important stuff.

"You're a fine woman, Victoria, and someday you'll meet the man who'll make you understand." Katherine reached into her pocket and removed a delicate necklace wrought from gold and gems. Starfire burned within each of the jewels, and a filigree of precious metal bound them together.

Victoria gasped. *"Brísingamen."*

The necklace was Freya's most prized possession. Being permitted to wear it was an immense honor.

"Turn around." Katherine created a circular motion with her hand. Victoria spun and lifted her hair. She held still while her mother fastened the clasp. The necklace settled warm and living upon her bare skin.

"Freya wants her necklace back when you're done," Katherine said.

Victoria bobbed her head. "Of course."

"Freya said to let you know it will render you irresistible to all men, except those related to you, such as your father."

"Can I borrow a scarf then?" Victoria asked. "I'll have to cover it or I don't stand a chance of getting across the dining hall unmolested."

Katherine snickered and located a white silk scarf. She smoothed it out, folded it in half, and wrapped it around Victoria's neck. She secured it with a loose knot. "Don't forget to take this off."

"Right. When am I supposed to do that?"

"You'll know, Victoria. Here, let me fix your hair."

Katherine extracted a hand comb inlaid with amber from a pouch and set about taming her daughter's wild hair. She tugged and straightened until Victoria's tresses were under control. She secured her daughter's hair in a neat coif that showed off her throat, chest, and necklace to the best advantage.

"The necklace's magic won't affect Logan."

Victoria started and checked the impulse to fly to anger. "What? Why not? What is the point to it then?"

"There is a point and a very good one. You will see," Katherine said with a knowing smile. "But Logan must make the decision to leave Valhalla as the result of free will."

Her mouth formed a flat line. "You wouldn't say that if you knew him, Mom. He's a stubborn jackass."

Katherine only laughed and hugged her daughter goodbye. "Take care, Victoria. I love you."

"I love you too, Mom."

Victoria's initial attempts to locate Logan proved unsuccessful. She searched and grew tired and frustrated following a solid hour of wading through the dining hall's dense crowds. Droves of men gathered about tables drinking, smoking, and gambling, and not a single one looked familiar.

At last, Victoria spied a dark-haired serving wench carrying a tray laden with ale upon her hip. The woman wore a low-cut blouse and a tattered skirt, and she looked the sort to know the whereabouts of lusty young men.

Victoria stepped into the woman's path. "Logan Koenig."

The servant looked up and gave Victoria a quick once over. Then, with a careless shrug, she gestured across the hall. "Over there, but you'll have to wait your turn. Ása has already gotten her talons into him."

"We'll see about that." Victoria's mouth turned up at one corner. She crossed the dining hall, traveling in the direction the servant had indicated.

She located Logan tucked into a recessed alcove off the main hall. He sat upon a wooden chair with a buxom wench riding his lap. The servant, Ása, was a healthy looking lady of voluptuous curves and little clothing. The chair, constructed from the wooden pieces of other broken chairs bound together with twine, groaned and trembled under the strain of holding up the two bodies.

While she drew near, Victoria stomped her feet to alert the lip-locked pair to her approach, but they failed to notice her. Logan's shirt slithered serpentine to the floor. The sound of ripping fabric reached Victoria's reluctant ears, and the wench's blouse burst open to reveal her cleavage. Bras were not a fashion of Valhalla.

Victoria frowned and leaned over in order to inspect them up close. She expected Logan to scent her at any moment, and it disturbed her that he'd let his guard down to such an extent. She smelled ale and boar on his skin beneath the potent aroma of musky arousal.

Logan and his wench continued their vigorous game of tonsil hockey and still failed to take note. The pair assumed a more horizontal attitude; the wooden chair shuddered as it rocked onto the back legs.

Victoria could stand it no longer. She stepped to the side and balanced her weight on her left foot. She stepped in hard and brought the side of her foot down against the chair's rear leg. The wood split and the chair collapsed, sending an explosive shower of splinters everywhere.

The wench shrieked and gurgled. They went down in a flail of limbs, and Ása choked on Logan's tongue. Beneath the wench, Logan took the brunt of the impact, suffering the dual assault of pointy sticks and screeching female. Reaching down, Victoria grabbed hold of the servant's arm and hauled her off Logan.

The wench came up spitting mad. "What the fuck do you think you're about, bitch?"

Victoria smiled to show teeth and allowed her wolf to surface. She held up her hand and flexed her fingers tipped in razor-sharp claws. "Bitch is right. Leave. Unless you think he's worth it, because I'll gut you and take him anyway."

"Not bloody likely!" The wench's eyes widened to show whites, and she shrank from Victoria. Ása held her torn blouse closed and made a show of gathering her skirt. She cast a disgusted look at Logan and flounced away.

On the ground, Logan sprawled among the shattered remains of his chair. He gaped up at Victoria. The smell of booze assailed her nostrils, and she nudged him with her toe. "You stink, Logan. Are you going to get up?"

"Victoria?" Logan said in a strangled voice. He climbed to his feet, shaking the whole time, and stared at her with slack-jawed disbelief. His hands seized her arms so hard he hurt her.

"Oh, no! Fuck, no!" Logan moaned and gazed at her with unbearable anguish in his amazing amber eyes. He scared her senseless.

Victoria's hands rose to soothe him. "Logan, it's okay."

"No, he wouldn't," Logan said. "Not over me..."

"Who wouldn't? What?" Victoria arched her brow.

His chest felt hot and solid beneath her palm; his heart throbbed with great power. The eternal promise of Valhalla--life with all of the associated pleasure and pain--enjoyed or suffered until the end of days.

"Damn it. Tell me he didn't kill you." Logan's hands touched her, subjecting her to the sort of examination bestowed upon waifs and found pets.

Victoria knocked aside his hands. It disturbed her on so many levels to consider the source of his agitation. "What on earth are you babbling about?"

"Tell me he didn't!" Logan grabbed hold of her shoulders and shook her. His eyes communicated his fear to her.

She gripped his wrists and kept her tone soothing. "Logan, calm down! I'm fine! I'm not dead!"

Breathing hard, Logan fell away. He stared at her and recovered some of his natural aplomb. He stopped reaching for her. "What are you doing here, Vic?"

"I'm a Valkyrie," she said. "As choosers of the dead, Valkyries have the right to walk the halls of Valhalla."

"Oh." He nodded and slouched, once again exemplifying nonchalance. "Good to know. I don't recall Valkyrie being on your extensive resume."

"It doesn't mean what it once did," Victoria said. She noticed their little drama had attracted attention. The heads of curious onlookers turned toward them.

Logan's sides heaved as he cooled down. Victoria slid a hand onto his arm and edged him further back into the alcove to protect him from prying eyes. She kicked aside a broken chair leg in passing.

"Why are you here, Vic?"

"I came for you," she said. "To bring you home."

His look communicated pure disbelief. "In case you didn't notice, I'm dead."

Her lips thinned, and she smacked at him, landing a slap on his forearm. "I've healed your body, idiot."

Logan sneered. "That doesn't change my deadness, Vic."

"Deadness isn't a word! Don't call me that."

"Is so: The deadness of winter."

"Stop making shit up." Victoria crossed her arms and glared at Logan.

"I'm dead," Logan said. "As in dead to rights. Dead in the water. Dead as a doornail. As Dickens observed, a doornail is deader than the nail of a coffin lid."

"Goddess, you're obnoxious!" Victoria flashed her teeth. "Shut up! Or I swear I'll—"

"Kill me?" Logan smirked. "Too late, Vic. I'm already dead."

One, two, three... Victoria heaved a hard breath, struggling for control, as her hands grasped for an imaginary throat. Her thoughts were a jumble, running in a hundred different directions. She wondered if she should try to reason with him, explain the witch, or make an emotional appeal.

"Logan, I have permission to escort your soul from Valhalla and reunite you with your body," Victoria said. She spoke each word slow and carefully so he could understand. "If you'll come with me."

Her fingers closed on his hand, but he yanked away. "I don't want to leave. Things here don't hurt as much. Combat consumes the days; booze, women, and song dull the nights."

She gritted her teeth. "One of my pack gave his life so you could return."

"Not my problem, Vic. I didn't ask for any sacrifices."

"You asshole!" Victoria swore at him, full of bitterness, despising him for his selfishness.

Logan's mouth tugged into a cruel smile. "So you keep saying, Vic."

"How can you prefer this?" Victoria asked with a sweeping gesture to encompass all of Valhalla. "Compared to living, it's so... deficient."

"You seem to be overlooking the obvious, Vic. I *chose* to die, remember? I opted for death, so why the hell would I choose to go back with you, if it were possible?"

Victoria stared at Logan. "You selfish bastard. Have you given any thought at all to how your father feels? He killed his only child, and the knowledge of that is destroying him."

Awful guilt wiped out Logan's smug sarcasm. His expression betrayed his horror, and Victoria took no pleasure in it. "You have to go back to him then, Victoria. You have to give him a reason to live," Logan said.

Victoria shook her head before Logan finished speaking. "No. No, Arik doesn't love me. He barely knows me. Nothing I can offer him is going to take your place."

"I can't go back," Logan said with finality.

"Logan, he's going to kill himself." Tears squeezed from the corners of her eyes and spilled down her cheeks.

"Then you have to stop him."

"How?" Victoria asked. "Tell me how?"

"You'll give him the strong son he lacks."

A crushing weight struck her chest. Victoria's eyes widened, and she sucked down a hard breath. It was far crueler than she would have believed Logan capable, and it proved to her the true extent of his anger toward her. Her honor lay in tatters.

Victoria stepped forward so she stood before Logan. She met his gaze and then dropped it in a deliberate act of submission. She knelt at his feet, head bowed and palms turned up. Her dishonor demanded her complete abasement before her victim.

"Vic, what the hell are you doing?" Logan asked.

She stared at his feet. "I have wronged you and your father."

"Victoria, no—"

She ignored him. "My actions were selfish and manipulative and caused you to fight your own father—"

"No."

"I have brought dishonor upon myself and my entire bloodline."

"No. I don't want your fucking apology!"

"Your death was my fault."

"It wasn't! I chose!"

"Logan, I beg your forgiveness."

Logan bent and seized Victoria's arms. She did not resist as he lifted her from the ground. Furious, he slammed her against the wall of the alcove. The force of the impact against the back of her skull left her disoriented. Victoria recovered her senses and found herself staring straight into Logan's eyes, so close their noses touched and she inhaled his breath.

"I do not want your apology," Logan said through clenched teeth, enunciating every single word with perfect clarity.

She could not force his forgiveness. Victoria dropped her gaze to his bare chest and discovered a hand-shaped burn seared into his flesh over the breastbone. She reached out, laid her hand over the imprint, and discovered an exact match.

"I left a mark," Victoria said. His heart throbbed beneath her palm. She met his wide eyes, but for the life of her, she could not read the tormented emotions there.

She licked her lips and tried again. "Logan, I am sorry for what I did to you."

Logan blinked and let her go. Victoria landed on her feet, bereft of his contact. He bent and picked up his shirt. Without a word, he pulled the tee shirt over his head. He walked to the edge of the alcove and then turned back.

"Don't sweat it, Vic. I'll get over it."

Her emotions were numb. Victoria nodded.

Logan turned away from her and walked toward the dining hall.

Confused, she followed him. "Logan?"

Logan glanced over his shoulder.

"I'm not coming back with you, Victoria." He backed up a step. "You look hot. You're smokin'."

He presented her with his back. Victoria watched him walk away and knew the bitter taste of failure. The finality of it slammed home, crushing all hope.

A split second later, she saw red.

CHAPTER EIGHTEEN

The male mind —
    "Victoria, have you wondered why he changed his mind?"
    "Yes, but I'm not going to ask."
    "Why not?"
    "If he starts thinking, he might change it back."

Victoria's boots hit the dining table with a resounding *thud*. Her sudden impact caused every plate, platter, and tankard to jump and land with a clatter. The heads of a dozen or so Norsemen turned to see what had caused the disturbance. Many leered or produced rude sounds upon catching a glimpse of her cool beauty.

Victoria stood tall and straight, and then ripped away the scarf covering her throat. Revealed, *Brísingamen's* magic snaked out in a spiral, capturing the attention of every man present who happened to glance her way. The necklace exerted an irresistible attraction, and once ensnared, a man could not look away.

"Warriors! Einherjar, attend to me! I have something important to tell you!" Victoria shouted at the top of her lungs so that her voice carried to the furthest corners of the room.

She spread her arms and invoked her wolf, sending a wave of feminine power over the gathered men. Her pheromones attracted and aroused, lending her an allure that twisted and twined about their testicles. Around her, male nostrils flared and jaws worked, lecherous gazes undressed her body.

Victoria wove *Brísingamen's* magic and her personal power into a siren's song. More heads turned, curious onlookers looking to see what their friends were seeing. Curiosity spread as a ripple, and soon she had the attention of every man in the hall.

"My Lady, what 'ave you to say? We are listening." A bawdy Viking stood to speak to her; others shouted their encouragement.

"I am the Valkyrie Victoria! I have come here seeking a single strong warrior! I have the permission of Mighty Tyr to bring one of you with me when I return to Midgard!"

The room stirred with piqued interest at the offer. Such opportunities were unheard of, and not a single man, with the exception of Logan and her father, could have refused her. She could crook her finger at any one of them, and he'd bound to her side like an obedient dog.

"I am not looking for any old warrior. I am holding out for more than a hero! I require a champion! A man who will bear my standard and fight to defend my honor. A man who would die in the name of my cause with a smile and a song on his lips."

Victoria took a run down the center of the table and leapt to the next and then the next, walking the tables in order to flaunt her physical prowess. The low neckline of the corset showed off a healthy expanse of cleavage; the skin-tight leather pants emphasized her athletic legs. She was a fine female animal, and every male present sensed it. Every pair of eyes followed her, coveting and lusting after her.

Victoria reached Logan's table and stopped a few feet from him. Those brilliant amber eyes glared daggers

at her, his fist clenched the handle of a forgotten tankard. Victoria smirked and stomped her foot hard enough
to slosh ale from his cup.

She stood, legs splayed, arms raised, and conjured
drama with her voice. "Where I am from, there is a powerful winter witch threatening my people. She is a
cunning creature, a *seiðr* who commands the wind and
the ice and the beasts within men."

Twenty tables over, Rand towered over every man
around him when he stood. His bright red hair stood out
against the crowd. "Tell us about your people, My Lady!"

Victoria flashed him a smile of thanks. Thanks to the
necklace's magic, she held her audience captive, but she
needed to keep them focused on more than her body in
order to accomplish her goal.

"My people are shifters, wolves descended of Fenrir. Centuries ago, we were driven from the Norselands
and crossed the ocean to the shores of an unexplored
continent. In this New World, we settled, spread, and
prospered. For a time."

"We are a proud, strong people, and we keep the
old ways. We honor the gods; we aspire to die in the
glory of battle. Some of you are familiar with my
breed..."

Her gaze traveled the occupants of the room and
scanned the rapt faces. Here and there she saw people
she knew, men she'd escorted to Valhalla, and at least
one person she'd killed. "Some of you are my breed."

A shout went up, and then another; not a legion, but
a fair number. Rand and Paul joined the chorus and
cheered at the top of their lungs. Among the human
Einherjar arose the occasional voice lifted in support, a
smattering of applause, a stomping of feet.

Victoria hushed them with her hands. "The *seiðr*...
Years ago, she plagued a prosperous pack. She manipulated their beasts with malevolent magic and possessed

the weakest wolves. An entire pack endured her assault and only three members survived: a man, his mate, and their son."

Logan's tankard broke. If looks could kill, Logan would be standing over her corpse.

Victoria ignored him. "The man killed the witch. With his bare claws and his naked teeth, he ripped open her chest and ate her heart."

Murmurs of approval sprang from the audience. Vikings, one and all, approved of gory revenge, and more than that, they loved a good tale.

Victoria shouted out and her fist struck her palm. "Now, the *seiðr* comes again!"

The audience surged, shouted, and burst with rage and violence.

"The witch has possessed the son to murder his own mother! She has schemed and manipulated, and left that noble father with no choice but to kill his own son! I ask you, is this justice? Is this right?"

The dining hall rocked on the tumultuous sea of angry men. They jostled one another for position. Vikings, to the last, bellowed and growled, demanding justice, demanding blood. Distant, Thor joined in the uproar, shouting for justice to be done, because the God of Thunder loved to have his voice heard.

"Tell us more about this champion you seek!"

Victoria turned toward the speaker: Rand, bless his giant heart, flashed a wolfish grin and howled. She laughed so hard, her sides stitched. She rode an extraordinary high, buoyed on the rambunctious energy of the throng, and at the same time, she acknowledged the silliness of her cheerleading to an audience of long-dead soldiers.

Victoria drew a deep breath and launched into her soliloquy. "My champion will be the son of a king, birthed from the loins of the northern tempest. His heart will be that of a warrior, his hands shall shape kingdoms. Gods will tremble before his gaze. When he is thirsty, he shall suck down oceans, and when he is full, he shall piss forth rivers. His breath will bring forth storms, his rage demolish worlds. He shall wield a mighty sword and ride a fiery steed. Death will be his companion, and I shall be his mistress. My pleasure will be his bidding."

Laughter rocked the audience. With a swing of her hips, Victoria gave Logan her back and took wicked pleasure in the act. She spread her arms to the men as if to embrace all. She blew kisses and winked at them.

"Nothing less will do," she said.

"Take me, darling! I'll be your hero!"

"I'm a champion between the sheets!"

Other bawdy suggestions filled the hall; it rocked with the laughter of thousands of amused, horny warriors. An underlying tide of warmth, protectiveness, and bloodlust accompanied the humor. No, Victoria would have no trouble at all finding a willing volunteer.

"Make no mistake, nothing less than the most courageous and fiercest man will do." Victoria stopped before a great hulk of a Norseman. The bear of a Viking sat across from Logan. She bent to stroke her fingers through his bristling beard and scratched his jaw with her nails.

He reached for her; she smacked his cheek. The audience roared, some men guffawing so hard they fell over. Victoria straightened and at long last looked at Logan.

She leveled an accusing finger at Logan. When she spoke, she addressed their audience. "I have already erred once and chosen the wrong man. You see, I offered *the son* of the man the witch has wronged the opportunity to avenge his family and father."

Her eyes bored into Logan's. He smoldered with pent up fury, lips pulling back in a silent snarl. Victoria bent toward him and sneered. "He refused because he's too craven to face his fears."

Logan rose to his feet.

"Vic, I'm warning you," he said, low and threatening.

Victoria ignored him. She shouted at the top of her lungs, "Logan Koenig is a bloody coward!"

Logan spread his arms and growled. "I'm going to kill you, bitch!"

Paul's shout rose above the audience's disgusted murmur. "What will it take to prove my worth, My Lady?"

Victoria marshaled all of her strength and used her influence to thrust frenzy into the heart of every man present. "*Fight!* Prove to me who is the best among you, and the last man standing may be my champion!"

Logan roared his fury. He overturned the table under Victoria's feet, causing her to leap without looking. Plates of food and tankards of ale flew through the air, and the disruption knocked an entire row of men to the ground.

With the deft grace of a cat, Victoria landed on the next table over. A bloodthirsty howl tore from Logan's throat, and he lowered his head in a bull's rush. He charged straight toward her, plowing into men and furniture in his single-minded pursuit, so intent was he upon tearing her limb from limb.

A collective roar arose among the warriors of the hall. Violence erupted all around Victoria. More tables overturned, plates shattered, mugs and fists flew. It was man against man, and in the midst of it all, Logan came after her with murder on his mind.

Victoria threw back her head and laughed with delight. Then she ran for her life.

Logan lumbered with all the stealth of a charging rhinoceros, pounding feet and labored breathing, but he also brought on that spectacular speed that frightened Victoria witless. She ran flat out through the riot erupting in the dining hall, dodging objects and people. She took advantage of her petite size to squeeze through openings where Logan had no choice but to plow through or over the same obstacles.

Exhilaration caused her heart to race, and she loved every second of the chase. Still, Victoria ran scared and ran fast. She ran because she suspected Logan might really kill her if he caught her, and she didn't want to die.

Logan caught her at the edge of the dining hall. With the enraged bellow of a wounded beast, he snagged a handful of hair and stopped. Victoria's head jerked back, and he yanked her off her feet. She crashed to the ground and landed on her back.

A chair struck Logan from the side and knocked him off his feet. He flew into the wall. Sides heaving, Victoria scrambled to her feet. She grinned up at the man standing over her.

"Thanks, Daddy."

"Is this boy bugging you, Victoria?" Adair Storm scowled toward Logan, who was sprawled on the ground.

Victoria grinned. "Thanks, but I've got it under control."

"If you say so, Victory." Adair looked dubious.

Victoria pulled off *Brísingamen* and pressed the necklace into her father's hand. "Give this to mom, and tell her thanks."

Adair spared the talisman a glance. His brow rose. "Don't you need it to recruit your champion?"

She glanced at Logan. "I've got my champion already."

Logan sat up. He shook his head and blinked his vision into focus.

"Sorry, Daddy, gotta run. Give mom my love." Victoria smooched her father's cheek and dashed toward the ceiling-high entrance to the hall.

Inside the great double doors, she glanced back to

be sure Logan continued to follow. She needn't have worried. Logan chased her in hot pursuit. An expression of fierce determination had replaced the unthinking rage on his face. Her father's blow must have knocked some sense into him, which scared her that much more.

Satisfied that he gave chase, Victoria turned and ran once again, redoubling her pace in the wide-open hallways of the vast keep. They passed at least one set of guards, who stirred at the sight of them, but did not abandon their posts to pursue as the wolves raced past.

They were outside the great halls of Valhalla before Logan caught her again. His arm closed on her waist, and he yanked her from her feet and swung her around. Her legs milled in the air. Then Logan let go and pitched her to the side. She hit the ground rolling, and he grabbed for her again.

As they tumbled, Victoria seized hold of Logan's arms and brought her legs between. She planted her feet on his chest and used his momentum in conjunction with all of her strength to flip him. She threw him over her head, and he landed flat on his back.

Free of his grasp, Victoria scrambled away, but he came after her. He landed on top of her and pinned her with his lower body to the ground, so she felt his arousal pressing against her inner thigh. His hot breath huffed against her throat while they wrestled for superior position. She placed more than one warning nip upon his arms and chest. His skin tasted of perspiration, ale, and healthy male animal. The harder he tried to hold her, the harder she fought.

Logan's nostrils flared with frustration. "Damn it, stop struggling!"

"Get off!" Victoria snarled and bit his neck, nothing more than a quick nip. She bucked, rocking them both, but failed to dislodge him. He managed to remain on top of her due to his superior weight and strength.

"I bet you're one hell of an eight-second ride, little

girl."

"You're disgusting."

"And I'm sick to death of you harassing me at every turn. Let's settle this once and for all." Logan stopped fighting and caught her gaze. His eyes were solid gold. His power unfurled and loomed over her. Logan's wolf was a long, lanky beast that slinked out of hiding, unfolding his limbs, opening a great mouth to drink in her scent.

Victoria's breathing stuttered, and she grew still. Logan had spent so much time and effort dodging a battle of wills, it caught her unprepared when he finally initiated a dominance contest. He had evaded direct conflict with her and even tried to protect her from Arik's challenge. She burst with questions but also with fear.

Why now? What will he do if he wins?

Victoria's wolf rose bright white and blazing, every bit as bold and beautiful as the northern stars. Instead of proceeding with caution, she launched her power against Logan and invested all of her strength in the initial assault. She came at him head on, her light against his darkness, and drove him back.

Logan's power yielded, flowing to the sides about her, so that Victoria drove straight at the heart of him. He floated around her, an amorphous cloud, a silken caress on her skin, a tempting whisper. She lost track of everything else around her. He did not assault; he seduced. He wasn't a hammer, but rather a slippery slope.

Stubborn to the bitter end, Victoria clung to her power and refused to submit, even while she felt her strength ebb. Submission scared her more than death. Logan's magic transformed from darkness to amber, a honeyed stickiness, pulling her under.

"Shh, Vic, it's okay. Don't be scared. Let it happen." Logan's hand stroked her hair, smoothing strands soaked with perspiration from her face.

Victoria gasped for air. "No."

"Trust me."

Her face contorted. She recalled his rage and his refusal to forgive her. "I can't."

Her jaw clenched, and she made a vicious decision out of cowardice and fear. Victoria brought her knee up, aiming for Logan's crotch, and scored a direct hit. He wasn't prepared with a defense to lessen the pain, because dominance contests never relied on violence.

Logan roared and rolled to the side, clutching a hand to his balls. "Bitch!"

"You know it." Victoria scrambled to her feet and stood over him. For a split second, she considered kicking his kidneys, but it was an instinctive impulse rooted in fear.

Once he recovered, if he chose to beat her, she had it coming. Dominance was supposed to be a pure contest of wills. She had cheated in the worst possible way.

Logan dragged himself to the wall and slouched against it, still holding a protective hand across his privates. He glared and gave her the silent treatment, sulking with a sullen pout.

Victoria sighed and crouched across from him. "Look, I'm sorry. I shouldn't have done that."

"That was a dirty trick."

"You're right. I'm sorry."

"I won," Logan said.

Her jaw developed a defiant jut. "You didn't subdue me. I'm more dominant than you. You're just... bigger."

Logan snorted. "What a load. Physical size has nothing to do with dominance."

"It does. Males are more dominant than females because they're larger."

"A smart female doesn't need to be dominant. Males are naturally more dominant because..."

"Their 'nads are bigger than their brains."

Logan gave her the evil eye. "Well, yeah." He paused to consider. "There's the whole attracting a mate and protecting cubs thing, too."

"Right, because women don't need to attract mates or protect their children."

"If you think being able to throw down with the boys makes you more attractive..." Logan tapped his temple. "Sister, you're loco."

"Don't even," Victoria said. "I've never met a more conceited, chauvinistic—"

"You're more of a chauvinist than I am." With a grimace, Logan shifted his position to sit straighter.

Nausea churned her gut. There were times when she said things, did things, without really understanding why. She hated those parts of herself.

"I'm sorry," she said.

"You usually fight fair," Logan said. He glared at her with justified resentment.

Victoria laughed but stopped at the look on his face. "I'm not laughing at you, Logan. I'm laughing at the fact that even though we met less than a week ago, you're familiar with how I fight. When I look back, most of our conflicts seem pretty trivial."

"You called me a coward."

"I've called you worse than that. That wasn't why you lost your temper," Victoria said. "It was because I did it in front of witnesses."

He regarded her with keen understanding in his bright eyes. "You wanted to piss me off. You wanted me to chase you."

Victoria rolled one shoulder in a casual shrug. "It got your head back in the game."

"That was clever." Logan crossed his arms.

"Thank you."

"What happened to you being sorry?"

Victoria arched her brow. "You rejected my apology. What's the point to feeling bad if the other person doesn't give a crap?"

A reluctant chuckle escaped Logan. "That's one of

the most self-serving excuses I've ever heard."

She shrugged again. "Whatever works."

"Why didn't you try to tell me about the witch?" Logan cocked his head and looked at her in a way that made her gut twist into knots.

"I'm not sure. I guess I wasn't sure you'd believe me."

"You could try giving me the benefit of the doubt sometime, Vic," Logan said with cutting sarcasm.

Victoria looked away. "I guess."

Logan swore. "This is such a fucking waste of time."

He picked himself up off the floor; Victoria also climbed to her feet. She caught his arm at the elbow. "I'm not giving up on you, Logan. Suicide is stupid."

"M'kay, thanks for the visit, Ms. Suicide Prevention." He waggled his fingers at her. "By the way, you're too late. That'd be a big *fail*."

"You're an idiot!" Fury transformed her; she wanted to kill him again. Life was worth too much to waste like this.

Logan scoffed and jerked his elbow from her grasp. "My day is complete. I've been accused of being a coward and an idiot by a crazy little blonde stalker."

He turned his back on her again, for the second time in one day, and started back toward the hall. With a burst of speed, Victoria shot past him. She got between Logan and his destination and stood in his way.

"I'm not leaving without you," she said.

Logan advanced and got right up in her personal space, so they stood toe-to-toe. Victoria's nose only came to his breastbone, which reduced her overall ability to intimidate him. Still, she refused to budge.

"What're you going to do, Vic? Force me to come with you?"

She lifted her chin in order to look him straight in the eyes. "If I have to."

"Allow me to point out the obvious. You're half my

size. You're not even normal girl height. You're short." He advanced a step and chest-butted her, driving Victoria back a pace.

"I am *not* short!" Victoria rebounded and struck Logan's chest with both palms, but he did not budge.

"Are so."

"Argh!" Victoria gnashed her teeth and swallowed the mandatory '*am not*' rejoinder. Her hands opened and closed about his imaginary throat.

"I'm sick to death of you and your Napoleon complex!" Logan shouted full in her face.

"Aarrhhh!" Struggling for control, she shoved her hot temper down and took a step back to consider the situation. Arguing with Logan wasn't getting her anywhere, and he had a valid point about the difference in their respective sizes. Trickery and deceit hadn't served her any better than self-abasement at his feet. She evaluated what she had left in her arsenal.

She exhaled, her entire attitude altered, and she shifted to the side, moving out of his path. "What will it take, Logan?"

His eyes widened, and he adjusted his position to face her. "Is that a loaded question or is that a loaded question, Vic?"

"You win." Victoria smiled and held up her hands to demonstrate surrender. She slid sideways; he followed again.

He eyed her with suspicion. "What exactly have I won? Is there a big cereal box behind your back, tricky one?"

"You win it all. The fight. The argument. I'm done. Name your price. Tell me what it's going to take to get you to come with me." Victoria stepped again to the right one last time, coming half circle.

"Oh, so you think I can be bought, do you?" Logan arched his brow, smirked.

"I do."

He watched her with comical wariness and followed when she retreated. Once again, they were underway, headed away from the dining hall and toward the rainbow bridge.

"All right, fine." Logan's grin took a turn for the worse, becoming wolfish and suggestive. "But if I name my price, and you refuse to meet it, I want your word that you'll leave me alone."

Victoria's eyes narrowed and she decided to gamble. "You have my word. Name your price."

Logan smirked. "I'll come back with you if you'll have sex with me."

Victoria stared at him. His smug nonchalance infuriated her, so she took a great deal of satisfaction in wiping the smirk from his face.

"Okay," she said. "Done."

"Just like that?" Logan rocked back on his heels. His eyebrows shot up and his mouth opened, then closed. The surprise lasted a mere flame flicker before suspicion took its place.

"Just like that. I have sex with you; you come back with me. Do we have a deal?" Victoria settled her hand over his heart. The steady throbbing beneath her palm reminded her of a caged beast, so fierce, so strong, so eager.

Logan's jaw worked while he dropped his gaze from her face to her body. A teasing smile curved Victoria's lips. "Would you like me to take something off so you can get a better look?"

"Thanks, but I've seen the goods."

Victoria slid her arms higher so her breasts flattened. She leaned forward so her chest brushed his and kissed the underside of his jaw. "Then you know I'm well worth the price."

Logan shuddered with arousal. "Ha, why do I get the feeling the markup on this purchase is more than I can afford? So how much is this little joke gonna cost me? For some strange reason, my 'nads are urging me to caution."

Victoria snickered. "You're a werewolf. Your gnads take about five minutes to heal. It's been ten." Her hand slipped lower, stroking his washboard belly, and located a bulge against the front of his jeans.

Logan drew in a sharp breath. "You must think I'm an idiot to fall for something this transparent."

Victoria wrapped her arms around his neck and her legs around his hips. She shimmied up his body and clung to him. She licked the curve of his ear and laughed, husky. "I do."

Logan's hands grasped Victoria's backside, providing support. She rubbed her face against the stubble of his jaw and placed her lips against his cheek in a full kiss.

Logan produced a strangled sound. "Okay, I'm an idiot, but I really think—"

"Shh, don't think." Victoria shushed him and trailed kisses along his jaw toward his ear. The hair on the back of his neck felt like silk. "Don't hurt yourself."

Victoria's teeth closed on Logan's earlobe. He produced a strangled sound; his heart slammed against his ribcage. She worked the tasty bit of flesh with her teeth and tongue.

Victoria hitched herself high enough on his torso to reach his mouth. She exhaled against his lips. "What's wrong, Logan? Are you out of smart ass remarks?"

His hands massaged her buttocks. "Right now my ass is about the smartest part of me."

Her mouth met his in full contact, lips full and pliable, pressed together. Her tongue licked his lower lip. Logan kissed her with his wary eyes wide open. Victoria knew because they never broke eye contact.

She ended the kiss and turned her face into his throat to hide her smile. Logan felt and tasted delicious. Even though only four years separated them, she still felt like she was cradle robbing. Her relationship with his father intensified the taboo associated with touching him. It was wrong, wrong, wrong. Goddess, he felt so fucking right.

"Fuck." Logan exhaled hard. "Okay, yeah, we have a deal."

Victoria slid down his body and landed on her feet. She took his hand and tugged it. "Do you have a room?"

"Yeah." He took the lead.

Victoria followed, noticing how their footsteps echoed through the stone hallways. It took self-control not to fidget. Her inner reflections were loud and recriminatory. Even with Arik's sanction, infidelity violated her ethics. She was about to sell out her principles yet again.

The sound of Logan's voice startled her, and Victoria glanced at him, guilt plain on her face. His brow rose; perceptive eyes saw far too much. She flushed and forced her features into an inscrutable mask.

"I'm sorry," Victoria said. "What did you say?"

Logan shot her an odd look. "How much time has passed since I died?"

Victoria rolled her shoulders, creating an expansive gesture with her hands. "It's been over a day, almost two, since the fight with your father," she said. "But time flows differently in Valhalla than Midgard. How much time has passed since you came here?

Logan thought on it. "Two weeks, give or take."

Victoria sighed with relief. "Good. If the pattern holds steady, we won't be gone from the world for too long."

Logan stopped in front of a door. "This is it."

"I hope you don't have a roommate."

"Nah, I've got my own room." He led her inside and closed the door behind them. A cot occupied one corner of the room; a trunk for storing personal effects was on the opposite wall. Logan hadn't done anything to personalize the area.

Logan stopped several feet from her. He stood apart from everything in the room, including her, and wore an expression of guarded suspicion. He still seemed to expect her to haul off and hit him at any moment. Overall, he conveyed the impression of reluctance or shyness, and she had no idea what to make of it.

Victoria placed her hands on his chest, giving Logan a gentle push toward the cot. "Sit."

Logan pretended to shiver. "Do you do a dominatrix bit, Vic? You're already got the black leather covered. Are you gonna spank me?"

"That depends. Have you been bad?" Victoria straddled Logan's lap. She balanced her hands atop his broad shoulders. Strong shoulders. Her nails dug into his skin, testing the taut sinew. "You know, I rather like you like this."

"Reduced to your miniscule height?"

"Obedient." Victoria leaned in closer to scent his throat. Her nostrils flared; her breath exhaled against his skin. Logan's body surged against her, an undulation of his hips thrusting his arousal against her inner thigh.

They didn't have much time, and it sucked. Having to keep an eye on the clock robbed her of the pleasure she would have otherwise taken in his superb physique. All business, she started to unlace the corset.

Her tone dropped to a husky taunt. "Want to give me a hand?"

"Yeah, sure." Logan's deft fingers located the top of the bodice and started working the lacing loose. His heart rate spiked as even more cleavage became visible and perspiration beaded on his upper lip. He finished undoing the corset but made no further attempt to touch her.

"What happened after I died?" he asked.

Victoria's brow pinched. "What's wrong?"

"Just tell me what happened after I died."

She reached for his hands and caught his wrists.

Tossing her head back, Victoria thrust her chest forward and pressed her breasts into his palms. His hands covered her; his hot skin burned her. Under her watchful gaze, his pupils dilated until his eyes appeared solid black.

"We healed your body, but your soul had already departed," she said. "Freya told us that we had three days to bring your soul back. I'd have come sooner except the witch possessed Morena, and she attacked me. Then I got ambushed and shot by a hunter. We managed to free Morena, and we escorted the pack out to Desolation Wilderness."

Logan's thumb stroked her nipple and she produced a sound of pleasure.

"Oh, and your uncle dropped by."

Logan reacted with surprise, progressed to disbelief, and finally, smiled in amusement. "Sounds like I missed a lot. Nothing ever happened in Sierra Pines before you came to town, Vic."

Victoria's spine stiffened. "Something happened before I came, or we wouldn't be where we are now. Stop calling me that."

Logan smirked at her. His palms teased her alert nipples, feather soft. "True enough. What would you rather I call you?"

Victoria frowned and shifted her hips forward in order to rub her lower body against his. His erection remained prominent against the front of his pants.

Victoria bit her lower lip. She hesitated to ask. "Logan...?"

His gaze rose to hers. "Yeah?"

"Are you... inexperienced?"

His eyes widened; he emitted a bark of denial. "What? No! I've tons of experience. Most recently with the willing wenches of the dining halls. You can ask..." He struggled to remember.

"Ása," Victoria said. The name came out sounding

far too prim for her liking.

"Who?" Logan's expression registered blankness.

"The willing slut from the dining hall. The one from earlier tonight."

"Oh, yeah. Her." He shut his mouth.

Victoria tried again. "Have you ever been with another shifter?"

Logan's brow knit. "No, I haven't been with another shifter."

"It can be scary the first time..."

"Damn it, I'm not worried about it! And no, I'm not gay!"

"I didn't ask that."

"I was helping you out," he said.

Victoria left his lap and moved to the cot. "If you're not a virgin, not nervous, not gay, then what the hell is the problem?"

Logan's emphatic gesture involved his hand sweeping the width of the room. "I never said there was a problem. You did."

Victoria crossed her arms over her breasts. "Any normal teenage boy would be rutting on top of me right now. You're holding back on purpose."

Logan reared back, offense plain on his face. "A) I'm not a teenage boy. B) You're bitching because I'm not grunting and tearing off your clothes?"

Victoria reached for his hands and sought to regain control of the situation before they came to blows again. She caught his wrists and knelt before him.

"This is because I tricked you with those damned breath mints, isn't it? I left you with no choice but to fight—"

Logan interrupted her. "Vic, I'm not as stupid as you think I am." The ambient aura vibrated with the intensity of his restrained anger.

She started to offer a platitude, or maybe an apology, but he cut her off before she knew what she had intended to say.

"Look, I'm not rutting because I don't want to. I do."

She arched her brow. "So you do want to rut?"

"Fuck yeah!"

"What's the problem then?"

Logan shot to his feet. "The problem is that I don't think of you like that. And fuck! I'm going to kick myself for this later!"

Stunned, Victoria stared at him. "How do you think of me?"

His gaze never wavered. "I think of you as strong and proud, not someone who would sell out her principles. If we have sex now, it would be demeaning for both of us. And you're going to give me no end of shit about this, but I don't want you like that."

Victoria regarded him in honest amazement. She felt as if she were seeing Logan for the first time ever. The oddest sense of pride in him filled her. He wasn't the lecherous, unprincipled lout she'd taken him for. It shamed her to realize how she'd underestimated his integrity.

"Stop that," he said.

"Stop what?"

"Stop smiling like that." Logan snarled in annoyance.

Victoria kept smirking. "How do you want me?

"Willing, for one."

Victoria laughed. "Logan, I'm in heat, and you're strong and virile. I love the way you move. This isn't the terrible hardship you're making it out to be."

His jaw set, and he looked at her with fire in his eyes. "I want it to mean something."

"What?" Victoria gestured. "What could it possibly mean?"

"You know what I'm talking about."

Her mouth went dry, and she shook her head. "I can't give you that. Not ever. All I can offer you is the here and now. Physical pleasure, once, never to be repeated. After we leave, you can't ever have me again. Do you understand?"

His golden eyes were piercing. "What happened with you and my dad?"

"The truth?" Her gut churned, and she felt herself tumbling into a moral abyss. If she lied to him, he would never trust her again. If she told the truth, he would refuse to return with her.

"I'm an idiot, and I'm gonna curse myself for this later. Yeah, the truth."

Victoria exhaled long and slow. "Your father and I sealed the mate bond."

Logan absorbed what she told him. She caught a glimpse of disappointment on his face before he adopted an inscrutable mask.

"I can't do this," he said with finality. "I don't always get along with my father, but I respect him too damned much to sleep with his mate."

Victoria scrambled off the cot and fastened the bodice of the corset. "I understand."

Logan chuckled, a cynical sound that cut. "You sound relieved."

Victoria hesitated, but she would not speak of her relief any more than of her disappointment. "Your father and I discussed this beforehand. I had his leave."

"No way." Pure disbelief shone on Logan's face.

"Believe what you will." She felt cold and tired, way too exhausted to argue. "Does this mean you're going to refuse again to come back with me?"

Logan made a show of biding his time. "Let me ask you a question."

"Okay." She would answer because she had no other options left.

"You have your choice of any warrior in the Einherjar?"

"Correct," Victoria said, watching him for trickery.

She had no idea where he was going, and she didn't trust the destination.

"The chosen warrior is to be your champion?" Logan asked.

Victoria nodded. "That's what was said."

"And you not only chose me, you *insisted* on me above all others?" Logan's smirk rivaled Thor's hammer for the strength of his smugness.

Victoria kept her demeanor skeptical. "I'm not sure you have the necessary qualifications to be my champion. Do you have a fiery steed?"

Logan snapped his fingers. "Damn, I left that in my other pants."

Victoria whacked his arm hard. "Are you coming?"

"Apparently not," Logan said.

But he followed her from the room.

CHAPTER NINETEEN

The plot thickens —
    "Goddess, I swear to you, I'm going to get him a leash."
    "A delightful thought. He's still young enough to be trained to it."

The bridge's end deposited them upon the Koenig's front porch. Victoria stepped from the shimmering path of light; Logan followed her. As soon as the travelers were clear, Bifröst vanished in a brilliant flash.

"That was so fucking cool," Logan said with a chuckle.

"It is a privilege not to be abused," Victoria said with more severity than she actually felt. "Not for bar-hopping or whatever other juvenile pastime entered your mind."

Logan snapped his fingers. "Damn, there go my plans for Mardi Gras."

Victoria glanced around in order to get her bearings. The sun occupied a position above the horizon, late afternoon. Victoria studied it for a minute, shading her eyes against the direct light. The sky was clear and the worker hired to shovel the walkways was nowhere in sight.

She bit her lower lip and worried.

Beside her, Logan stirred. "What's wrong?"

"It's late. We're running out of time."

"Well, my body's right inside," Logan said. "We're in the home stretch. Relax. No need to go getting your panties in a twist."

"I don't wear panties." Victoria yanked her belt dagger from its sheath.

"Good to know." Logan flashed a feral grin.

"I'll relax after we have your soul safe inside your body," Victoria said.

Logan regarded her with a hint of caution in his amber eyes, but he did not flinch when Victoria thrust the blade in the air in order to catch the fading sunlight. She used the reflective surface in order to complete the transition to the physical world. Logan remained trapped within the Shadowlands, a disembodied spirit, perceivable only to mediums.

"What just happened?" Logan asked. "What'd you do?"

"Right now you're a spirit," she said. "In Valhalla, your spirit has substance and experiences pain, hunger, and lust the same as if you were flesh and blood. When you traveled to Midgard, your spiritual essence became more..."

"Ghostly?"

"Immaterial," she said. "Be careful, Logan. When you're in Valhalla, the body can be wounded, but you always heal... Here in the mortal realm, your spirit body can be damaged and your soul can die."

"This is gonna suck, isn't it?"

Victoria grunted, a neutral reply. She tried the front door and found it locked. She pushed the bell, waited over a minute, and then rang it again. She glanced at Logan. "Is there a spare key anywhere?"

Logan shook his head and then stepped out to look toward the carport. "Dad's SUV isn't here."

"Where would he go?" Victoria asked.

Logan's mouth twisted into a bitter smile. "Work.

It's where he's spent the last twenty years, so why not now?"

Victoria frowned and shook her head. "That's unfair."

"It's perfectly fair. You barely know the man; I'm his son."

Victoria sighed. "Look, can you Casper through the front door and open it?"

Logan appeared startled. "I can do that?"

"Sure, you're a ghost," she said with a shrug. "Passing through solid objects should come naturally to you."

Logan approached the front door. With an experimental thrust, he stuck his arm through the wood. He withdrew his hand and then inserted it into the door again.

"Look at that."

"Stop screwing around."

"Aye, aye, Captain Ahab." Logan stepped through the door and disappeared. A second later, his face appeared through the wood. "How am I supposed to touch it if I pass right through it?"

Rolling her eyes heavenward, Victoria entreated Freya for patience. "Even the weakest spirits can manage to poltergeist stuff about," Victoria said. "By all accounts, you should be a powerful ghost right now. Grab the knob and turn it. If you want it bad enough, it'll happen."

"Right." Logan managed to pack an incredible amount of skepticism into that single word. He withdrew, and a few seconds later the front door popped open.

"Nice work," she said.

"I try." Logan moved out of her way.

Victoria stepped into the entryway and closed the door behind her. She threw the deadbolt for good measure. Then she performed a quick inspection of the foyer. Nothing appeared amiss.

Why do I have gooseflesh on my arms?

"It's quiet," Logan said. "Dad definitely isn't here."

"Let's get this thing done."

Victoria led the way down the hallway to Logan's room and pushed open the door. She came to a stunned halt within the doorway and surveyed the mess. It looked like a tornado had struck the bedroom dead center.

"Shit," Victoria swore. She clenched her fists and stomped her feet. "Shit. Shit Shit!"

"What's wrong?" Logan ducked into the room after her. Once he got a look at the destruction, he scowled.

"First your damn soul goes missing and now your fucking body!" Victoria shoved her finger into Logan's face. "You're more trouble than you're worth! Do you hear me, Logan?"

"Where's my body?"

Victoria dropped her accusatory finger. "How should I know where your body is? I was with you, *remember?*"

"What do you mean you don't know where it is? It's my fucking *body*, for Christ's sake! It's not the sort of thing you lose!"

Hands pressed to the sides of her face, Victoria turned her back on Logan to survey the destruction throughout his bedroom. The bed had been overturned, and debris strewn everywhere. The curtains beside the window produced a constant fluttering as the wind blew into the room.

"Vic, if this is a joke, you can be damn sure I'm gonna get even." Logan slammed his fist into his palm. His ire exceeded hers, if such a thing were possible.

"Be quiet for a second, please." With each passing second, Victoria felt the throbbing in her temples build, ready to explode into a migraine. Nausea pushed bile into the back of her throat.

"Somebody is playing *Weekend at Bernie's* with my

body, and you want me to be quiet?"

"Shut up so I can think!"

"Yeah, well don't hurt yourself, sweet cheeks."

Cool air caressed her face, and Victoria approached the window beside Logan's bed.

"This is broken outward," she said, touching the pane full of glittering shards with her fingers.

"Yeah, so?" Logan moved closer to inspect the damage also.

"So it means whoever took your body probably left this way," Victoria said.

Logan grumbled something beneath his breath and turned away. He marched straight through the wall of his room, passing through the solid barrier without a hint of hesitation or doubt. He'd gotten a fast handle on the ghost business.

"Showoff." Victoria crossed the broken glass and boosted herself out the window.

Logan stood outside in the snow where a single set of tracks led away from the window. Thanks to his incorporeal condition, he moved about without creating any additional prints. He glanced up at her approach. "Bare footprint, size twelve."

"How can you be sure?" Victoria eyed the tracks with skepticism. She lacked the advantage of being a ghost, so she broke a fresh trail in the snow.

With a narrow-eyed glare, Logan stuck his booted ghost foot into the track. "Why did you take my shoes off, Vic?"

"What?" Victoria stared at him. "You're crazy."

"Am I? You've dragged my soul out of Valhalla and lost my body, and I'm the one that's crazy! From where I'm standing, this is on you." Logan glared at her. All of his frustration over the mysterious disappearance of his body focused on her.

Victoria dropped to her knees in the snow and buried her nose in one of the tracks. She closed her eyes and inhaled, drinking in the scent.

Logan.

She followed the trail for a hundred feet and turned back to Logan once it became clear it led deeper into the woods. Tracking it would be an undertaking.

Logan waited in expectant silence.

He wants me to provide answers, only I've got none. Her brow pinched as her forehead furrowed, and an epic headache exploded against her temples.

"Well?" Logan asked.

"We need to find your dad."

"Call him on your cell," Logan said.

"I can't! My cellphone got trashed when you tossed my car into the lake!"

"Use the house phone then."

"I don't know his number."

"You had time to get horizontal with the old man but don't know his phone number?" Logan said with a crude leer.

Victoria arched her brow. Her smile grew provocative. "We were never... horizontal."

Logan's features set in stone. "I know his number."

"Fine. Where's the closest phone?"

"In the kitchen."

Logan accompanied Victoria to the kitchen where an old-fashioned rotary phone hung on the wall beside the fridge. He supplied the number, and she dialed.

It rang without an answer and went to voicemail.

Victoria hung up. "Arik's not answering."

"Why didn't you leave a message?"

Victoria rubbed her temple, trying to think over the throbbing in her head. "Exactly what sort of message do you propose I leave? 'Hi! Logan and I are back from Valhalla, but his body is missing. Call me! Okay, bye!'"

"It'd be a start."

"Leave your own damned message."

Logan rushed at her, arms raised. "I would, except

I'm a fucking ghost!"

"And from the looks of it, your body is a fucking zombie," Victoria said with perfect deadpan delivery.

Logan took a swipe at her, expecting his hand to pass through her, and Victoria caught his wrist. With a quick twist, she flipped Logan so he landed on his ass.

Logan wore a comical expression; his mouth hung open. "What the fuck!"

"Quick lesson: Valkyries can touch the dead in addition to being able to see and speak with them."

With great dignity, Logan rose from the ground and brushed off his backside. "Thanks for the heads up."

Victoria walked away, heading out the backdoor of the house to the patio. Logan followed her. "Where are you going?"

"Out."

"Vic, stop and think. Don't you think we ought to find my dad and regroup? Have a game plan before we go charging off?"

"That's rich, coming from you." Victoria halted in her tracks. Fuming, she clenched her fists.

Damn him for being right.

She took a deep breath and glared at Logan. He stared back, arms crossed over his chest. Just once, it would be great to be able to agree with him on something. Anything. She opened her mouth and then closed it again. Her head throbbed with violent energy, part frustration and part fear. Without his cooperation, she might track down his body but have no means of wresting it from the witch's control.

"Logan," she said, and it hurt to speak his name. Her anxiety carried in her voice and he looked at her with suspicion in his eyes. She questioned what to do. So far, he'd proven resistant to her attempts to bully, cajole, or trick him into doing what she wanted. Her options were limited.

"What?" he asked. "What is it?"

She realized her hands formed fists, so she took a deep breath and tried to relax.

Trust.

It didn't have to be difficult. One of them had to take the first step.

"If I tell you something, no matter how crazy, would you listen?"

Logan tried and failed to conceal his surprise. "And what's that?"

"Promise me you'll listen. Please?"

"I'm listening," he said.

"We need to work together to find your body. We don't have time to wait for your dad to show. This is the third day since you died, which means time's running out to reunite your body and soul. I know you're angry with me, but I didn't expect this to happen. Please believe me."

Logan stared a long time. "Yeah, I believe you."

A weight lifted off her chest, and she breathed easier. "I have a theory."

"What's that?"

"The witch has possessed your body and taken it joyriding," Victoria said. "Like before, when she murdered your mother. It's the only thing that makes any sense."

The silence dragged for so long, Victoria figured Logan didn't believe her. Disgusted, Victoria resumed her trek around the back of the house to where the trail began. Despite his insistence they ought to wait, Logan followed her anyway.

"You still believe I didn't kill my mom."

Victoria's breath exhaled in a long thin stream. Her shoulders started to sag in relief; she aborted the gesture before it completed. To communicate weakness bespoke doubt. She looked up with tears in her eyes. "I do believe you're innocent. It might have been your body that committed the act, but it wasn't you."

"You sound so damned sure of that."

"I am."

"Why?"

She turned and looked him straight in the eye. "Because... you're a nice guy, Logan."

"Gee, thanks. Just what every guy wants to hear." He looked away to hide his expression; a convulsive swallow bobbed his Adam's apple.

"You're not a berserker, and you're not a killer," she said. "The witch has targeted Arik for revenge, and the surest way to get to him was through his family. She manipulated you while you were young and defenseless, the same way she turned Morena against me."

Logan finally looked at her. He stared, expression unreadable, wearing a damned fine poker face. "How do you know that? So far it sounds like the same old conjecture and speculation."

Victoria glared and lapsed into silence. Her breath came in rapid huffs. "I know. I just know. I can see it in the ice — flickering images. I hear it when she laughs. I feel it in my soul."

"So you've gone all Oracle at Delphi, and I'm just supposed to take your word for it?"

"Yes," Victoria said. "I follow my instincts. I'm asking you to trust me."

He remained silent for a moment. "Okay."

"Okay?"

He nodded. "Okay."

"Just like that?"

He shrugged. "Yeah, sure. If you can believe in me, I can believe in you."

Tears filled her eyes, and her throat clenched. She produced a strangled sound.

Dismay crossed his face. "What is it? What's wrong?"

"Nothing," she said. "I... thank you."

He tilted his head to the side, regarded her with a

gaze that saw too much. "What's next?"

"There are a few things I need to tell you."

He opened his arms, and gestured with his hands for her to bring it. "Let's have it. Pour your infinite wisdom into me, oh my Yoda."

Relief suffused her. She was grateful he'd resumed his flippancy, his irreverence toward all things big and small. She couldn't handle anymore intimacy, and neither of them were the sort to put their feelings into words. She adopted a lecturing tone. "Logan, you need to take this seriously. If your spirit dies, it means the destruction of your soul."

"Blah. Blah. Blah." Logan smirked and crossed his arms over his chest. "Yeah, I get it. You want me to be careful. Anything else?"

Victoria curbed the impulse to whack him. "If we find your body, you need to get your spiritual ass back in the driver's seat."

Logan smacked his forehead. "Doh! Why didn't I think of that? Okay, any other obvious advice?"

Victoria squeezed her eyes shut and wished upon the stars for an anvil to fall out of the sky... preferably on his head.

Oh, and a couple painkillers too please...

"How do you know all this stuff?" Logan asked.

"I'm a shaman. Just like you."

She waited for him to ask more about that but was surprised when he instead made a shooing gesture. "Well, lead on, Vic. My body is wreaking havoc while we're standing around jawin'."

It required no great tracking ability to follow the trail in the broken snow. Victoria didn't bother catching the scent again. She followed the footsteps in the snow and conserved her energy for the upcoming confrontation.

Time passed before Logan spoke again. "What did you mean? Calling me a shaman?"

Victoria shot him a dubious look. "I'm not qualified to teach you this."

"Do you see anyone else lining up with the syllabus to Spirits 101?"

Victoria stopped walking. She drew in a deep breath and took a second to organize her thoughts. "Okay. Crash course then: As a shaman, you possess the innate ability to communicate with spirits. The whole nine yards—sight, sound, smell, touch..."

"Taste?"

Victoria narrowed her eyes.

"Seriously, what do spirits taste like?"

"You're pushing it," she answered in a sing-song voice.

Logan laughed and squeezed her arm. "Sorry, keep going."

"As a shaman, you should have the ability to enter the spirit world via a reflective surface. A mirror works best, but a pool of water, ice, polished metal, all potential entry points," Victoria said.

"Does it have a name?"

"Different cultures and religions call it by a variety of names, but my mother always called it the Shadowlands. It's part of and apart from the living world."

"Which is where I am now."

"Yes."

"Where is Valhalla in relation to everything else?"

Victoria shook her head. "There's no map. Don't try to draw relational locations for places. It all moves around. The only constant is Bifröst, the rainbow bridge."

"Of course, silly me, thinking it should make sense."

"Don't whine to me," Victoria said. "I didn't want the responsibility of telling you all of this in the first place."

Logan cocked his head to the side. "Is that what I am? A responsibility?"

Victoria licked her lips. Whether she liked it or not, he was.

"Yes," she said. "Once this is all over, I'll teach you how to enter and exit the Shadowlands and summon Bifröst. Now that you've died for the first time, you'll undergo certain changes once you're reborn. Your becoming..."

"Becoming what?"

"Whatever it is you're going to be."

"Why is it," he said, "that I always feel like I'm going in circles when I'm talking to you?"

Victoria said, "I try to use simple words so you'll understand, but some of the ideas are big."

Logan snorted but failed to rise to the bait. "Okay, how do shaman happen? Is it birth? Destiny? What does it take to win the spiritual lotto?"

Victoria pressed her lips together. Logan noticed her reluctance because his brow rose. The throbbing in her head reached a crescendo.

"Vic?"

"Okay, fine," she said. "A god touches an unborn fetus in the womb and opens the child. Freya touched me, so I am called to her."

"Whoa! Wait a sec! So I was touched by a god?"

"Touched for certain," Victoria said beneath her breath.

"Do you know which one?"

Victoria crossed her arms. "How the hell am I supposed to know? If your god isn't speaking to you, that's not on me."

Logan seized her shoulders and bent forward so their noses touched. "You know more than you're saying. I can see it in your eyes."

Victoria ripped free of Logan's grip and marched away. He followed with dogged determination, unwilling to let the topic go. "How is my god supposed to talk to me, Vic? Premonition? Phone call? Do gods have a rate plan?"

"Don't be an idiot."

"Then stop being evasive."

"Fine. I'll tell you what I think, but there's no guarantee I'm right."

"All right, share your insight with me," Logan said with obvious amusement.

Victoria came to a dead stop. She stared at the tracks on the ground, and her frown turned to a scowl. She exhaled a long stream of hot breath that hung in the air, a long finger, writhing and curling. The ribbon of mist floated toward the trees, joining with a thick curtain of fog coalescing out of the air with unnatural speed.

Gooseflesh rose on Victoria's arms, and a leaden weight formed in her stomach. Logan, her own restless dead, fidgeted beside her.

"Vic? What's wrong?"

"The tracks have changed. Your body has shifted to a wolf," Victoria said.

"The growth is heavy here, and the ground is getting rough. Four legs are probably the easiest going," Logan said.

"True enough. I think I see a house up ahead." Victoria stared at Logan, waiting for him to reach the obvious conclusion. However, he remained clueless.

"You're trying to change the topic."

"Logan, do you understand what this means?" Victoria scanned the surrounding forest, searching for any trace of movement, but the bank of fog continued to close from all sides. It cut off the afternoon sunlight, leaving them shrouded in shadows.

"Yeah, it means my zombie body has four legs instead of two."

Victoria grabbed Logan's hand. "It means the witch has complete control over your abilities, all of your abilities."

"I don't see how that changes what we already

knew," Logan said. "Stop evading and tell me what you think about the Godspeak."

"Goddess, you're the most thick-headed ass." She turned to him. "Fine, I don't think it's a coincidence that you bear the mark of the World Serpent."

Logan's expression grew disbelieving, and he scoffed. "What? You're talking about my tattoo?"

"The World Serpent is the second child of Loki."

"Yeah, well Fenrir is the first child of Loki," Logan retorted. "Father of our kind—if you believe a bunch of old stories."

"Logan, how can you even question?" Victoria asked, aghast at his skepticism. His words were blasphemy. "You've been to Valhalla and walked its halls. You've seen Odin and Frigg—"

"That doesn't prove any of the old legends, and even if it did, what does it matter? What would being touched by Loki mean?"

Victoria stared at him and shook her head. "Twice blessed, twice cursed."

"Shit! Vic, look out!"

Caught from behind, Victoria went down beneath the weight of her attacker. The male wolf ripped open long parallel gouges upon her shoulder with his fangs.

Find Logan's body: check.

CHAPTER TWENTY

Gone—
  "Goddess, he's gone."
  "Have faith, Victoria. In him."

Victoria hit the ground rolling with the great black wolf right at her back. Her injured shoulder took the brunt of the impact and sent lancing pain throughout her upper body. She left blood splatters upon the white snow. Before she came to a halt, her hands transformed to claws and her teeth to fangs.

When she rolled against the base of a pine tree, great jaws snapped shut and teeth grazed her cheek. A huff of scalding hot breath exploded in her face; spittle sprayed over her. She smelled Logan in his scent, felt Logan in his touch. The familiarity made the violence all that much worse, as if a member of her own pack had turned on her.

Victoria came to her knees and lunged to her feet, dodging past the rabid wolf. "Logan!"

"Over here!" Logan's answering shout emerged from the fog.

She glanced about, but the fog bank surrounded her on all sides and limited visibility to a few inches. The cloud moved with deliberation, prowling the woods with restless determination. Magic stank bitter upon the mist.

"I could use your help!" she said.

"I've got my hands full!" In the distance, Logan growled at some unseen menace in the fog. A terrible wail rose up and filled Victoria with dread. She placed the sound: the fiendish wraith she'd confronted at Sanders's grave.

Blazing eyes appeared in the fog; a murderous roar thundered through the air. The black wolf charged her again, employing all of the remarkable speed Victoria associated with Logan but none of his grace. The beast lumbered where Logan lolloped.

Retreating into a thick stand of trees, Victoria took advantage of her diminutive size to slip through the growth. The tips of clingy branches caught on her hair. Branches snapped and scratched her face, leaving long, thin scrapes. Others bent and allowed her to pass.

Behind her, the wolf collided with the living barrier and attempted to plow it down with brutish force instead of working through the maze of branches and undergrowth. Broken timbers cracked, the thunder of felled trees marked his impact, and for a moment, it seemed the forest might give before him.

More wood split and snapped, and the mighty groan of an uprooted tree marked the forest's resistance. As a falling pine struck the ground, Victoria squirmed free of the undergrowth, and the wolf bellowed his frustration. He thrashed like a giant through the trees, fighting to break free, but his immense size worked to his disadvantage.

Victoria ran blindly into the fog, allowing Logan's growl to act as her guide. While she sprinted across unbroken snow, her awareness divided and time slowed. She listened to the distinct halves of the world: a spiritual combat unfolding within the Shadowlands and the rampage of Logan's beast within the physical. The fragmentation threatened to destroy her sanity, and she knew she could not maintain the duality for long.

Without warning, the brush ended. Victoria burst from between two large redwood trees and came upon Logan and three spirits. She recognized Gregory Sanders. The other two specters were not familiar, although, they bore a striking similarity to the bloated wraith that had attacked her in the cemetery.

Logan stood with his back to a boulder and held his ground against the surrounding foes. A partial transformation provided him the benefit of claw and fang, but his left arm was limp at his side. His flagging strength showed, and the wraiths foamed with bloodlust, having scented a weakened opponent.

A wraith circled to Logan's left, seeking to take advantage of his vulnerable state.

Victoria let out a roar and leapt across the clearing to his aid. With bared teeth and ready claws, she fell upon the closest spirit and ripped into it from behind. She fought with ferocious energy, as if one of her pack were under attack.

Her claws opened long slashes in the wraith, causing it to bellow in agony. It twisted about and took a swipe at her, opening parallel gouges across her bicep. A killing fury overtook Victoria, and she attacked the spirit, rending it with tooth and nail until the last wispy bit of its essence bled away beneath her hands.

More wolf than man, Logan held another of the spirits in a death grip between his jaws. He raked the captive wraith with both claws. The spirit shrieked and writhed as it lost form and substance. Black ooze flowed from Logan's jaws and hands, dripping to the ground to form a pool of goo.

"Logan!" Her shout alerted him to the approach of the third wraith. Logan turned to confront it, head low, claws ready.

The spirit of Sanders rushed Logan. The wraith's body distorted at the edges, causing it to undulate in a fashion sickening to see. Sanders's mouth opened wide — too wide — to reveal a black void. Gravity shifted, sucking everything and everyone toward that maw with irresistible force.

The portal led straight into an unfathomable nightmare.

Victoria sprang at Sanders from behind, determined to destroy the dangerous spirit. Instead, a great black form collided with her mid-leap and knocked her out of the air. The wolf's teeth tore into her injured shoulder and deepened the bleeding gouges. Victoria fought like the devil, screaming Logan's name at the top of her lungs.

Her teeth sank into the wolf's shoulder, ripping open a wound in his flesh. Blood filled her mouth, flooded her nostrils, and pushed into the back of her throat. She choked, unwilling to swallow Logan's blood. The weight of the wolf pinned her to the ground. She clawed at his head, but her desperate struggles failed to loosen his hold.

Abruptly, the wolf released his hold on her shoulder, and permitted her a brief respite. He caught Victoria's throat between his powerful jaws, and his unbreakable hold prevented her from tumbling toward Sanders's mouth. The pit — the bottomless maw headed straight to hell.

In an attempt to loosen his grip, Victoria pried at those jaws with both her hands. She fought for her next breath; each inhalation was hard won and shorter than the last. She sliced open her fingers on the beast's razor-sharp teeth. Blood flowed down her forearms and splattered her face.

Twisting within the beast's jaws, Victoria caught a glimpse of Logan. His heels dug into the ground in a futile attempt to resist as he slid toward the spirit's gaping mouth. She saw Logan's foot slip, his leg falling out from under him, and witnessed his desperation as his claws dug into the icy ground. Clods of dirt and rocks flew and then he lost his grip. Logan flew headlong into that void, and Sanders closed his mouth.

Logan, gone without a trace.

Victoria never stopped fighting, but her strength waned as she suffocated. Her struggles lessened until she grew too weak to move. She dangled from the wolf's jaws, body limp but spirit unbroken, and waited for the beast to crush her throat and end her life. The wolf snarled long and low, and maintained a stranglehold that prevented Victoria from drawing a breath. Her lungs burned in her chest. She felt her consciousness fading, and a great blackness closed about her.

A woman's icy voice penetrated the darkness. "Wait, my wolf. Don't kill her yet. I may have a use for her."

The black wolf loosened its grasp upon Victoria's throat, and she gasped with her mouth wide open. Air inflated her starved lungs, and she thought of nothing other than gulping great draughts of fresh air. Her head cleared, and the pain of her injuries resolved, letting her thoughts come into sharper focus.

"Bring her." The woman — *the witch* — commanded the wolf. Power touched her voice, and Logan's beast obeyed his mistress with alacrity. He maintained a stranglehold on Victoria's throat, allowing her enough air to live, but his jaws never loosened enough to permit her to escape.

She dangled from the creature's jaws, and he dragged her through the frozen snow, over jagged terrain and rough rocks until her legs were bloody with scrapes and bruises. They traveled for about half a mile until they reached a rustic cabin within a pine tree copse. The witch followed in her beast's wake and remained out of Victoria's line of sight. Snow, sky, and trees filled her line of vision.

The hated wraith wearing Gregory Sanders's face

accompanied them.

The door of the cabin swung open, and the black wolf pinned Victoria against the hardwood floor with a huge paw. The witch's footsteps receded and returned with the sinister clank of dragged chains. Facing the threat of restraint, Victoria resumed her struggle. She twisted and snapped her teeth, attempting to bite his shoulder or leg.

The larger wolf growled and tightened his grip on Victoria's throat, once again cutting off her air supply. Following a brief skirmish, the witch managed to snap the silver shackles around Victoria's wrists and ankles. Her tattered clothing provided some protection from the silver, but not enough. Bright, bold pain caused her to scream.

The stench of burning flesh filled the cabin, and Victoria wailed in agony. She fought that much harder, but to no avail. Female hands pushed heavy chains toward her and wrapped them around her torso. The silver left her feeble, and finally, the black wolf opened his mouth and dropped her to the floor.

The wolf stepped away, and Victoria got her first good look at the witch. She snarled and glared daggers at the woman.

"You."

"Oh, yes. Me." Delores, the librarian, smirked in triumph. "I was right under your nose the entire time, and yet you had no clue. Our dear Arik has handled my legal affairs for years. He's a simple fool, so easy to deceive."

"Where is Logan?" Victoria refused to give the witch the reaction she wanted. The Sanders wraith sidled around behind the witch in order to smirk at Victoria. His malformed mouth dropped open, mocking her. Past charred lips and yellowed teeth, his bloated tongue writhed like a fat caterpillar.

"Of course, Arik would recognize me *now*." Delores's appearance flickered, a series of still shots belonging to a malfunctioning movie projector. The severe middle-aged librarian vanished; a frozen queen took her place.

The woman from the ice.

The *seiðr* wore a blue-hooded cloak of lambskin trimmed in white fur. Inlaid gems weighted the skirt; strands of matching jewels encircled her throat. Talismans of bone and bags made of human skin decorated her thick leather belt. She held a crooked staff in her hand.

"What have you done to Logan?" Victoria tested her restraints. Flesh hissed and sizzled when her struggles exposed unburned skin to the silver, but the chains held.

"Do you recognize me, wolf? I am Hrafnar." The witch's blue eyes burned from her pale face. She tilted her head to the side so her silver-blonde hair curled upon her shoulders. The blunt end of her staff struck the ground, adding emphasis to her declaration.

"You're the librarian. Where... Is... Logan...?"

The witch laughed, a cruel sound, and settled her hand atop the black wolf's head. Her pet sat, his big tongue lolled from his mouth and his tail curled behind him. "Logan is right here, my beast, my faithful servant."

Victoria gritted her teeth and used the pain to fuel her rage. "I mean his soul. What have you done to his soul?"

"Oh, *that*." Hrafnar shrugged as if Logan's soul were of no consequence.

A snarl peeled Victoria's lips from her teeth, and a deep growl rolled from her throat. Vicious, abiding hatred found a place in her heart. "Where is he?"

The witch smirked. "He's gone to a place of pure chaos; a place that spawns creatures so foul and awful they defy imagination. It is a place of darkness and demons. I assure you, his soul will be gobbled whole, a tasty tidbit for the hungry things."

"You're wrong. He'll survive, and he'll find a way back," Victoria said.

"If he does, you should be afraid. No good returns from the Abyss. He will no longer be recognizable; he will be a monster."

Victoria showed the witch her teeth. "We're already monsters."

"Stupid, foolish bitch," Hrafnar said and chuckled. "It's been amusing playing with you and your pack. I admit, your arrival caught me unprepared. I improvised to work you into my plan, and quite brilliantly, if I do say so. You proved the perfect tool to drive a decisive wedge between Logan and his father."

"It was you this entire time," Victoria said. It was not a question but confirmation.

"Oh, yes." Hrafnar nodded, eager to take credit for her handiwork. "It was always me. For almost two decades, I've watched and waited for my opportunity to take revenge upon Arik Koenig. *My heart!* That beast stole my heart! He ripped it from my breast and swallowed it whole."

The witch parted her mantle, revealing a great gaping hole in her chest. At the center, torn veins and arteries dangled, limp and useless, where her heart should have connected to the bloody mass.

Victoria's upper lip curled in disgust.

"Are you the world's worst procrastinator or just an idiot? That happened ages ago," Victoria said.

Hrafnar's eyes burned with blue flame. She closed her mantle. "All this time, I've existed as a mere shadow, relegated to places and times where the sun cannot shine. In the hottest part of summer, I must retreat to the deepest crevices in the earth, skulking and hiding like a worm. I only approach the pinnacle of my true power when the winter winds blow, bringing the ice and snow."

Victoria said, "I'm going to crush you beneath my

heel, witch."

Hrafnar glowed with an unholy fury. "To recover my heart intact, I must break the Alpha, his heart, his will, his spirit. I orchestrated the murder of Arik's wife at the hand of his son. That stupid, stubborn beast refused to kill Logan. I destroyed everything in the world Koenig loved, and yet he refused to break. I waited and watched for my opportunity to create a division between father and son."

Victoria stared, unable to speak, filled with a terrible sense of guilt. The witch had employed her as a weapon intended to destroy Arik. She knew what came next, and in the face of her own recrimination, lacked any rebuttal. The witch had used her to drive a wedge between Logan and Arik.

"You know, I can see it on your face," Hrafnar said. "Yes, it was you who provided me the means to split father and son. You created conflict; you let me in. You gave me so much more than I dared dream. Because of you, Arik murdered Logan and he broke. I felt it."

"He didn't!" Victoria said.

"He did! He should have been mine then, but you couldn't leave well enough alone. You had to keep interfering..." Bitter accusation twisted Hrafnar's beautiful features into a mask of ugliness.

Victoria smirked and bared her teeth. "The classic form is: *And I would have gotten away with it too, if it weren't for you meddling kids!*"

The witch's face went blank with momentary confusion. Victoria snickered harder, ignoring the threatening rumble from the black wolf.

"Oh, you are such a formidable badass," Victoria said. "You forced a teenaged boy to murder his mother and commanded an Omega wolf too weak to resist your magic. But when it comes to confronting a powerful adversary, you hide behind smoke and mirrors. You're a coward."

The witch took a firm hold of her staff with both hands. "That boy, as you call him, is my masterpiece. I chose him when his family still dwelled in Ironwood, and I nurtured him. I took a human child, destined to be nothing, and awakened his beast. He is a wolf because of me."

Victoria stared at the witch in patent disbelief. "That's impossible."

Hrafnar smiled with wicked delight. "Oh, no, quite possible. While your meddling cost me an opportunity to destroy Arik, you have presented me with a valuable gift. I should thank you. Without a soul, this wolf is the perfect servant, pliable to my will. You have once again placed the means to break the Alpha within my grasp."

The witch caressed the head of her soulless pet. "He is an animal that can't help but love his master. Now, let's see if you can be turned into an obedient puppet, Victoria."

The assault came as bitter guilt pressing against the walls surrounding Victoria's heart. So heavy, so dreadful. So many people were dead because of her: her mother, her father, her pack, Logan. The terrible knowledge weighed Victoria down worse than the great silver chains. It sapped her strength, burned her soul. She felt weary and desired nothing more than to lie down and sleep.

Victoria's head drooped forward, and her eyelids grew heavy. She fought to remain awake, but minutes ticked past and the witch did not speak again. Hrafnar, the black wolf, and the Sanders wraith watched and waited while Victoria wallowed in her guilt. Her lethargy became a great pit with slippery sides and a bottomless depth, sucking her down.

In desperation, Victoria turned her gaze toward the black wolf. She saw none of Logan's soul in those amber eyes, but—as always—she found inspiration.

Victoria tilted back her head and howled to raise the

roof. She poured all of her great guilt and despair into the call, channeling the power of those dark emotions. The howl seemed to go on forever, and before it faded, an answering howl originated from deep in the night.

His power touched them all. *The Alpha.*

The witch cried out in rage and drew back her arm in fear. Hrafnar delivered a sharp smack to the side of Victoria's face, forcing her head to the side. The spell fragmented into millions of pieces, bits of broken glass, still sharp and painful, but too small to do more than cut.

"He's coming," Victoria said with the most ruthless smile ever. "You'd better run or he'll gobble up what's left of you, little witch."

Hrafnar wrapped both hands around her staff, for contemplation, for courage, for concentration. "No, quite the contrary. This is the opportunity I've been waiting for. My wolf will destroy Arik, and he will be unwilling to risk harming his son in order to defend himself. At long last, I shall have my heart."

The witch turned to command the Sanders wraith. "Devour her. Don't leave as much as a hair behind."

The spirit started forward with a lascivious leer and stopped within a pace of Victoria. With malicious anticipation, he allowed that cavernous maw of his mouth to fall open. Gravity within the cabin shifted, all things drawn toward that awful nothingness.

A slimy black-furred claw burst through Sanders's chest.

The wraith shrieked and staggered, clutching at the gaping hole. The limb protruded to the wrist from the wraith's perforated form. Another claw appeared and ripped at Sanders's torso from within, widening the opening. Black ooze gushed forth from the wound, larva poured to the floor. The muzzle of a great black wolf appeared, pushing at the distended opening.

With a tormented shriek, Sanders's chest bloated

and his ribcage ballooned outward. The bones stretched beyond capacity, and the wraith burst with a sickening *pop*. Sludge flowed everywhere, spilling from Sanders to the floor, spreading as a slick. With its death, the wraith birthed a monstrosity.

Logan's soul fell from the wraith's body and landed as a slimy heap upon the floor. He slid several feet upon the pool of ooze, and lay on his side, pushing with his legs. Like a deflating balloon, the wraith collapsed in upon himself, losing form and substance. He melted away until nothing remained but a pool of black goo.

Horrified, Hrafnar retreated. No longer under her control, Logan's wolf sprang to his feet, tail wagging when he greeted his soul. The beast welcomed home his true master. Logan pulled himself upright with a determined grunt and then lurched to his feet. He fell forward into his own body.

Hrafnar reversed her direction and reached for the black wolf's head. "Soul or not, you're still my beast, Logan."

The witch rallied her magic, and the temperature inside the cabin underwent a precipitous drop. Ice particles formed in the air, and it became colder and colder until Victoria's breath emerged as streams of hot steam. Hrafnar stroked Logan's head with perceptible possessiveness.

"No, Logan!" Victoria's skin crawled, and her stomach cramped in reaction to the magic.

Logan cocked his head and his tongue rolled out of the side of his mouth. His eyes glinted with amusement. Quick as a flash, the great black wolf chomped off the witch's hand at the wrist. He swallowed it in one gulp.

Hrafnar fell back screaming, clutching the bloody stump.

"Your pet bites," Victoria said, and she smirked.

The witch fled, leaving behind the sound of her horrified shriek.

CHAPTER TWENTY-ONE

In hot pursuit—
  "Thank you, Goddess. She can't fly."
  "You're welcome, but I can hardly take credit for that."

The cabin's front door slammed shut behind the witch. Logan sprang to his feet, his entire body vibrating with the excitement of the hunt. He held his head and tail high. His claws created a clattering on the wooden floor of the cabin while he chased after the witch.

"Logan?" Victoria's voice came out weaker than she liked and contained a definite note of pleading. It hurt her to think Logan would abandon her to silver chains, and the prospect of being helpless scared her even more. Judging by the distance of his howl, it was possible Arik would not arrive for another several minutes.

After the briefest hesitation, Logan returned to Victoria. While he walked, he underwent a lightning-fast transformation from wolf to man. He stood naked before her and bent his head to examine the silver cuffs on her wrists. His fingers touched the toxic metal without a hint of burning or blistering.

"You okay, Vic?"

"I've been better." She bit back a cry of pain when Logan tested the cuffs.

"Where are the keys?"

"The witch has the key. Rip them off."

Logan stroked a comforting finger across the back of her hand and hesitated. "That's gonna take an awful lot of skin off with it."

"Do it," Victoria said between clenched teeth.

His lashes lowered to hood his eyes and his mouth hardened. Logan nodded and Victoria tensed, but nothing could have prepared her for the excruciating pain she felt when he ripped off first her wrist shackles and then her ankle cuffs. The silver chains across her midsection took thick sections of her skin with them, leaving her bloody and raw.

Victoria staggered, and Logan caught her and kept her upright. When he touched her, energy coursed across her skin, and a mystical connection bound them together. Victoria exhaled a soft sigh of resignation and acceptance. Despite her best efforts to remain impartial, her wolf had forged a pack bond with Logan.

"What is that?" Logan stared at his hand on her arm.

"Nothing," Victoria said. Later, she would explain the pack bond, when all was said and done, if they were both alive.

Logan shot her an accusatory glance, well aware of deception, but he did not challenge her. He had an odd look in his eyes, a scary light, a callousness and cunning unlike anything she had ever witnessed on his face before. His trip into the belly of the wraith appeared to have changed him in a fundamental way she could not quantify. Within him, she sensed a restless energy and malevolent anger.

He frightened her senseless. Victoria's nails drove into her palms, and her eyes widened. She caught a glimpse of the darkness before Logan shut her out.

"Logan, what did you..."

Logan lowered his mouth so it was close to her ear. "What did I what, Vic?"

Her unhealed injuries hurt, and weakness from the

silver chains lingered. Victoria shook from the pain. Something of the original Logan remained at his core, the essential goodness. She had to believe that or despair.

"What happened to your soul, Logan? Where did you go?"

Anger shimmered in his eyes. He lowered her to the floor. "You should sit down. Get some rest until you heal."

A powerful howl announced Arik's arrival. The front door of the cabin splintered and burst inward, flying off its hinges. Arik's massive black form skidded to a halt within yards of them. His eyes glowed with ferocious golden light.

Arik undertook an immediate transformation to human. As a man, he stood naked before them. The Alpha held his ground, brown eyes watchful. "Logan, Victoria, are you hurt?"

"Dad." Logan wore an expression of tormented ambivalence. He took a tentative step toward his father and then stopped. He reached for Arik and then froze.

"I'm okay." Victoria shoved Logan hard from behind toward his father, providing the initiative he needed to start the journey. Several feet away, Arik took the motion as a signal to charge toward his son.

The males met in the middle of the cabin in one of those awkward man hugs—right hands locked in a handshake, left arms wrapped around the other, bodies touching only at the shoulders. Arik pounded Logan across the back with his fist, and his son replied in kind.

Victoria rolled her eyes heavenward and sagged in relief. She averted her gaze and tried to give them a semblance of privacy.

"Son, I'm so sorry." Arik smacked Logan's shoulder one final time, and the men broke apart. "Can you forgive me?"

"Nothing to forgive," Logan said, scrubbing at a

streak of conspicuous wetness from his cheek. "Let it go, Dad. We're good."

Logan might as well have slapped her. The unintentional slight caused her to cringe. She shrank from him. How could he forgive Arik with such ease and deny her with such vehemence? She had begged on her knees for his forgiveness. Jealousy ate at her despite the irrational, unreasoning nature of the feeling.

Arik knelt beside Victoria and laid his hands on her shoulders. The mate bond flared to life between them, and she strived to conceal her bitterness from him. The last thing he needed was to become embroiled in her complicated conflict with Logan.

"You're hurt, Victory." Arik inspected her wounds with care and concern. His fingers were cool on her hot flesh, and his tender touch brought her relief. Physical contact with her mate sped her regeneration.

"The witch used silver chains." Victoria jerked her head to indicate the discarded restraints. "I'm fine. See, I'm healing already."

"What are you two doing here?" Arik asked. "I smell the *seiðr*. She was here."

"We tracked my body here," Logan said. "The bitch patrol took it joyriding while my soul was absent."

Arik scowled. "Did she kill anyone?"

"Oh, Goddess, I hope not." Victoria tilted her head toward Logan. "Cujo here bit off her hand, and she fled."

Arik and Logan traded a glance. The Alpha looked insufferably proud of his son. He chuckled. "Nice."

Logan grinned. "Thanks."

Victoria gripped her mate's hand. "Arik, the witch is Delores Sanders. She used her magic to conceal her true identity."

Arik appeared chagrined. "I know. Mike and I went to her house. We found some things there."

"What sort of things?" Victoria asked.

"Witchy things," Arik said. His reserve made it clear

he did not wish to elaborate.

Logan cleared his throat. "Dad, as much as I hate to break up your touching reunion with my new step-mom—"

"Logan..." She snarled in warning.

Logan flashed his teeth in a wolf grin. "I'd sure as hell like to know how the *seiðr* got hold of my body."

Arik grimaced, his expression sheepish. He ran a hand through his hair. "It was my fault, but I swear, I only left you unattended for an hour, Logan."

"Urgent business at the office?" Logan asked. "Did Gayle Patterson need to update her trust again?"

"It was a mistake, but I never imagined this could happen." Arik's inclusive gesture encompassed everything around them.

"We need to stop yammering and go after the witch," Victoria said, changing the subject with her standard lack of diplomacy. Her wounds had almost healed.

Through her mate bond with Arik, she sensed his agreement. He looked up and met Victoria's gaze in a wordless exchange.

"We should tell him," Arik said.

"Yes, we should."

Logan made a face. "Uh, you two are creeping me out."

Arik turned toward his son. "Logan, your mother's spirit visited your Uncle Mike while you were in the coma. He came to see us to deliver her message."

Logan's face froze. "She did?"

"Yeah." Victoria's voice slid into a soothing tone, her power sought to calm Logan's wildcatting emotions. "She told us how to kill the witch."

Logan inhaled and clapped his hands together. "Okay, great. So how do we ice old Witch Hazel?"

"Water," Arik said.

"Water?" Logan's brow arched.

"Water will end the witch," Arik said.

A heartbeat passed, then another. Logan looked from Arik to Victoria and then back again. His intelligent eyes searched their faces.

Logan threw his hands into the air. "You're fucking kidding me!"

"What?" Victoria asked, but Logan cut her off.

A terrifying screech rose up from Logan. "I'm melting! Melting!"

Victoria gaped at Logan, afraid for his sanity. She traded a quick glance with Arik who also appeared baffled. Victoria opened her mouth to say something but could think of no appropriate reply, so she shook her head.

"Killjoys," Logan said with clear disgust. "I've never met two such clueless people."

All of the sudden, Arik choked and started to laugh, a rusty sound as if the Alpha had forgotten how. His laughter grew from a rough rev to a mellow rumble. Arik clasped his son on the shoulder and shook his head. He wiped tears from his eyes.

"It's good to have you back, son," Arik said.

Victoria hid a smile behind her hand. "Let's get back on topic before the wicked witch gets away."

"Sure thing, Dorothy," Logan said. "Can you stand?"

"Better than you, Toto."

Too fast, Victoria shot to her feet and reeled as a wave of weakness swept over her. Only Arik's steady hands kept her from toppling.

"Okay, maybe I can hobble," she said.

"Victoria, I want you to stay behind," Arik said. "Logan and I can go after the witch."

Gathering her strength, Victoria found her footing and pulled away from Arik's supporting hands. "No way. I'm not sitting this out. This is my fight, too."

Victoria locked gazes with her mate and glared at him in defiance. She refused to remain on the sidelines like an invalid or a liability.

"I'll be outside waiting until you two resolve your pissing contest," Logan announced. He hesitated for a moment. "Or maybe I won't wait at all."

The door slammed shut behind him.

Arik broke eye contact and sighed. "Fine, but I want your word that you'll try to stay out of the fight."

"Done. You have my word." Victoria smiled, agreeable once she had her way. She accompanied Arik outside to where Logan stood at the edge of the forest. By mutual consent, both males underwent a complete transformation to wolves. Only Victoria remained human.

Outside, the sun had set. Great clouds darkened the sky, hiding both moon and stars, and the wind lashed the earth. A trail in the snow led into the woods. There was a lot of fresh blood. Victoria inspected the footprints and studied the storm front moving in overhead. The scent of cold, fresh moisture filled her flared nostrils.

"It's starting to snow." To prove her prediction, the first snowflake drifted past her nose.

Victoria turned to Logan and Arik, tapping into the stream of emotions and impressions that flowed between pack members. A bright, vibrant pack bond bound them together. As wolves, the males could not manage speech, but the magic enabled a deeper and nuanced communication.

The distant roar of an engine announced the approach of an SUV before the headlights rounded a curve on the road. The wolves turned toward the sound and watched a gray Jeep pull into the cabin's turnoff. Victoria recognized the vehicle.

The engine turned off, and the headlights dimmed. Mike Trash jumped from the vehicle and approached them at a jog. His breath formed great puffs in the frozen air. He wore a heavy jacket and gloves with a red hunting hat with flaps that covered his ears, and carried a rifle, stock toward the ground, barrel aimed in the air.

The sheriff skidded to a halt. "I want to hunt with you."

Victoria turned an inquiring look toward Arik and arched her brow. She understood the man's desire for revenge, but this was not her decision to make. Arik bobbed his head once, and Victoria sensed the Alpha's acceptance through their bond. She gave a single curt nod and turned back to wait for the human. The black wolves, father and son, melted into the night and ran on ahead, pursuing their prey.

"Good evening, sheriff," Victoria said. "We're hunting the witch who murdered your sister. If you'd like to join me, we'll be following the trail while Arik and Logan flank her."

Mike regarded Victoria with narrowed eyes. His jaw worked, and he indicated his assent with a jerk of his head. "I take it you're a member of the family now?"

"I guess so," Victoria said, surprised at how wonderful that sounded when he said it. She turned back to the witch's blood trail and took the lead.

Tilting back her head, Victoria let loose a long, full-bodied howl. In the distance, Arik answered and Logan followed suit.

The final witch hunt had begun.

The snowfall thickened from a flurry to a blizzard, decreasing visibility to the point it was difficult for her to even see her hand in front of her face. It was a frozen gale, and the wolves struggled to produce howls loud enough to penetrate the storm's constant moaning. Victoria kept her nose close to the ground and followed the blood trail. Mike trudged along in her wake, relying on her for direction.

Victoria moved closer to the sheriff and touched his elbow to gain his attention. He turned a reddened face toward her, suffering from the cold despite his winter clothing. As uncomfortable as the man's presence made her, Victoria felt for him. She understood his desire to avenge his sister. However, his frailty worried her, because the responsibility for keeping him alive fell on her.

"Where are we going?" Mike asked.

"This way!" Victoria gave Mike's arm a tug to indicate direction. The witch had fled toward the lake on foot. The sheriff adjusted his course, trudging into the thick wind in an attempt to gain headway.

Logan's howl penetrated the wind, coming from ahead in the woods to her right. Victoria waited until the final note faded before she released a thin cry in reply. Afterward, she listened and waited, but Arik remained silent.

Mike and Victoria plowed on through snow and wind, stopping every few yards to allow her to gauge their bearings. Several times the human beside her stumbled, and Victoria kept him from falling. With the passage of time, it became impossible to judge the distance traveled. Even with her heightened perception, she lost track of their surroundings.

The sheriff ground to a stop and expressed his frustration, shouting and gesticulating. "Shouldn't we be to the water by now?"

"Yes." Victoria stopped dead in her tracks. An intense sense of foreboding swept over her, causing her entire body to quicken with an adrenaline rush. She looked down, staring at the icy ground, and she knew.

"Shit. The lake is frozen." Victoria grabbed for Mike's arm at the same time a great black blur rushed at them from the blizzard. The sheriff brought his rifle up and fired a single blast at the phantasm as it strafed them. The cloud of darkness passed, and a whirling flight of ravens became distinguishable from the mass. *Craas* echoed while the birds pecked at their faces. Victoria threw up her hands to protect her eyes from the razor-sharp beaks, but one of the ravens left a long diagonal slash across her cheek.

Mike shouted at the top of his lungs and fired another shot into the air, missing the flock. Victoria ducked out of instinct. Mike's lack of control scared her. Normal ammunition hurt, not as much as silver, but enough to make her jumpy at the prospect.

Beneath their feet, a thunderous crack split the frozen surface of the lake, both felt and heard. It widened and elongated with alarming speed, too fast to allow a calculated reaction. Victoria grabbed for Mike's arm but missed. The ice separated farther, and they plunged into cold water.

Victoria caught a breath before her head submerged. As soon as she hit the water, she struck out with her arms and legs, a powerful stroke to propel her upward. Chunks of ice hit her face and arms, forcing her to fight her way around them in order to break through. Finally, she surfaced and gasped for air.

At the edge of the broken ice, Hrafnar stood in righteous fury, her wind-torn blue cloak whipping about her. Her arm ended in a bloody stump and dangled at her side. Her remaining hand clutched her staff. The witch shouted words lost to the blizzard and lowered the end of her staff into the lake's water, causing it to freeze. The effect spread, and the breathing hole began to close.

Victoria kicked hard to keep her head above water and glanced about, searching for any sign of the sheriff. She did not find him. For a second, she considered getting out, but her responsibility to the human kept her in the water and turned her from self-preservation. She sucked down a deep draught of air, and then she dived when the surface froze, sealing her breathing hole and trapping her beneath the ice.

Eyes open, Victoria pushed off the ice and used the force to propel her deeper into the lake. She relegated fear to a distant corner of her mind and closed the door, focusing on locating Mike. She treaded water with her hands and kicked with her legs, going deeper. She released some air and sank. The water turned dark blue and then black, and her range of vision decreased.

The pressure built, causing Victoria's ear canal to ache. She worked her jaw back and forth in an attempt to clear her eardrums. It failed. She grabbed hold of her nose to seal her nostrils and forced air into her sinuses. Finally, the pressure behind her eardrums popped, alleviating the pain.

Her lungs burned. She released some air and continued to dive, all too aware of the ticking clock. If she failed to locate the sheriff and return to the surface before her air supply ran out, they would both die. Drowning, decapitation, fire, and silver were among the few things that could kill a werewolf.

In the darkness, her foot brushed something solid, and it startled her so she released precious air. Victoria performed a quick flip and used her fingers to probe. She found Mike's unmoving body floating in the dark water. She seized hold of his arms and kicked with all of her strength, heading toward the surface. She kept her figurative fingers crossed, hoping her sense of direction held true.

Victoria swam in absolute uncertainty, trusting her instincts. Lungs on fire, she finally ran into the ice sheet blanketing the surface of the lake. Several thick inches served as the final barrier between her and air. She kicked with her legs and kept her left arm wrapped about Mike's torso. She used her other hand to pound at the ice, attempting to create a crack. When the ice failed to split, she used a clawed hand to scratch at the barrier. She struck the ice sheet over and over, each blow growing weaker and more desperate.

Right before her strength failed, the ice cracked and shattered due to a violent blow from above. Broken chunks of ice crowded the fresh air hole, and Victoria struggled to thrust her face past the obstructions. She tried and failed, gulping down water instead of air, which filled her throat and lungs. She choked and floundered, and then a hand caught hold of her arm. The welcome sight of Logan filled her vision.

Victoria used her remaining strength to cling to Mike while Logan hauled them both out of the water. He dragged them several yards through the blistering wind and driven snow and deposited them on the lakeshore. The moment Logan released her, Victoria staggered two steps and retched up the entire contents of her stomach. Great wracking coughs forced soupy lake water from her lungs.

Victoria turned to find Logan crouched over Mike. The sheriff lay on his stomach while Logan attempted to force water from the man's lungs. Victoria hurried to them.

"He's not breathing, and I can't find a pulse," Logan said.

"He's lucky to have drowned in freezing water. There's less chance of brain damage," Victoria said, pushing Logan aside. "Let me do this."

"That's only lucky if we can get him breathing again. Do you know what you're doing?" Logan asked. He shot her a dubious look while she flipped Mike onto his side.

Victoria took over administering first aid to Mike, first clearing his lungs of water. She started chest compressions and rescue breathing. "I'm a nurse. Where's Arik?"

"I didn't know that. Dad's keeping the witch busy. He told me to help you."

"Lots of things you don't know about me," Victoria said. "Find a way to call for an ambulance, then go help your dad."

"There's a radio in Uncle Mike's Jeep."

Victoria told Logan where they had met Mike. She watched from the corner of her eye when Logan took off running. She continued CPR. His departure allowed Victoria to concentrate her energy on helping Mike. She sent a pulse of healing magic through his chest, and his heart rewarded her with a thud.

A short time later, Logan passed her in a flash, heading toward the lake. "Help's on the way," he shouted.

"Good," she said, controlling the impulse to chase after him. She had an obligation to help the sheriff before she returned to the fight.

Victoria continued to administer first aid until the sheriff's heartbeat and breathing were regular. At last, Mike opened his eyes, conscious but groggy. His lips were blue, and he shook from the cold. Hypothermia posed the greatest risk to the man's life, but Victoria lacked the resources necessary to keep him warm and dry.

"There's nothing else I can do to help you," she told Mike. "An ambulance has been called. I'm going to help Arik and Logan."

"I understand," Mike said, teeth chattering. He managed to nod.

Springing to her feet, Victoria followed Logan's path onto the frozen lake. When she found them, the fight between the wolves and witch created a great commotion, roars and screams that penetrated the storm. Due to the terrible visibility, she burst onto the scene moving at a sprint and overshot, passing Logan.

Victoria skidded to a halt and spun around in a dizzying turn. It took her a second to process everything. As wolves, Logan and Arik fought side-by-side. A block of ice imprisoned the lower half of Arik's body, encasing his rear legs. He struggled to be free even while a widening crack in the ice threatened to swallow him whole. In an effort to break loose, Arik undertook the transformation to human.

Great bloody slashes crisscrossed Hrafnar's torso and face, and she knelt with her staff raised before her,

her hand wrapped around the base. Logan gripped the other end in his mouth. The witch shouted words, lost to the wind.

Horrified, Victoria watched while ice engulfed Logan's jaws and then spread to encase his head. It became impossible for him to breathe. Logan made a frantic grab for his head, tearing at the ice with his claws while he suffocated. The staff also became stuck in the ice.

Hrafnar tugged at her staff, but Logan's wild thrashing wrenched it from her grasp. As soon as the witch lost her grip, the blizzard died away with a whimpering howl from the wind. The blinding snowfall ceased. The frozen sheet of ice covering the lake cracked and broke apart.

Panicking, Logan ran in the direction of the shore, moving in leaps and bounds. His charge carried him away from the dissolving ice sheet but also from Hrafnar and Arik. Victoria was not able to reach him to help, so she started toward her mate.

Arik's shout stopped her in her tracks. "Victoria, help Logan!"

Midway between man and wolf, Arik let out a ferocious howl. With a heroic effort, the Alpha dug his claws into the ice and used his arms to drag his entire body toward Hrafnar. The ice sheet continued to split, noisy and capricious, exposing the black water beneath. The growing fault followed Arik, moving toward him with frightening speed.

Arik reached Hrafnar and latched onto her, sinking both claws into her flesh. The witch's shriek pierced the night. The Alpha's triumphant howl carried for miles. The ice sheet under their feet shattered, and they plunged into the water. Victoria caught one final glimpse of wolf and witch, locked together, as they vanished beneath the lake's surface.

For a split second, the impulse to go after Arik seized her, but Victoria recalled all too well his determination and his love for his son. Besides, he had given her a command, one she felt compelled to obey out of respect for the man. Casting instinct aside, Victoria went after Logan like her mate had asked. She caught up with him on the lakeshore, still struggling to free his head from the block of ice.

Victoria tackled him and took them both to the ground. Logan kicked at her with his hind legs, unable to distinguish between friend and foe in his panic. She wrestled with him for the upper hand in the fight. His strength far exceeded hers, but suffocation weakened him.

Victoria grabbed hold of the witch's staff; the ends protruded from either side of the ice encasing Logan's head. The staff provided the control she needed to pin him beneath her. She straddled his back and pressed against him so he could sense her through the pack magic. "Logan! It's me! Stop!"

Logan bucked a final time and subsided, resisting her no longer. Victoria used her claws to tear into the ice block. She ripped off great chunks until the entire thing split under her assault. The pieces fell away, and Logan labored to breathe. The staff dropped from his mouth.

Victoria rose to her feet, preparing to launch back into the fight. Beside her, Logan also lurched to all fours even though he staggered to the side. With a groan, he rose to his hind legs and shifted to a man.

"Where is he?" Logan asked, gasping for air.

She turned toward the lake where the blizzard decayed upon the water. She saw no sign of Arik, no trace. "I don't know."

Together, they reached the edge of the lake in time to see the last of the ice disappear. Victoria searched the surface in desperation, but the impenetrable depths kept their secrets. The vast expanse of water stretched before them.

Logan seized her arms again and spun her around.

"Where is he?"

Victoria shook her head. "I don't know."

"You must have seen them go under! Damn it, Victoria! My head was encased in ice!"

Tears streamed down her cheeks. "I'm sorry. I don't know!"

Suddenly, the other half of her soul died. Victoria screamed and staggered, experiencing the severance of the mate bond she shared with Arik. The terrible loss left her bereft.

Only Logan's arms kept her from running into the lake. Caught in his grip, she wailed, a mournful howl that soared to the starry sky, and she sank to her knees on the snowy shore.

"What is it? What's happened?"

"He's dead," she said, unable to see past her tears.

"No. No fucking way." With a howl of denial, Logan plunged into the icy water.

CHAPTER TWENTY-TWO

Revelations —

    "Goddess, he's gone."

    "I am so sorry, My Priestess. Take comfort in knowing, he is with me now. They both are."

    "Thank you, My Lady."

    "Victoria, will you ever tell Logan what the witch said?"

    "That she made him? No, he deserves better."

"Logan, wait."

Exhausted, Victoria swayed on her feet, but she marshaled her remaining strength and staggered after Logan. She made it within ten feet of the shore when an apparition blocked her path. Startled, she stopped and blinked, double-checking her vision.

Her heart skipped a beat, then resumed, and in her gut, she knew.

The visage of Arik resolved from an insubstantial whorl; his body manifested and gained cohesion. He met her tired gaze with those familiar honey-brown eyes, amused and cynical all at once.

"Stop Logan before he drowns himself, Victoria," he said.

Victoria released a resigned sigh and gave Arik a curt nod. She waded after Logan, sprinting in order to catch up with him before he made it to deep water. When Victoria seized his elbow, Logan stood waist deep in the lake, but the water came to her chest.

"Logan, wait up a sec. Please."

Logan turned to her, his agony and agitation plain upon his face, and she flinched to see the depth of his pain.

"What?" he asked.

"Look," she said, pointing toward where Arik's spirit waited on the shore. She grabbed his head and forced him to look. He froze and stared and then flinched.

Calling upon the last of her reserves, Victoria hauled the unresisting Logan from the water. For several paces, she dragged him as dead weight, but finally his feet cooperated, and he followed her out of the lake and onto the shore. They came to rest fifty feet from where Mike Trash shivered on the ground in a sodden huddle.

Logan grabbed hold of his father's arms. "Dad, tell us where your body is, and we'll pull you out."

Arik smiled and shook his head. "No, Logan, this is final."

"Fuck final! Dad, Victoria can bring you back! Uncle Mike was dead and she resurrected him! I was dead! She brought me back!"

From his vantage, the sheriff's head jerked toward them. Mike stared at the wolves with round eyes, startled and confused. Could the human perceive Arik's spirit? He'd seen and spoken with Lori. On the other hand, she and Logan might just seem to have gone mad to the man. She sighed and ignored him. Explanations would have to come later.

"Logan, the sheriff wasn't beyond conventional first aid," Victoria said. "And I only brought you back with the help of my goddess." She turned toward the lake anyway, considering the daunting task.

"Does that mean you won't try?" Logan asked.

"Of course not," she said. "Arik, Logan's right. We'll

need to recover your body."

Arik shook his head and placed his hands on his son's shoulders. "Logan, listen to me. The witch is dead, forever this time. She was a vile creature that inflicted nothing but suffering on our kind for generations. My death was necessary to assure she never returns."

"Fine, she's dead. What the hell stops us from restoring your life?" Logan choked on his grief, and a cough wracked his chest.

"Freya has called me to her service and I must answer, Logan. She is waiting to take me to her hall. I'm only here because I needed to tell you... I love you, and I'm so damn proud of you. A father couldn't ask for a finer son." Arik hugged Logan hard.

"Dad..." Logan strangled on emotion.

"Live a good life, Logan," Arik said. "Protect our line. It all falls to you now."

"No." Logan shook his head, cheeks wet with tears.

Victoria swallowed a painful lump and panted to keep pace with her racing heart. She noted a golden glow emanating from the Alpha, effusive and effulgent as the sun in the sky. She stared hard at that radiance, and then sighed in relief upon recognizing the source.

"Freya," Victoria said.

"Your goddess has called me to serve her. She has done me a great honor, Victory." Arik smiled and stepped away from Logan to embrace Victoria. She welcomed him, open arms and open heart, but when they touched, she no longer sensed his soul connection to her.

Our mate bond, gone.

Arik drew away. "I'm sorry, Victoria. I wish we'd had more time."

She blinked, and tears spilled down her cheeks. "It's not fair. We only had a day together.."

Arik's expression grew grim. "It is the way of things."

She longed to argue with him but saw no point in

ruining their final moments.

"What is done is done," she said, striving to keep the bitterness from her voice.

"It was an honor to be your mate," Arik said with finality.

"As it was my honor to be yours," Victoria said with a brave smile. She took her tears and banished them, shoved her grief down deep. She walled it off so the pain would not cripple her.

Arik laughed and embraced her tenderly in farewell. "You turned my neatly ordered life upside down." He released her and backed away with concern in his beautiful eyes. "Are you going to be okay, Victoria?"

Victoria flashed Arik a bold grin, showing teeth, standing proud. "I'm good. I'll see you again in my lady's hall, Arik."

Arik's spirit began to fade.

Logan stepped forward and touched his father's shoulder. "Wait."

Arik looked to his son.

"I love you too, Dad."

Arik smiled to acknowledge Logan, and then the spirit dissolved in a golden shimmer. He went with Freya upon a chariot pulled by great cats to her hall where half of the Norse warriors slain in combat resided. He would never meet Victoria's mother or father, and it made her sad.

In the distance, Victoria heard the distinctive whir of a helicopter's approach from across the lake. Even further, sirens echoed through the snowy valley. Help was on the way.

Victoria turned and walked away from Logan, heading toward where Mike sat alone on the shore of the lake. Midway, her foot kicked something hard, and she glanced down. The witch's staff laid forgotten upon the snow. Victoria contemplated the thing for a long moment and then she bent to pick it up.

"What do you want with that?" Logan asked from behind her.

"Nothing. I just don't want it falling into the wrong hands. Imagine some innocent person picking it up. What might happen?"

"Maybe nothing," Logan said, drawing alongside her.

"Maybe, but do you really want to risk that?"

When Logan made no reply, Victoria jerked her head toward Mike. "Come on. Let's go see if we can help warm him up."

"Yeah." Logan looked at her with hurt, loss, and anger revealed clearly in his eyes.

So much anger.

He walked on alone.

As the eastern sky turned rosy with the first hint of dawn, Victoria and Logan returned to the Koenig home on the lake in the sheriff's Jeep. Mike Trash stopped in front of the house and peered at Logan with obvious concern. The sheriff had suffered from his ordeal, but thanks to Victoria's healing magic, the EMTs had cleared him without taking him to the hospital.

Logan opened the passenger door, and Mike leaned over to place a staying hand on his nephew's shoulder. "Logan?"

Logan stopped in the act of sliding out of the passenger seat to look back at his uncle. "Yeah, Uncle Mike?"

The sheriff passed Logan a heavy-duty plastic bag. "These are your father's personal effects. He left them with me before he shifted."

Logan accepted the bag, regarded it with a blank stare, and then tucked it under his arm. "Thanks."

"The authorities are already dredging the lake,"

Mike said. "But I want you to know, even if Arik's body isn't recovered, I'll see to it the official death report lists your father's death as a drowning accident so there won't be any problems with the insurance company. I'll call you tomorrow about funeral arrangements. You'll want to bury him with your mom."

Unintentional or not, the snub made Victoria wince. The sheriff never so much as glanced her way or asked her opinion about her mate's death. Before she had to hear anymore, Victoria slid from the backseat of the vehicle and closed the door behind her. She carried the witch's staff with her for lack of a means of disposing of it.

Victoria moved to the relative privacy of a pine tree and took refuge beneath the vast branches. Head bowed, she stared into the silent night, debating whether to slip into her wolf form and leave. The Koenig home did not feel like a place where she belonged, not without Arik there to welcome her inside. At the same time, she refused to leave Logan alone without as much as a word of goodbye.

The crunch of boots on snow announced Logan's approach, and Victoria waited for him. He wore borrowed clothing that fit poorly but served their purpose.

"Vic?"

"Yeah?"

"Are you going to take off?"

Victoria glanced around the snowy night and considered where she would go. On foot, it would take her days to reach her pack in the middle of Desolation Wilderness. Her injuries had not fully healed, and she needed both sleep and food, not to mention a change of clothes.

"Do you want me to go?" she asked.

Logan moved closer and took her elbow. He tugged her toward the house. "I'm too tired to play games tonight. Stop being contrary and come inside. If there's something to have out, we can do it tomorrow."

Victoria curtly nodded and followed him up the front walk. Logan arrived at the front door and grabbed the knob and then uttered a vehement curse when it refused to turn. "No way, no fucking way! You've got to be kidding me!"

He spun on his heel, hands swinging toward his face, as if searching for something to strike. His restrained violence caused her to tense. For a second Victoria expected Logan to rip the locked door off the hinges. She stared at him with wide eyes, and he stared back, seething with murderous fury. She wanted to laugh but feared for his sanity. She retained a tenuous control over her own brittle emotions.

Reaching out, Victoria caught his hand. "Come on."

"Come where?" He resisted, but she tugged hard enough to propel him to motion. Through the pack magic, she experienced his rage and grief but also knew that physical contact with another wolf would soothe him.

"This way," she said and led him without offering an explanation. They circled the house until they reached Logan's shattered window.

"Good thinking," he said. He boosted Victoria through the window before she could protest and then followed her into the bedroom.

Victoria stood beside the window and watched while Logan performed a quick, disinterested inspection of the room. He bent to open a dresser drawer and removed a pair of sweat pants. "I'm gonna grab a shower."

Logan tossed the words over his shoulder and left Victoria standing alone in the room. She crossed and uncrossed her arms, fidgeting while she tried to decide on a course of action. Finally, she left Logan's room and tracked down the hallway to the kitchen. She hid the witch's staff in the broom closet, closed the door, and forgot about it.

In the refrigerator, Victoria found deli meat, cheese,

and all the fixings; in the pantry, she located a package of sourdough rolls. Welcoming an opportunity for busywork, she spread everything out on the kitchen's center island and set to work assembling a platter of sandwiches.

After a time, Logan joined her. He wore black sweatpants and a dark green shirt. His wet hair stuck out all over the place from having been towel dried. They stood, not sat, and fell on the food with the single-minded hunger of wolves. Neither spoke. Afterward, Victoria put away the condiment jars, and Logan loaded the dishwasher.

Logan broke the silence. He shoved a piece of silk across the countertop toward her. "This was in my dad's things. I don't recognize it, so I figure it must be yours."

Victoria stared at the scrap of silk, and after a long delay, she picked it up. She allowed the neat square to open. A lock of golden hair wrapped in a blue ribbon dropped into her palm.

"Is that your hair?" Logan asked. "The shade is all wrong."

Victoria shook her head. "It belongs to Freya," she said with a bittersweet smile. "I gave it to Arik when we first met."

"A whole week ago?"

"Goddess, has it been that long?" Victoria rubbed the silky hair between her fingers. It spoke to her, communicating the wrongness of returning to her. Victoria considered the talisman for a while and she closed her fingers about it. Knowledge dawned on her with certainty.

She knew what she must do.

"Come on." Victoria headed for the backdoor leading out to the patio. She moved so fast she ran.

Logan followed. "Where are you going?"

"I want to see if your mother's spirit has moved on," Victoria said, calling over her shoulder. She hurried past the covered swimming pool and out past the edge of the patio. Her journey ended in the snowy field where Lori Koenig had met her brutal death. Victoria opened all of her senses and circled the clearing. Expression dark, Logan stood on the edge of the field, reluctant to enter.

"Lori?" Victoria said. "Please, come out. I can feel you."

Victoria waited, and finally, the spirit rewarded her patience. Lori Koenig appeared in a shimmer of silvery light. Her light brown hair flowed long and free about her lovely face. Red slashes no longer crisscrossed her torso, and her amber eyes shone with serenity.

The spirit came to rest upon the spot of her death.

Victoria backed up until she stood beside Logan. Transfixed, he did not move and only reacted when Victoria put a hand against the middle of his back and urged him forward. She shoved him, and he staggered a couple of steps before he came to a halt.

"What?" Logan asked, giving her a startled glance.

"She's not here for me, you simpleton." Victoria spoke slowly and clearly as if addressing the dimmest child. Her tone provoked Logan, creating a flare of anger within his eyes. Victoria chuckled, pleased to have penetrated his withdrawn stupor.

Lips compressed, Logan walked to his mother. "Mom?"

"Oh, Logan..." The spirit sighed, and her hands rose, reaching for her son. "I'm so sorry for what you've been through. I've wanted to reach you, tried so many times."

Logan stepped forward and engulfed his mother in a hug. His cheeks glistened with wetness, visible due to the spirit's silvery light. "God, mom, I'm so sorry. I'm so sorry."

Lori's hands framed Logan's face, and she kissed his forehead. "Shh, don't apologize, my love. It wasn't your fault. Do you hear me? It wasn't your fault."

A hard knot in Victoria's throat made swallowing

hurt; another knot in her chest pained her heart. She reached with both hands for her cheeks to rub away tears and turned away. She retreated from the clearing, determined to allow mother and son privacy and give herself a chance to recover.

Minutes passed and the sounds of their hushed voices filled the night. Victoria fiddled with her broken nails, longing for the luxury of a good manicure, and sent her mind along a myriad of paths in order to avoid eavesdropping. She did not turn back until Logan called out.

"Vic?"

Victoria approached the pair, noting how Logan's eyes were bright and red-rimmed. Lori's spirit seemed to know genuine peace.

"What is it?" Victoria asked.

"We need your help," Logan said and appeared sheepish.

"I sense I must move on, but I do not know how," Lori said. "It is as if I've been lost for so long..."

"Oh!" Victoria aborted the impulse to smack her forehead. "Give me a second. Logan, pay attention! I'm only going to show you this once. I hate repeating myself."

"Lead on, little one."

Victoria bared her teeth in a mock snarl. She reached for the dagger that always hung over her right shoulder. She opened her hand, palm up, and passed Lori the lock of Freya's hair. The spirit accepted the talisman with a curious look. She waited while Victoria used the enchanted dagger to carve the rune summoning Bifröst into the air. The bridge appeared as a shimmering path, glowing with every color of the rainbow.

"Present the lock of hair to the God Heimdallr, guardian of the bridge," Victoria said to Lori. "Ask to be taken to Freya's hall in Fólkvangr. My goddess will welcome you as an honored guest."

Lori blessed Victoria with a beaming smile. "Thank you, Victoria, for everything."

The spirit started toward the bridge. Without meaning to, Victoria cleared her throat.

Lori turned back with a curious look. "Yes?"

"I have one thing to ask of you," Victoria said. "A favor."

Lori nodded. "Ask. Anything I can do or give. It is yours."

Victoria swallowed. The painful lump had returned to her throat, making it difficult to speak. "Seek out Arik and forgive him for whatever bad feelings persist toward him in your heart. Please. He'll be in Sessrúmnir."

Lori's expression softened with gratitude and agreement. She nodded. "I will do as you ask, Victoria."

"Thank you."

Mother turned one final time to son, and her radiance shined upon him. "I love you, Logan. Always."

"I love you too, Mom."

The spirit stepped onto the shimmering path, which faded and became lost from sight. Victoria watched her go with a deep sense of satisfaction. It might be a day or forever before she saw Lori Koenig again. Either way, Victoria considered her obligation to the spirit satisfied, and more than that, she experienced no qualms about bestowing a congratulatory mental pat upon her own back for a job well done.

Victoria accompanied Logan inside, and they wound up in the family room where they had eaten pizza and bickered a few nights before. The room offered a neutral setting free of uncomfortable memories and intimate scents.

Victoria curled next to Logan on the couch and leaned against him, seeking the comforting touch of the only present member of her pack. He wrapped his arms around her, and she settled her head upon his shoulder.

"Thank you," Logan said in a gruff voice.

His voice startled Victoria out of her drowsy state. "Huh? What?"

"What you did for my parents."

"Oh." A faint flush stained her cheeks. "Arik was a great man. I did no more than was honorable."

Logan snorted his skepticism. "You're still convinced that it was a marriage of convenience."

Her brow drew together in a frown, her lips pulled back from her teeth. "I didn't love your father. I admired and respected him, nothing more."

"Whatever you say, Vic. Keep telling yourself that," he said. "You loved him. No one else would have gone to this much trouble for strangers."

"He was my lifemate." She spoke without thinking, in a voice full of bitterness.

Logan stirred beside her. He grew tense. "What do you mean?"

"Freya sent me to Sierra Pines to find my lifemate," she said. Tears blinded her. "We had one night together. How's that for fair?"

"Hate to be the one to say it, Vic, but life isn't fair." Logan's laugh echoed with rage. Once again, that awful darkness stirred within him, and she shivered.

He terrifies me.

She levered her torso off Logan and leaned back to stare into his eyes. "Logan, what happened to you in that place? Can I help? Did something hurt you?"

Logan shook his head, denying her, denying everything. "Nothing happened, Vic. Let it go."

Victoria could not do as he asked; she would not. "Logan? If you'll tell me—"

"Why should I be any better at asking for help than you?"

Victoria bit her lip. As always, Logan's points were sharp.

"No reason," she said.

Logan got to his feet and gave her his back. He paced a stride and swung back. "I met my god, Vic, and that's all I have to say. All I'm going to say, all right?"

From the look on his face, Victoria knew not to push him further. She nodded and curled into a ball, drawing her knees to her chest. Breathing hard, Logan stared down at her, and he joined her again on the couch.

In his arms, she slept.

The sun shone bright and warm the day they laid Arik to rest in an empty grave beside his wife. The entire community turned out to honor a respected and popular man. Many said fine words of remembrance, many shed tears in tribute.

Logan wore a dark suit and stood at the center of the crowd. Victoria kept to the far edges of the gathering and wore the same clothing she had worn the day she and Arik had met. She was not part of the community, and none in it acknowledged her status as the man's mate. However brief her time with him had been, it had not been long enough.

From her vantage, Victoria watched while Logan handled the people, offering condolences with extraordinary aplomb. He exuded confidence and command, the mark of a true dominant male. For the first time, she saw him as his father's son, in every sense of the word, his latent potential realized.

Following the services, Logan came to stand with her near a copse of small trees, without touching, without words. Logan shoved his hands into the pockets of his suit jacket and removed them in an expression of his restlessness. Finally, he stripped the jacket away and folded it over his forearm.

Logan broke the silence first. "Whatcha thinkin'?"

Victoria sighed. "I can't keep mooching off you. I

need to get a job, find a place to stay, and provide my pack with a home, which means I need to deal with my hunter problem or none of that is possible."

Logan stirred, regarding her with a startled expression, as if coming to an unexpected realization. "I wasn't aware your hunter problem was ongoing. Do you need help?"

Victoria chewed her lower lip.

Yes.

She needed the assistance of another dominant wolf to shoulder the burden of protecting and providing for the pack. She could not deal with droves of hunters alone or fight the entire world with no one to watch her back.

She met Logan's gaze and thought about everything he had already lost. She refused to draw Logan into her mess and risk getting him killed. Again. She put on her game face and grinned.

"Nope, I've got it, but thanks."

"Maybe I can help some other way." Logan's hand dipped into the pocket of his jacket and pulled out an envelope. He offered it to Victoria, and she regarded it with suspicion.

"Go on," Logan said. "It won't blow up."

Victoria smiled despite her reservations. "You sure about that?"

"Positive."

She took it from him and opened it while he watched. Inside, she found a ring with three keys on it and an ATM card.

"What the hell is this?"

"Those are keys to the house and my dad's SUV. There's an account with enough cash to take care of expenses for at least a year. Don't worry about the mortgage; it's paid off. I've arranged with my dad's financial guy to cover the utilities. You're welcome to stay as long as you need to."

Victoria's stomach knotted and turned over. A terrible sense of finality inundated her, but she was not surprised. "You're leaving."

Logan's head dipped. "I'm leaving."

She shoved the envelope toward him. "I don't need your charity."

Logan refused to take it. "We're pack."

He shut her up for a full minute while she processed that. No one could call him a slow learner. He knew the exact words, the right words, the words she had no defenses against.

"It's charity," she said with far less certainty. Her hand remained extended and steady, holding out the envelope.

"Bullshit. Would you hesitate to offer anything you owned—anything needed—to the others? Sylvie or Morie?"

"No."

"Then how am I any different?"

Victoria stared at him. "I don't know. You just are."

"Because it wasn't a choice? I just happened." Bitterness flavored his tone. Logan seemed determined to provoke a vehement reaction from her, as if he craved conflict. Maybe he wanted things to end badly so it would make leaving easier on him.

Victoria stared at him. She inhaled a deep breath. "No, you were a choice, Logan. I feel bad about taking from you when I have nothing to give in return."

She shut him up. His spitefulness vanished and a look of chagrin crossed his face. Then he smiled with grudging affection and laughed from the diaphragm. "Christ, Vic, you really believe that, don't you?"

Victoria withdrew her hand and tucked the envelope inside of her black clutch purse. "Thank you. Do you know where you're going?"

He shook his head. "No, but it's all about the journey, not the destination, right? It doesn't seem to surprise you that I'm leaving."

"I get it. You've been through a lot. It makes sense for you to want to get away from here. I hope you find whatever it is you're looking for, Logan."

His smile turned sardonic. "I expected a sarcastic quip about the cowardice of running from my problems."

Victoria's blue eyes lit with humor. "I can't do that without being the pot calling the kettle black." She hesitated for the space of a heartbeat. "Logan, you're not leaving to do anything stupid or suicidal, are you?"

He shook his head. "At least, not intentionally. The stupid or suicidal parts may happen, but not on purpose."

"Do you remember everything I taught you?"

"Yes, mum."

"Logan, can the stepmom jokes, or I swear to Freya, I'll put you back in the grave. Do you hear me?"

"Loud and clear. Any other choice words of wisdom?"

Victoria thought for a second. "Yeah, I should explain that the pack bond will weaken with time and distance. It's not a forever thing, so you're free to seek out a new pack or found your own, whatever you want."

It hurt to contemplate losing yet another member of her pack. Logan hadn't been a member for long, but she had so few wolves left, making every individual all that more precious. As for the personal cost, she did not want to go there. If Logan remained, she'd have sex with him, complicating their already convoluted relationship.

An expression of pure belligerence crossed Logan's face. Victoria registered the darkness in his eyes before he hid it away behind a facile smile. "Good to know. Thanks."

Victoria gathered her strength, muscles bunching, and launched herself at Logan. Her arms wrapped about his waist hard enough to crack the ribs of a lesser man.

Logan held back, arms straight at his sides, and Victoria hugged him harder, determined to provoke a final honest reaction from him.

Finally, his arms crept around her, and he hugged her back.

"Gonna miss me?" he asked.

"No. Just so we're clear," Victoria said. "I hate you."

Logan laughed. "I hate you too, Vic."

"Be careful." She released him and stepped back.

"I'd say the same to you, but it would do no good."

Victoria tilted her head back and shot him a wolf grin. "Maybe we'll hunt together again someday, Logan."

"Maybe we will." Logan turned on his heel and strode away.

"Take care."

"Yeah, you too," he said over his shoulder.

She watched until he reached the perimeter of the cemetery, almost gone from view. He whirled then and raised his hand, two fingers forming a V. He saluted her.

She remembered Logan, in that moment, defiant and mocking, always mocking, an image captured in her mind and carried in her heart.

EPILOGUE

Joy-

"Goddess, my pack is everything."
"That they are, Priestess."

"Woo-hoo-hoo!" Victoria's cry of excitement turned to a howl that carried for miles through the desolate wilderness, touching every gully and peak of the valley. Her bare feet left tracks in the melting snow that collapsed inward, filling with slush.

Running at breakneck speed, Victoria charged straight down the steep slope of the mountain. Her braid whipped behind her like a tail, white-blonde in the morning sunlight. She reached a precipice overlooking a fifty-foot drop off and soared straight over the edge.

She landed in a crouch in the soft snow, kneel-ing among tender shoots of green. A bright dot of red, a single ladybug, clung to the tip of a long blade of grass. Her explosive descent frightened robins and mourning doves into flight upon beating wings. Panting, she tilted back her head and howled again.

In the distance, a wolf sang out a welcome. *Sylvie.* The others followed suit, adding their voices to the impromptu chorus until they numbered six strong: Morena, Sophia, the three pups. All had survived the harsh, hungry winter. The month of the hunger moon was past. Spring had come to the mountains.

Victoria grinned and ran again, traveling on two legs through terrain better suited to four. However, she lacked the patience to stop and transform to a wolf. She skipped over a small stream composed of runoff from the melting snow and followed it down into the valley. Her stream merged with others until the capillaries converged to become a rushing creek.

Victoria burst into a clearing and startled a doe and her fawn, sending the deer bounding for safety. Eyes bright, she pursued the animals and sprinted in order to draw alongside the doe. For a moment, Victoria ran neck and neck with the deer, glorying in their thudding heartbeats, drinking in the scent of fear. At the last moment, she swerved right and passed on an easy kill.

At the bottom of the valley, Victoria skidded to a halt and dropped to her knees. A wolf burst from the trees and headed for her at a full run. Victoria spread her arms in welcome, and Morena leapt straight at her. She caught the Omega wolf with open arms, and the impact knocked her flat on her back.

Laughing with joy, Victoria hugged the squirming wolf. Morena's warm tongue lapped kisses across Victoria's cheeks and forehead, and the Omega's tail wagged with ferocious verve. Seconds later, the rest of the pack joined them. They pranced, barked, and wrestled, rejoicing in their reunion, celebrating life.

Of course, her troubles with the hunters remained unresolved. Victoria still needed to contact Sawyer and negotiate peace—if at all possible. The future was far from secure, but for the moment, she reveled in being with her family once again.

"Good news! We're going home!" Victoria gasped and struggled to sit up amid the furry bodies. Mick almost pushed her over, and she wrapped her arms around his neck. The pups had grown so big it amazed her.

Sylvie sat on her haunches and smiled a wolf's smile. Her tail thumped a steady cadence upon the ground. Her hazel eyes held a distinct question. Her hope and curiosity communicated through the pack bond.

Victoria sank to a crouch beside her old friend and hugged her close. She whispered into Sylvie's ear. "You'd better start knitting, my friend."

About the Author

Melissa Snark is a resident of Northern California, where she lives with her husband, three children, and three cats.

Visit Melissa at:

www.melissasnark.com

or

melissasnark.blogspot.com

Coming Soon

Battle Cry

by

Melissa Snark

"Victoria, you do realize you've taken *Jake Barrett* hostage?" Morena said, casting the injured hunter a worried glance over her shoulder. The teenaged werewolf gazed at her leader with huge, round eyes.

"I hadn't, but now I do. Thanks for pointing that out for me." Victoria took her eyes off the road and grinned at her companion. "Relax, Morie. It's going to be okay."

Victoria adjusted the rearview mirror and checked on her captive. Barrett appeared still to be unconscious. No doubt, once he woke there would be hell to pay. After so many months of running and hiding, she looked forward to confronting the man responsible for so many deaths of the people she loved.

Morena's eyes bulged.

"Okay! Okay!" she squawked with dismay. "We've kidnapped the most dangerous man alive. His son has threatened to come after you. Once word gets out, every hunter in five states will be looking to kill us. Our getaway vehicle is a fire-engine-red convertible, but *you* think we're going to be okay!"

Victoria chuckled and reached over to drop a reassuring pat on Morena's shoulder.

"More like six states," she said. "Don't forget Utah."

Morena muttered an expletive that a girl her age shouldn't have even known. She stared at Victoria and her mouth opened. An accusing finger leveled at her packmate. "You're enjoying this!"

Victoria flashed a wolf's smile. "Hell, yeah, I am."